D1456948

*Also by Andrew H. Malcolm*

This Far and No More

Final Harvest: An American Tragedy

The Canadians

Unknown America

*Someday*

*Beatrice Bowles Malcolm, 1936*

# Someday

## ANDREW H. MALCOLM

*Alfred A. Knopf*

NEW YORK

1991

THIS IS A BORZOI BOOK
PUBLISHED BY ALFRED A. KNOPF, INC.

Copyright © 1991 by Unlimited Words, Ltd./Andrew H. Malcolm

Library of Congress Cataloging-in-Publication Data

Malcolm, Andrew H., [date]
   Someday / Andrew H. Malcolm. — 1st ed.
     p.  cm.
   ISBN 0-394-58782-0
     1. Terminal care—Moral and ethical aspects.   2. Right to die.
3. Malcolm, Beatrice Bowles.   4. Terminally ill—United States—
Biography.   5. Malcolm, Andrew H., 1943-     .   6. Journalists—
United States—Biography.   7. Mothers and sons.   I. Title.
R726.M29   1991
179'.7—dc20                                                90-5048
                                                            CIP

Manufactured in the United States of America

FIRST EDITION

*To Con, who made a new life possible.*

# *Acknowledgments*

This book is my responsibility only. But it is also the sum total of many experiences with many people, some near, some very far.

Some I cannot mention by name, but they know who they are and how much I appreciate their consideration, time, and friendship for me and my parents. I am especially indebted to three for their conscientious and loving caring of my mother. These would include Mom's bookkeeper and friend, her nurse and friend, and her doctor, who was so careful and thoughtful in those dwindling days and, in the end, so sensitive to her needs and Dad's. Although Mother never knew her intensive care nurse, I should also express appreciation for her kindnesses. The memories of each of these professionals will, unlike all other good things, never come to an end.

I can name but a few of the others, but I must thank them all for their guidance, understanding, and patience, and many for their friendship as well. These would include numerous colleagues at *The New York Times*, especially David R. Jones, Fred Andrews, William Borders, Gerald Walker, and James Greenfield, editor of *The New York Times Magazine*, whose sympathetic receptivity was so crucial in the early stages of this last story. I should also mention an array of the senior editors there who, through their decisions on newsplay and allocation of resources in recent years, encouraged my initial investigations into this sensitive subject, and a bevy of very helpful copy editors who helped shape the early pieces of this puzzle.

# *Acknowledgments*

Not least, I am indebted to the many, many folks who had the confidence, or at least the willingness, to allow a stranger to peer into their private lives, often at the most difficult moments, and to share with me their hard-earned insights for safe passage on to many others. I do hope I have been true to their trust.

I must also acknowledge the important influence on my life of two places—one the community of Hudson, Ohio, and the other an institution, Culver Military Academy—where so many of my values were observed, instilled, and nurtured.

I would like to express my deepest gratitude to some people who, in their own individual ways and with a goodly lump of patience and understanding, have over many years been my teachers in the truest sense of the word and shared their life-wisdom. They include Arthur G. Hughes, Richard Gimbel, Ronald J. Gleason, Jock Sutherland, Chet Marshall, Robert A. Reichley, Fred Whiting, Ben Baldwin, David Karno, Richard Gray, John LaHoud, Orvil Dryfoos, Marty Gansberg, Seymour Topping, Cleve Matthews, Wallace Turner, Allan Siegal, Evan Jenkins, Gene Roberts, Henry Lieberman, Henry Kamm, Robert Semple, Richard Freeman, C. Conway Smith, Elizabeth Granfield, and William Hale.

I should also like to thank Jon Segal, my editor, and Julian Bach and Ann Rittenberg, my agents, for their enthusiasm and patience in past times and during this book's sometimes painful pregnancy.

I owe a debt of gratitude, too, to my family—Christopher, Spencer, Emily, and little Keddy. One of them may be too young now to understand how important their patience, acceptance, and insights have been to me. I trust that over time they all will know. But so much goes dangerously unsaid between parent and child that I'll say it now anyway, to make sure.

I have tried, above all, to make this book as brutally honest as possible in keeping with the lessons of my parents and other teachers. In a way, the entire work is, I hope, a kind of tribute to them. I thank them again nonetheless and will let my later words speak for themselves.

Last but first, I must thank my wife, Connie, from the bottom of my heart and soul for her life-support—her vital early-morning notes of encouragement, her patience, understanding, acceptance, yes, and even her copyediting. If any mistakes survive in here, they are, of course, her fault.

—A. H. M.

# *Preface*

This is a true story about a little boy and his mother at the beginning of life and a man and his mother at the end. In between, they lived and loved and laughed and learned and fought a while. And that is told here, too. It was easier to live this story than it was to write because mere living has a momentum of its own and can require little thought.

And in our society, little thought is precisely what most of us give to the end of life. We plan for births, for college, for taxes and retirement. But this is the first generation in which progress and life-prolonging technology have allowed us to fool ourselves into ignoring the largest inevitability of our time here on earth. Whenever a wonderful party or afternoon was ending in my childhood, one of my parents would always say, "All good things must come to an end." And I would think, Why? Why can't it be, say, visits to the dentist's office that must come to an end? I never did get an answer, of course. But during all these months of writing and looking back over the nearly half-century that I knew my parents, the thought briefly crossed my mind the other day: All good things must come to an end, thank goodness.

This book, in a way, is also the tale of a professional writer's quest to discover how that mysterious end comes, quietly, out of sight and mind, and beyond the old rules that have developed over the centuries. When I was a child, a majority of people died at home, quietly and sadly but naturally, surrounded by familiar possessions, relatives, smells. Today, more than 80 percent of all deaths occur in institutions, where the technology is gathered, the insurance pays, and the scents are antiseptic. And those of us who can still stay outside may feel pained, but we can feel good about placing the ill ones there out of our misery.

In a very few years, we have leaped from meekly accepting each demise to blatantly challenging the necessity of going now. Why not later? We detour blood flows around congested areas or scope the inside of unseen arteries. We restart failed hearts, implant mechanical ones, or install somebody else's. We replace leg bones with steel shafts, hips with plastic ones. We cleanse a body's entire blood supply by machine while the person sits reading a magazine. It is an awesome power with at least two sides.

Americans now spend more than $650 billion every year on health care, about one-eighth of the gross national product, and twice as much as they do on education. And no end is in sight.

Yet, as medical prices continue to mount almost as fast as expectations, we have developed no real list of priorities. About 30 to 40 percent of all Medicare money is spent on just 5 percent of the patients in their waning months of life. Which is better for the patient and society, a $150,000 liver transplant for one experienced adult or 150 courses of pre-natal treatments for pregnant women and the next generation? Does my desire for a longer life require you to pay for it in a new world of fiercely competing interests and finite finances?

More importantly, when don't we do what we can do? At what point does the ability to prolong life become instead the power to inflict prolonged dying? And how do we leave room for individual choice? Not so long ago, society was consumed with the debate over removing the artificial breathing machine of a comatose young woman named Karen Ann Quinlan. Now the emotional debate focuses on withholding the precisely mixed chemical slurries that can be pumped into patients for sustenance. In some countries the terminally ill can arrange for their own death through poisoning. Others force such souls to do it themselves. In the United States in some years, the suicide rate of elderly people is twice that of the young. Suicide there is not illegal, but assisting one is.

How can a free society protect its broader values and legitimate concerns for protecting life while preserving the individual's freedom of choice in a delicate area where few ever think about the choice until they must? And then, often, it is too late. So it is left to frightened families and wary medical practitioners or worse, distant courts to decide when, or if, to pull the plug.

One problem is that just as social consensus seems to develop over one marvelous medical advance, a whole series of new ones comes along, moving the gates of decision ahead.

And one person's blessed extra months of life are another's living hell. Every year, thousands of people on artificial kidney machines choose to quit and die within days. The American Hospital Association estimates that 70 percent of the six thousand deaths that occur in the United States every day are somehow negotiated and timed as experienced doctors, fearful of lawsuits and criminal prosecution, confront distraught and divided families, who have successfully dodged contemplating what their loved one would want. And how *they* feel about it.

The United States has a puzzling attitude about death. Every night on television while munching popcorn and dodging commercials on another channel, Americans watch countless killings and demises for entertainment. Then they stretch and go off for a good night's sleep, never contemplating their own end; only a third of Americans has a will. This is the same society that demands the death penalty for murder, but every year drunken drivers kill 23,500 people, 3,500 more than other murderers. The drunks are sometimes sent to school to practice abstinence. But let one Missouri family's members seek permission to let their permanently comatose daughter die, and they must go before the Supreme Court, which acknowledged a constitutional right to refuse treatment and die but said Nancy Cruzan had not made her wishes clear. The result: her body was kept going.

In most families, death is the *d*-word, not to be spoken. One day Grandma, now comfortable with her own approaching mortality, speaks over Sunday dinner. "Someday when I'm gone—," she says. But her voice is drowned out by her offspring and their spouses. "Oh, Grams," they say amid nervous laughter, "you're going to outlive us all." And the children, peering out from behind their mashed potatoes, get the message that death is right up there with sex on the list of family unmentionables.

It should not be surprising, I suppose, that a society that cannot agree on when life begins has yet to reach a consensus on when it may end. But the result is that, besides squandering uncountable sums of money, this indecision, stubborn ignorance, and willful inattention condemns many patients to endless months of unwanted life and suffering and their families to matching emotional anguish and often financial destitution. An estimated ten thousand Americans now float in a permanent vegetative state in institutions because no one knows or wants to ask what they would have wanted.

In the final conversation with my father, I suddenly realized he did not want to continue living as he knew he would, in pain and fatigue. This was a deeply disturbing discovery for his only son, who had worshipped the man and his words for so many years.

That Tuesday-evening bedside conversation launched me on a long journey of professional and personal discovery over several years into the arcane world of modern medicine and the shadowy one of modern death. I wrote about it in *The New York Times*. It was a fascinating journey, watching the wins and the losses, the struggles and tensions, the hopes and fears of all those years. I learned a lot about how life and death are negotiated in our allegedly enlightened and certainly inattentive society.

But I never thought I'd have to live it, too.

This is, then, the story of two parallel journeys by the same person, one by a young boy who absorbed the values of his father and mother for unanticipated use someday, and the other by a middle-aged journalist whose curiosity and training led him to learn some of the darker secrets of our society today. And how these values, childhood lessons, adult insights, and immature fears came to merge on a trying, sunny autumn afternoon in a dim room on the third floor of a hospital where my mother lay in suspended animation.

As I looked down at this sad woman who had so controlled my life and thinking for better and worse, I knew in my heart and gut what was about to happen. I determined in those long, numbing hours to donate her beautiful Irish eyes to someone without eyesight. A few days later, at the urging of a wise professional friend, I determined to donate her story to those without foresight. I hope I never need these lessons again. But I also hope the lessons and insights, inadvertent and intentional, will prove useful for many others, who, like me before that day, are seemingly so successful in ignoring what is surely coming for us all.

It is not a perfect story. My relationship with Mom had many joys and laughs, numerous shouts and some slaps, a good deal of puzzlement on both sides, I think, and a fair number of scars, I know. In her own way with me, Mom did the best she could with what she knew. And, in finally letting her go when I never really had her, so did I.

Andrew H. Malcolm
The Yaak, Montana
August, 1990

# Someday

O n silent hinges, the oversized wooden door yielded heavily to my hand. It revealed a square room four paces wide, dark, dominated by walls, lit only by the feeble green glow of digital readouts and dials discerning the innermost processes of something alien, somewhere. Alertly, quietly, blindly, the costly screens gave out their numbers, which moved up and down, as did the lines on a moving green graph, communicating with impeccable obedience their vital messages to no knowledgeable eye at the moment.

The indoor window on one wall was long and tall, and blinded by metal slats slanted, for now, against the eyes of omniscient strangers in white coats who would gather there in the hall some mornings to watch and move their lips, though no sound could be heard from inside this safe room.

From the far dark wall came clear hoses hauling invisible cargoes from secret storage. Hanging high on silvered hooks were plastic bags of several colors. Down from them ran more networks of plastic tubes that, like the others, converged on the middle of the room, leaped the silver-steel railings of a tall bed to merge, and then to plunge through a tunnel of adhesive tape into a human nose.

Someone was suspended within that chrome network of bars and rails that could only be opened by the deftly initiated. That someone was very small, judging by the nondescript ridges and mounds vaguely indicated beneath the sheet. And very still, too. Except for the chest, which rose with a whooshing sound, clicked, and then fell with an exact rhythm that was simultaneously admirable and frightening for its non-human precision.

On each side of the bed one frail hand, bony and spotted with age, stuck out from the sheet. Strips of knotted gauze held them firmly to adjacent rails. The fingers were gently curved, not clenched. The right forefinger glowed red through the nail and from there another thin wire ran off with its steady flow of secrets.

"Mom?" I said, as if there were only one in the world. "Mom, is that you?" The nurse had motioned generally toward this room. But I spoke so tentatively, so softly, and so naïvely in that seemingly sacred darkness that one might have thought I hoped to be wrong.

I wasn't. And I winced. Was this really the strong-willed woman who had shaped and ruled my life for so long? The woman who told me when and how to eat what, when to get up, and when to sleep? The woman who bought my clothes, washed them, and each morning laid out the ones I was to wear that day? The woman who cooked the favored potatoes, bought the right cereals, poured the milk, and assembled over the long early years enough packets of cut carrots and gooey peanut-butter-and-jelly sandwiches to feed a Napoleonic army? The woman who tied my toddler shoes and then had them bronzed, who constructed all the Halloween costumes, who hummed by me at night when I was ill, and drove many miles to deliver and fetch from practice an amateur athlete who would spend so much time between plays scanning the sidelines for that familiar face, as if being watched by her would give worth to what he did?

Could this be the same woman who was always so damned effusive and happy with friends and then often picky and angry at home, the woman who slapped me now and then for my impudence and her ignorance, who was so silent at my college graduation, so pouty at times and jealous at others, always eager to be hugged but ever so stingy at hugging?

And now here she was before me with her mouth open as if frozen in mid-scream, so embarrassingly helpless, so bony and pathetic in wrinkled pajamas and a diaper. Unable to talk and move and chew and give orders. Food flushed up her nose. Medicines and liquids pumped into her immobile arms. Urine dripping out the other end into a plastic bag to be measured and studied to the last milliliter by faceless technicians whose findings were vital in determining her future on this conveyor belt of technology.

I was disgusted—at her for being like this, at myself for seeing it and thinking it, at the world for allowing it and calling it progress. Parents should be parents and children should be children. But now here was I forced to be a parent to my sole surviving parent. My father whispers in exasperation from the past, "So? Just do it then." But what was I to do? To know? Did I know enough? Did I know too much? "Young man," she used to say, "you think you're too smart for your own good." Could I care enough for her own good? And mine? Could I care too much? What was right? What was wrong? And how do you tell the difference today? Hanging over it all in these days of routine medical miracles was the unfocused thought: Is this me in thirty years? Or sooner.

And I was secretly terrified. I knew then that someday was very close. I would have one last chance to please her or blow it all for good, forever. And either way I'd be left behind to wonder.

Parents have always been there; therefore, they always will be. I don't think anyone is ever fully prepared for the death of a parent, or any loved one really, although in the back of my mind I knew it was inevitable someday. In recent years I thought about this, for a moment, every time I said goodbye; I worked on those farewells in case they had to last quite a while. I wanted no seams for guilt to seep through, although there was nothing I could do about it either way, I had thought.

It was bad enough in past years when death came quietly, inevitably, upstairs in a family bedroom with no appeals to a higher mechanical authority. And no especially agonizing decisions were necessary because nothing special could be done.

Except maybe, on his own, the family doctor would administer an extra shot of morphine, which slowed the breathing but eased the pain. It is much worse now when death nears, or seems to near, in a sterilized hospital room full of bewildering equipment that can do so much. But without foresight and planning, families are rarely sure whether they are prolonging a life or a death, if they are strong and quick enough to think.

In the past, sons or daughters had to accept the inevitable loss and handle the funeral arrangements. Terrible enough, to be sure. But today, in addition to that properly painful burden, middle-aged men and women—including this still-shaky son— are routinely asked to participate in deciding when and how a parent dies. Loving repayment, perhaps, for a parent's long-term commitment of time and worry. And these modern-day decisions should not be easy. But none of my high-school classes, my university degrees, my hours in church, my walks in the woods wondering at their awesome scale and order and rhythm—nothing in my fairly normal life had begun to prepare me for the enormity of that final episode. The roller coaster had reached the top of the climb and there was no way off now. I sensed in my stomach the approaching time: what I, like most people, had successfully ignored for so long, what I was going to be asked to decide, and what would likely happen as a result. And I knew, too, what that would mean—she'd be relieved, I hoped, and dead. And I'd be relieved for her, and alone.

And there never would be any of those hugs.


An only child is very good at being alone. And the only child of two only children is especially good at being alone. I got so much practice. No brothers or sisters to fight or share with. No genuine uncles or aunts to entertain. No cousins to abide. No need to visit anyone on Christmas, or share the early-morning gift-wrap-tearing frenzy. Fewer folks to drift away from in later years. Fewer trusts to be broken.

An only child may be more self-centered than those raised in larger families, where parental attentions must be shared. Lone children are very often more independent, ambitious, and eager to impress superiors—like all seven of the original American astronauts, for instance. Only children are also becoming increasingly common, by design, given their pre-packaged convenience for carefully planned two-career families, who schedule the arrival of children between major purchases. Mine was an old-fashioned two-career household; there was the father's career, which brought in the money, and my mother's career, which was our house and me, not counting the bridge club or church guild afternoons, and not always in that order.

I wasn't meant to be an only child, though. In the more private days of the 1940s, before the omniscient eye of television created endless cadres of celebrities-by-overexposure timing their public confidences to the release of their latest movie, such things as pregnancies were intensely private matters. To a naïve Midwestern youngster, especially one like myself without a big brother or sister to surreptitiously pass on worldly wisdom, such happy things just happened innocently, although sometimes it happened to a high-school junior, which was very different in those days.

I remember one night, after Dad returned from his factory office in the city, my parents coming to my bedroom to confide in happy whispers, as if there ever was anyone else anywhere near our rural house, that someday soon I would have a brother or sister, which they seemed very excited about. But, of course, we mustn't talk about it outside the family. Which was great with me because that created a warm sense of belonging to a special club—or, more accurately, it created that superior comfort that comes from knowing that many people do not belong to your club, even if they don't realize it. It would be just the three of us in the know.

Since everyone in my family seemed happy enough with me —and since my mother was somewhat older than a high-school junior—I remember the impending arrival as pretty good news, especially because they both took the time, together, to tell me privately. That's how I knew when something was really important, when the Supreme Parental Secretariat arrived, father just behind the mother's shoulder in proper parental protocol, to issue a joint communiqué in my bedroom. My turf.

Usually, it was just my mother calling upstairs to tell me something because she was very organized and had her list and she wanted me to know about it—now. Or it was just my father dropping by to examine with interest the latest entries in my Cleveland Indians scrapbook and to ask me, seemingly offhandedly, how I felt about something. Except those encounters always seemed to end up with me asking lots of questions about life and girls and sports and even mothers, and him kind of remembering things that had happened in his exotic life in other lands and the lessons and values he had learned from all that—which, come to think of it, he would say, might be useful to me someday. Then he would roughly pat my knee or shoulder a couple of times, in that comradely way that men use to punctuate their conversations with boys, and he'd go away to read the evening paper, leaving me and my teddy bear sitting in the wooden bed he had built, feeling as if we had just been a big help to him again.

Now, with this other kid coming, I was sure Dad would need my help, you know, getting him off to the right start like me. Finally, I would outrank someone around the house; more importantly, I'd be bigger. He could be second base and chase the fly balls in the evening baseball games with my father. At last, there would be somebody to unload—er, trade—my extra Andy Pafko baseball cards to. Sometimes I would probably let this brother play with my dog. This little newcomer could have my old little-boy toys. Except for the Lionel train set, of course. And the toy soldiers. And my autographed baseball. And some other playthings to be named later. I'd get the new stuff.

As the days and weeks went by, the idea of a baby brother

began to grow on me. I was excited, in a hidden sort of way, which I've learned is the safest, in case you're mistaken about what's coming. It never occurred to me that it would be a girl. Anyway, this little guy and I would be buddies and I could show him the ropes out in the woods and teach him about following animal tracks and whistling birdcalls so well that they'd talk back to you for the longest time. The baby could also help with the horse and I'd teach him to ride as soon as he got home from the hospital, which seemed to be the local delivery point for babies.

I knew about waiting from the dentist's chamber, which was my definition of soul-numbing waiting. But this baby was taking longer to arrive than some of the cereal-box offers I sent in for. Impatient because baseball's spring training was about to begin, which is what my yearly calendar was built around in those days, I determined to discuss the subject at dinner, when the three club members were gathered. But the instant I said the word "baby," I got such a sharp frown and a quick headshake from my father that I froze in midsentence. My mother didn't say anything. But she didn't finish her dinner that night, not even her favorite scalloped potatoes. I felt as if I should say I was sorry, but I never could figure out what I'd done that would cause such sadness. The baby never did come home. No one ever talked about it again—at least not with me around. And I remained an only child, although a wiser one who knew now that even within private clubs of three, one member is still always on the outside.

Outside is a wonderful place to be. Of course, before television there wasn't much choice. In my earliest childhood years we lived in a city neighborhood where everyone knew everyone. That is fine if you're a member in good standing but not so good if you're up to mischief, which is why neighborhoods worked in those days. Few families may have known each other well enough, say, to share Thanksgiving dinner. But all the adults knew whom the children belonged to, and misbehavior in a garden or with a hardball would surely prompt a visit between adults and an immediate summons indoors, causing your play group to disperse rather quickly lest there be other names on the indoor indictment.

By day, the youngsters would wash with the tide of play back and forth, past the Italian greengrocer selling from the back of his little green truck and across the tiny lawns, with a complete time-out for lunches at home and a partial time-out for those who required naps—or, rather, for those whose mothers would require naps indoors.

I hated naps. They ruined everything. It was hard enough waking once a day. Then to waste all that good daylight inside. I told my mother I hated naps. "I hate naps," I said, which had as much impact as a mother saying, "Now don't get dirty out there." So I said, "I hate naps!" Which, depending on how badly she needed one, could draw the favored conversation-closer: "Don't you talk to me that way!" But she liked naps, so much so that she'd always take one, too. One day, in genuine anger, I called over to her room: "If I do fall asleep, it'll be purely accidental." That became so much of a family legend it should have been carved over my bedroom door. Or, better yet, on my tombstone: "Andrew H. Malcolm. He Hated Naps."

One afternoon I tried to sneak out after the warden had gone to sleep. Having trouble with the buttons on the straps of my overalls, I instinctively went to the only person who could help. She opened one eye and inquired what I thought I was doing. Standing there with two buttonholes that were far too small for the buttons under my chin, I thought the answer was rather obvious. So did she. And, moments later, the overalls were back on the chair. My fanny was back in bed. And I was a mite wiser.

Slowly, the Nap Wars escalated. For a while the "I Forgot" ploy worked. Magically, about 2 p.m. every weekday afternoon this Andy Malcolm would disappear into the house of a friend who was not sentenced to his bed for the best part of the afternoon. But then, oh, no, I had forgotten about the telephone. Thanks a lot, Alexander Graham Bell. "Watson, come here. It's time for your nap." Sure enough, my friend's phone would ring. And from out of nowhere would come another mother—gosh, they were everywhere in those days—holding the heavy black receiver up to her ear, then slowly turning to look right at me. And, naturally, being a faithful member of the ruthless Council of Moms, she would turn me in.

So I took to playing musical friends. These other kids could be my best friend for most of an afternoon if they'd hide me for a while. I think it worked a few times if they were fringe friends and their numbers were not circled in my family's phone book. It occurs to me now that I could have erased some of the circles. But you don't think of such things in the heat of battle.

Finally, I could not take it anymore. With an accomplice named Tim, a real best friend, I ran away right around naptime with plans to return just before dinnertime, in case we were having steak and mashed potatoes. We went to no house, which eliminated the phone threat. We played through old folks' yards a block away, which eliminated both the mother and the familiarity factors. I was hiding in the bushes up behind the drugstore when I saw Mom walk by in her apron, calling out my name over and over. I didn't answer. She looked really upset. It was great.

When the coast was clear, we lit out for Tim's house because his mother would be asleep by now. But she wasn't; she was on lookout duty at the front window. She grabbed him as an accessory and she told me to go home immediately because my mother was worried sick. I suggested perhaps she was thinking of someone else's mother—mine was just fine the last time I saw her. But nothing would do but that I head home, straight home. Outside, according to a school theme I wrote a few years later, I considered really running away, maybe to join the Cleveland Browns. "But then I remembered what my father had said, 'You can't run away from trouble because it will always catch up with you.' So I went home." There, as I walked in, my mother was

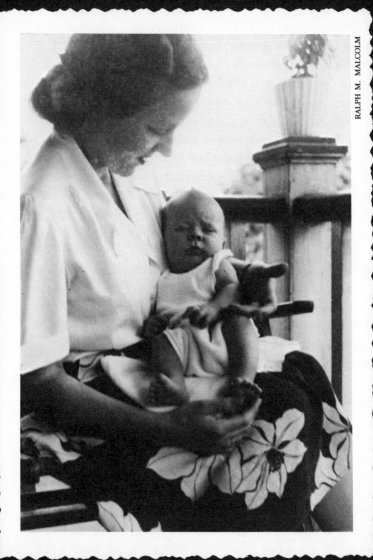

*A new mother and her son*

on the phone saying, "Red hair, freckles, forty-six inches tall . . . No, wait, he just walked in."

Then, according to the theme, which was titled "What I Did Wrong and Faced Up To," "My mother took me into my bedroom and tried out the new hair brush on me."

At least I got 95 on the theme.


My first memory was of my father and how strong he was. It happened in the late afternoon in a house under construction not far from that neighborhood drugstore. The unfinished wooden floor of the house had a large terrifying hole whose yawning darkness I knew led to nowhere good. Dad's powerful hands, then age thirty-three, wrapped all the way around my tiny arms, then age four, and easily swung me up to his shoulders to command all I surveyed.

I don't have a first memory of Mom, only a few jumbled early recollections. The pregnancy with me was several years coming, according to family legend, and she was very sick during it, especially near the birth, which was described not so much as a Blessed Event as a Blessed Relief. I was a little late—not for the last time—being born and needed some encouragement with forceps. But there are no snapshots of a tired though happy Mom cuddling her firstborn son, it being wartime and film being scarce and Mom being Mom. Her hair would have been mussed, her makeup gone. There was some illness or weakness afterwards, too, such that nursing the baby was out of the question. A professional nurse was hired at night, and my mother's mother came all the way from Ontario to help for a while. All in all, something of a scary ordeal, everyone recalled. Each time I heard the story, I felt I should apologize.

Both my parents were immigrants from Canada. The Depression ended sooner in the States than in Canada, and my father, the young consulting engineer fresh out of the University of Glasgow with an engraved graduation pocket watch from his parents to prove it, found work in Cleveland. He was a prairie product, born in Calgary in 1914 six months before my mother emerged as the cherished daughter of a small but quite successful haberdasher in Toronto.

My father grew up in a log house in rural Manitoba on a hardscrabble family farm where his morning chores included breaking the ice on the washbasin and milking the cows. Then he and his mother, the local schoolmarm, walked the two miles to the schoolhouse where he had his lessons drilled into his mind and rapped into his knuckles.

My mother had a fairly normal city childhood for those days. Her father, one of three boys from a hardworking small-town family of oil workers in southwestern Ontario, had married one of the two Hunt girls, a well-known local family of serious singers and painters. The newlyweds moved to Toronto where my grand-father opened his shop. Times were very good in those days, once the end of the killer flu epidemic marked the close of World War I. As the twenties roared on, a strong scent of social change was in the air, even in conservative English Canada, which was stuffy but not so stuffy as to try to impose Prohibition on its people.

Then, of course, came the Great Depression, that series of mystifying financial setbacks that seared a generation of parents and their offspring, who watched their family's affluence and their will wither in the face of forces so strong that the era's name must be capitalized. Later, listening to the survivors talk of those days, it reminded me of the way people feel and talk about earthquakes, so awesome and overpowering in their muscular strength, so seemingly random in their destructiveness, yet so terrifying in their demonstration of the fragility of something as fundamental as the ground we walk on. Life could never feel exactly the same after experiencing either. It may be sunny today, and maybe even tomorrow, too. But someday soon, eventually for sure, very bad things will happen. And this time we must be prepared.

My mother's father lost his business in the Depression. And something of his spirit, too, it seems. And, I think, in an ill-defined and pre-feminist way, his daughter did too; they were so close. Halfway through university, my mother was forced to drop out and go to work, selling handbags in Eaton's department store in Toronto. Her inherited painting skills, which were impressive, also were abandoned.

Walking home from another futile job-hunt one midday, my grandfather rounded a corner just in time to have his ankle crushed by a door falling off a passing soft-drink truck. For the rest of his days he would wince and limp, which he never mentioned, although his daughter often did protectively.

My grandparents had to sell their large city house and buy a small parcel of sandy soil beyond nowhere outside Toronto where they farmed chickens, asparagus, and apples. Mom said this prompted derisive comment among family members: another hopeless investment by that hardworking small-town boy. He would, along with those very same relatives, be gone by the day his widow sold just one field to a shopping center for many times her husband's original investment.

Though both sets of grandparents were tied to the land—and that tie nurtures a set of values as much as any plants—they could not have been more starkly different. Grandpa Malcolm, who had four older brothers, was a country boy, tall and Lincolnesque. Until settling down with his wife and son in Manitoba's wilds, he was a restless soul, wandering the western Canadian frontier, working on ranches, running pack trains. Grandpa once wrote about the humility he felt when finally, at the age of eighteen, he bent his six-foot-two-inch adult frame into the tiny desks of an elementary school to learn to read and write and escape the harsh prairies, which he did, in part. He entered federal civil service, becoming Canada's immigration officer in Scotland, rounding up stolid Scots to help populate his infant nation.

But a part of Grandpa Malcolm never left the farm and, in

the end, he was remembered more for what he did for others. Years after his death I found in his papers numerous crumbling letters of handwritten appreciation from the immigrants he had approved for settlement in Canada, the new country having no Statue of Liberty and not bound to accept all of the world's huddled masses, just a few select ones. Then, when I returned to his comfortable suburban Toronto neighborhood, I did find the tiny, tidy house but not anyone who remembered him. Until I mentioned his love of gardening. Oh, The Gardener, they said, my yes, we remember him tending the huge garden in his straw hat and white suit and all the crisp vegetables he would distribute to his neighbors. Sure, Mr. Malcolm, the gardener. So you're his grandson, eh? He was a good bit taller than you.

I have similar memories: even in his later years, living in that comfortable, now urban Toronto house, he could most often be found outdoors, tending his vast garden, now part parking lot. Whenever he visited our house in rural Ohio, he would spend the entire day outdoors laboring mightily on some project he had asked his son to assign. And I would watch. Sometimes, on a break, he would hike up his suspenders, wipe his forehead with a handkerchief, replace his straw fedora, and look way down at me. "Andrew," he'd say, "let's go for a walk." That was great, a masculine walk. I had noticed that women like to sit, look at each other, and talk; it's more intimate. Men prefer to walk, look straight ahead, and talk; it keeps a supply of potential distractions streaming by for emergency escapes, if necessary. And Grandpa and I would stroll off toward the woods. Actually, Grandpa strolled; I scurried to match those big strides.

Like most men I knew in those days before Alan Alda was invented, Grandpa Malcolm never talked much. He didn't tell jokes, make wisecracks, or blow a lot of hot air like math teachers. He spoke plain and simple like the prairies that produced him. And sometimes, if you were a newcomer to the country from the city, especially a young bride whose daddy lavished constant praise on her, those prairies and those words could seem mighty harsh. My mother called him "Daddy Jim" and around him she was unusually quiet, which was fine for him, but for me it meant it was probably better to be outside, safe, for a while.

Whenever Grandpa Malcolm talked, he seemed to have something to say. When he didn't, he didn't. Around Mom or Grandma Malcolm I tried not to talk too much, because any sound that came out of my mouth was subject to correction. If my idea didn't need correcting, then the grammar or pronunciation did.

My Grandmother Malcolm was a tough lady, no doubt loving in her way. I wanted to like her a lot, but she was more than a little frightening, seemingly stern, and, like her husband, constantly called me Andrew, which my mother used only when I was in trouble. Grandma Malcolm always wore her hair pulled back severely and she held her head turned to the side, like Long John Silver, so that her single good eye could scan everything to the front. I knew about her partial blindness, but to me she seemed capable of a vicious right-cross at any moment. She always looked askance, as if she were about to say, "Come now, young man, what *really* happened?"

She had grown up in Saskatoon, Saskatchewan, in those early-twentieth-century days when Canada's urban communities contained log houses and the streets come spring were quagmires. Then she moved to become a farm wife, cooking on a wood stove round the clock at branding and harvest times, and a schoolmarm, which brought in extra money because she also chopped the wood for the school's heat. Being the only schoolmistress for five miles around also insured that her young Ralph would get the proper education, which was important since she expected so much more of her own son. Years later, she was still at it; Grandma would sometimes return her grown son's letters corrected for grammar. At one point in those early days she had to run the farm alone with my father for a year; her husband had gone abroad and was establishing family living quarters in Scotland, which everyone in my family called "the old country" because, eighty years previously, my great-great-grandfather John had left there to find his future in the New World.

In Scotland, my grandmother sent her son to regular schools. But with their posting time and money running low, she pulled him out to tutor him by herself at home—two years' schooling in one to prepare for university entrance exams. As a result, my father never received a high-school diploma but earned a master's degree in economics in three years, which made Grandma Malcolm very proud. So they gave him the pocket watch to prove it. It still runs.

I remember showing her around my room one day. That was during my Early Airplane Era, so the walls were covered with color photos of jets and World War II fighters, including a Spitfire just like the one a distant cousin had died in over Britain. "Do you know what equilibrium is?" my grandmother asked.

"What?" I said.

"No," she replied. "Pardon me."

"Why?"

"Because it is more polite."

For a second I looked for the third person in this baffling conversation. "Oh," I said, "yes, ma'am." And turned to show off my model aircraft carrier.

"Well?"

Completely lost in my own room, I did the safest thing. I smiled, politely, inanely.

"Well?"

"Well, what, Grandma?"

"Do you know what equilibrium is?"

"Uh, no. I'm sorry. I don't." So she taught me about that word and I became smarter for it, which was her whole idea.

"Do you know how to spell it?"

"No, ma'am."

So she had me sound it out—"eee-kwah—no, kwi—lib-ree-um." Then she showed me the word printed beneath one of my airplane photos. And I never forgot it.

I had heard my parents grumble slightly before Grandma Malcolm's visits, which my mother saw more as Presbyterian inspection tours. All signs of alcohol in our household had to be eradicated before my grandparents' pale-green Studebaker arrived. But I knew there was no use taking my complaints about Grandma Malcolm to Mom. Although the two women did not share the world's warmest feelings toward each other—my father is said to have said that his mother once told him he could have done better than marry my mother, a department-store clerk— Mom and Grandma M. were both card-carrying Moms. And in those days when most families had two parents living together, frontal assaults by any child on any adult member caused a firm tightening in the ranks, hairbrushes at the ready.

These barrages by major women in my young life had a way of landing when I was the most enthusiastic and least expected an admonition. "Hey, Mom," I'd say, bubbling over as I ran up to the house clutching my precious Daisy BB gun, "I just got four straight bull's-eyes!"

"Well," she'd say, "just make sure you don't hit anything else by mistake."

Around Dad and Grandpa, it was safer. "That is good shooting!" they'd say.

"Let's move the target away from the shed so a ricochet doesn't hit the window."

Ricoshay? Oh, right. Those things you couldn't control. "Good idea."

"Life is a little like shooting," Grandpa would say. "A little foresight helps your aim." Around him, I wanted to avoid saying anything foolish. But during our walks alone, outdoors, it was safe to talk, and wonder, and I think my boyish enthusiasms and curiosities melted his masculine guard. He would point out things—wildlife tracks, animal droppings, where certain trees grew because secretly they liked all that moisture, how broken branches at certain heights hinted at the size and identity of previous passersby.

These were the lessons he had learned helping put food on the family table out West. It was exciting having a grandfather who had lived on a frontier just like Davy Crockett. Unfortunately, that involved hunting. Killing disgusted me. Actually, it terrified me. I think I felt very vulnerable. And this straightforward admission to killing helpless animals by my own grandfather bothered me deeply in my youthful world of black-and-white right or wrong. So strong was this taboo that I never saw the end of Walt Disney's *Bambi*; when the baby deer's mother was killed just offscreen in that long-ago Saturday matinee, I became so distressed that my father had to take me home early. I remember asking my father about Grandpa's killing days—in private, because it ran against everything Dad had warned me about. Who had given me the right to decide if some little wild creature should live or die? he had asked. Had the animal done anything to hurt me? What if the bird had a nest of babies at home waiting for food?

I don't remember ever shooting anything alive, although I was a good enough shot once, even shooting left-handed, to win a target shoot against adults in a nearby community; Mom cooked the prize for a special Sunday family dinner, Sundays being a particularly dangerous time to be a chicken in those days. Until the Hunting Lesson, I had never thought beyond the challenge of hitting something moving, which seemed very exciting from behind the weapon. Put yourself in the animal's place, Dad had suggested. How'd you like to die because of someone else's decision? That sure didn't seem right; therefore it couldn't be right. So I promptly adopted the Bambi Taboo for everything, even stepping around ants. I still have a problem pruning trees and thinning corn. I also admonished my mother, who saw bugs in her kitchen as another hostile attempt to make a mess inside her fortress. After another one of my tiresome lectures, parroting his perceived preachments, I recall my father impatiently saying, "Look, when the bugs run the world, then they can wipe *us* out for being in the kitchen."

However, my rigid anti-killing regulation was amended one day to exclude flies after I spotted a dead possum near my dog's water bucket. It seemed to be still moving. Then I realized it was actually a thousand swarming flies feeding on the carcass. Over the years I took pointed parental ribbing for this sudden change in philosophy, for being so disgusted by the natural course of events. But no one ever answered my question: Is death always so sudden and ugly?

And now here was my own grandfather talking about shooting rabbits and deer, maybe even Bambi's cousins. I remember my father's patient explanation of the difference between killing wantonly for fun or sport and killing only enough to eat. How did I think hamburger got on my plate? It didn't walk there. It was killed by someone else for our food. That was a good enough explanation to get Grandpa off the hook, although it elevated the evilness of those faceless men with expensive shotguns who appeared in nearby fields every autumn, when my mother made me wear a red jacket and my outdoor play was curtailed long before dusk.

Needless killing was one of those lessons etched into the supple granite of my childhood memory. As a teen, I was driving to a summer job early one morning when a sparrow flashed out of the roadside bushes in front of my car and perished on the grille. When I saw its spindly legs and little feathered body so limp and lifeless just seconds after being so alive, I vomited on my shoes.

And when, in tears muffled to avoid detection by co-workers, I called my father from the factory to announce my awful deed, he was his usual calm self. "Were you speeding?" he asked. No. "Did you try to hit him?" No! "Can you think of anything you could have done to avoid it?" Well, um, no, not really. "Then it wasn't your fault, was it? You know, son, sometimes when creatures get old and sick, their minds get muddy and they do strange things that can lead to their death. In a way they're ready to die. We may not understand that, but we must learn to accept it. That's a very old cycle."

How could anything ever be ready to die? Life had to go on as long as possible. Death was the black hole, The End. What he said didn't make perfect sense. But it sure made me feel better. "The bird didn't suffer. Nothing lives forever, son."

I saw my Malcolm grandparents at least three times a year—on their way to Florida in late fall, on their way home to Canada in late winter, and at their house during the summer. Most of my summers were spent in a little farmhouse with my Bowles grandparents where I felt very safe and welcome. When we arrived, after a fourteen- to sixteen-hour drive over 340 miles of back road from our house in another country, Grandma would bring out a loaf of fresh bread and her old toaster with the doors on the side by the electric coils. And while everyone talked excitedly about adult things, she sat with me at the kitchen table and made me as many pieces of toast as I could consume, each smothered with her homemade blackberry jam. "Andy, just look at you," she would say. "How you have grown!" Then we would all adjourn to the darkened front porch where, as soon as Grandma would sit in her rocker, I would climb up into her lap, lean my head against her big, soft chest, and drift off to sleep with her arms enveloping me. There would be many other nights we could play Our Game.

Next morning I would awaken upstairs, with the windows wide open to admit a stream of warm sunlight and the fresh, familiar sound of dozens of chickens clucking their way across pens out back. Throwing on my clothes as I dashed down the stairs and out the back door, I prayed I wasn't too late for feeding time, a very important help for Grandpa, my mother said. Somehow I never was late. There by the gate was the waiting bucket, brimming with golden grain. And under the smile of my grandfather I would toss out tiny fistful after tiny fistful. And the birds with their beautiful, shiny colored feathers would cluster around my feet, pecking, and crowd each other, and sometimes flap their

RALPH M. MALCOLM

*A daughter and a mother*

wings so hard they would fly by my face briefly, sending feathers furiously drifting everywhere. They seemed to like me a lot. And I liked being liked.

I could play with them anytime I wanted. Sometimes I would sneak up behind one, grab her by the legs, and hold her upside down for a moment, which was deemed terribly cute by everyone except the chicken concerned. Of course, there were eggs to collect, buckets of water to haul—keeping at least some of the liquid in the pail—and I would throw inside the fence clumps of grass, which interested a fair number of the pens' residents. But often I would just squat down in the fine dirt and watch this animal community. They had different personalities and status —pecking order, Grandpa called it. Some could go anywhere they wanted; others went more hesitantly and often were shooed away by their feathered brethren. Some would stay far away from me, wary. Others would never even notice this redheaded tyke. Others, brazen, would come up close, turn their head sideways, cock it, start to leave, and then come back. I practiced my clucks down there at chicken level and sometimes they would cluck back and I felt good, as if I'd made a friend.

But chickens, I discovered, are not raised by farmers to be friends. Some become dinner, a messy process which, I now suspect, was timed for one of my afternoon absences. Those were the days before chickens came in bite-sized McNuggets, so everyone received one or two recognizable body parts on their plate. So innocent was I that I don't ever remember thinking that this meal might well have been one of the birds I had been feeding the previous day.

Then, every so often, a few chickens were herded into an orange crate with a dish for food and water and taken to the railroad depot to spread the breed in chicken pens on distant farms. Grandpa would remove the trunk lid on his 1932 Ford coupe. Two crates would be stuck in. We would climb inside the two-seater, slide the steel bolt into place to latch the door closed, and chug off toward town in the slow lane. But, first, as we eased down the dusty driveway with the grass growing thickly in the middle, he would have me turn the aaah-oogah horn lever so the women would know of our departure.

These were largely silent trips we made together, which is the way men often travel. It seemed to me that the women in my life talked to talk. The content was irrelevant; it was the intimate exchange of words they cherished, as if talking was a shared pat on the arm, a touching reminder of their continued togetherness in this life. The men were more wary, as if talking would some-how breach their protective ramparts, word by word, stone by stone, ultimately revealing a weakness.

Grandpa Bowles was very nice to me, friendly, accepting, if somehow uncertain at times. He was always ready to listen and to answer my questions, but he didn't ask many and hardly ever volunteered anything. We made windmills together with juice-can lids for the propeller. And we sailed kites over the asparagus patch while other family members debated if the craft had too much tail or not enough. Grandpa B. was never stern. Until near the end, when he would fly off the handle at me for things that weren't happening, like all the noise I was making sitting in a chair reading. That was strange, but it was no big deal because my mother had sat me down, several times, and told me his arteries were hardening. All I had to do was ignore him politely. Then a few hours after his outburst, always before bedtime, Mom and Grandma would stand in the door while he shuffled into the room. He told me he was sorry, that Grandma had said he'd said some mean things, which he didn't remember, but he was sorry. I said, "That's okay, Grandpa. I don't remember either." And we would shake hands and change the subject.

Grandpa could be talkative with other men, especially if the conversation was fueled by cigars, which made old men remin-isce. But he never had much to say when we were alone. And his wife was the only one who sent any letters. I loved getting mail so much that I sent away for every cereal-box offer in history, so much so that Dad had to place a weekly ceiling on my orders.

Mail from far away was a kind of recognition of me, I guess. One time I asked my parents if Grandpa Bowles knew how to write because he never did. They laughed and a week or so later I got my own letter from Grandpa. He said the chickens missed me.

I never did understand why Mom gushed on about her father. Well, I mean I understood gushing on about a father; they were very special guys. But not her father. He always called her Babe. And he didn't seem to need all the protection Mom gave him. The number of times I heard about what the Depression did to him and what the door falling off the truck did to his ankle and how sure she was that everyone sniggered at his move to a small farm. He showed me his hairless ankle once; it was like a straight shaft and had a perpetual purple bruise all around. But I never heard him complain about it or the Depression.

Gripping the chair arm, he sat down as old-fashioned old men did, slowly, carefully, under control until the last few inches, when he just gave up and plunked down on the cushion, aiming his body, knowing gravity would win yet another skirmish. And the chain on his old gold pocket watch would settle around his middle. Grandpa seemed to move especially slowly around Christmas, which had a ritual air about it in my family. On a dark early-December evening Grandma would arrive in Cleveland by train, wearing her black fur coat that felt so soft. It was such a happy time. My father drove the car, of course. Mom sat in the mother's seat. And Grandma and I sat close together in the back, clutching each other's arms. She said I was her young man for the evening.

On the way home we'd join the throngs of motorists cruising by the office buildings and scores of houses brightly decorated with colorful bulbs that no one ever thought of vandalizing. Some of the displays were immense, with Santa's sleigh on the lawn and a long string of lighted reindeer suspended all the way up toward the roof. It was a magical transformation of an aging city, like the first overnight snowfall each year that turned the world into a momentarily trouble-free fantasyland. Everyone was so happy, cruising by all the homes with the large front windows filled with folks happily watching the folks watching them. The evening was perfectly capped in our living room by homemade Christmas cookies, which Dad baked, and by Mom-made hot chocolate.

I always thought my mother thought of Christmas not so much as a private family holiday with members sharing it and each other as a time when people were more likely to drop in to judge her homemaking skills. Mom worked very hard at everything she undertook. Everyone said our home was exquisitely decorated— the antiques, the colors, the wood grains, and pleated curtains. Each season some decorations changed—late-winter daffodils, spring flowers, dried autumn posies and some meticulously arranged dried cornstalks leaning just so, and at Christmas lots of evergreen boughs, evergreen wreaths, and, of course, the tree capped with my crayoned green-and-yellow paper angel from second grade.

I swear Mom could hear a Christmas-tree needle hit the carpet, even from upstairs. Either the needle was fed to the Hoover the instant it landed or, more likely, the tree was afraid to shed any with her around. There never were any needles on the floor until Dad and I dragged the old tree out in January. Then they all fell down in a chaotic path that was somehow sucked up before we got back in the house. One spring I remember walking across the living room in my bare feet and painfully stepping on a Christmas-tree needle. I felt pretty special because my mother was so concerned, until I realized her attention was focused not on my foot but on the escaped needle. I'm certain she had it carbon-dated to determine guilt.

At our well-organized church, Mom founded and worked long hours effectively running an ambitious craft shop that attracted many customers and raised substantial sums from the items she assigned her friends to make and donate for sale. She invested long hours in the yard, tidying up with her clippers around trees and garden edges where our mower could not graze. And the inside of our house always looked so neat and tidy, as if no child lived there. Later, when we had a little more money, Mom hired a cleaning lady to come every Friday, not to do all the basic housecleaning, but so the two of them could get even more cleaning done. I don't remember all that many people stopping by to check on her housecleaning, but you never knew, way out there in the country.

Nor could I ever see all the dirt—it was called "filth"—that my mother could sense lurking in every corner. I honestly never knew what a dustball was until I went away to school and they magically sprung up under my bed. In my teens, Mrs. Tidy and I had some run-ins over her passion for spotlessness and precisely placed knickknacks. In those days I consumed paperback books like candy. They were my best friends, carrying me into a fantasy world of non-fiction and home again safely. I'd clear off a space of the table by my father's big easy chair for a stack of books, along with a portable radio and a bottle of Coke (yes, yes, I used a coaster). In a while I'd go to the bathroom. My mother was nowhere in sight. When I returned, some commando maid had swooped through and erased all trace of my presence. The bottle was gone. The coaster was restacked. And the radio and books had disappeared, to be found later neatly piled on the stairs for portage to my room. Even the pillow had been re-puffed. "Mom!" I'd whine toward the kitchen. "Where did all my stuff go?"

"Well, you just left everything lying there."

"I left it there because I wasn't through."

"Well, how could I know that after all this time?"

"All this time? Mom, I was only gone forty-five seconds to take a pee."

"Watch your language, young man."

"Why couldn't you just leave everything alone for three minutes? Then if I'm still missing in action, you can fix it up."

"Because *I* care about how this place looks."

"But there's nobody looking right now."

"I can see that mess and I care."

"Well, maybe you could care a little less about this corner just for a while."

"Don't you talk to me in that tone, young man."

"Mom, c'mon."

"That's enough."

"I'll say!"

Her head appeared at the kitchen door. "What did you say?"

"Nothing."

"*What* did you say?"

"I said, 'I'll say.' "

"That is definitely enough."

I would stare at that door debating: college or the electric chair. But I would act as if it didn't bother me, maybe mutter a few silent words toward the now empty doorway and then retreat outdoors, away from her. Except the fumes of fury must have hung in the air, because that evening my father would find an occasion when he and I were alone and he'd say, "What happened between you and your mother this time?"

---

*I suppose the emotional fingerprint of a parent's death is different for everyone. I thought I had prepared pretty well. But I didn't have a clue.*

*When I got Mom's call on that Sunday morning some years ago, I knew something was very wrong because she began with my name. "Andy," she said, "it's your mother." And then, of course, I knew what was coming across that phone line on weekend rates.*

*A switch clicked in my mind; I went on automatic pilot —calm, cool, practical, determined, unemotional. How did it happen? How are you holding up? What did the doctor say? Where is he now? Who's there with you? I'll be there as soon as possible. Let me talk with your nurse. What happened? How is she holding up? Why are the paramedics still there? Oh, what mortuary?*

*I looked at my wife. Her hands were pressed together by her mouth, her face colored with grief. I became even calmer. It must have been quick, I said, hoping.*

*I called the airline. One aisle seat, please, near the front, but not the bulkhead. I packed quickly but neatly. Do it right the first time, he would have said. I picked up my children at their friends'. I let on nothing. I sat them down at home; they knew something was wrong. Their dad was frighteningly calm, like an engineer who has just spotted cracks growing in a new dam. There was going to be a family funeral in a few days. We would make arrangements if they wanted to attend. We would understand if they did not. No one did. I was leaving in a minute. Any questions? In his sleep, it looks like. She sounded okay. It was very sad. But a relief also, in a way. Maybe they could say a prayer.*

*There was no time for tears then. I had to get in the car, get to the airport, get a parking space, get a bus, get to the gate, and take my seat. There was no one else in my row. I did my expense accounts. They were overdue.*

---

Every year, my parents had one or two large parties, not counting my father's annual office poker get-together where, my mother said, little boys and moms were not allowed after initial greetings. My parents' parties were held in the living room, and those being the days before children deserved their own TV set, it meant I got no Lone Ranger or Jackie Gleason that night. All these noisy adults invading our house all at once, the place reeking of smoke for days after, and every sign of my existence—my books, my little chair, even my parakeet—banished to hidden storage for days beforehand. I had to be dressed up, too, to greet everyone, to shake their hands firmly, and then to lug their coats up to the guest bedroom. (Furs were big in those days; more little animals getting killed. So it secretly puzzled me when Dad bought Mom a mink coat, an inconsistency I never wanted to ask him about.

But she loved it, I mean gushing-loved it, and then I understood his reasoning.)

At some point I would be summoned down to the party to perform; my specialty was lip-synching to rowdy Spike Jones records, which I practiced and practiced until I had every bang, every siren, every word and grimace timed perfectly. I enjoyed that greatly because I made everyone laugh and then they clapped. Come to think of it, I enjoyed making my classmates laugh in school, especially during show-and-tell, that sacred time that was to school days what live TV programming is to modern evenings, rare and delightfully unpredictable. One Saturday afternoon in college, I smuggled a police whistle into the football stadium and mimicked the drum major's signals, which got the band moving in many different directions on national TV and thousands of people laughing, although the band director was not among them. It was a high point in my career of mischief and defiance of authority, although she probably wasn't watching that day.

Inevitably, after the Spike Jones laughter my mother, a true Victorian though that Queen and her era were long dead, would suggest that her child play the drums for the people. Since I only had one and didn't think of myself as all that good, certainly not as good as I imagined Dad was in university, these were excruciating and silent moments. I would stare daggers at her then, but she was oblivious to me, or pretended to be. And when I turned to Dad for rescue, he looked elsewhere. I felt like saying, "What would you like to hear on the drum, Mom? 'Moon River'? A little Glenn Miller?" But I would stumble through a couple of marching cadences and the room would be dead silent, except for the drum. Then I would notice my mother wasn't listening anyway. She had begun chatting with someone, so I'd finish up and quietly sneak away to read yet another book on World War II, with its distant, relaxing devastation.

A few days before Christmas, having arranged a caretaker for the chickens, Grandpa Bowles would arrive on an evening train.

The adults would open their presents on Christmas Eve, leaving The Day all to me. I would put out cookies and milk for Santa and, of course, some carrots for the reindeer. In the morning I monitored my clock until two seconds after the minimum sleep-in time established by my parents. This was usually 7 a.m., although once I think I whined it down to 6:45. Everyone would don their dressing gowns and brush their teeth. And Grandpa was always last. "Dad," my grandmother would call out, more impatient than I, "hurry up. The boy's waiting."

"I'm coming. I'm coming." Finally, he'd slowly shuffle up to join the grand family procession into the living room to see the wonder that Santa had secretly wrought during our slumber.

In those days there was a discipline to a child's life, at least this child's, even at Christmas. And this discipline, including the naps, had an inexorable and very comforting rhythm to it, as if we youngsters were fitting into a pre-established system of acceptable behaviors and values generally and specifically shared by virtually everyone in our neighborhoods. These were the years before television's addictive wonders reorganized families into audience segments by age groups, before family members waited for commercials to converse with each other, and before days were divided into precise half-hour time slots, showing us other behaviors that must be acceptable, otherwise why would they be on TV.

First in required behavior in those days was the handshake. No fishy little finger grip, but a good firm squeeze accompanied by an equally strong gaze into the other person's eyes. "The first thing anyone knows about you is your handshake," my father would say. And we'd practice it every night on his return from work. There was the toddler in his battered Cleveland Indians baseball cap, trying to be serious beyond his size, bursting out the screen door to run up to the father, who seemed a giant, to shake hands again and again until it was firm enough. Then came a toss in the air and a hug. When I grew up, the tosses disappeared, of course. The hugs were always there when I wanted them, although for an awkward spell in teen hell they were embarrassing. The handshake, however, lived on as the symbol of our link. In fact, the last time I touched my father, it was a handshake.

After dinner most non-winter evenings, the first to emerge out the front door of the duplexes lining the streets of the city where I spent my first seven years were the children. We picked up our bikes, baseball bats, and jump ropes right from where they were dropped when our mothers had called us; these women had appeared at their respective doors and, almost in unison, shouted, "Dinner!" We were followed back outside by the fathers, who came down to the curb to umpire and talk with each other. And then came the moms, who stayed nearer the houses, chatting with each other across the driveway and only seeming to pay attention to the street when one of theirs was performing a particularly wonderful feat of derring-do, worthy of applause and the obligatory, "Be careful now!" If a parent or set of parents was missing for an evening, the neighbors became parental surrogates, distributing praise and admonishments in appropriate portions to their friends' offspring and, to my knowledge, never pondering for a moment the possibility of a lawsuit or personal retaliation for such audacity toward a family across the shrubs.

When the streetlights came on, that was the official curfew and impartial arbiter of the end of playtime ("Now, you come in when the streetlights come on"). The city worker who threw the big streetlight switch probably had no inkling of his larger social role, closing down the city nightly. There was no higher appeal from the streetlights' illumination. The families drifted inside with many waves and "See ya tomorrow"s. Down in the basement then, my father and I would work on our alphabet. Receiving the keys to language from my father was almost as exciting as getting the keys to the car more than a decade later. Plus the fact we did the letters together on Dad's workbench; he lavished his time on me and we got to use his holy, otherwise untouchable, woodworking tools. I reveled in his ardent attention. I knew even before "Sesame Street" that letters and words were the most important things in the world.

First came a review of all the letters already completed. If that was successful, under his direction I would trace the night's letter on a block of wood with a pencil stub. Then from behind me his powerful arms would reach over my shoulders, his left hand enveloping my left and his right on mine. And slowly and firmly, with the wood block held tightly in the vise, our hands would grip and guide the jigsaw. We were so close then; I could feel his breath on my hair, could smell his familiar father scent. My stubby fingers would hold on so tightly while my teeth gripped my little tongue in intense concentration. Then came the hand drill for the holes in A, B, and P. And the sanding, which was very tiring to the hands and very boring to the mind, but made such a difference in the feel of the letters and the words they could build; the more I sanded and wiped, sanded and wiped, the smoother were the letters and words I could make. "Do you feel the difference, Andy? If something is worth doing, it's worth doing right—the first time."

I could choose any paint color for any letter except the vowels, which had to be red because they were somehow special. Then it was upstairs for the prideful announcement to Mom: "Tonight we made L." And, if I was lucky, the dishes would be already dried. If I hadn't, she'd stand there and check my drying work. She never said when I did a good job, just when I missed a streak.

There was even an order to the presentation of Christmas presents in my family, beginning with our stockings, then the trivial parcels, then the symbolic ones (the useless matching belts and ties from the distant cousin I never did meet), the clothing (blah), the books (better), and moving right along up to the big surprise (the record player, which I had inadvertently discovered the previous week in the attic over the garage). Most presents had a clue to them, perhaps a code Dad had written on the label.

And I had to try and decipher it. Mom handed her favorite presents to me and Dad did the same. They both handed me the BB gun, but Mom didn't say anything about that one.

Getting around the tree in clumsy slippers and dressing gown amidst all the wrapping paper could be tricky, since hidden beneath the festive refuse was my electric train set. For two or three weeks every year I was allowed to control one corner of the living room with tracks, sidings, tunnels, crossings, signals, and bridges linking piles of books. The main line ran around the tree and under the davenport, with sidings for shunting, loading, and unloading inside and outside the loop. Every year, we added a new car and some track. And Mom was surprisingly patient about the whole mess; come to think of it, that was her typical reaction when I became consumed by intense preoccupations such as becoming a BB-gun marksman, moving pretend-railroad cargoes efficiently, lifting weights, or playing ferocious football.

Mom herself was consumed that day by preparations for The Meal, which was very traditional and very organized. Some people could help as bit players. I ripped up the bread for the stuffing, for instance. Dad did his famous mashed potatoes with onion bits. And Grandma B. did a couple of pies—mincemeat because there were going to be adults present and they liked little black things in their pies, and apple because I would be there and apples were her trademark (well, rhubarb, too, but that doesn't count). However, Mom was in charge of everything, from the fresh turkey and the family's old silverware down to the crisp green tablecloth and the new red candles. (The poinsettias had already been precisely placed and would not be moved by anyone fond of living until that same placer removed them in several weeks.)

Unless summoned, the males had best stay out of the kitchen because they got in the way, as always. And the women knew the only thing that men were after anyway, to snitch food before it had been appreciated by everyone and photographed for the record on the dining-room table with the new camera that a certain young man was caressing in the living room. And although Mom did make squash, on this day I could leave that orange pile of muck on my plate and get away with it, even if there were starving children in Korea.

She was a real Anglo-Saxon meat-and-potatoes kind of Mom. Nothing ethnic; I never knew pizza existed until high school. Nothing resembling fish; if it couldn't walk, we didn't eat it. To insure no disorder took root in our house, eating was a semi-rigid affair. No platters of meat, vegetables, and salad making the rounds of our kitchen table. My food was what she put on my plate over by her stove. Her menus. Her cooking. Her spoons. Her portions. A prayer. Now, eat. All of it. It's good for you.

Some days breakfast could be flexible in terms of timing, but not in content—cereal, two fried eggs, toast, in winter hot chocolate, and, for years, orange juice. I said orange juice made me feel funny in the morning, which was too bad but orange juice was still good for me. That was the Mothers' Health Credo in those days: if it tastes bad, it's good for you. Now, of course, the opposite is true: if it tastes good, it's bad for you. One day Mom saw me throwing up in the grass after my orange juice; from then on, I could skip morning juice, as long as I drank it right after school. I never saw her or Dad drink it once.

Somehow in all those culinary struggles, I managed to control lunch—peanut butter and jelly, day in and day out, year after year after year. What varied was the celery or carrot sticks. The peanut butter came in jars decorated with flying ducks, which, when emptied, became milk glasses. Many years later, whenever I visited my mother, she'd serve my Coke in one of those duck glasses and then stand there to see if I'd notice. "Do you remember—" she would start.

"Oh, yeh, sure," I'd say. "I really like peanut butter and jelly."

"I'll say," she'd say. "I was so sick of making peanut-butter-and-jelly sandwiches all those years. We had more than ninety of those duck glasses, you know."

One time I perversely suggested she should have thrown them

out if she had too many. But she looked hurt. So from then on, whenever the duck-glass skit was playing at her house, I just recited my lines perfectly. One day, cleaning out her apartment for the last time, I found a lone peanut-butter duck glass tucked up with the wineglasses. I didn't throw it out either.

When I was not in school, which was more frequently than I remember, weekday lunches came on a precise schedule determined by the radio soap operas, primarily "The Romance of Helen Trent" and "The Guiding Light," which, like everything on the radio then, had to be listened to sitting down. When I was home sick, I'd watch her listen to these lunchtime tales. If I tried to talk then, I'd get a stern, "Shhh." My mother listened so intently there had to be something to those shows. But as far as I could tell, nothing ever happened on the programs, because the next time I'd be home sick, the same people were doing the same things, unless one of them had caught amnesia. Years later, I suggested every listener must also have amnesia to accept such plots. But she didn't laugh.

On school days shortly before four, the bus delivered me home for orange juice, followed by cod-liver oil, unless the gods were good and she forgot. My mother had a rule: no TV before five —"You'll become a vegetable!" A fate worse than death, and cousin to a couch potato. But that rule was okay because "Howdy Doody" wasn't on until 5:30. I'd be sitting there on my own little chair watching intently the front of our 12-inch Dumont set, which Mom and Dad bought used. Mom would arrive with her daily delivery of one cereal bowl of potato chips, which I could nurse until about 5:45. Dad would arrive at six like clockwork. They would have a drink—martini for him, Manhattan for her. And by 6:45 we were eating.

I didn't mind not watching television until five. Some days I even missed Howdy. There was so much outdoors. I had exploring to do, especially if it was a Frontierland Tuesday when Davy Crockett was due on the Disney show. I had chores to do. "Do it now!" my father was always saying. "You've got something

*Mother of a growing son*

to do, do it now. Then you'll have time to do other things later."
He drew me two signs for my bedroom. One said, "Do it now!"
The other said, "Think."

I was often lent out as a small but willing extra set of hands
to neighboring farmers. In those days our school year ended
around May 20 so everyone could help plant. At corn-planting
time my job was to ride the planter, monitoring the level of the
weathered wooden boxes of outgoing seeds and signaling when
it was time to reload. Or, later, I'd help haul hay bales for stacking
in the barn where they made great cushions for us to fall on
during cap-gun shoot-outs. Or I'd be assigned to pick up all the
loose cobs that were mislaid during harvest and storing. In return,
the farmer might let me drive his red tractor around the yard and
sell my parents a quarter of beef at a cheap rate.

I learned about the inexorable rhythms of the land during those
long hot and cold hours. And through animals I learned a lot
about the rhythms of life and the inevitability and sometimes
sickening pain of death unless, out of humanity if not love, the
man of the family put the dying animal out of its misery to prevent
further suffering. I never fully got on the hay wagon on that one,
since I couldn't talk with the creature and discover maybe he
thought his suffering wasn't so bad, given the alternative. And I
found that while the departed one may have been relieved, those
remaining were stuck with that hollow gut grief that looms so
large in its finality. Death was not a welcome visitor in my
childhood world, although it was a fact of life. I could cry about
an animal's passing. But "death" and "family" were two words
that could not appear in the same sentence. The word death was
like a swearword, the dread d-word. Only worse, because I didn't
know why I couldn't say it. And sometimes I would go to fearsome
lengths to avoid confronting it.

One day, Mitzi, the dog of my friend Johnny O'Dell, caught
a rabbit a few seconds before I caught her. The bunny was terrified
and pretty badly chewed, but I carried it home for repairs. My
mother and father were aghast because, they said, wild rabbits

have some equally wild diseases. They held my hands under the hot-water faucet for five minutes. But under the barrage of my non-stop pleadings, and probably feeling embarrassed, Dad took the rabbit to the vet's for stitching. A few days later, fortified by injections and a mountain of proffered carrots, Herman, as he had become known, escaped from our garage to become the healthiest wild bunny in history. And the best remembered in our family's lore. Forevermore, whenever we saw a rabbit, Dad, Mom, or I was sure to say, "Ah, one of Herman's cousins." Sometimes we said it simultaneously. Saving a life was a very good feeling. Maybe I should become a doctor—or, better yet, a veterinarian?

Some years later I came upon a dead field mouse and a nest of her sightless newborns. It was a difficult decision. Walk away, let them starve or be eaten, or kill them myself now, according to my perceived code of humanity, and prevent suffering. I drowned them. And felt very sad. And the next day I felt worse; I got a terrible case of poison ivy on my hands, arms, and face, even around the eyes. I never told anyone, but I thought perhaps my suffering was some kind of divine comment on what I'd done.

Animals loomed large in our country life in those pre-teen years. First came a cat. His name was Rusty. Mr. Weaver, who ran an old general store near Grandma Bowles's house, gave him to me after one of our long afternoon chats. I smuggled him into the United States, which was probably illegal with the government but it was all right with a higher authority, Mom.

Then came a dog, something long-promised. One Saturday, Dad and I set out for the city dog pound with my mother's twin admonitions in our ears: the dog could not be too big and he'd have to sleep outside. Well, one out of two isn't bad. "How big will he get?" we asked the elderly city widow who was offering her dog for adoption.

"Oh," she said, "eighty, ninety pounds." Dad and I looked at each other and nodded. Didn't seem too big to us. Anyway, he might be a small Saint Bernard. No way to tell at that stage.

At home, we may have forgotten to mention to Mom the ninety-pound business. He was so cute and affectionate she would surely love him, too. And while she didn't exactly get down and cuddle with him, she did pat him and she didn't object—not to me anyway. What she said was, "Now, remember. He's not coming inside." I quickly nodded since he probably wouldn't fit in the door anyway. "Well, I'm glad you like him so much," she said, returning to the house, then turning, "And he is still a puppy, eh?"

But an hour later she was in our old Mercury station wagon with the wooden trim, driving the fifteen miles to the grocery store for a large bag of dog food. The baby who didn't arrive was forgotten that day as I reveled with my new friend. I dubbed him Buddy.

We had a new leash for him and a bright-red leather harness that spanned his huge chest. I tied him up to the porch railing that first night. Just after Sunday dawn, I tiptoed downstairs in my bare feet to peek at my slumbering pet through the back door. He was gone! The leash was broken in the middle. And pieces of red harness lay strewn about the porch. Oh, no! I flung open the door and ran out on the cold wood. In the corner, Buddy raised his big head. It was the last time he was ever confined, even in the mud-filled springtime when all the neighborhood dogs would run about in semi-wild packs for a couple of weeks until they each returned home, spent, filthy, and matted with burrs.

That was about the time Rusty went missing, probably on another long-range hunting expedition. Buddy and I grew up together. He was always there. When I'd go out the back door, he'd be there. On the porch. In the field and barn. We ran in the woods for hours. When he wanted to play, he'd stand on his back legs and bang the back door with his right paw—so much for that screen. We tried to play hide-and-seek, but he always cheated. He never could wait until I'd found a hiding place. I'd hear his feet thundering on the ground behind me and then, I swear, he'd trip me so I went sprawling in the grass where he could place one mammoth paw on my chest, which was heaving with laughter.

When I got off school bus No. 1 each weekday afternoon, there he would be in the same place, stretched out, waiting, his huge head resting on his huge feet, big eyes staring up. Then he'd jump up, place both front feet on my shoulders, and look down on me. Dad and I built him a large doghouse, so large that at some somber times I could crawl in there with him and pour out my heart to my brown-and-white buddy. He would listen and then we'd fall asleep together until dinnertime. And he always kept my secrets.

That's where I went after I found Rusty. He was in the grass alongside the road. It was the right color for Rusty. But his head had been flattened. My parents seemed strangely uncomfortable about this possible death in the family. Mom suggested it was perhaps some other cat; in fact, she was sure of it and I shouldn't think another thing about it. And Dad was strangely quiet. But Buddy and I decided it was Rusty. For some days I felt badly that I hadn't done something—what, I don't know—to protect my cat. It didn't seem right that he had been so alone in death. So I buried him out back with a handmade wooden cross that I could see from my bedroom window.

Having animals who depended on you for their well-being, my father said, was the best way for a young man, even a very young man, to learn a sense of responsibility and duty and reality, whatever that meant. "It'll do the boy good someday," he said.

I don't remember asking, but when the idea came up, I sure didn't resist getting a small horse. He was more of a large pony really, dark brown with a shaggy black mane, a rowdy forelock, and mischief in his eye. I named him Happy Rascal. The first school day after his arrival, I leaped off the bus and ran to the barn. Happy had ingeniously shed his halter, broken the stall gate, tipped over the oat barrel, and was lying between that golden mound and a bale of hay, stuffing himself. He didn't even look guilty.

His care was my job. Virtually every morning of that childhood era of mine (except four days when I had the mumps) before anyone else awoke, Buddy and I were out in the barn, feeding, watering, combing, and exercising this frisky fellow and cleaning his stall, which was pretty disgusting at first. But since it would have been unacceptable, bordering on the precious, to say that in my family, I got over the disgust at my duties. Happy was always happy to see me; I could tell by his little hello whinny. It felt good to be needed.

If I finished in the barn early enough, Buddy and I would walk back in the woods and listen to the night close down and the day world wake up. The stars would fade. The crickets would drift off. So would most other insects. A deer might pass by, heading for hiding. A pheasant family, too. One or two birds would stir and then be joined by numerous others. I'd try to imitate their calls. Sometimes if my lips were in good form, we'd exchange whistles and chirps for several minutes. Making that link with the wild world was strangely but wonderfully satisfying to me, as if I were some kind of Christopher Columbus stepping through an invisible window in those woods to discover there were hidden layers to life all around us that other people could not see. Understanding those layers could come later, maybe. For now, just knowing of their existence was sufficient. And I would head home with Buddy, feeling somehow richer, although it never occurred to me to tell anyone.


Animals, in their individual splendors, keep you from becoming too self-centered. Our pets even got Christmas gifts—a catnip mouse for each cat, a huge bone for the dog, extra birdseed by the feeder and scraps for the raccoons, a fresh red bow on Happy's halter and a big red apple. He loved apples.

Animals always seemed to me a lot smarter and full of personality than some people were or could see. Happy learned where sugar cubes came from, which was more than I knew. So when I wasn't looking, he would nip at my jacket pocket. He learned how flimsy was the board fence Dad and I built as his corral. He backed his large rear end into the wood. The fence would crack apart. And the pony would nimbly step over the debris to prance about our rural neighborhood for a few hours, leaving my frantic mother to call for help on the phone and then, with her apron tied firmly in place, chase that infuriating creature from field to field. Finally cornered, he'd stand tense, his head held high, his eyeballs turned so far you could see the whites. Then just as your hand was inches from the halter, he'd feint as if he planned to run you down. When you flinched, he was gone, until he tired of the game or got hungry for oats.

And he knew how to administer humility, too. One big day when Mrs. Guy, my fourth-grade teacher, came by for tea, I saddled him to show off my equestrian skills. With Mrs. Guy watching, he and I gleefully galloped the length of the corral. Then he turned sideways and suddenly stopped. I went flying over the fence. According to Dad's rules, I had to get right back on to show him who was boss and to stifle my own fears. So, of course, I did.

Dogs learned tricks and daily schedules and they had different barks and moves for communication. By and large, cats didn't learn tricks, which made them pretty smart in my book. But they could spot good people and steer clear of others. One night long after Rusty's disappearance, Dad arrived home from work with a strange passenger, a tomcat, all black save for four white paws and a white star beneath his chin. He had been hanging around my father's factory and that night adopted the boss, following him to his car and curling up in the backseat. "Okay," said my father.

The cat was named Edgar. He would be a family member for a quarter-century, patrolling the barn or basement for unwanted creatures, occasionally condescending to be scratched by a human hand, fathering sixty-nine infants with his wife, Irene, a dog-pound refugee, and eventually retiring, a wise widower, to a soft chair in a high-rise city apartment. One Sunday afternoon in our mutual youths, the great black hunter stepped out of the high grass out back with a half-dead bird in his mouth. The cat was terribly proud. I was furious. I pried open his mouth and began pummeling him.

That prompted Dad to sit down there in the grass and start up a conversation about something called "instinked," which Nature had put in most living things. It was very powerful, he said, and, like a lot of natural forces, we couldn't, shouldn't, try to change it. You had to accept some things in life. Ed was always going to hunt. It was a part of him, a part of life and death. How could I expect a cat to know that it was all right to hunt mice in the barn but not birds in the bushes?

But I feed him everyday, I said.

That didn't matter. Someday I would understand; he seemed sure of that. But for now I would just have to accept these things.

But he hurt the bird.

That was too bad to us. But maybe Nature thought there were too many of these birds. Did I think I knew more than Nature?

Well, no, but it didn't seem right that there was suffering. Why didn't Ed just kill it? He was being cruel, wasn't he?

It can seem that way. But he didn't think my cat was hurting the bird on purpose. Maybe Ed thought he was showing off what he'd done.

But how could anyone, especially my cat, be proud of hurting something?

I had to understand that I wouldn't always understand everything. That was part of life, too.

Good, that explained the existence of long division. But, gee, look at the poor bird flopping around here.

The will to live is very strong in every living thing, he said. Nothing wants to die. The strong ones won't. The weak ones will. Someday the strong will be weak. That's the cycle. But we don't control that. Remember, Nature works in mysterious ways.

The bird died anyway. That may have been when I began thinking of death not so much as a distant event but as a dark, unseen force lurking nearby, watching for targets of opportunity. Sometimes you could duck it. But someday you wouldn't.

Intellectually, I was aware that things were dying and being born all the time—presumably in balance—although it was so hard to keep track. Every spring I'd see baby bunnies hopping about uncertainly and baby birds and, later, butterflies fluttering around, and I'd find one or two lonely carcasses in the bushes where they had crawled to expire, unnoticed, while life went on around their throes. There were no babies in my family, but I knew people died, too. Now and then, my parents would put on dark clothes and go somewhere for an entire morning. I was very curious, but they wouldn't take me. I knew that parents couldn't die. But although they appeared extremely uncomfortable talking about it, they agreed that if any of my relatives ever died, I could go to the funeral. I said I'd need dark clothes.

---

*When I got there, to their one-bedroom apartment, she was sitting, only slightly bent over in those days, watching television, always television. But it was Sunday, so at least we were spared the game shows where everyone gets a round of fullsome applause just for saying their name. "Oh, Andy," she said, "I'm so sorry." She acted as if it were my husband who had been removed from the bedroom that morning by a couple of truck drivers in ill-fitting black suits.*

*She was in her pajamas still, or already. I hugged her. Her back was bony. We agreed it was all for the best; he had been in such constant pain. I said I had to go to the bathroom. I went into the bedroom instead. There was his bed, still unmade just the way he left it, or they left it. There on the dresser was the glass jar nearly full of coins for his grand-*

*children's college accounts. Their pictures in color. He and I and Mom on the very green grass at my college graduation. His parents in black-and-white. His key chain. The pocketknife I gave him. The gold pocket watch his parents had saved so hard for. With my arm, I scraped all those little plastic bottles of pills into a wastebasket. And that oxygen tank with the chipped green paint was going out of there first thing in the morning.*

*The nurse left. I was feeling very tired. It was nearly midnight my time. But Mom wanted to talk, about everything but It. So I listened; everyone has their own lifeboat. I could actually feel my strength waning, like the grains of white sand that seep into the bottom of those old egg timers, leaving nothing behind in the tiny glass globe on top. And my stomach was beginning to feel weak.*

*"Would you like something to eat?" she asked.*

*"Oh, uh, no. No, thanks, Mom. I'm really exhausted. And it's going to be a busy week."*

*"Oh," she said. "Busy?" As if I had just popped in for a visit with her and there was nothing to do but sit there by the tube and talk during the commercials.*

*I really didn't know if I had the strength to make it down the hall. I never wanted to sleep so much in my life. I'd settle, desperately, for a nap. And my gut was feeling completely hollow, as if a cannonball had blithely passed through my body and left a large hole open to the cool air. And I still had to take a shower, a very hot shower that would wash away everything. I felt so filthy. How can you get so dirty hurtling by seven miles above the nearest sandbox? I hung my dark suit inside the humid bathroom, hoping the wrinkles would fall out.*

*Ten minutes later, I crawled from the steaming bathroom. Mom was smoking a cigarette. The radio was on. I laid my glasses on the tiny table by his bed, but my foggy eyes were caught by an apple-shaped picture frame standing there, a*

*window on the past. I put my glasses back on and peered in,
like someone leaning over the mossy bank to look deep into
some serene forest pool. It was a thumbnail-sized, black-and-
white photo of a little boy dressed as an acolyte. He looked
very familiar but very far away. My head hit the pillow. It
smelled very much of him, in the basement, cutting wooden
letters. I was falling away fast when she spoke.*

*"You know, your father took baths."*

Illness occurred more often than death in my childhood. My
mother was wonderful when there was sickness about. Even with
the animals. When Edgar was deathly ill—somehow poisoned,
perhaps—and he wouldn't eat, he was allowed to sleep in the
kitchen. When I went down to see him in the middle of the
night, he was gone. My mother's voice came out of the living-
room darkness. "He's over here, Andy."

There was the family's beloved black cat on his back in Mom's
arms sucking on a doll's bottle full of milk. And the rocking chair
creaked and creaked all night.

According to family lore, I was sick a lot as a child. A fair
amount of more serious ailments such as whooping cough, the
usual measles, mumps, and chicken pox, something that looked
suspiciously like polio for a few days but wasn't, and perhaps a
bit more of the colds, flus, and aches and pains than might be
expected in an average span of youth in the fume-free countryside. There was one affliction about age five that sealed my eyes
shut every night so that when I awoke, I was unable to see. That
was scary. But as soon as I cried out, Mom was there with her
soothing voice and gobs of warm, wet Kleenex to loosen the crust
and end my blindness.

If I had any health problem, I had my mother's undiluted
attention. Even if it was just a passing pain. That's when she
would hover helpfully. One morning in the second grade after
nine full innings of Sunday baseball with my father (I had to hit

and pitch both right- and left-handed because he said it made me a more valuable player), my throwing arm felt very sore. Mom said it sounded like I had caught a bad case of baseball-arm ache. And I agreed. So she made a sling, which I proudly wore onto the school bus and right through until it got in the way during the first recess.

When I was sick in bed, I had my mother all to myself all day. If I was sick on a bridge-club day, she'd even stay home. If I lost my voice, there was a little bell by my bed to ring. She would bring ginger ale anytime I wanted. She was always asking how I felt and taking my temperature and doling out pills—and orange juice, of course. I got my toast cut a special way when I was sick, and Mom might sit down on the bed and review the stamps I had just put in my album or talk about when she was a young girl and sick. I had never thought of her as being a child.

At these times she taught me how to sew, or she might get out the old family photo album and pore over the aging black-and-white pictures and her colorful memories. She'd remind me of who all my relatives were (that was the boring part) and what kind of cousins they were and where they lived and what they did. She must have read something in my face because every time she would pause. "Listen carefully now, Andy, because someday you'll want to know all this." I could not imagine why.

She would describe her youth and being a Girl Guide, working in a department store and how Dad courted her relentlessly—she really liked that part—and how when she first met him, she didn't like him, so when he phoned for a date, she came up with phony excuses why she couldn't go out. One time she told him on the kitchen phone that she was taking her mother to an evening lecture. This was news to her mother. But when the appointed evening came, there was Grandma Bowles all dressed to go out. My mom said, "Oh, it was just an excuse. We don't really have to go." To which Grandma replied, "Oh, yes, you do." And so the two women went to the most boring lecture in the history of Ontario. That was the only way to undo the lie.

And if she didn't tell me, I always asked to hear the story about how long and eagerly they had awaited my arrival (the good part). Then I might fall asleep and pretty soon Dad was home, bringing a surprise supply of new comic books, if I had been good, which, of course, I always was.

During the day, I could listen to the radio: the "Breakfast Club," then the Arthur Godfrey show, and music. Just before lunch there was a bizarre show called "Queen for a Day" where three or four women got up and told the saddest stories about their families, their illnesses, tragedies, and financial misfortunes. The woman who got the studio audience crying—and clapping—the most won a refrigerator or something. At night there was music too, but the evenings of illness were very long unless Mom, Dad, and I played some Parcheesi or Chinese checkers. And when, later, I couldn't go to sleep, Mom would come by and I'd feel her sitting on my bed right next to me. If I was hot, she'd put a wet washcloth on my forehead. If I was cold, she'd tuck me in tighter. It felt very secure. If I was throwing up, she'd hold my head. "Everything's going to be okay," she said. If I was just fussy, she'd scratch my back and hum "Silent Night," even if it wasn't Christmas. And I would drift off to sleep and try not to feel that much better by morning so we could do it all over again.

I didn't mind missing a few days of school here and there. It reduced the times I got in trouble for telling jokes during class. I had my very first day of school when we lived in Shaker Heights, next to Cleveland. Mom walked me all the way, all seven blocks, to kindergarten. The plan was that each day she would walk me one block less until I was a big boy and could do the whole thing by myself. That first day she waved me across the last street and up the steps and then she set out for home. When she arrived, she turned around and there, about twenty steps behind, was her little boy who had decided he'd had enough of school. The next week on the first day that I was to make the journey all by myself, I got as far as the first corner before rushing back home because I had just realized how much my hamsters needed me and they could obviously not survive a whole day without me. My mother had a different thought. And somehow the hamsters did survive without me.

By the first grade I was learning the warm satisfactions of pleasing a teacher—they were all women in those days—with answers, any answers. I had also learned the delights of raiding kindergartners. This was a relaxing after-school pastime adapted, I believe, from stagecoach holdups in the black-and-white Westerns on the Saturday-morning "Buckskin Billy Show." Raiding kindergartners was really very simple: a few first-grade boys hid in the bushes on the trail home. When the five-year-olds shuffled by with their bunny lunch pails, the six-year-olds jumped out of the bushes and began screaming. Although this happened most days, the kindergartners reacted by standing frozen in shock for a few seconds. They then began screaming and running into each other and falling down in the snow.

It was great sport and fairly safe, too, because if anyone ever asked, the first-graders could honestly say, "I never touched them." Being raided was a rite of passage for all kindergartners walking westbound on Lomond Boulevard, something the first-graders had experienced the previous year and something long-forgotten by the time any of the youngsters reached home—until one of those sneaky little people told. Next day, some first-grade boys were summoned to the office of the principal, who was always a man in those days. I happened to be caught in this dragnet. I listened with appropriate attentiveness to the principal's admonition. Some of my cronies said, "We never touched them." I took the Fifth, safe silence.

But I was addicted to raiding, which I knew was absolutely harmless because it made people—well, some people—laugh. And although the ranks of raiders dwindled, the afternoon forays continued. I was a leader of the bad guys. I assume this prompted a telephone call to my mother, because one day after school she sat me down. I expected the hairbrush again. But instead she gave me a long boring talk about being a bully, which I clearly was not because I never touched them, and about giving up one of the real joys of my life because of some little kindergarten fraidy cats. Mom's talk was surprisingly mild, however, which should have set off danger signals.

But it didn't. And a few days later I was blithely walking down the dark hallway toward the safety of my room when Mom leaped out of the door and screamed unintelligibly at me. My feet and mind went in different directions and I ended up sprawled on the floor. "How do *you* like being raided?" she asked. I was speechless. But that incident did bring to an end my life in crime. Except for the assault on Joey.

In retrospect, Mom's disciplinary approach did fit a pattern. A few years before, I had been found guilty of biting a playmate in the sandbox. Punishment was swift. My mother took my finger. And she bit it. That was the last time I recall being involved in a biting incident. It also, I believe, eventually helped firm my total belief that you do reap as you sow, even if sometimes you must take justice into your own hands. Like the time that Joey Andrews, one of my two best friends, hit me on the head with a lead soldier during a dispute over a crucial land battle in his bedroom. My mother was summoned. There was a lot of blood. People looked very worried. My T-shirt was soaked red. But I survived.

Two weeks later, the time for retribution presented itself. At the end of a backyard play session Joey turned for his back porch. I whipped out my metal toy pistol, ran up behind, and hit him on the head as hard as I could. There was considerable crying, a fair amount of blood, and everything seemed back in balance. Our parents negotiated a peace treaty, which blossomed again into full-scale friendship for many more years.

. . .

*A mother and a teacher*

Do unto others as they did unto you. If that represented a distortion of the Golden Rule I heard so much about in Sunday school, it made sense to me for a long while. How my parents could inflict on me some school that didn't even have a recess was a matter of silent, seemingly respectful wonderment.

I first went to Sunday school at the age of four and a quarter. It was a big deal, "good" clothes all chosen and laid out by Mom, which wasn't the big-deal part since she did that every day. First suit. Buttoned collar. Tiny tie. Pressed shorts. Shiny shoes. Combed hair. Family photos. The works. I had to look "nice," otherwise what would people say about her?

Sunday school at that church was simultaneous with the big people's service, kind of like a religious baby-sitter, which wasn't so bad because they had color comic books, although they weren't exactly Captain Marvel. Then all three of us went out to lunch afterwards. "Why don't you try something new this time?"

"No, thank you. Peanut butter and jelly, please."

But then as I grew a little older and we had our own young people's service before the adults', certain inconsistencies began to emerge. Seeing the intricate connections between so many natural things in our country life, including the wonder of a kitten's birth and growth, I had no problem believing in a God overseeing most everything. I respectfully said my prayers every night and thought I had a pretty good direct relationship with Him without having to deal through middlemen who wore their shirts backwards. But I wondered sometimes if He was paying attention all the time, because there were some awfully hypocritical, meaningless, and really cruel things going on down here pretty often. And I didn't see the culprits getting caught or having to pay.

Also, how come He had so many truly boring people working for Him? If they wanted to get His message out so badly, why were all the readings in such murky olde English designed to trip up young tongues? Why were cushions okay at home but not on those hard wooden pews? I didn't see any paintings of God or Jesus when they weren't wearing a wraparound sheet, so why did I have to wear the shirt and tie Mom laid out? How could there be much personal meaning in saying the same things so many times you didn't need to read the prayer book anymore, you just mumbled like a robot? And how come the only time He was available to be formally worshipped by young people was early Sunday morning Eastern time? Why not, say, Wednesday evening or later Sunday morning after breakfast but before the Browns game? Later, when confirmation classes were required, I saw a human conspiracy when they were scheduled for early Saturday morning, the one day of the week that had heretofore been blessedly free of a school.

After confirmation, which was such a big deal that the Bishop came to officiate, my parents signed me up for acolyting, which was supposed to be an honor. But being the junior-most acolyte, I was assigned the 8 a.m. communion service, so there weren't all that many people around to be impressed by my red-and-white starched robe and the proper order in which I lit the candles. And after the first weekend, when they took pictures of me at the front door, my parents threw their overcoats on over their pajamas to deliver and retrieve me from my assigned Sunday-morning religious calling.

I think I tried once or twice to ask my father about some of this. My mother always took general questions so personally, as if I were trying to find the chink in her armor or challenge her authority, and somehow we'd often end up shouting. I could ask my father the questions safely, although that didn't guarantee a helpful answer. I didn't exactly say, "How come I have to go to church early every single Sunday, but you and Mom don't?" But that was the gist of it, I think he thought. And his reply was a little harder than usual, harder and useless. "When you grow up, then you can go when you want." Thanks a lot. I decided, silently, not to go as soon as I could.

I did, with a fury that frightened me. She was wrong again. How could she know? She didn't know anything, not anything about anything.

Did I realize I had broken the new thermos?

The what? So what? So it's broken. You want broken? There! I kicked it across the floor with the new paratrooper boots she'd bought me. I didn't care. I didn't even care about the stupid Joe Palooka lunch pail she had picked out. Buddy was hurt. That was the important thing. He needed help. What was so difficult to understand here? Didn't she want Buddy to get better?

No, Andrew. Buddy was dead. And the sooner I accepted that the sooner I could get on with life. Now come have some orange juice.

Orange juice? Orange juice! How could she think about that crap at a time like this?

What was wrong here? Why wasn't she responding to this obvious crisis? She didn't know anything about football and seemed strangely proud of that. But could she really be this stupid? I'll bet if it was a crisis for her, like snow threatening her blessed Friday bridge club, then she'd get excited. But she was so calm and uninvolved. Goddammit, didn't she realize what would happen unless she began to care about something important for once? And we ended up shouting at each other, as we would many more times in the years to come. Dad said it was because we were so much alike. But no amount of shouting at her or being shouted at by her could explain the pain or bring Buddy back from the animal hospital. And I ran back into the woods, alone.

They had no explanation either. When Dad came home, he was there, with his big arms and his own tears and some thoughts on the natural order of life and death. Although what was natural about a speeding car that didn't stop always escaped me.

"It's very sad," he said. "And it's very painful. But you'll sur-vive."

"No, I won't."

"And I'll survive."

"You? What do you have to do with this?"

"I loved Buddy, too. I was there when we met him, don't you remember?"

"Well, I don't want to survive."

"You can do whatever you have to do. Always remember that."

"It's too late."

"You have your whole life ahead of you."

"Without Buddy!"

"Everything dies sometime, son. Dogs, cats, trees, people, plants."

"I don't care about plants."

"Sometimes it's just sooner than we'd like."

Pause.

"But it hurts so much."

"Yes, I know. I hurt, too. That means you really love him. And he loved you very much. He had a good life with us. But you wouldn't want him crawling around here, always in pain, all crippled."

"Yes, I would. I'd take care of him. Forever."

"No, you wouldn't do that to him. Make him suffer. That's not my Andy. That would be selfish. That wouldn't be kind to him. That wouldn't be loving. And that wouldn't be the real Buddy, would it? He always wanted to be free, not tethered to pain or anything. Remember the leash that first night? And every spring when he'd run away?"

"But he always came back."

"This was his home. You were here. You'll always have his memory."

"But I don't want a memory. I want him."

"Well, we don't always get what we want in life. And memories aren't so bad to have, Andy. Better than nothing."

"But I'll miss him, Dad."

"Of course you will. And I will, too. But— And your mother does, too. But life goes on."

"I don't care."

"It has to."

"I don't care."

"Well, you better start caring. You've got a lot to do in life."

"What? Like what?"

"I don't know. That's the mystery. It's exciting. Don't you want to know what you were meant to do?"

Pause.

"No. I don't. And I don't care."

"Maybe you don't right now. Give it time. You will someday."

Someday. Someday. I was interested in angry revenge right now. First, I didn't talk to my mother for several days. I think there was a fight or two at school. And for a couple of weeks every afternoon I'd sit out by the highway under the big elm with a pad of paper noting the estimated speeds and at least part of the license number of every vehicle that seemed to be going too fast. That made me feel some better, as if somehow in this world justice had a chance. For many years after, whenever I'd see another roadside victim, I'd think of Buddy bounding about on the clouds and say a prayer and think of how crowded Heaven must be getting with crunched little creatures because there didn't seem to be any room for them down here on earth anymore.

Then one Sunday I decided to run away from home, which I announced about midafternoon. There was a brief silence. My parents said they really wanted me to stay. They hoped I would reconsider.

I packed up my wagon with all the essentials I could think of—blanket, hunting knife, BB gun, toothbrush, PJs, teddy bear. I told my parents it had been good to know them. They said they loved me. And, after an awkward pause, I put on my Indians cap, strode out the back door, and headed down the sidewalk. Mom and Dad watched from the window but did not move.

# Someday

That's when it occurred to me that I had nowhere to go. Also, it was raining.

---

*"This is a lovely one," said the funeral director.*

*"Where are the wooden ones?" I said. I was quite firm. I had never planned a funeral before, which he could tell. My wife would arrive for support in a day or two. But Mom was at home being closely cared for and enjoying every minute of such intense attention. She said her hip was bothering her. I was out determined to take care of Dad. Everything was up to me. As each choice was presented, I made the decision. Which burial plot; I examined several and settled definitely on the hillside one. I thought he would like the vast openness of the view. What kind of headstone; I looked at the samples and chose the mottled gray one, along with the simplest lettering. How long was the visitation to be; one hour was plenty. Which clothes to take; his favorite summer-weight with a bright-red tie. I even took his best shoes. But there was no choice about the coffin.*

*"Just dump me in a wooden box," Mom remembered him saying years before. "Use the money on the living." Like most everyone, that was as close as we ever brought ourselves to making any advance final plans. Seems like courting bad luck. Who needs it now? Maybe someday. But maybe, like a persistent pain, it'll go away.*

*But not the memories. Whenever I see raw lumber, Dad's image flashes through my mind, a pencil behind his ear. Dad in a slightly dirty T-shirt, measuring the fresh planks. Dad marking it with the pencil stub. Dad sawing it. Dad nailing. Dad sanding. Dad perusing. Dad staining. He used to work with pine, sometimes mahogany, on his sacred basement workbench. He loved bringing out the deep grains in furniture, bowls, even my toy chest, my cars, and some of* the toy trucks he made for the neighborhood children whose fathers were away in the war. Like his mother, he had but one good eye, which kept him at home.

"Do you have anything in pine?"

"No, sir," said the funeral director as if he'd just suffered a bad burp. "I'm afraid we don't carry anything like that." So I chose an oak coffin. It had a deep, blond grain. But wood apparently is not so funeral-fashionable these days, which convinced me it was the perfect choice.

For two days I had been getting along just fine, burying myself in minutiae, until we began the funeral paperwork and the man said, "How many copies would you like of the death certificate?"

I froze. A hurricane of something was boiling up within me. I couldn't speak. Tears began rolling down my cheeks. I could make no sound. The man opened the desk drawer. He had a half-dozen tiny tissue boxes in there. He handed me the open one, and waited. When enough pressure had seeped out, we were able to continue. "I'm really going to miss him."

He smiled and nodded and waited with pen in hand. "What was the question?" I said.

The service went smoothly. My dark suit still fit. I got a wheelchair for Mom to ride to the gravesite. And I remembered to bring her favorite cushion. I found a copy of Dad's favorite prayer, the one he had read at his mother's service, and that day his minister read it, too.

I was fine, except for some persistent stomach trouble. I had kind of lost my appetite. And I sort of fell at the end of the visitation. But my wife caught me and we sat there together, just the two of us, with him for a few final minutes.

That afternoon I took his clothes to the collection box for the day-care center where he had done volunteer work. I kept one jacket.

Mine was, by and large, a peaceful childhood. When a few friends and I staged a children's circus in our yard complete with a dressed-dog parade, trapeze-hanging, and some attempted juggling, my mother bought tickets for the reserved-seat lawn chairs and attended the matinee. We lived a few miles outside of a small rural Ohio town that would, in another generation, become something of a quaint, affluent suburb. I think of those times generally in black-and-white. There were rules to follow, both written and unspoken. Shop signs, for instance, had to be flush with the building, nothing ugly sticking out to block the views of the broad, leafy elms that hadn't died yet. That sign rule was written. So were the zoning rules encouraging houses and roofs to look like New England, which some felt was the natural repository of all culture and important values.

But people didn't need a law to know never to honk their horn at the stoplight: too pushy. Or spit on the sidewalk: disgusting. The town crews needed no law to know when to close down College Street by the hill for sledding. And most of the children didn't need a law to know they were never to leave their bicycles on the sidewalk in front of any shop; bicycles belonged across the street. Children also knew that if they asked politely, Harvey at the drugstore would permit use of the store phone to call home. If they didn't, he didn't. Politeness paid.

Not by chance, the diagonal parking spaces out front were large enough to hold tractors. A squad of them appeared magically at the morning coffee hour when beefy men in overalls, some of them school-bus drivers, would share a table, a pot of coffee, and not many words. Men went to the restaurant. Women— that is, mothers on errands—patronized the drugstore, which also served soft drinks and all kinds of salad sandwiches for the ladies. Around the village square, which was really more of a village rectangle, the town also had all the usual establishments—a bank, a jewelry store, a clothing shop, record store, real-estate office, hardware, post office, a library, Town Hall, retirement home, a Catholic church, and, at the other end, a Protestant church.

The square was the summer site of the Ice Cream Social, that festive evening in June when every organization of women in town merged to sell baked goods and ice cream to raise money. The parents chatted and the kids walked around all sticky and gooey, and if I had Little League that night, I'd get there so late I might miss the Christ Church chocolate cakes with the white icing. In the winter, hundreds of townsfolk, and those like mine from the countryside, too, would end up in the square one December Monday evening after snaking down snowy local streets from all directions, sharing carols and their sense of belonging to a place, that place. The old red-brick sides of the village clock tower would be decorated with lights and the large stuffed Christmas mouse that mysteriously appeared every holiday from its honored but secret hiding place in a select someone's garage.

It was such a happy time, everyone bundled tightly, having thrown fashion to the brisk winds. I remember the first year I came of age caroling: I got to carry our family's oil lantern. Afterwards everyone would adjourn to a church for refreshments, the Catholics, Episcopalians, and Congregationalists taking turns doing the marshmallow hot-chocolate honors.

The fall brought hayrides with real hay, real horses, and real kisses safely exchanged in the dark because the driver had promised not to turn around. In the spring, there was mud.

The town—actually, it was a genuine community—was a special place to grow up safely and sanely drawing on a reservoir of values that had been stored there, unpolluted, for many generations, although few of my classmates could afford to stay when that process was complete and jobs were required. It was no paradise. It had all the fables and foibles of small-town life, the containerized fame and shame, the hidden loneliness and public joy, and the occasional headshaking social scandal that would now draw barely a shrug. As the years swept by, there was so much to do and to learn, usually in that order in those swirling times of teendom. There were the girls who were determined pretty in grade school and thus destined eventually to ascend to the May Court. There were the guys, some handsome, many awkward, some powerful, some gangly, others lithe and lean, and a few just mean. The coaches began sorting them by junior high.

Some of these young males played varsity baseball on the field behind the bus garage and nobody knew. A few played basketball and a few knew. But every male with any ambition, any dreams, aspired to play football, the community's complete focus every fall Friday night. Not every boy played, which was all right; it was the trying that mattered and each team member got a uniform. As a youngster sitting in the children's reading room of the town library consuming the addictive adventures of Kit Carson and Jim Bridger, I could hear the fabled future pounding down Division Street in the afternoon soon after 3 p.m. En route to the field, the football team, clad in its once-white practice uniforms, its bulging pads and battered blue helmets, would come rhythmically running down the sidewalk, hundreds of metal spikes banging the pavement in a clattering pattern of power that was so awesome to behold from the sixth grade. Without their numbered jerseys these guys were frighteningly anonymous and also huge. I would have said very huge, some of them being as old as sixteen and seventeen—eighteen if they'd flunked once. Anyway, they could drive cars without a parent, which was the parole date from childhood's confinement.

That daily scene—the chanting pack pounding off to practice full of energy and enthusiasm and, 150 minutes later, straggling back toward the lockers full of fatigue—was as regular as the smell of cut grass in May or the noon siren every day of the week but one (the Lord's Day was quieter, although this wasn't written either). Would-be knights of the Midwest learning to be men through legal aggression, and woe to the weak in the way. The meek might inherit the earth, but they'd never beat Mogadore:

shouldering the honor of their town against this week's dread enemy, who ventured out from their own fortress twelve miles down the road; being of one in a solid group united in self-protection against the opposing knights in their own colors and anonymous armor; and striving for victory beneath the warmth of hometown cheers, the glamorous glare of the field's floodlights, and the even more powerful beams of the girls' eyes. And if, as it did, victory came less often than defeat, that pain was soon overshadowed by the social anguish at the ensuing dance—the studied but soft consolation offered by the girls and its awkward acceptance by the boys—and the prospect of the suffering which the dissatisfied coach had promised to inflict during the next week's 170-minute practices.

Those were my days and years for dreaming. If I just thought about something long and hard enough, it would surely happen; wishing hard made things so. Staring out that library window at the darkening street, I planned touchdown runs that shook the stands, interceptions that gagged the enemy's fans, and tackles that sent their leaders into a different dreamland and set my coaches to smiling at me. In study halls I drew colored sketches of my ideal bobsled, always with an intimidating set of shark's teeth at the front. At lunch I dreamed of owning Grandpa Bowles's '32 Ford, an easy extrapolation from his passing promise that I could drive it someday. In my dreams that car was so hot that it had to have red-and-yellow painted flames streaming from the engine compartment. In math class my mind's eye pictured me owning a pickup truck and hitting the road, any road, for anywhere far away, maybe even Chicago or the uncharted wilds of Kansas where so many unknown adventures awaited me that I couldn't even conceive of them.

The reality of life then seemed more mundane. The simul-taneously crushing and comforting routine of chores, school, chores, and bed placed such a premium on learning and surviving and seemed to leave such precious little time for doing anything real. My mind could only be occupied so long by gluing tiny turrets onto model destroyers. There were books, of course, and regular outings with Dad into the real world for Indians or Browns games; all you did was flag down the afternoon Greyhound bus and, an hour later, get off in the city terminal, where Dad would be waiting.

I took up serious target-shooting with my BB gun and earned more medals-by-mail than my jacket would properly carry. By mowing, picking up rotten crab apples from our wild orchard, and sometimes helping a friend with his newspaper route, I saved the $49.95, plus tax, necessary to buy a Hallicrafter's shortwave radio. The earphones came on the next birthday; it never occurred to me that they were perhaps less a thoughtful gift and more to relieve my parents' ears of the aural clutter of exotic static. I used the earphones to secretly cruise the world's airways, listening in on conversations and programs without anyone knowing, except my radio diary. Alone in the darkness of my carefully appointed room, where Mom had neatly arranged my books on shelves by descending order of height and perfectly coordinated and hung my pennant collection around the ceiling's rim, I would twist the wanly lit dial and go anywhere I wanted, even if I had no idea where I had arrived. Often in the summer, when my pillow was damp from the humidity and my heat, I'd listen to Indians night games, hoping against hope and occasionally being rewarded. "Well," I'd tell myself, "I'll just listen for one more inning." Sometimes I'd get unrecognizable languages or alien accents. "Well," I'd tell myself, "I'll just make one more tour of the dial." I was fond of entering postcard contests on Texas and Louisiana stations, though I never won. I kept notes on the dates, times, and frequencies of these radio encounters and hid them inside my comic-book stash.

It was around then that I determined to build a car, a little one, to be sure, made of wood and without a grinning shark's mouth. But it would go like lightning, I was certain, and I would settle for menacing yellow dragon eyes up front. These little vehicles are metal nowadays and called go-karts. But mine would have an aerodynamic body, an airplane-style steering wheel, lightweight front wheels, heavy-duty drive wheels, and one of the most unnecessarily complicated cable-and-lever braking systems in the history of motordom, although it worked. It was a point of personal honor that no one work on this vehicle except me, although I did seek the hands-off engineering advice of my father a couple of times. I found a used lawn-mower motor for sale and installed it, complete with chrome tail pipe, directly behind the driver so I could swim in the deep-throated power of its unharnessed noise.

I worked on my creation at any free moment, emerging for personal refueling at dinnertime and then disappearing under its gangly frame immediately after. It took me a year to finish. It didn't look pretty, but it was beautiful. I made the first test drive alone, in case it fell apart. But it worked perfectly. At its first public run, my parents applauded. Mom said it was really good and was I absolutely sure the brakes worked? Dad said it was great and took lots of pictures. He also wanted to drive it.

Soon after, I drove it into town, my mother driving closely behind with her right-turn signal flashing a protective warning to other traffic. My friends waited in line to try it out. But many afternoons I would take it out myself for slightly wreckless spins down an absent neighbor's paved driveway whose twists became a demanding road course. Even without a crowd's "oooh"s, those private skids were worth all the skinned knuckles I had endured during construction.

A few years later, having long outgrown the personal satisfaction as well as the cockpit, I sold my little car for forty-two dollars, about four times what it cost me to build. Dad said he was very proud. Mom said it was great to have that half of the garage back.

In those years I made little time for social life, a pattern my wife might suggest has been preserved in later years; aloneness was safer. I had halting crushes from time to time and remember vividly the exhilaration one day of exchanging ID bracelets with a girl. That amorous allegiance was an automatic ticket to and through many parties. But, of course, that too was destined to die.

What females really thought about anything was a true puzzlement to me. From their notebook covers I was pretty sure many of them loved horses, just loved them. And judging from Mom's comments they didn't think much of us guys. Girls giggled a lot. And talked about talking on the phone a lot. They were believed more by teachers, too. Sometimes they were completely bizarre; I remember one recess a tomboy named Lynn downing a pair of dog biscuits to prove her masculine mettle when what our team really needed was a solid double to left.

But mostly girls were just downright puzzling. They gave off one set of signals with their eyes and then reversed them with their words. They dispatched female Cyranos with promising messages of ardor. Why didn't they just say what they meant outright? Why did we have to superimpose a game with the most confounding unwritten rules onto one of the world's most confusing chemical reactions? It was absolutely infuriating, not to mention terrifying. I didn't like that awkwardness, that phoniness, and I didn't like me when I was around it. So I didn't spend much time around it.

I remember trying to balance the scales of adolescent justice on one dark hayride. "Eleanor," I cooed loud enough for the other guys to hear, "are your hands cold?"

"Yes, Andy," came the eager reply.

"Well, then, put your gloves on."

Humor was always safe. If everyone laughed, I got the credit. If the object of the joke acted hurt, I could deflect the blame: "Oh, c'mon now. It was just a joke." But I had gotten the shot in anyway. It could be risky to be around me. I liked it that way. Safer to keep things at a distance. Gave you more reaction time when the unexpected happened.

I don't think I really thought that the most beautiful—or at least the second most beautiful—girl in the seventh grade would go to the movies with me; I forget her name now. Maybe I needed a rejection right about then. Maybe she had seen that movie already. It took me a week to construct the courage to telephone. Reach out to touch someone, safely, from a distance.

When, as expected, she turned me down with one of those eminently transparent or purely plausible excuses, depending on my mood, Dad just happened to be passing by the kitchen phone. "This may be hard to believe right now," he said, "but someday you won't even remember her name."

There were in those junior-high years required dancing classes in the gym one night a week all fall, proper attire required. These tedious sessions were designed to practice proper footwork and social graces. But they also created a brief freedom from homework and an excuse to stay in town after school, which one day led to a most puzzling experience.

It was arranged for me to spend that afternoon at Toby's house. His mother went shopping, leaving behind the stern instruction not to play any football in the house. We hadn't thought of that at the time, but her reminder made in-house football seem like the best possible way to pass an unchaperoned hour in the downstairs hallway. I went for a deep pass past the living room and, because as the visiting team I was unfamiliar with the exact dimensions of Toby's home field, I went right through the front storm door. It was a completion for a touchdown. But the sound of shattering glass shattering even more on the front porch detracted somewhat from our celebration.

"What are we going to tell my mom?" my friend inquired desperately as we picked up a thousand pieces of evidence from the crime scene.

"I think the truth," I suggested naïvely. When in danger, fall back on your father's most sacred rules. Honesty was his, at least as it related to our discussions. He called it "right kind." With a serious frown, he would ask me what happened. I would tell him most of it. "Right kind?" he would say, looking inside my eyes for the entire truth. Well, uh, yeh, I would say. Oh, well, there was one other thing. And I'd tell him the rest of it. He'd nod. And we'd shake hands, which was the last chance for truthful amendment before what I had said was set in cement. Nothing could be more serious between us than having a lie fixed in cement because it set the course of the road incorrectly from then on.

The only way to avoid that was to tell the truth or not say anything. Which I had tried years before in the notorious raiding case, and also after breaking a neighbor's garage window with a high fastball. For ten days I had lived with that festering secret. Where would I ever get the thirty-five cents the neighbor demanded to replace the glass pane? Finally, I realized the only way out was to tell the truth. I took forever to get home that night. I told Dad I had something to tell him, right kind. And I confessed my accidental destructiveness. He hadn't seemed angry. Instead, he'd seemed, oddly, to have been waiting for something. He thanked me for telling the truth. And then he handed me a quarter and a dime.

I suspected that Toby's parents' storm door would cost more than thirty-five cents. But the absence of any viable alternative tale and the presence of my instincts made honesty the only way out.

Then I realized that I must have cut myself picking up the glass. My left hand was all bloody. Except it wasn't coming out of my hand. It was coming from under my wristwatch. Or wait, no, it was coming down my arm. In a pretty large stream here. Geez, it was getting all over everything. I hoped I hadn't cut my new jacket too. Mom would be furious.

In the bathroom I held my elbow up to the mirror. There was a hole in my jacket sleeve. And there also was a hole, a very large hole, in my arm. It couldn't be too bad. It didn't hurt at all. But the blood was surging out of that place like a new well.

I decided to go to the doctor's two blocks away, which, not by coincidence, would place me somewhere else when Toby's mom got home. So I walked to the doctor's office, which was closed. However, when I held up my elbow to the nurse standing inside the door, she quickly let me in, held a towel to the new cavity, and then sent me directly back out toward the other doctor's office, the town's new young doctor, the one my mother liked because he didn't get impatient with all her calls about me. It was several blocks away and I was feeling a little woozy, but I could do whatever I had to do. So I plowed on. From a block away I could see Sharon, the pretty nurse, leaning out the new doctor's door and waving. She shepherded me, all gushing, right through the waiting room; no old magazines today. And onto the table where the usually talkative but now silent doctor proceeded to sew me up with nine stitches and a bandage that meant I'd have to move with my arm in a funny position at dancing class.

I was on time for the class, which seemed to last eighteen hours. And, feeling fairly brave, I got my ride home to announce my injury, which was beginning to throb a lot. My mother was at the door to greet me, which was weird, it being after the usual dinnertime when her regular duties required her perpetual presence elsewhere. And, was that right, she looked mad?

That was putting it mildly. She was furious.

How could I?

How could I what?

Why would I do such a thing?

Why would I do what?

What ever crossed my mind?

When? What? Wait. What's going o—

What must I have been thinking about?

Mom, wait, Mom. I hurt my arm today and—

She knew all about it. Sharon had called. How's Andy doing? she had asked.

Uh, fine, said my mother. Why, how's he doing? He's not home yet.

Tell him, Sharon said, if his arm hurts tonight, he should take some aspirin.

What arm?

The left one.

No. What is wrong with Andy's arm? That he would need to take aspirin?

Well, usually after that kind of accident—

Accident!

—in a few hours that many stitches really begin to hurt.

*Stitches?*

Oh, Mom didn't know? Well, Sharon didn't know all the details. Something had happened at Toby's house. But Doctor had fixed pretty much everything. And Sharon had suggested Andy go home and lie down.

Andrew had not come home early. He had dancing class on Wednesday evenings. He had not phoned either. So she hadn't talked with him since that morning. But she would definitely talk with him on his arrival. That was certain. She was so very glad Sharon had called.

Well, the nurse was sure everything was going to be fine. Just fine. Mom shouldn't worry. The artery was barely nicked. Bring him in late next week to have the stitches out.

I could only imagine the fury of the fingers immediately dialing Toby's mother, who would know only enough about the day's destructive doings to mention the need for a new storm door and for rug cleaners to work on all the blood. Toby and I never did have a chance to get our stories straight. But I was in shock, not from the self-inflicted stupidity of going long through a storm door, but from the deeply disturbing reaction of my mother. She had always been reliable—cool if I was well but consummately concerned if otherwise. And now here I was with nine stitches —the first ever on her side of the family, I was later informed, as if it was a normal statistical record every family kept. But it seemed to me that what really consumed her was anticipation of the town's opinion of her momentary ignorance about the accident. It was clear that she didn't give a damn about me.

"Now, Andy, calm down," my father said after another silent dinner. "Of course she cares. She cares a great deal."

"Funny way of showing it."

"Well, sometimes when parents get very scared about something they care a lot about and then they find out everything is okay, instead of being very relieved they get very angry."

"What for?"

"Uh, no real reason. That's just the way they feel. It's relief. But it comes out anger. You'll understand someday."

"You didn't get angry at me because I was okay."

"She wasn't angry because you were okay. She was angry because for a while she was afraid you weren't."

"Oh, come on, Dad. She was just worried someone would know something before she did. And she'd look dumb."

"And I was a little annoyed, too, son. The thoughtful thing would have been to call to say you were all right."

"That's ridiculous, Dad. People don't call to say, 'Hi, I'm still fine. Don't worry about a thing.' You call if something is wrong. And by the time I could get to a phone, nothing was wrong. But, all right, okay, fine. I'll call my mommy every afternoon to say I'm okay so in case someone calls and asks how Andy is, she won't be embarrassed and then she won't get angry at me that night because I'm fine."

"Don't be a horse's ass."

"I'm not the horse's ass."

"Watch it, boy."


Mom and I seemed to get along better as long as Dad was around. He gave me more room, even to make mistakes. He gave me a list of things that had to be done and a deadline when they had to be done. How or when they got done was up to me, as long as they got done. With Mom, she was always hovering. Did you do this yet? Did you do that yet? No, Mom, Dad said it didn't need to be done until Sunday. Well, don't leave it till the last minute. Thursday is not the last minute, Mom.

I remember one weekend trying to start the lawn mower and

being blatantly unsuccessful, pulling on the rope time after time and getting not even a stutter, though I began to mutter. Dad casually walked by. "I'm sure you checked the gas tank," he said. "Yeh, yeh, yeh," I said.

Then, when he was gone, I did check the gas tank. Bone dry. It was a very useful lesson; I still check the tank before trying to start anything. And learning it from him that way didn't cost me a public mortification. "Go on, stupid. Check the tank. I'll bet it's bone dry. There, see, what did I tell you?"

By those uncertain teen years, he wasn't telling me what to do anymore so much as he was showing me different ways the job might be done. Different routes to the same destination, he would say. And it was up to me to be the bright observer and then pick the manner that suited me best, even though at that point the unpracticed choice was more a matter of whim than informed decision. "In college," he said, "there won't be anyone hanging around to tell you what to do and when to do it." Which sounded great—no mothers in sight. And while there never was any choice given me about going to college, this was all very heady stuff, even when it concerned just starting a lawn mower. And it was a little scary. Like getting your driver's license without the lessons.

Dad provided perspective, not telling me what was around the great corner of life, but letting me know there was a lot more than just today and the next, which I hadn't thought of. This was not enough to force me to apply myself to life's most unpleasant tasks, such as algebra. But it did suggest a scale of existence I had never imagined. And I began to question my lifelong assumption—being an industrial engineer like Dad, with all the math and stuff—although I didn't actually say this for fear of hurting his feelings. He never did try to shape my job goals—except that first time, after another family automobile vacation, when I announced my long-term career plans and he suggested that driving the big rigs was probably not my calling.

But going places always excited me. Him, too. The early-morning excitement of departure for new unknown locales. Even familiar places were all right, as long as we were on the road. Every turn offered a surprise; before Interstates, there were turns in the road. Dad said when he retired, he was going to do nothing but travel—no mortgage payments, no lawn to mow, no snow to shovel—just constant movement from one new place to another. Mom said nothing about that. But she went along on the vacation trips. To Canada. To Michigan. To Atlantic City before the neon. And upstate New York. I loved these trips so much. He wore short-sleeved shirts then and no tie. I got more of his time on these vacation days. And because he listened, Mom seemed to listen more also. And Dad laughed a lot.

Of course, we took the required Revolutionary War swing through New England, which seemed to be modeled after our Ohio hometown, except New England was boring until we got to the U.S.S. *Constitution*. If we stayed somewhere, we'd get a temporary library card and a stack of books for the evenings and rainy days. And on the sunny ones, the two of us, Dad and I, would do something outrageous together like go for a wild, wet ride in a black speedboat with deep-throated engines so noisy that no one could hear our whoops in the backseat. Mom said she saw us from the shore.

One quiet Sunday afternoon he drove right up close to a pier so I could see a real aircraft carrier. It was the *Midway* that I had read about from World War II days. All I could say, time after time, was "Wow!"

Then Dad did a strange thing. He said, "No time like the present." He got out of the car and walked up the ship's ramp as if it were his. In about ten minutes he came back.

"How'd you like to take a tour of the *Midway*?" he said.

I nearly died. There was an officer at the ramp and he took us all over the ship. We saw the engines and the pilots' ready room and the bridge and I sat in the captain's chair, and then we rode on the huge elevator that lifts the planes up to the flight

*A wife and mother*

deck. I stood right where they landed, just like in "Victory at Sea." I told Dad that night in the tourist home that I would never forget that day.

Dad and I also went fishing a lot, which was tough on the worms but gave us lots of time to sit and maybe talk. Of course, we'd throw all the fish back in; they might have families, you know. Except one time when I caught a very big fish and it was flopping around and Dad sent me to the other end of the pier to get the bucket. But when I got back, the big fish was very still. Dad didn't look me in the eye. But he made a big deal at dinner about me being provider of the night's meal.

When we traveled to Grandma Bowles's in Canada, I would rush to the nearby railroad tracks to see and feel the big steam engines and their heavy followers heading off down the rails and I'd wonder where they were going. And while Grandma didn't seem to travel much, except to come see me, my favorite childhood game, Our Game, had to do with a family trip. I would crawl up in her broad lap just before I went to sleep at night and I'd start telling her about the time we were on a train in New York state, in the observation car, when I saw something shiny under the radiator and reached down to get it, but my mother said, "Get your hand out of there—it's dirty," and then I pulled out a dime. It was a silly story, though true. But as soon as I started telling it for perhaps the seven-hundredth time, Grandma would begin tickling me. I had to finish the bedtime story before laughing, or else she won. I never could get enough of Our Game.

Grandma and I also made outings together. Every summer she and I had Our Day in the city. We would take every means of land transportation except my horse and bicycle to get into Toronto and back—car, bus, streetcar, train. We would buy a toy at Eaton's, the big downtown department store where Mom once worked. We would have lunch. And we would see a safe Jerry Lewis movie, before heading home, holding hands.

One summer Mom, Dad, and I took a train trip across the

United States and then back across Canada. The trip had its share of teen-sullen moments, I guess. There was one color snapshot of a happy Mom admiring a red rosebush in some famous California garden while her only son stood behind doing a James Dean impersonation. But I remember the massive scale of the landscape and sitting up in the darkened dome car late at night with Dad, soaking up the vast openness of the view together without a word being spoken. He just stared out at the land, which was empty as far as I could see. But he saw things. I wasn't sure exactly what he was doing then, but I wanted very much to do it, too. So I stared out there as well. It did feel good. And I felt so close to him those nights. I still do. Mom had gone to bed, tired, because there wasn't anything to see.

The phone rang about three on a sunny summer afternoon. Mom was gardening out back. I must have been trying to please her that day; I was hauling away her weeds. I ran into the house. I knew the call was for her; kids didn't call each other in midafternoon. What a pleasant surprise! It was Aunt Bea, Grandma Bowles's sister, Mom's namesake. Her favorite relative.

"It's for you," I called, saving the nice surprise part for last, just as she reached the door. I smiled. "It's Aunt Bea!"

"Oh, my God," said Mom, stricken with horror. She brushed past, knocking me into the doorjamb.

"Yes! Hello. Hello?"

I watched and listened from a safe distance, arranging cans of cat food in the cupboard so the labels all faced the front. I pictured Aunt Bea calling from Grandma's big wooden wall phone with the separate earpiece and the hand crank where everyone who called was named Central. "Hello, Central." Within moments, Mom was turning a frightening shade of white, as if the receiver at her ear were draining all the color in this one-sided conversation.

"I'm fine. Fine. What is it?"

Pause.

"What?"

Pause.

"Oh, my God."

Pause.

"Oh, my God."

Pause.

"When?"

Pause.

"How is he now?"

Pause.

"Where?"

Pause.

"What did the doctor say?"

Pause.

"Oh, my God. . . .

"Are you at the house now?"

I never noticed it before, but when Mom talked on the phone, she played with her other ear. And she always looked down, so the words could fall out of her mouth into the receiver easier.

"Are you going to stay? . . .

"Oh, yes. Yes, of course I will. . . .

"As soon as I can."

Suddenly, those eyes that could be so pretty were aimed straight at me.

"I don't know. I don't know. We'll have to see."

What had I done now?

"He comes home about six. . . .

"How's Mom taking this? . . .

"That's good. It'll do her good. . . .

"I hope so. I hope so. . . .

"We'll pray, too. . . .

"I'll ring you back in a couple of hours. . . .

"Thanks. . . .

"I love you, too. Very much. . . .

"What? Yes. Yes, I know. Of course, you always know, but you don't think about it. You know what I mean? You hope it never will. . . .

"Whose hands? . . .

"Oh, His. Yes, I suppose He will."

Grandpa Bowles had no choice. He died that afternoon. Which, according to my calculations, would put him in Heaven by Saturday evening.

He died in his own home, as most people did in the 1950s. In his own bed that creaked on the left side. Right by the light switch I bought for his birthday. Beneath the photos of his mother and father, his brothers and daughter. Next to the dark wood dresser decorated with a large doiley and a wooden dish of buttons and coins he stashed there. In his wrinkled, collarless white shirt and those wool trousers. With his old vest on and the pocket watch and chain in their proper place. His arteries finally too hard.

No one thought to take him to a big hospital. They weren't so big then, and when your time was up, what could a hospital do about it anyway? Trying to fix his shattered ankle was one thing, but there was something vaguely blasphemous and presumptuous then about trying to interfere in the natural course of events when it was so sadly but obviously sliding. It was a time for bowing heads and accepting, regretfully but respectfully. The sun would have been streaming through the old lace curtains of Grandpa's bedroom at that time of day. But he was in a blessed fog. The family members who got to the bedside in time remembered his last words exactly: "Get this big stone off my chest."

They were each saddened, of course, but not destroyed. Family members had no choice in the matter either. Yet. And the aging family doctor, who also wore wool trousers and a vest with a pocket watch, could only stand there too and make his trusted old friend Harry comfortable at the other moment that we all have in common.


I got my first airplane ride that Thursday. We were in a little DC-3 of Trans Canada Airlines, just like the one in a drawing on my bedroom wall. It was very noisy in that plane, which was great, and very bumpy, which was not. Mom threw up in a bag in the seat behind me, which I knew was horrible for her because the man across the aisle probably saw the whole thing. Also it may have ruined her lipstick. I didn't get sick; I was too busy trying to act not excited about my first plane ride and my first funeral, two more inch markers on the ruler of growing up. Even if it was mysterious, you weren't supposed to act excited at sad times; excitement and best clothes—dark ones anyway—didn't go together, which didn't make sense, like a lot of things. This growing up was a tricky business, learning all the different feelings you were supposed to show instead of the ones you were really feeling. Control and camouflage yourself—with women anyway.

I didn't really decipher this until well after high-school algebra class, which took me two years. First, in that class I figured out what computation method made maximum sense to me, and then I did the opposite. It was right most every time. When you felt the most excited was when you should act the calmest, unless you were at the football stadium, where practically every emotion was acceptable, which is why so many people go to those stadiums nowadays. When you were frightened, you shouldn't be. And when something didn't seem to matter at all, it almost always did to someone in authority. The trick was figuring out which one in time to protect yourself. Sometimes I'd forget and drop my guard. And, bam, I'd get a surprise reaction from the blind side, which is another time when it's far better to give than to receive. But over time I got better and better at controlling and camouflaging and feigning care.

I overheard some adults comforting Mom with essentially the same words as I had used. She acted very pleased to hear theirs. So I knew children—or at least this child—weren't supposed to say comforting things. I had just learned that. She had been running down the hall toward the bathroom after Aunt Bea's call. When I asked what was happening, I guess she didn't hear me. When I followed, suggesting that maybe everything would turn out all right because Grandpa was just sick—his arteries were hardening, you know—that got her attention. She froze in her tracks. She flung herself around sharply. She leaned down right in front of my face. "Everything is *not* going to be all right!" she shouted. "My father's dying!"

Well, everything dies some day. "How do you know?" I said in genuine puzzlement. Aunt Bea was no doctor. I knew that kittens all bent up had gotten better. I knew my dog died getting better. Where was the pattern? The rules? We hadn't even begun to pray for Grandpa. How could anyone know for sure about death until it was over? Who better to ask than the person who had brought our poisoned cat back from death?

"Well!" Mom said. "*You* don't know! That's for sure." And she stormed away.

Mothers. They have a way of declaring the obvious and making it sound like a revelation. Of course I didn't know. That's why I was asking. "How do you know someone's dying until they're dead?" She kept on walking away. "How do you *know* someone's dying until they're dead?

"I'll say some prayers, okay?" I had a pretty good line up there. It might help. It couldn't hurt. She slammed the door. I hadn't pleased her, though at least I had gotten her attention. Then I retreated outside and into silence. Who was going to feed the chickens now?

The funeral at the funeral home was just as I had imagined, though I didn't know they kept more dead people in other rooms.

The same people were there as had been at Grandpa and Grandma's fiftieth-anniversary party the previous year. Almost all old. Lots of gray hair and black clothes. I was the only child again. But at least I would not be told to play my drums. Everyone stood around talking softly, as if their mother had said to be quiet because someone was sleeping somewhere. Just about every person there told me how big I was getting, so it must have been true.

Wow, there was the big ring of flowers Mom said I sent: "From Your Loving Grandson." No mistake about who that was. But, just to make sure, I told the people next to us in line, "Those are my flowers." And they nodded. The line moved slowly across the room. Oh, and here was Grandpa. He looked just like Grandpa, only in a suit. Everyone was saying he looked so natural. But natural would have been him making something with his short, thick fingers. I thought he looked to be sleeping, only more formal than usual because his mouth was closed this time and he wasn't snoring. He was very still. And his hair was brushed a little funny. But Grandma fixed that later with her hand.

I told Grandma again how sorry I was she didn't have Grandpa anymore and I would still help with the chickens. She gave me one of her huge hugs. And I started to cry. Just like that. Bawling away uncontrollably like a little kid. But Mom said to hush up now. "Get ahold of yourself," she'd say. So I did.

We were seated on one side of the room because we were family. I thought this was special until they closed the curtains in front of us. "What are they doing?" I whispered to Dad. "Shhh," he said gently. Then they opened the curtains. The coffin was closed, like magic. We sang some more and filed out to the cars. We got into a fancy black car that was not like our Plymouth. We sat there forever. I was impatient.

"What's your hurry?" Dad asked.

He was always saying things like that that made me shift gears from just doing to thinking, from feigning to knowing. Come to think of it, I didn't know what the hurry was, except to get past this sobbing part. But I did want to make sure the car's headlights were on. That was important at funerals, even in the daytime. And this was my grandpa's funeral. I don't remember much about the cemetery except it was way out in the country in those days and had lots of birds and some rabbits too, judging by the chewed leaves and droppings along the bushes. The minister said some familiar prayers. Everyone whispered again. And they didn't lower the coffin while we were there. It was a bright, sunny day and a number of people said it was so fortunate that Grandpa did not suffer, which I had tried to tell Mom. But she smiled at these other folks.

----

*My father's death had seemed normal and natural—cardiac arrest, the documents said. The cause was worked out in a phone call between the paramedics, who looked Dad over, and his doctor, who never saw the body. There was no sign of foul play, nothing at all to suggest the need for any further inquiry, unless perhaps you were a haunted only child whose father took that black-and-white photo of you as an acolyte early one chilled Sunday morning. And then on that last Sunday morning he put it by his bed.*

*Some time later I asked a doctor friend if that had been routine, the paramedics conferring by phone, the doctor signing the death certificate the next day at the office. Oh, sure, he said. An elderly man in deteriorating health dies quietly in his sleep. His elderly wife sleeps blissfully on by his side, even talks to him in the morning for a minute or two before sensing an unusual stillness that quickly moves from annoying to frightening. The ambulance crew leaves their breakfast dishes on the firehouse table to rush through the streets, sirens whup-whupping and briefly waking dozens of dozing people who think, Someone's in trouble—I'm glad it's not me, before falling back to sleep and never again thinking a thing about that signal of someone's passing. As they say in the army, if you hear it coming, then it's not for you. One more chance, anyway.*

*There was nothing suspicious in any of this. There was relief and normalness and a developing sense of yeh-so-what routine for those in the business of health and death. He died now instead of, say, next spring or summer. This way there was a little less pain. Why bother pursuing the case? It happens every day. What good would come from probing further? For those in the once-simple business of just living, it was becoming harder to ignore death because now, maybe, it could be postponed. But that required a decision. And maybe even some thought.*

*But was death still so normal? In my mind, it had always been an unwelcome visitor wherever it knocked. In our final conversations Dad gave me a quick peek suggesting otherwise. I began to look with a sharper, more skeptical eye at the clichéd news of other deaths that briefly bump into the lives of us healthy ones. In obituaries, the end is always sad. The actual details are sanitized by language and the perceived proprieties of breakfast-table reading. The living always sound stricken, as I would have had anyone been so thoughtless as to question me on that Sunday—as I have done to survivors on many of my workdays. But interviews were no longer possible with the real subject of that article, the one for whom the death may not have been a shock, a surprise, a sadness.*

*Of course, I would never welcome death, never having suffered much physically and still being able to deny its inevitability, although I did start reading the obituaries just out of curiosity. But most of them are written by people under forty, probably thirty. And for them, death is something very distant that happens to Ethiopians without names or to movie stars whom their parents used to talk about. Or, once in a while, it is a freakish little incident that breaks out locally like a pimple.*

However, I was getting older, becoming more aware of the shadows, present and future. But I still kept my youthful curiosity. And this little-known business of dying in modern times seemed far too tidy for my professional mind. All my instincts said there was more going on here, although whether I really wanted to know about it was another matter. At the very least, Dad was expecting that last grim visitor and had left the door unlocked. I began to wonder if maybe, when that solemn knock came, there might well be some very sane people who answered the door saying, "Where have you been all this time?"

Then, by chance, on an airplane with a strange newspaper in my hands I happened to turn to a page and happened to scan down to the corner and happened to read a short item from Texas. Isn't it amazing, my father would ask me with a wink, how every day just enough news happens to fill every newspaper? This item wasn't really an obituary. It was presented as a news story, one of those freakish things that happen, like the family dog that gets lost on the auto vacation in California and finds his way home to Nebraska in time for Thanksgiving. As strange as they sound, these things seem to happen with a stunning regularity and just as regularly are thrown into the paper as bizarre brighteners that almost everyone will read and marvel at if they happen across them. Only, of course, this little item had to be written like some Sergeant Friday police report because it involved death.

It seemed that this old man in Texas had walked into the hospital to visit his wife of fifty-odd years. She had been stricken with Alzheimer's disease some time ago. She would start screaming in church or at home for reasons that probably even she did not know. Her family had put her in a home. Now, after all these months, she had contracted something life-threatening. But, thank God, a young nursing-home staff had caught it in time. They got her to the hospital, where the pros in the white clothes got this body stabilized and operating fairly smoothly before their shift-change, so now her frail little partner for life could shuffle in every day to visit and be yelled at by the familiar voice controlled by the unfamiliar mind.

But this day, the day before I read the newspaper item, had been awfully different. The old man had walked into his wife's room. When the nurse left, the man pulled out a pistol. He shot his wife in the heart. And as shocked hospital staff burst open the door, the man pointed the weapon at his own heart. He pulled the trigger and slumped into a chair, also dead.

It was a compelling story. It had everything—love, sadness, death, tragedy. Innocent victims to make us wince. No remaining bad guys to be tried. They were obviously two troubled minds. Two sad deaths. In one weird newspaper story. But they were old. The plane was landing. And life must go on for everyone else, even if you knew the dead couple.

Still, I was intrigued. A few weeks later, haunted by what I imagined this man's story could be, I telephoned the hospital. I told the spokesman I was a reporter. I wanted to know more about the old man who had killed his chronically ill wife there.

And the hospital spokesman said to me, "Which one?"

---

Hot summer days made Mom anxious and irritable. Too young to work legally, I could always hibernate from the heat with a book. So could Dad, who said he'd had enough cold in that prairie cabin with its icicles inside. He liked the heat. The hotter the better. In fact, he said he liked it so hot and humid that you'd sweat just lifting up your hand.

I don't remember ever seeing Mom curl up with a book even in the winter. She was always moving, doing something. And in the summer she was always talking about how the heat got to her, as if the climate of northern Ohio was so much more oppressively tropical than southern Ontario next door. Air-conditioning was something for the movie theaters. In the summer daytime, our house was usually sealed against the heat, even though by 1 or 2 p.m. it seemed to me as if the battle had been lost. Doors had to be closed immediately lest there be any movement of air. And to keep out every dot of dust. The curtains were closed, too, to give it that homey tomb-like feel.

At night, the windows could be opened to let in the cooler air, although I usually thought of it as fresher hot air. Sometimes I would lie on the living-room couch, which was a little prickly but nice and long and it had a table for my portable radio. Radios and the TV were assigned to reside in another room, a little den that seemed to soak up the sun well after it had set over Indiana. But I could bring my radio into the larger, shadier living room temporarily some evenings and stretch out on the couch and read or doze off, until Mom had that piece of furniture shortened.

Some men took it away and a few weeks later it was back as a little settee, a stubby thing for two women to sip tea on. Mom said it fit in more, although I didn't fit it now. And she said it looked much better. I thought furniture was something to use, not look at. But she must have been right because the following summer her house was chosen as one of eight on the town's annual house tour. It drew thousands of people, mostly women, for many miles around to munch tuna-fish lunches at one of the churches and purchase tickets to stroll and drive the town and visit the set of selected homes. The paper ran a large picture of Mom sitting by the fireplace looking at the large oil painting of her mother. She was really smiling, Mom was. A lot of people commented on the photo and us kids knew this was a big deal among parents; we needn't know why.

Mom gave a class for the tour hostesses assigned to our house, providing the history and meaning of everything—the usual stuff about her grandfather, the Canadian artist, and his son, and who the people were not smiling in the portraits, and the antique chair that had rocked five generations of Malcolm babies, and the marble table, and so forth, though she skipped mentioning the spot where the cats threw up the previous winter. Dad and I had very specific mowing and pruning instructions for the weekends preceding the tour. Mom arranged for perfect weather, though she rejected an offer to park my go-kart by the front door for public viewing.

For four weekdays it was like living in a museum. We could visit our home downstairs if our shoes were clean, but couldn't touch or move anything because the next day's visitors would know somehow. Every evening she went on dust patrol. Hundreds of people, all shapes and sizes and looks, paid money to stroll through our yard and first floor, evaluating Mom's taste and decorating skills.

I thought these were the kinds of strangers you locked your doors against. And they were so stupid they maneuvered their mammoth Oldsmobiles all over the lawn trying to find the gravel driveway. The cats hid out all week. And by nighttime each day the house had accumulated the unaccustomed perfumed scents of many strangers. But it was for a good cause, Mom said. And I don't ever remember seeing her happier.

We ate out every night to preserve the kitchen and a nervous mother's sanity. Our living room was off limits even after closing hours, which didn't bother Dad so it didn't bother me. And Mom had the newspaper photo enlarged and framed for the den. She had it hanging somewhere everywhere she ever lived after that.

We were supposed to be out of the house all day while the official tour hostesses herded everyone through. But one day I stayed in my room upstairs, and when I walked out I caught

Mom leaning over the bannister listening to the strangers' "ooh"s and "aah"s; she didn't even notice me. And somehow that scene made her seem very human that day.

Those hot summer nights were somnolent affairs in the country. You could almost hear the corn growing all around. The resting fields were moist and simmering. The mosquitoes were dining on anything that breathed. The swallows and martins were swooping silently about, dining on those diners. A dog might bark at a distant house and a moth flutter on the screen. And in the distant distance was the faint whine of truck tires on the new turnpike, implying others going about other lives differently, moving to other places at other paces, creating the only breezes that rustled that countryside for days.

There was always ample outdoor work at our place. Dad was always building something—a rock wall, perhaps, so I'd be assigned to pry the stones loose from the grasping soil where Nature had put them and place them where Dad said they should go. Or he was building a patio and I'd haul the sand.

One day one year, Dad announced he was going to build a pond out front. For me, it was very exciting—my own swimming hole just out the door. For him, it was exciting, too—one less acre to mow. The construction work—the steam shovel and all the dump trucks—was all exciting.

But then it was decided by the Parental Presidium that some of us might have more summer fun if I went away to a camp for not a few weeks—eight, to be exact. I thought I knew whose idea that was. Years before, I had been sent off to day camp once or twice. The milk tasted funny there. I also learned how to lose towels, how to make friends with the cook in charge of leftover sandwiches, and how, no matter how cool you think it looks, you should never slide into first base; it made people laugh, which was not funny. I also learned not to carry an entire bottle-cap collection in my jeans pockets on a hot summer day.

But actually sleeping at a camp overnight, for weeks of overnights, with strangers who wore funny pajamas and took showers naked at the same time I did—that had not been part of my experience. Which was just fine with me. "It's time he got out in the world," I imagine my father saying. "At thirteen I was driving a horse team to town to deliver milk." And I picture my mother saying, "Are you sure? About his going away, I mean?"

But one late-June day Mom and I and one of her bridge-club partners set out for the wild West of central Indiana, which didn't invent summer humidity but did perfect it. It's like living in a sauna under a huge wet towel.

We lived in framed tents, twelve kids to a counselor. I couldn't believe that the tidy blue uniforms included shorts. But at least no one I really knew was there to see. My roommate was a nice guy, also from Ohio—also, of course, a Browns fan. "I'm sure you'll be good friends," said my mother, as if she weren't going to be there. This had a disturbing tone to it. It stopped me short—an imminent future without her? Now just hold on. Of course, I knew it was not a camp for parents; there were no tents for them. But emotionally it hadn't dawned on me. Or maybe it had but I'd been very successful at denying its imminence. At the last innocent moment I began to realize, horribly, that when this car was unloaded, Mom was going to leave. To go far away. And leave me there.

That's why she'd brought the friend. It was a trick. She wouldn't be alone. But I would. Dad was always going away to work, and just as regularly coming home. But mothers didn't go away, not farther than bridge club anyway, which got them home by 5:15. But now here we were standing in a dusty parking lot in the middle of a foreign country among hundreds of sweating strangers. And in a moment I was going to be alone, completely and totally alone in this noisy crowd. At the mercy of men who wore shorts. Unaware of where to eat. What to do. Not even a dog to talk to. Abandoned. All alone. Wait. Mom, don't go.

It would be nearly thirty-four years before I had that awful feeling again. People called it homesick. I called it Momsick. When she was gone, my life was suddenly so hollow. What was the point to anything? My head throbbed. My stomach ached. And hearing from the jolly camp counselor that everyone goes through this was no help whatsoever. I was supposed to say, "Well, then everything'll be just fine." But instead I just thought, Well, then why does anyone come?

It was my last night, I was certain. The tears flowed abundantly, though silently. And when I woke up, I was surprised that I had been asleep. It was sunny, but there still wasn't much hope for the future. We marched off to breakfast and then somebody began talking about the walks in the woods. Woods? And the afternoon's softball game. Baseball! And swimming in the lake. Well, that didn't sound too bad for a first afternoon. And the roommate was turning out to be a really good guy. Maybe I could take a few days of this after all.

Returning to my tent after breakfast, I saw her. Mom! My mother came back! I was free at last! I ran up and hugged her and began describing how bad I was feeling and what an awful place this was and how I missed her so. And I started crying again. Now we could get out of there.

Well, wait, no, she said. After yesterday's farewell scene she had gone to the motel, and now before heading home she just wanted to stop for a minute to make sure everything was all right, which may have been a mistake, she was beginning to think now.

Mistake? Oh, no, it wasn't, I said. The mistake was my being there. And everything wasn't okay. I wanted out now.

No, no. No! I was there. They'd paid a lot of money. I was going to have a nice time. Everything was going to be fine. It took time to get acquainted. But I was going to make many new friends. And she and Dad would be visiting in a few weeks.

Now, get ahold of yourself, she said. Would you want your father to see you like this?

Invoking the deity's name brought me up short. That's right. He would be waiting at home, expecting me to do whatever I had to do. I didn't want to stay at camp. But I definitely didn't want to walk in on Dad after not staying at camp. So I let her drive away again, without me. And, sniffling, I went back to my group for morning inspection, when it was very important not to let a wrinkle sneak onto your bed blanket. Did these guys have Mom for a mother too?

The remaining seven weeks and five days were pretty good, as Mom had predicted, even with the daily remedial math class. I wrote home every day so I could feel a link to there. I knew they wouldn't want to miss a single detail of my life, so as soon as one letter was posted, I began another. "If I don't get this off," I wrote once, "you won't have heard from me for three days." These vital missives, which cost three cents to move from Indiana to Ohio, were full of the details of my life, the meaningful and meaningless, which take on import only later as part of a larger pattern of living, revealing habits, tastes, fears, a few joys. "Boy," I wrote one afternoon, "I think losing things gives you the worst feeling." I forgot to say what I had lost.

I was hitting .764 until a not-so-minor shower scuffle with a Chicago kid caused me to throw a few return punches, some of which landed, one of which broke my right hand. The camp doctor said there would be no more athletics for three weeks, which I may have forgotten to mention to my counselor. The cast ended my summer's swimming, and after a few days it smelled real funny. But Dad had been right; it was useful to be able to throw and bat both ways. And the cast made me the star volleyball server of the drum-and-bugle corps.

When I reluctantly reappeared at the infirmary with a broken cast, the doctor examined the cracked plaster closely. Since he had banned athletics, he said, he knew that couldn't have caused this kind of strange break, which he had never seen before. He suggested perhaps I had rolled over in bed and hit it on the tent frame while asleep, a theory which drew my emphatic endorsement and nods. He also said he was much too busy to remove the broken cast. So he simply added another heavy one on top of the old one.

I think it was during that first summer at camp—I know it

wasn't the third—that my counselor said after dinner that the head of the entire camp wanted to see me in his office. I had never been in the Big Tent. So there was an element of awe and not a little worry attached to this summons. I quickly ran down the list of potential causes: broken cast; talking after Taps; joking loudly at Campfire; tripping that Chicago kid during the Sunday parade so he fell over his drum, making a complete fool of himself in front of hundreds of chuckling spectators while I marched on by, smiling safely. None of these felonies seemed worthy of a summons to the Big Tent. But you never knew, especially if the complainant was someone's mother. I would have to be very careful on this new ground. And in control of myself.

"Sit down, Mr. Malcolm," he said. "Are you having a good camp?"

Watch it. This guy was up to something.

"Oh, yes, sir."

"Well, good. Your—"

"It's a—"

"Sorry?"

"Excuse me, sir."

"No, go ahead. You were saying."

"It's a lot of fun here, sir."

"Good. I'm glad."

"Me, too, sir."

What was this guy not getting at?

"You're a drummer, I understand."

"Yes, sir. I play the drum. In the drum-and-bugle corps."

Pause.

"Your counselor tells me you're doing very well."

So it wasn't the Campfire.

"Thank you, sir."

"Yes, well, Andrew, or is it Andy?"

That depends on why you called me in here. "Andy's fine, sir."

"Andy, I got a telephone call from your father this afternoon."

But he wasn't at that Sunday parade.

The camp commander leaned forward, closer to me.

"He wanted me to tell you, I'm afraid, that your grandmother has passed away."

Passed where? Away. Oh, that's the adult code for dead. Dead!

"Oh, Jes— I mean geez."

He smiled yes, painfully.

Grandma dead? Grandma Bowles dead! Oh, no. Our Game. Our Day. Not Grandma. That was awful. But she wouldn't just leave like that. No, wait, hold on a minute.

"Which one?"

"Pardon me?"

"Which grandmother, sir?"

"Oh, my. Now I'm not sure. I remember your father said he and your mother had gone to her house on a spur-of-the-moment visit and it must have happened while they were out in the garden with your grandfather because—"

With my grandfather? Well, then, phew, it was Grandma Malcolm. Oh, Grandma Malcolm. Gone? Forever?

"She was a teacher."

"Your grandmother?"

"My Grandma Malcolm. She was a teacher. She taught my father. And me, too, sometimes. She doesn't like liquor."

"Well, I'm very sorry. I mean, it's nice she was a teacher. I'm very sorry she's gone. Unfortunately, these things happen in life. And your father said he was sure you would take it like a man."

It would have been nice to take this one like a grandson, but I got the message. "Yes, sir."

Pause.

"You can sit here some more, if you like. I'll tell your counselor and you can come see me anytime, if you feel the need."

"Yes, sir. Uh—"

"Yes?"

"How did it happen, sir?"

"Oh. Well, your father said it was very peaceful."

Well, of course it was peaceful. This wasn't Korea.

"Her heart just gave out. Your mother found her on the kitchen floor."

I'll bet she was cooking a big dinner.

"She was cooking a big dinner."

"That's Grandma."

The head of camp smiled. He put his hand on my shoulder for a few seconds. In Man Talk that means, "You're not alone, though I can't actually say it out loud." On the way back to my tent I remembered the time Grandma found me with the dictionary, troubled. She was always saying, "If you don't know how to spell a word, look it up in the dictionary." Which made no sense since how do you look it up without knowing how to spell it? She found me muttering through the F's. I couldn't find "foursight." But this night I checked my memory, silently spelling "equilibrium," and getting it right. Words, I could do now.

It seemed to me the earth should have moved or stopped, or at least paused for a moment. After all, my grandmother had died. But the world wasn't paying attention, or it was but chose to ignore the event for its own good. I didn't know what ought to happen during such a terrestrial pause. But doing everything normally suddenly seemed somehow disrespectful and, well, noisy. Something serious had been lost forever, which was longer than I had been alive. But I couldn't think where to look or what to do that would help—the woods were off limits after dark. And crying was out of the question, something a thirteen-year-old would do. Hush up now. Get ahold of yourself. So I went to the camp movies. Later, after prayers, when the lights were out, I cried privately. But just a little.

---

*"I think," I told my boss, "that there's something going on with how some people die in this country."*

*I started talking with some middle-aged people who work*

*for groups that lobby for the elderly. Elderly suicides? they said, shocked. No, they knew nothing about that. Nothing at all. They couldn't imagine the elderly being any different than any other group. The statistics of death are the same for everyone, one man told me: one per person. Which was funny at the time and also indisputable.*

*Then one day I heard about a young nurse who had sided with a dying patient's family to defy the doctor; the nurse unplugged the patient's respirator and was charged with illegally practicing medicine. I read about a terminally ill woman who had jumped off a balcony, destroying herself and a car down below. Someone whispered there was one organization, maybe two, that helped a few people with such decisions.*

*What decisions? I asked. What is there to decide? Silence.*

*I found the nurse who unplugged the man. The nurse was a man. He would talk with me if his lawyer approved. The lawyer approved, saying, "It's time we got this out from behind the curtain."*

*Got what out?*

*I found the organizations. There were three of them—Concern for Dying and the Society for the Right to Die, both in New York and now merging into one, the National Council on Death and Dying. There also was the Hemlock Society, in California, of course (now it's in Eugene, Oregon). I visited each. They had file after file of newspaper clippings from large and small cities and towns all over the country.*

*The files were full of articles about freakish incidents: an old man taking his bedridden wife home from the hospital, shooting her, and then himself. An older couple, contemplating an approaching life in separate nursing homes, dismissing their housekeeper early one sunny afternoon, then sipping poison together from the same glass of wine. After several hospital stays, another couple, both in steadily de-*

clining health, drive into the country and have a picnic.
Then they spread a plastic covering over the front car seat.
He shoots her in the heart and then himself. They leave a
note apologizing for any inconvenience. I spent days sifting
through these accounts.

My God, I said, it's happening all over.

That's right, said the organizations' workers.

Each case seems so isolated until you pull them together
like this.

That's right, they said.

I researched the statistics on suicides among the elderly; it
was twice the rate for young people. "And those are just the
ones we know about," said a veteran statistician.

What do you mean? I asked.

"Listen," he said, "a person gets old, gets sick, then sicker.
One day they find that person dead on the couch or in bed.
There are no signs of violence. He or she probably would have
died soon anyway. So, hey, what's the point in pursuing the
matter and confronting a family with the stigma of suicide?"

You mean, I said, knowing full well what he meant, a lot
of the natural deaths in this country really are something
else?

"Welcome to the wonderful world of the future."

I tracked down details on many of the individual cases. I
talked to the doctors and coroners, the police and families.
They said their relatives were so afraid of being alone and,
worse yet, terrified of what would happen once they got back
onto the conveyor belt of medical technology. They would
lose all control to strangers. The elderly had tried to talk
about this fear with the family, but the younger, healthier
people couldn't conceive of someone not wanting to get help
to get healthy again. It was amazing what medical technology
could do in today's hospitals. Now the survivors wondered,
late at night after flying back home far away, if they had
missed some significant signals somewhere. But they consoled

*themselves with the knowledge that their relatives were probably the only ones ever to do such a thing.*

*I understand, I said. I really do.*

*I wrote the story then. It was published, almost an entire page. Isn't it amazing how just enough news happened that day? That was supposed to be it, one more story out of thousands I've done. Scanned by a million or so pairs of eyes and then forgotten by lunch. I went on to my next assignment.*

---

The school years seemed to roll by inexorably, like a large wave working its way methodically across an ocean on its unwritten natural schedule. The days seemed longer then, and each was significant and separate, not merged like now. Some days were stormy. Some overcast. Some were sunny. Those were the ones to be careful with; things could change unexpectedly. Rain or shine, the junior-high-school bus came at the same time every morning. The seats weren't assigned but they were taken by regulars. And woe to the new kid who sat in a bigger kid's regular seat. "That's mine. Get outta there." I know why Welcome Wagon doesn't hire teenagers.

In good weather, and sometimes pretty nippy times, too, I took to riding my bike to school. It was several miles. But I liked being alone and independent like that. And I didn't like the closed-in feeling on the crowded bus, where someone was always eating an orange or hugging a bouquet of flowers for a favorite teacher, and those fragrant whiffs mingled with regular blasts of diesel exhaust. I also liked the exercise on the bike; I could feel my legs getting more powerful for when I played football someday. And I cherished feeling the brisk air chilling my lungs after the hill.

I bought some red saddlebags from the Western Auto Store and strapped them on the back fender. I didn't have enough books to fill them properly, so I added a dictionary. And it looked great.

Everything seemed the same and fine at home. The sets of kittens also came and went, mostly to employees at my father's factory. Weaning was my job. One by one I'd take those little balls of fur with the outsized ears. I'd dip their faces in a bowl of milk. You had to get their noses all the way in so they'd open their mouths. Then, after a couple of seconds, I'd let go. They'd sit back up, sneeze, and lick their faces clean and, oh, by golly, they'd get a taste of this funny white stuff that didn't come from a nipple. And after a couple of days they got the lick of it, though they'd sometimes choose to stand inside the bowl to do their licking. And stumble away leaving little furry white paw prints on the linoleum.

A week before this weaning, Dad would walk around the plant smiling and asking the workers if they liked their jobs and if they also wanted a kitten, each one a guaranteed male. Pretty much everyone seemed to like both their work and the kittens. Later, some sent photos of the kittens that their male cat just had.

We had also gotten a new dog—or, rather, someone had given us a new dog. Another one of those shiny clean cars from the city stopped out by the mailbox. Clean cars were notorious for dumping unwanted pets, garbage, and other refuse on country roadsides. I knew it wasn't the mailman's car but didn't think anything about it, except maybe I'd have to pick up more litter; I could see they weren't trying to take the mailbox again. But, later, when I went to fetch the mail, there was a pile of wet brown fur in the ditch. It was quivering uncontrollably.

It was a dog, actually a mutt, golden brown with black eyes and a bushy tail. A skinny little thing that wouldn't move. Wherever you put her, she'd stay curled up and quivering. I told Mom we had to keep her. She said we'd talk it over when Dad got home. It wasn't so much a talking over as a pleading. There was a moment of silence; after all, we still lived on a road. "You can keep her if—" he said, but his qualification was drowned out by cheers. "If the vet says she's not sick with something."

I was not in the strongest bargaining position at that moment. ("Never ever let the other side know how much you want something," Dad would advise years later.) But that "if" didn't seem too bad, though it occasioned an anxious twenty-four hours while the dog was checked. Right after school I wanted Mom to call for the results. But she wouldn't. That was Dad's job, which I badgered him to do before he even got his coat off.

"Yes," said Dad, on the phone.

"Uh-huh. . . .

"She is? . . .

"What kind? . . .

"How long? . . .

"Well, I wondered. . . .

"All right. Well, thanks very much." He hung up. He turned to me.

"She's fine. Just undernourished. You'll have to make sure she eats well."

"Oh, I will. I will."

"She's a lucky orphan to be dumped out near someone like you who loves her so much."

I hadn't thought of that. "But when can we get her?"

"After dinner. Do you want to come along?"

"Funny man."

"She'll have to stay in the garage," Mom added. I said sure, sure, because I knew she was a soft touch later. On cold winter days if I asked nicely and cleaned her paws first, I could take the dog and her blanket down to the basement and make a corner for her by the furnace.

I named the newcomer Wendy.


Grandpa Bowles had kept a pistol in his dresser drawer, a little silver .38, which Grandma didn't want around anymore. So Dad brought it home, and one Sunday he taught me how to use it out back in the woods. I don't think Mom liked that idea, but

Dad said it was important to know how to handle them properly because of what they could do, and someday I might encounter a weapon and not be around a parent.

I wasn't sure what he meant. But I was excited that first Sunday when we set up a board against a crab-apple tree out back. Dad said the gun was not loaded and I should get the feel of it first. He had it in his right hand and was turning to hand it to me. Suddenly, it went off. It actually fired, with the loudest, most terrifying BANG I had ever heard. I screamed. Wendy ran back to the house.

I could see no hole in me. Or Dad. I looked at the board. The bullet had blown a large hole right through it. And then had buried itself deep in another wound in the tree. Jesus, what if it had been pointed at someone instead of something?

In shock, I looked up at Dad.

What the—He was smiling.

"Scare ya?" he asked.

Scare me? I had to go to the bathroom real bad. Still unable to speak, I nodded.

"Good! Now you know what these things can do to you, or someone else."

"But you said it wasn't loaded."

"That's what everyone says just before the gun goes off. Every single gun is loaded until you see the empty chambers yourself like this. Understand?"

"Yeah. Yeah. Sure . . . But you really scared the daylights out of me."

"Maybe you'll remember better now."

I dug the bullet out of the wood, drilled a hole in it, and put it on my key chain. It's still there.


He did the same sort of thing about cigarettes and drinking. He smoked like a furnace. Camels, the man's smoke, a pack or two a day. Mom smoked Chesterfields. Women's cigarettes. Dad said I might want to smoke someday when I got older; it wasn't that good for me. But if I ever did want to try it, he wanted me to promise, right kind, to come to him first.

He said he'd buy my first pack. No questions asked. But he didn't want me sneaking around out behind the garage like he had with his cousin. One kind of sneaky leads to other kinds, he said. We shook on it.

A couple of years later, all the guys seemed to be smoking, which led me to believe there might be something to it beyond its innate coolness. I went to Dad. I said I wanted to start smoking. We went to the store. I picked out a pack of Salems. He paid. And I tried smoking.

It was awful. I coughed and coughed. I felt dizzy and nauseous. Over the course of several days I tried, I really did. I must have smoked half the pack. I couldn't see the point. I stopped starting to smoke.

Dad made the same offer about beer. So I never got much pleasure out of that forbidden-fruit business my friends enjoyed with such relish and satisfaction, even in university. Being congenitally straight had its costs, I know now, but there didn't seem to be any choice in the matter.


One summer, Dad had business in Europe so all three of us took a steamship from Montreal. Every day, I put messages in bottles and tossed them overboard and got several replies over many months. I also had a brief shipboard infatuation. Over there, we saw Dad's old university buddies in Scotland, some relative's statue in Westminster Abbey, and friends in Holland and Switzerland. We arrived in Paris at a railroad station along with half the population of France.

It was a bewildering crowd going every which way in another language, though Dad seemed to know where to go. We were

in a mob at the taxi stand. People were yelling. I was guarding
the luggage with Mom while Dad fought for a cab. Next to me
at the curb, an old woman was helping her very old husband out
of his wheelchair. He was standing up. Then he was crumpling,
backward, toward me. I grabbed him under the arms. His head,
with lots of wispy white hair, snapped back on my arm. His black
beret fell on the pavement. He looked at me, startled. I smiled
at him reassuringly. Then he gurgled. And he puffed in my face
the foulest-smelling air I had ever smelled. His eyes rolled back.
He went limp. His wife began screaming. The crowd gasped and
drew back. I set him gently in the wheelchair. The woman
screamed louder. She ran her hands over his face again and again.
She kissed him. A policeman came. The old man's gray pants
were wet between his legs.

Mom grabbed my hand and yanked me away. Dad pushed us
into the taxi. And we escaped, in absolute silence. "Uh," I said.
"I didn't do anything wrong."

"Just be quiet," said my mother.

Okay. "But I didn't do anything."

The world didn't pause that day either. We went up in the
Eiffel Tower after lunch, a normal day for nearly everyone.
France being an alien culture, for dinner we had fish with little
shavings of nuts sprinkled on it. Shortly after going to bed, I got
up and wandered out into my parents' room. There was a purpose
to such encounters in my family; nothing like that happened by
chance. They looked up, demanding the reason without a word.

"That was really interesting what happened at the train station
this morning," I said.

"Just don't think about it," said my mother a little too quickly.
"And get a good night's sleep."

My father said nothing.

So they had been frightened, too. I didn't close the door all
the way. And when I lay down in that shaft of safe light, I couldn't
think of anything else I could have done for the old man. I walked

through my memory of that morning maybe twenty times. It always moved in slow motion and it always ended the same. From a distance, death is always very clean. But it had landed very close this time. And it certainly didn't smell very good.

One winter's day I went out to the garage to feed Wendy. But she wouldn't leave the little wooden bed Dad and I had made. She hadn't done that since we got her. "Yum-yum, girl. Look at this, the smelliest can of food I've ever opened. Don't you want some? C'mon." But nothing would budge her. I went over to the bed and patted her. And holy smokes! There were three dogs there—Wendy and two tiny little wet balls of blind fluff sucking away. We didn't even know she'd had a caller, let alone gotten pregnant.

This was so exciting. New life in midwinter. Full of promise. And all the playing and learning—and messing—they had to do. I told everyone at school, and the girls seemed to care. I put Wendy and her new brood down in the warm basement. Each puppy fit in one hand. And she pranced alongside all the way down the hall and stairs, proud but alert. She would never leave them alone; we had to put papers on the floor because she wouldn't go outside alone, even for a minute. I liked to watch her devotion a lot. She knew just what to do with them.

That was actually my last year living at home full time. My income from good grades had declined as the A's (fifty cents) and B's (twenty-five cents) slipped more into C's (a dime). My best friend Dan could have retired early on his report-card income, but as the course difficulty increased, my interest in it diminished, unless it was English. Studying often consisted of looking at the book and wishing I wasn't. There was always something to do outside or another wave band to cruise on my shortwave.

To my mother's mild dismay, I had wired the metal mattress frame of the top bunk on my bed into the largest radio antenna in the township. "This won't electrocute anyone up here, will it, Andy?"

"No, Mom. There's no electricity in this wire. See. Look. No, look."

"All right. All right. I'll take your word for it."

I could get almost anywhere at night on that radio—Moscow, Canada, Nashville, France, Spain, Texas, the Greenwich time signal, Cuba, and Africa, I think. I knew by heart the precise spot to put both needles to hear foreign people talking about things in places I'd never been. But, like a lot of things I could do well—play the drum, shoot a BB gun with amazing accuracy, break the two-minute-mile barrier on my bike, and talk to animals—there wasn't much call for such skills where I spent the rest of my life. And there was even less appreciation anywhere out there, which I understood because these were minor things in the world and they only mattered to me.

So that when lightning struck and I got called on in math class, she wanted to hear the formula for determining the area inside an isosceles triangle, not how close I got to petting a wild rabbit the previous evening. The rabbit had a regular routine every day at the same time; he liked this one bush and I'd watch from afar, him munching away, his ears forever alert, always tuning in for danger and not finding any, yet, in me. And the next day I'd move a step closer and watch again, always standing still so I'd become part of the scenery. Each afternoon, I'd watch the clock for my appointment with Nature. Until after some weeks the rabbit and I were just a few feet and a world apart. And I offered him a piece of carrot and after much thought, sniffing, and turning his head, he hopped over and took it from me. Right out of my hand. He went away, of course; everything always does. But he left me smiling. If there had been anyone else around, I'd have let them congratulate me. I treasured that moment. And there was always a chance he might stay someday.

But there was no class in Animal Communication or Shortwave Appreciation. Such things had nothing to do with isosceles triangles. I didn't blame anyone for my feeling so completely outside the normal scheme of living; that would have been too aggressive; to be acceptable, aggression had to be sanctioned through games. I was better at defense anyway. Neither were my skills in the woods or with the radio effective at attracting members of the opposite sex, risky as that might be, or even keeping them interested if they happened to cross my path.

Awkwardly moving, sort of, to the corny tones of Glenn Miller in someone's basement rec room while holding a girl in my arms and feeling beneath the back of her dress the outline of the second bra she'd ever worn was not the best time to volunteer on what frequency I had gotten Germany the previous night. Though, Lord knows, I tried it anyway. Nor did my limited store of personal chatter for the opposite sex leave much room for a meaningful response that would carry the conversation forward. And she'd say something like "Uh, that's nice."

"Have you ever listened to a shortwave radio?"

"No. I haven't."

"You should sometime. It's really neat." I was going to offer use of my set, but it was in my bedroom. So that would be way out of line, the formal engagement not yet having been revealed, even to the young lady involved.

"Your radio sounds, uh, interesting."

"Yes. It is. Well, I think so anyway."

"Uh-huh. . . . Do you listen often?"

"Every night."

"Every night?"

"Yup. It's fun. But I said that."

"Yes, you did. Do you want to sit down?"

"Oh, okay. Would you like a ginger ale?"

"No, thank you. Excuse me, I'm going to the ladies' room."

"Okay. Thanks for the dance."

"Sure."

"Maybe we can dance another one later."

"Maybe."

The other guys were dancing. So I'd sit down on a bench and pretend to be resting from that arduous fox-trot and kind of look around at the slowly darkening room and wish that I was dead. Because that had to be less painful than this. Or at least that I was somewhere else. Somewhere far away. And safe. Where I needn't deal with these baffling equations and formulas, where I didn't even know the questions let alone the answers.

I'd find the host's parents and for a while talk with them adultly, which they'd comment on to my parents sometime in the coming weeks. Then I'd ask to use their phone. The dial system was in by then. I'd dial Olympic 3-5542 and ask Dad to come rescue me. The party was pretty much over anyway, I said.


Where better to flee from half the world's population than a boy's school? It was decided that I would go to high school at a boarding school in another state. I was in on this crucial decision in part, I think, because my parents knew I would like it. The school was a military academy, the winter school of the summer camps I had been attending; military things had interested me since I discovered the Spitfire. The school was in the country—rural Indiana. It reeked of tradition, involved uniforms, real military gear, which fascinated me, and its staff had an intimidating reputation for education, excellence, and self-discipline. One day, many years later when the rest of the country had become concerned over excellence in education and teaching values to drifting youths, a network television documentary would focus on the school and its now coeducational system, as if these teachers and administrators had just invented a new process, instead of carrying on a tradition.

Every day began at 6:28 a.m., not 6:29. Every day ended at ten, unless you had earned a special thirty-minute extension. Everybody had a new roommate every year, whom you learned to abide and then appreciate. And he did the same. Everyone put in a year of servitude as a plebe while the upperclassmen, with only a sprinkling of shouted stupidities, instilled the traditions and standards they themselves had learned the same way. There was an unbreachable Honor Code, enforced by a student court that was far sterner than most faculty would be. There were manners and signs of respect that were required at first and then seemed to come naturally; since teachers deserved to be called "Mr." by the students because of their age, rank, knowledge, and academic achievement, then the teachers would return the respect because of who these young men were, how hard they were working, and what they would become because of it, although the teachers would likely never see the full blossoming they ignited.

There was also an array of rules and regulations whose boundaries seemed more guiding and comforting than confining. There were times to be serious. Times to work. Times to sleep. Times to play. Times to pray. Times to study. Times to choose. Times to win. And times to lose. And you'd best learn which was which and what behavior was appropriate when.

There was, however, no time for excuses; every academic day began with a free period when every teacher was available to any student for help on the previous night's lesson. So when class time came, no one could say, "I couldn't do the work last night." It was up to each of us to figure out when we needed help, when we didn't, and to pay the price when we were wrong. Many of our books were written by the teachers who handed them out. When accused, there were always opportunities to explain, possible mitigations, and sentences. There were punishments that warned, punishments that nudged, and punishments that humiliated, according to the severity of the breach, and I could accept that. Well, there really wasn't any choice. But that spawned a sense of justice—right was right and wrong was unacceptable and punished, swiftly and certainly—a system which I carried far beyond those ivied walls. It was up to each graduate to use those values in his own life later, which often made notable achievement much easier in a wide, wide world where values were things to profess and then change like jewelry, depending on the occasion.

There were 859 other young men at that school, from practically every state and numerous countries. We lived in groups of eighty or so. Though we came in 860 different shapes, we dressed alike, precisely alike, which eliminated clothes status and worry. It also taught me how different each guy was inside those similar-looking clothes, which I had never thought about. We had our own vocabulary, our own slang, and our own system of humor. Everyone did sports; no choice there either. Everyone at his own level. The teachers lived on campus. They coached both sports and classes, which seemed to merge into a seamless system of living, not forty-six-minute academic periods.

Each class began with all students rising in respect to the teacher, which he acknowledged with a nod and a "Thank you." And then the search began. Always challenges to meet. Methods to learn. Mysteries to decipher. Mistakes to make safely. Always some way to earn praise. Always something new to strive for. "There's so much I don't know about," I wrote home once, "but I'm not worried. I'll just learn about them as I go." It was all mostly exciting, even math, and exhausting. Ten o'clock came and my light went out fast. No problem. Too tired for mischief.

Almost every teacher was like a father, or grandfather. Somehow they knew my name and every other student's, even if I wasn't in their class. I'd be walking around campus with friends. I'd pass a faculty member. He'd nod, "Mr. Malcolm." And those two words acknowledged my existence and made me feel a little special, as if sometime out of my presence these respected teachers had discussed the cadets and decided I was worth noting. And his nod also calmed me down a bit; maybe I had been telling the joke a little too loudly for a young person of my aspiring station. "Sorry, sir," you might say, which meant you understood.

There were no mothers in sight, except on set weekends when they came to pose next to their uniformed sons in front of the chapel and say, "How big you're getting." The sisters came then, too; the little ones were, well, little and with all these big buildings and big guys in uniform around perhaps a little less goofy than usual. The teen sisters, windblown hair hastily rearranged before emerging from the station wagon's backseat, tried to act calm and regal and to pretend they were nowhere near their parents at that moment. These young ladies, of course, did not return the looks lobbed their way. But for the guys—we had all these brothers around. Guys doing the silliest, neatest, zaniest, toughest, cruelest, funniest, smartest things. And I belonged to this immense family, just by being myself and following the rules. I didn't have to be somebody else, or even try.

I had no idea what I wanted to do with my life, but I knew I wanted to be right there in that place with those people. "What I like about this place," I wrote once, "is that everything presents a challenge, not a chore. Instead of dreading a coming job, I kinda look forward to it to see how well I can do it." I knew the secret to my future resided on that sprawling, leafy campus with the worn paths that led everywhere, where so many had trod before and gone out to do exciting things, and where so many had now returned to watch their boys walk the same paths. I had endured homesickness that first year at camp, so I had none of that even the first year. Home was becoming somewhere the guys weren't.

And there was football. No more two-hands-below-the-belt park stuff. This was real knock-'em-down, pick-yourself-up, grunt-and-groan, physical football, with uniforms, plays, grudges, giving and taking bruises, handling losses, and savoring victories.

The first play of my first game, a junior on the other team kneed me so hard between the legs it hurt to pee for two days. I was complaining in the huddle when a teammate interrupted. "So what're you gonna do about it?" I had no idea I could do anything about it, let alone what. There was no mother in the huddle to ask. I wasn't a father yet, so how could I know? (And the way I was feeling at that moment, I didn't think I ever could be a father, either.) By the next year I had it figured out. That same guy was coming across the line when he caught an elbow on the chin so hard it sent him to Toledo. He never saw me coming. But I was standing over him with the doctor when he came to, just to make sure he knew. I smiled. He nodded. Or maybe he was still woozy.

I loved the contact—knocking people down and being knocked down and getting back up and feeling good about giving and taking, trying to act oblivious about it all, and going on about trying again. When I had the ball, I would look for people to run through—might as well, I wasn't fast enough to outrun them. My legs were thick, thanks to all those bicycle races against myself. The tackler would come at me. If he came in high, that was the easiest; I'd hit his face mask with my shoulder pads and bring my forearm up into his belly. I'd twist my shoulders and drive off toward the goal. If he tried low, I'd give him some hip, then pull it back. Up would come my knees, and if he didn't catch some stars on his chin, my legs were lifting free out of his arms. I was gone. And I had won. I had won! At least for a yard or two. Then two of them would sandwich me. And if I still hung on to the ball—and my senses—I had still won.

One time in a scrimmage, I took a handoff and went into the line bent over, head up, shoulders twisting, legs pumping, ball safely covered, stretching out another yard while falling. I only picked up maybe seven or eight yards, but when I came back to the huddle, the coach said, "Mr. Malcolm, where did you learn to run like that?"

I was stunned. What could have been wrong? I ran down my mental checklist again, as I had just before the snap: left arm up for the handoff, right hand cupped, shoulders down, head up, eyes open, knees pumping. What had I missed watching the pro and college teams play on TV? Position by position, I would watch each man for series after series. Then I'd go outside in my paratrooper boots and my department-store Christmas football uniform with the cardboard thigh pads and I'd run around the field taking handoffs from the right and then the left and running into and out of unseen tackles. Or being a pulling guard to the right or left. It was harder to practice defense because the TV camera always followed the ball and you couldn't see the line-backer until the last second, when he'd flash into view like a missile and level his target with admirable violence.

"I don't know, sir. Did I miss something?"

"No, son. You did fine. Keep it up."

Actually, I liked defense best. Fewer rules. More reaction. More devastation. There were so many other things to learn about the game. Controlling emotions, especially the down ones when nothing seemed to work against the other guys. And if you didn't figure out what went wrong, it would happen again and again, mercilessly. And the clock was running down and we needed six points, but the coach was ordering us, time and again, to think instead about just this one handoff or block and then the next one, and the next one, step by step, down the field and then do it again. One step after another throughout practice, then the game, and then life. But how come some quarters are longer than others?

I'm sure I tried twice at least, but the wonders of those intense joys and subterranean lows shared with buddies were impossible to describe to mothers—at least mine. I don't know why I tried. If there was any reasonable excuse, even too much mud, the cold, the possibility of rain that week, she would not come to my game. Even if she was there, I'd hear Dad's familiar voice: "Attaboy! You can do it." But I never heard her. And afterwards she might ask, "I understand you had to tackle that other boy, but why did you have to knock him down so hard?"

But the neatest thing about football was the camaraderie of the team. We all went through so much shared sweat and struggle, practice and fear, joy and despair together that we became very close. We knew each other's thoughts or words before they could be said. We had our own running jokes and nicknames. Walking to class, we'd acknowledge that bond with a quick nod, a secret reminder of the link. After someone made a mistake, the two closest guys would pat the culprit and say, "That's all right. Next time." At night just before Taps we would instinctively congregate to run through plays together outdoors without the coach. We could hear the leaves crunching underfoot, but we couldn't see each other in the darkness, which was the point. Each of us had to know our own assignment and what every other guy's was, too. We thought it was a pretty good timing practice when we could run play after play without bumping into each other in the black. And we'd go to bed feeling even more exhausted than usual, and better for it.

Since it was a boys' school, there were, of course, not that many girls around to cheer, like back home. There were, in fact, nine girls in the entire school, all faculty daughters, which didn't make for much perfume in the hallways. Because of our raging hormones, we all secretly wondered what was underneath those soft sweaters they wore. But dealing with girls was not a routine part of our existence, which was just fine. There were three or four formal dances a year when the school would bus in a couple of hundred young ladies from girls' schools not so close by. The big decision every time was whether to sign up for a blind date, not knowing the same thoughts and fears were running through the minds of these composed young things stepping off the bus with their overnight bags. My thoughts on this were summed up many years later by my oldest son, who as a youngster fed a quarter into a Las Vegas slot machine, imagining instant wealth and happiness and discovering instead the end of his allowance. His resulting definition of gambling: "Sometimes you lose and sometimes you don't."

It was safer to keep that quarter in your pocket. And I never felt myself to be much of a desirable catch for the equally terrified young lady being matched by height with me by the chaperone with The List on the clipboard.

Mobs of parents, including both of mine, visited their sons on occasional special weekends; frequent visits were discouraged. So these official visits were special; I counted down to them in my letters—"See you in 17¼ days"—certain that my parents were as excited as I, though perhaps too busy to keep such a close count. "Why don't you make a list of what I ask you to bring so you won't forget anything? P.S. Please don't forget my shortwave radio." The parents would dine out with their offspring and watch a parade. And the adults would marvel at how their little boys were becoming young men, wheeling huge howitzers around, controlling mammoth horses, whipping impotent combat rifles about in precise, impressive drills that had nothing to do with what those weapons were really designed for. My parents didn't make it to all my football games. Dad had a high-pressure career and it meant driving most of Friday night. But for all the big games when I looked over at our sideline, there was that familiar fedora. And, by God, did the opposing team captain ever get a firm handshake and a gaze he would not soon forget!

Mom would likely be standing there, too, huddled in her fur coat and smiling wanly when the game was over, as if her mind were more on her freezing feet. Dad hadn't played American football; he had played rugby, which seemed more like unorganized pushing to me. But, like football, there was more going on than met the spectator's eye. He'd meet me at midfield after the gun and reach out for a muddy but firm handshake. "Good game, son," he'd say, and that made it so, whatever the score. I knew Mom didn't want to get dirty. So I didn't touch her.

It wasn't always wins, of course. "Handling victory is easy, Mr. Malcolm," the coach said after one loss. "I want to see what you do with defeat." Which I thought was a pretty dumb thing to practice. So we went out and destroyed next week's opponent. And afterwards he said, "That's what I meant."

Off the field I remember one time, which was followed by others, when a fact discovered in school contradicted something Dad had said. Impossible that he could be wrong, but there it was in black-and-white. These accumulated over time, along with a widening range of personal experiences and acquaintances, primarily with these coaches and teachers to buttress my own slowly developing sense of person and values. Home became somewhere I visited at Thanksgiving, Christmas, and spring break. Then I returned to the main highway of my life.

I still kept in close touch with my parents, at times desperately. I wrote regular letters, dated, and even lines that were marked with the time I wrote them, so that my parents could live right along with me, and we were each to imagine what we were doing at all those parallel moments. I knew this was important to them. "Too bad I'm not there to cut the grass—bring it with you."

Mom would write brief comments on the envelopes of her favorites before stashing them in a drawer somewhere, which I did not discover for many years. "How sweet!" she'd write. Or, "Funny!" One favorite observation of her teenage son: "Mr. Hayes was telling me about how the Navy ROTC works for you when you're in college. They pay everything, he says (and Brutus is an honorable man)."

I might phone—collect, of course—every couple of weeks. Parents weren't encouraged to do so officially, but every month or so a Care package would arrive from home, usually Dad's homemade fudge, a high-value currency in boarding-school barter. I would share this tin of dark-brown goodness with my roommate and those others who had shared the cookies in their last package from home. My regular letters home ("I'll write on Tuesday, Thursday, and Sunday and you reply in between, okay?") were filled with the hourly minutiae of my life and immature plans and ideas, which I knew they wanted to know desperately: "6:40 Wed. Hi! B-fast in 10 mins. All well. Gotta go. . . . 7:48 Off to class. Bye. . . . 3 Now FOOTBALL! Yeah!! More later." But gradually I spent my limited free time less imagining what Mom and Dad were doing back home and more aimed at accomplishing what I had to do. And then writing them about it, if Dad had included stamps in the previous week's fudge. "Don't they sell stamps in Indiana?" he once asked.

There were a few rocky periods when the grades slipped and my energy overflowed acceptable bounds. I was to learn that an angry father was narrowly dissuaded from withdrawing me by one grandfatherly counselor's citations of progress and gentle urgings for patience. The bonds with others were strengthening.

These teachers seemed so accepting of each of us and to know and to see so many amazing things, even in me. I loved English and reading and writing and communicating my feelings and discoveries; it was safe to do that on paper because I wasn't around when the reader saw them and perhaps laughed at the wrong parts. And I guess my fascination showed. The English Department took those kinds of people under their wing, as Math and Science did with their favorites. They gave us tougher classes, more demanding tests, supplemental reading lists, and optional extra reading lists, which had nothing optional about them. I remember my parents getting one report-card comment by a man renowned as the sternest English instructor: "Mr. Malcolm sometimes falls asleep in class but does it so unobtrusively I wake him with regret." My parents were puzzled. I couldn't explain it either, but I knew there was a special link there.

Some of these men would invite cadets to their homes on Sunday afternoons. Their wives would serve popcorn or hot chocolate. These teachers were always so interested in what we were thinking. It was a lot easier to talk about what I'd been doing, but this thinking business required a whole new set of muscles and they would exercise them, hour after hour, back and forth, stretching them like rubber bands with new ideas at either end. They would gently challenge my simplistic replies—not that they said they were wrong, mind you, just that surely I could think deeper. They forced me to make an argument, and they only seemed hurt if I couldn't produce some evidence to buttress my stand. So they'd suggest where to find some.

I began to read newspapers and magazines, not just for the funnies and sports. This time I had to read to remember the ideas. And that really required practice. Sometimes I'd put a publication down and I couldn't remember more than one or two things from the last page. So I'd read it again and again until I could not only summarize it, but remember specific phrases. I'd be ready this time.

Then, the next Sunday, I'd spout off and feel pretty pleased about myself as the other students threw in their thoughts. The teacher said that was all mildly interesting, but he wanted to warn us that some people thought that thinking meant reciting what others had written in, say, *Time* magazine. And since he could read that himself, he would be very interested someday in hearing what we ourselves thought about what others had written.

So I walked back to my room thinking that this thinking business could get pretty darn complicated.

But it could also be exciting. I remember one class when the teacher, the chairman of the English Department, a towering, deep-voiced presence who dominates many memories, wanted to discuss the sledding scene from *Ethan Frome*. He assumed we'd all read it by now; he'd told us three weeks ago we should. Now what had we noticed about those two pages?

Silence.

One boy said it was about two lovers taking a sled ride down a hill. Darn. I knew that much. I could've gotten it right.

Yes, said the teacher, that was an obvious answer. Then I was glad I hadn't made a fool of myself with an obvious answer.

The teacher said he was looking for more.

Silence. More? More what?

What kind of sled ride?

What kind of sled ride? we all thought. Oh, come on. How many different kinds are there?

A snowy sled ride, someone said, which prompted the teacher

to completely ignore him and squelched any more jokes that might have been hatching.

It was a fast sled ride, said one student.

Yes, we murmured. It was definitely fast.

Oh? said the teacher. How did we know that? Was the word "fast" in there anywhere?

Suddenly, many pages were ruffling. We might be on to something here.

Silence.

No. No "fast" anywhere.

Then, he said, how did you know it was fast?

It just seemed fast.

Precisely!

We had the scent now.

And why did it seem fast?

It went fast.

That's right! Why?

We were so close. Who would be first?

It read fast.

Why?

The sentences were short.

*Yes.* And?

So close!

The sentences were shorter.

Ah, ha! Shorter than what?

Shorter than before.

Yes. Yes. Before what?

Before the sled started.

Right! Now put it all together.

The sentences were long and slow when the sled was at the top of the hill and just starting to move. And as the sled got moving, the sentences did, too. Until the sled was speeding. And so was the reader. Faster and faster. Without saying so.

We had done it! Our literary guide raced to the front blackboard.

"Gentlemen," he said. "You have just discovered this—" And, as excited as we were, he scrawled on the board: "FORM CONTRIB- UTES TO CONTENT." He broke the chalk, so enthusiastically did he underline the discovery.

And he turned around and beamed at us proudly. And we beamed back, verbal explorers who had just found the promised land. Or one of them, anyway.

---

_The reaction to my newspaper story on elderly suicides was immediate and continued long after lunch. Handwritten notes on flowered stationery from women—some mothers, some daughters—who echoed the published fears. Badly typed mis- sives from fathers and sons. Some were soaked in guilt. Others were a flood of relief; "Thank God," said several, as if one person had written them. "I thought I was the only one." Dictated notes from doctors, who understood what they were doing but were so afraid not to, for their own tangled legal sake. And then came a phone call from a deputy attorney general in Minnesota._

_"Yes, yes," he said. "We know it's happening. And we don't know what to do. But where are we working out the answers?"_

_"Good question," I said._

_"Find out," said my boss._

---

It happened in December. The previous year Grandma Bowles had gotten some stomach bug while visiting our house for Christ- mas. But it wouldn't go away for weeks and then months. She stayed in the guest room next to mine, and I'd go in to talk a lot every day. But she was old and tired easily. And Mom was always interrupting because Grandma needed a nap, which sounded annoyingly familiar.

The doctor visited numerous times, but eventually Grandma

went home to Canada with her cancer. Her writing changed in that next year, becoming not as bad as Mom's tight scrawl but less controlled than before. She couldn't just sit and write. One letter might take more days than pages to complete, which was unusual. And some other old lady had come to live with her.

Then came the first Christmas we did not spend at home. We stayed at her house. Grandma was in a big hospital. We had no decorated tree, but they had allowed a small one in her hospital room. I remember some debate about whether I would visit her, though there was no doubt in my mind. And then when that was decided, Mom wanted me to wear my school uniform. Mom also gave me a long lecture about how to act, because Grandma was very, very ill and there were many, many things not to do and only a few to do. It was her stomach again, or still. She might not know me.

Not know me? What a laugh! I was her only grandson. We had Our Game. Grandma B. would know me, no matter what.

The hospital room was almost all dark. A half-dozen people stood along the wall hiding in the shadows like frightened vultures. There was Grandma stretched out in the bed in the light. She looked worse alive than Grandpa did dead. She was yellow and drawn, as if the body had shrunk inside the skin. She wasn't moving except—wait, yes, little breaths. The nurse backed away from her when it was my turn to visit. It was like walking onto a stage and, right off, I blew my lines big time.

"How're ya doing, Grandma?"

I heard Mom suck in air behind me.

Grandma's head turned slightly. Her eyes opened a little.

"Hi!" I chirped. "It's Andy."

Slowly, she smiled faintly. Grandma smiled! See, I knew she'd remember. I turned to the audience. "See," I said, "she knows me." Mom shook her head. Wrong again.

"It's very good to see you, Grandma."

I heard Mom wince again. What could have been wrong with that?

Grandma's lips moved. I leaned down close. Closer. Mustn't get too close. I wasn't supposed to hurt her. And, of course, I knew you weren't supposed to touch dying people; somehow that violates the approaching aloneness. And dying might be catching. But this was Grandma. I couldn't hear what she was trying to say. I put my ear right by her mouth.

Oh, what the hell. I gave her a big hug around the chest and over the top of her head. "I love you, Grandma." I kissed her cheek. It was bony. I put my head on her chest. It wasn't.

She raised her hand slightly. I took it in mine. Then I leaned down by her ear. And I told her a story about a little boy on a train in New York state, in the observation car, when he saw something shiny under the radiator and reached down to get it, but his mother said, "Get your hand out of there—it's dirty" and then the little boy pulled out a dime. And when I got done telling her that bedtime story, Grandma tickled my hand. I knew all along she was still in there.

Then it was her turn to sleep. That was the last time we talked.


It never occurred to me to share that moment with anyone later, at home or school. You could say that death came. But only obliquely, like remarking on the weather—"My grandmother passed away over Christmas." You couldn't actually talk about it with anyone—"I really miss her, you know." Too morbid. It made other people think about their dead grandparents or their dead grandparents-to-be, which might not be such a bad thing since memories are all that's left of anyone in the end anyway. And there could be worse things than a grandchild comfortably savoring the thought of an old lady's lap and enfolding arms.

I knew too it is absolutely forbidden to feel good about any part of her death, because she wasn't a dog or horse so we couldn't note how her suffering was over now, no more painful stomach, no more vomiting or moaning. She was supposed to stick around for as long as we thought possible, to postpone our sadness as long as possible, and thereby somehow our own departure. Nor should I say how good it felt to make her feel good at the end. How could anyone actually dare to feel good at a time like that? Or enjoy her hand in mine, tickling away weakly, secretly, while everybody else watched without comprehending?

So I got on with the business of living and forgetting. And I got pretty good at it, too, except around Christmas or whenever I heard a train in the distance, or when I saw braided white hair wrapped around the back of a woman's head, or whenever I smelled rubbing alcohol or whatever it is that makes hospitals all smell the same kind of suspicious clean. And I never went to another Jerry Lewis movie.

Jerry Lewis never came to my school's theater. But many other outsiders did. They danced, modern and ballet. They sang, opera and otherwise. Basil Rathbone recited poetry. Others lectured. Hal Holbrook, who had walked those same school paths as a youth, performed Mark Twain. And before and after each appearance there were discussions in class and in teachers' living rooms. Everything had meaning, if only I could figure out how to examine it all and unlock the treasures. It was such a hungry time.

And then it happened. A bearded man named Robert St. John came to speak one Wednesday evening. He was a newspaper foreign correspondent. He had traveled all over the world, especially Africa where so many different lands were beginning to emerge from the enforced, starched-white tidiness of colonialism. He had witnessed all these goings-on, had talked with famous people, had seen the battles and aftermaths. He had written newspaper stories and books for millions of eager readers to rush out and buy and consume for their own good. And he had been paid to do it; that was my kind of math. After his talk I went straight to the podium and bored through a small crowd of admirers toward the goal line. How had he gotten that job? How did he know where to go? Whom to see? What to write? How to write? Even when his faculty host politely tried to rescue him, I tagged along.

"Mr. Malcolm, Mr. St. John has had a long day. He's going back to his room now."

Sure, fine. That's okay, I'm walking that way, too. I'll just come along. What's it like to be in the Congo? Is it really like *Heart of Darkness?* Where are you going next? When? Why? How do you get there? Who decides where you go? How do you decide what to write? Do readers ever write? What did you study in college?

"Mr. Malcolm, Mr. St. John is going to bed now."

Sure. Okay. When is he getting up for breakfast? When are you getting up for breakfast? I can show you where it is.

"He's leaving very early in the morning."

Oh. Okay. Fine. Where are you going? What will you do there? Why? Can I write you? What's your address?

When the door to the guest house closed, I stood there in a shaft of light from Heaven. I knew it! I knew I would belong someday. I had figured out the mystery. Just like Dad said I would.

I turned on my heel and strode into the future. On the way I made a phone call, collect.

Mom sounded sleepy. "Uh, yes, sure, we'll accept. . . . Hello. Andy?"

"Hi, Mom. It's Andy. The neatest thing. Tell Dad to get on the phone, too."

"What? Is everything all right?"

"Sure. Everything's great. Tell Dad to get on the phone."

"Now? Ralph, wake up. It's Andy. He wants you on the phone, too. . . . I don't know. He sounds okay. I don't know. He wants you on, too. . . . Your father is going downstairs."

Long pause.

"Hello?"

"Hi, Dad. It's Andy."

"Andy who?"

"Very funny. Is Mom there?"

"Yes, I'm here. What is it? Are you okay?"

"Yes. I'm fine. In fact, I'm great. I figured out what I'm going to be."

"Oh," said two voices in Ohio.

"I'm going to be a newspaper correspondent."

It was perfect—travel, writing, pay, new places, new ideas, finding out things and telling others, like show-and-tell for money. Editors would faint at the import of my stories and fall over each other rushing to get them into print on the front page. Readers would laugh and cry and marvel at the wisdom of those carefully chosen and accurately arranged words and perhaps buy an extra copy of the newspaper just as a souvenir. Plus, I'd get my name in the paper. And if they thought my stories were stupid, I wouldn't be around to know about it. Absolutely perfect.

The next day, I ran into English class. "I'm going to be a newspaper correspondent," I told my teacher.

"Well, then," he said, with the eye of a veteran, "you'll want to work for the best paper."

"Which one is that?"

"*The New York Times*," he said.

"Okay." Now that was settled. The only question left was when.

That afternoon I walked in on the adviser to the school newspaper. I introduced myself. I told him I had just decided what my career was going to be and said I wanted to learn how to be a newspaper writer. He gave me my first assignment, interview an opera singer who was coming Sunday night.

"Okay, fine. How do I do that?"

"Well, what do you want to know about her?"

"Nothing. I don't know anything about opera."

"Well, you've got three days to learn enough to ask questions."

Study? You mean you don't just sit down and begin writing? This newspaper-writing business had a little more to it than I imagined. But okay.

At dinner my counselor approached. My parents had phoned. "Are you okay?"

"Yes, sir. I'm fine. Why? What did they want?"

"Oh, nothing. Just a chat." The counselor wanted to make sure everything was all right.

"Yes, sir. Everything is great. I'm going to be a correspondent for *The New York Times.*"

"I see."

That night I phoned my parents again. Did they remember the call last night?

Yes, they thought they did.

Well, now I had decided I was going to work for *The New York Times.* That was the best newspaper, in case they didn't know. It was in New York. So I needed a subscription right away. Could they help? But they had to do it right away. There wasn't much time and every day lost was—well, another day lost. Also, what could they tell me about opera singers?

The second day of my journalism career, my English teacher produced a list of writers and novels I would have to taste deeply as preparation for my writing—Robert Penn Warren, Thomas Hardy, Stephen Crane, Upton Sinclair, Ernest Hemingway, Mark Twain, Edgar Allan Poe, Sinclair Lewis, Sherwood Anderson, Thomas Wolfe. I was delighted to see Nathaniel Hawthorne did not make the list. Well, said my English teacher, some of these writers had actually been newspaper correspondents.

"Really?"

"Why, sure. If you're going to develop your own style of writing, you'll have to shop around and see what has already been invented and then invent your own."

"My own writing style? You mean I could invent one that was just mine?"

"Why not, Mr. Malcolm? It's your life, your career."

We had read something by each of these men in class.

"Didn't you notice they all wrote differently?"

"Oh, sure. Yes. Most definitely. Yes. They were all different. Very. But that's them. This is just me."

"Well, you're different, Mr. Malcolm. You can have your own style, just like your own fingerprint. And if you read a lot and work hard enough at writing, maybe you'll write a book someday."

"A book? Me?"

"Why not? If you're a very careful observer of human nature, like Shakespeare and other writers, you can make an important contribution to society. That's the role of writers."

"A contribution to what?"

"To understanding the human condition."

"Gee, I don't know much about that, sir."

"Well, you have a very long way to go and a lot to learn about life and writing. A good way to start is to read how it's been done very well before."

That made sense. These guys had written an awful lot. The school library had them all. I started with the W's.

It must have taken more than a whole week for the newspapers to begin arriving. But when they did, I pored over page after page. At first, I knew nothing of their subject matter. But there were patterns to many stories; the boring, dry stuff was on top and the good stuff, the news about real people, was hidden way down below, if it was anywhere at all. I arranged the stories in piles by patterns and read them with passion several times. I noticed patterns too in the bylines of the stories I liked, the most thorough ones that answered questions I hadn't thought to ask. So I read them backwards to discern what question produced each detail. I never knew there could be so many different kinds of questions. Then I tried out the same type of question on whomever I was interviewing for the school paper. I remember

Vincent Price saying, "Are you writing an article, young man, or a book?"

The newspaper adviser would write all over my typewriter-pecked stories quite a bit and tell me why there were better ways to say things and why hadn't I included this and show me in your notebook where he said that. And, c'mon now, when was I ever going to learn that newspapermen don't use exclamation points?! When the school paper came out, I got such a thrill seeing my name in ink, **bolder type** than the rest of the story. I'd send the papers to my parents and mark my stories in red so they wouldn't miss them. And then someone like my English teacher would comment on my interesting article. And I'd float down the hall.

Reading *The Times*, I couldn't help learning about current events and decided to impress on friends how important they were. I'd organize them to watch space launchings on television because this was somehow important. So were Presidential speeches. Then came Election Day. I petitioned the dean. I told him evening study hall should be suspended because important national news was occurring and it was essential that the students, who were, after all, the voters of tomorrow, be exposed to the drama of vote-counting as it unfolded on television. And that everyone would learn a lot more from this than from sitting in their rooms.

He called me into his office. He said he was very impressed with my reasoned argument. I was right. But, unfortunately, owing to the shortness of time until the election, it would not be possible to change the entire school's schedule to allow every student to watch. However, since I was so interested and had made such a good argument, he wanted to invite me to his house on election night to watch with him and his wife. I was torn between my activist responsibility to lead the student body into becoming more educated about our democratic process or, since this didn't seem to be in the cards this time, to become more educated myself. I settled that night. We had popcorn and watched Huntley and Brinkley, and the dean told me about the history of the Democratic and Republican parties.

Suddenly, most of my classes had a lot more meaning and relevance; I might need to know that stuff for journalism. I read the memoirs of Eric Sevareid, a CBS correspondent. It was so good that I bought the book. I wrote him. What did he think I should do to further my journalism career? He wrote back from London and said I should take French, which I was doing already; suddenly, my French grades improved.

I was always reading James Reston in *The Times*. So I consulted with him by letter. What did he recommend to prepare for my career with *The Times*? Read a lot of history, he replied. So I did.

For our Honors English theses, everyone was picking subjects like "Changing Roles for Women in Shakespearean Tragedy," which might have been news to Shakespeare. I went to my English teacher. I said I had this weird idea for a thesis. What if I was to compare the writing styles of James Reston, Walter Lippmann, and Joseph Alsop? I know they're just newspaper columnists, but I thought that might really be interesting. I had already noticed many differences. And it was very interesting to me. But maybe the idea wasn't academic and boring enough. It wasn't Shakespeare, after all. And I knew what made academic papers important was their irrelevance to virtually everyone living.

Hmmm, he said, leaning back slightly and ignoring all the other student petitioners jostling for attention. Did those newspaper writers use words?

Well, of course. Yes, sir, they did.

Did these words reflect the times the writers lived in?

Yes, I thought so.

Were these words printed on paper?

Yes, sir.

And did people read them?

Yes. Millions of people.

And did they learn about the human condition—their society and their own lives—by reading these words?

Yes, indeed.

So then, what's the difference? Where was the problem? He was fairly sure, as chairman of the department, that he could persuade the committee to accept such a non-traditional subject.

Oh, good.

The committee members will probably examine you a bit more closely when the oral-presentation time comes.

Oh, good.

By the way, he wondered, had I thought about keeping a notebook?

How do you mean?

A little notebook in your pocket.

Like a diary, sir?

A writing diary. You write dated entries, something every single day: a thought, a phrase, a long description of something you've seen, a feeling you have, a new word—especially verbs. It's very good practice. And over time it will sharpen your writing skills. And your observation skills.

Yes, sir, I might try that.

Might?

I will definitely try that.

Good lad. And from time to time I shall ask to read it. So you must have it with you at all times. And it must always be up to date. Remember, there is no wrong entry—except no entry.

Yes, sir.

This had turned into something unexpected for me, something exciting and a little uncomfortable. All this positive attention and encouragement felt very warm, but also close.

Thank you, sir.

You're welcome, Mr. Malcolm.

When I got to the door of his classroom, I looked back. Other students were clamoring around. I felt he was still watching me expectantly. I still do.

I got a pocket notebook that afternoon. I still keep one.

As time passed, I realized I was no longer trying to please my parents, mainly Dad. I was trying to impress him. He was impressed by hard work, thorough preparation, the unexpected gesture or idea, and determination—silent, steely, seething determination that threatens to overcome anyone or anything in its path. He was not impressed by quitting, not at all.

I never could figure out what impressed Mom. It wasn't football—"It looks like a very rough game," she'd say, as if it were something to arrange and admire instead of a very physical chess game that soaked through my body and being, changing itself and me by the moment. Bad grades didn't overly impress her—"You'll just have to work harder." Neither did good grades—"Congratulations." Even a tidy room didn't work—"No, no, this goes over here."

But my uniform made her melt—"Oh, my, don't you look ever so handsome. Look at that!" I knew it was the uniform because she never said that any other time. She wanted me to wear the uniform everywhere, even on vacation, which was not my idea of vacation attire, especially if there might be someone around I knew.

Of course, I figured she cared. I never went without food and health care. My next doctor's, dentist's, and eye doctor's appointments were arranged before the end of the last one, and set to fall within minutes of the approved intervals. When that English teacher commented on my unobtrusive in-class dozing, I was sent through a major clinic for a full day's testing to determine the precise cause. I always imagined the medical team formally diagnosing it as something called "Teen Fatigue," generated by sixteen-hour days that included fourteen seconds when the body or mind was not in motion.

I never went without consolation if I sought it, although after the first fifty-two seconds of emotion she would steer me to my father. "I don't know what else to say," she would say when she felt her words were inevitably inadequate and failed to fix the situation immediately.

I never went without fine shelter and decent clothes; she selected my wardrobe with the keenest eye to matching color and texture. I had no interest whatsoever in such things, although I kind of liked her interest in my appearance. Even into my university years, on my vacation trips to visit, she would schedule an afternoon's shopping safari to acquire replacement and supplementary garments. I would stand by the rack fairly bored. She would bring over the new coat and trousers and shirts and ties and hold them up to my chest or waist for momentary study. Then she'd try another combination and another and another and another, and study each intensely, as if they gave off silent signals: "Appropriate." "Nice." "Too Loud." She liked green-and-brown combinations.

If we were at home going out, she would suggest what I should wear. Or if it was a particularly important occasion—such as, say, Thanksgiving at the home of Dad's former boss—she would simply lay the clothes on my bed without a word. I knew what it meant. We also went through a Plaid Era; Mom discovered the Malcolm tartan. So the mailbox, one set of curtains, some pillows, and, at times, all three family members were draped in that pretty green, red, and yellow pattern. Often she would suggest that we wear the plaid together. Of course, we did, though in the car Dad would profess fear of imminent arrest for not having a proper parade permit.

Before I returned to university, Mom would spread everything across my bed. It was a bewildering array that looked to me like just a pile of shirts and pants. To me, the one to wear next was the one on top. Then Mom would deliver the complex overlaying formulas for the garment combinations: "Now, this coat will go with these three pants and these two shirts and those ties—well, wait, maybe not this one but these two are okay."

"Do I have to wear both those ties with this shirt?"

"What? No, of course not. Andrew, stop fooling around."

"Well, how about this shirt and tie? They look nice."

"No, too busy. Stop it. Now, just pay attention. Do you want to learn about this or not?"

"No."

"Now, these go with those and those go with those. You could also wear this with this and this with this. And that might look —oh, that does look very nice. Doesn't it? Yes, very nice. But this doesn't go with this and that never should go with that. Also this combination would work if you're not going anywhere too formal."

Dad would appear at the door to my room to deliver a signal. "Your mother put a lot of work into getting all this together for you."

"I know, Dad. Thanks, Mom." And she would start to glow all over, though she'd never take her eyes off the clothes.

"They look great, Mom. They really do. I just hope I'll be able to remember the right ones."

"It's simple," she'd say, which is what someone says about school *after* their graduation. The clothes could be packed later. The game was on TV. And I'd move toward the door. "Thanks again, Mom."

"Mmmm," she'd say, still standing there staring at the bed, with her forefinger and thumb nervously squeezing the sides of her lower lip together, trying to discern just one more appropriate combination.

"Thanks again." I had found, the few times I knew what seemed to matter most to Mom, that I'd better score points when I could. "Really, thanks." There seemed to be so many times when I blew it, when I didn't notice the new curtains or bed-spread, the rearrangement of a room, the special place settings

for my ceremonial homecoming dinner, the mountains of radishes and mashed potatoes that accompanied the meal. It could
have been months since I'd seen that room and so what if it had
changed? I always felt like saying, "What was wrong with the old
room?" And sometimes I would say it, and the two of them would
just shake their heads silently at my stupidity. I tried to keep track
of the photos on the den wall, which was rapidly developing into
an Andy shrine. Andy marching in a parade. Andy playing drums
in a concert. Andy standing by proud parents in front of the
chapel. Andy tilting his head as ordered by the professional pho-
tographer for the annual yearbook pose. Andy with his goofy,
teenaged grin right up there with the smiling father, and the
great-great-grandfather, the Original Immigrant from Scotland
who lost part of his feet in a prairie blizzard, and all the stern-
looking grandfathers, the great-grandfather.

The homecoming dinners were always the same roast beef,
which was just fine with me. That was the point of favorite meals.
They were always delicious and I was going to say so afterwards,
but the proper timing had changed in my absence. Now I was
supposed to comment upon the first bite, if not before. "This
looks really nice. I can't wait to dig in." Or, "If it tastes half as
good as it smells, I'll eat the plate, too." Before I had left home,
if I had said something like that, my parents would have paused
in mid-bite to eye a smiling me suspiciously, and their unspoken
mutual thought would have been: Now, what's he up to? At times
these days, it was like walking through a minefield around home
without knowing I was in a war zone. At some fateful moment,
when least expected, the bomb would explode, as if a nightmare version of Ralph Edwards would leap out of a closet
clutching a large scrapbook and, smiling cheerily, exclaim,
"Andy Malcolm—This Is Your Death!" But I wouldn't feel the
shrapnel until sometime later; I would notice Mom had become
unusually quiet, and I'd mentally track back through the day
trying to figure out what I'd done to cause this. Sometimes I
could trace it all right, or thought I could, and I'd apologize or

attempt to cover my tracks: "Those pictures still look nice." As if I had remarked before.

At times that worked. At times I hadn't followed the tracks properly and the silence would still be brewing when Dad got home. But he'd changed too; he was less curious now about what caused the problem and more just plain annoyed that it had happened. So I'd get That Look a few times. As if I were making his life harder too, which I guess I was.

Even I could figure out that Mom also loved mushy greeting cards. The mushier the better. On Mother's Day the commercial sentiments had to flow copiously. And if they did, her tears would also. Christmas too. Also on her birthday, which she noted I had missed being born on by five days. "I'm sorry," I'd say, and she'd smile forgiveness. Even on St. Patrick's Day, which Mom fancied as a kind of national family holiday because of a distant relative's Irishness. Even on that March day, the maternal hurt would show through unless the family's males produced thick green cards with pages of rhymed sentiments sufficient to evoke tears from statues for miles around. Dad usually wore an orange tie on March 17, which Mom found outrageous for a few years and then ignored. I thought it was hilarious. And Dad annually vowed to bring home some haggis on Robbie Burns's birthday the next January.

When I was a youngster in postwar Cleveland, diverse ethnic heritages were an integral part of life. The city was filled with short Eastern Europeans who spoke no English. They had their own daily newspapers. Even the afternoon English newspaper had a full-time reporter wandering those lands writing features about the relatives left behind by the new Clevelanders.

My dad liked these people very much. They were called DPs then, for Displaced Persons. But he said we were all immigrants and they worked very hard; I think he must have hired every one of them who applied. Some Saturday mornings in my childhood, Dad would take me to work with him, with the promise of a lunch at my favorite restaurant and maybe an Indians game in the afternoon. I would always seem to jam the keys of the old-fashioned adding machine while he worked. Dad was the plant manager for a paper-box factory. He toured the plant at least once every day, talking to the foremen, waving to his favorite workers, checking the new printing press from Switzerland, and watching, always watching. He seemed so efficient; he aimed his mind and speech at the immediate issue at hand, solved the problem or suggested a solution, and moved on to the next stop or problem. I tried to watch what he watched and mention it later to see if what I saw was the same. Sometimes he smiled.

The immigrant women with babushkas confining their thick gray hair would leave their machines on the second floor to flock around him and chatter in Polish and Czech and Hungarian. Dad would smile and reach out to shake their hands, which prompted waves of giggles to roll back through the crowd. Some of the women would bow. If they were bold, they might seize his arm and squeeze it. I remember some older women trying to kiss his hand. Dad would turn then to introduce me. The women would "ooh" and "aah" and pat my little head and the red hair, and we'd all babble in different tongues and smile at each other. They didn't have very good teeth.

Frequently, a worker's daughter would be married and, naturally, the boss was invited. Dad did not go to the wedding, but he said it was important to pay his respects at the reception because he knew the parents. Usually, Mom and I waited in the car outside the grimy old assembly hall. But a few times Dad took me in with him. An usher kept us at the door until the bride's parents could run up and shake Dad's hand and lead us into the big, smokey hall where the accordionist and the band with the two clarinets would stop playing. The crowd moved back. And the bride's father addressed the throng in some language. I think he was talking about Dad, because everyone's head would turn to him. They would smile. Dad smiled back. Everyone applauded.

Then the bride's mother would tap her husband's arm and point to me. And he would say a few more foreign words to the silent crowd. And people leaned over each other's shoulders to peer down at this little redheaded stranger standing by Dad's pants pocket. Or a brother or an uncle or someone strong would pick me up above his head and turn me around to the crowd, living proof of the importance the big boss attached to this occasion. And everyone cheered and applauded enthusiastically, even without my Spike Jones impersonation.

We would be presented to the bride and groom. Dad would make a brief speech about what a joyous day it was for everyone to see so many families gathered together for this happy event, the joyous start of one more family. There would be silence. The father would translate the remarks. More applause. Dad said that as an immigrant himself, he knew the importance of families and their support. Pause. The father translated. Applause. He knew too that not every day in the life of everyone was this happy. But we could all see right there what hard work could do in the United States of America. Louder applause. And abundant nods.

The music would start again. The newlyweds would move awkwardly about the floor while everyone else watched, except me when I found the table of cabbage rolls. Then it was Dad's turn to dance with the bride and he'd sweep her about for a few minutes while the women cried and the men stood silently stolid in their ill-fitting suits. At the end Dad would smile and kind of bow. Then he would kiss the bride on the cheek and slip a white envelope into her hand.

And after a few more minutes and a round of trilingual thanks as the music resumed and the crowd began to dance, Dad and I would be escorted to the door, where it was always raining.

---

*I visited some hospitals. Their public-relations staffs were delighted to arrange tours of the sprawling facilities where innocent people looked for salvation in an age when anything*

ing on film a multidimensional image of her innermost parts for technicians to peer at in dark rooms nearby and predict what her future would be, some of which she would learn someday.

I ran down the halls with the doctors and nurses, stethoscopes gripped firmly in their hands like a relay baton. They were responding to the drop-everything Code Blue summons that the operator in the windowless phone room had just spoken on the building-wide intercom. "What's a Code Blue?" I said. We leapt down the stairs and burst inside through the fire-escape door. "You'll see," he said.

And there was the patient, not breathing, turning blue. They had shoved a huge tube down his throat. They were taking turns jamming his chest down. His white hair was all tousled. He had tubes in his arm. He was stark naked before this crowd of strangers. He had a tube up his limp penis.

Two paddles were slammed onto his chest. "Clear!" Everyone stepped back. Blam! The body convulsed on the table.

They closed in again. They all turned and looked at me. I didn't do anything, honest. No, wait, their eyes were aimed above me. At a screen with numbers and a straight line.

"Clear!"

Heads turned. Everyone stepped back again, except me; I couldn't get any more into the corner.

Blam!

The green line rippled overhead.

"C'mon, baby, c'mon."

So he did. Within an hour his eyes were open, giant saucers full of fear, darting about, alone in that crowd of people. The eyes looked from strange face to strange face, as if seeking something. Was this Heaven or the other place? And how could you tell the difference? But, of course, he couldn't talk with the hose down his throat. And his hands were tied to the bed rail to keep them out of the way. After some time someone saw that he was awake. "Everything's going to be fine," she said idly, without knowing. The remaining faces were busy, very busy; they were talking shorthand because they had a lot to do yet to this body. The other faces had gone for coffee. It had been quite an ordeal for them. But a satisfying one all around, just what they had been trained to do by all the books and the teachers. And it had worked this time, in case anyone was keeping score. There were, of course, no guarantees about tomorrow. Three out of four of these resuscitation subjects die for good soon after anyway, according to the literature. But how do you tell in advance which is the fourth one? Anyway, today they had saved his ass. And it felt real good.

There had been no time to thumb through all his records or talk with the floor nurses or the family about whether the patient wanted all that treatment. "Excuse me, sir. Sir, wake up. In another hundred and forty seconds your brain will start to decay irreversibly. Now, sign here if you want us to bring you back. And sign over here if you don't. I'm sorry, it's required by the Legal Department. Both copies, please." And, of course, the patient and his family hadn't initiated any of this in advance, if they knew they could. And the doctor, who did know, hadn't told them. In today's world, planning for the worst can too easily seem like preparing.

"Was that the man's wife and daughter huddling in the hall outside the room?" I asked.

"I suppose," said the young doctor, sipping his coffee.

"Why was that man here in the first place?"

A shrug. "Hey, Barb. That Blue Code up on two. What's he in for? No, in the first place? Well, we can get that for you later?"

"What was his name? I mean, what is his name?"

"I don't know."

I began to see some of my parents' blind spots and vaguely expressed prejudices, which were disturbing. My parents were supposed to be perfect, not human, since they had been here so long, would be here forever, and belonged to me. I tried to ignore these blemishes. That's when I also learned that Mom had never finished college, which was no big deal except I had been led to believe she had; one day I realized all the talk of her college days had never included the word "graduate." Which was her choice, of course, or more likely society's in those days of Depression and rigid marital expectations. But let me suggest that there was a philosophical foundation to Hitler, albeit evil and corrupt, and disgust and anger would wash across the face of this woman who had lost high-school friends to Nazi metal. For me to discover that there was far more to those series of bloody battles than cardboard good guys and bad guys pushing each other around was very exciting. To her, it was as if by examining the other side, merely by discussing it, I was endorsing it.

"But don't you see, Mom, by understanding the other side better you can maybe defeat it easier?"

"I don't want to understand 'Hitler's side.' He was evil. Period."

"No, see, they believed that—"

"It must be nice to be a teenager and know everything."

"Gee, I don't know everything. I just—"

"Well, that's good news!"

Once, I asked why she was being so defensive.

"I am not being defensive!" she said. "And don't you talk to me in that tone of voice!"

"What tone of voice? I just asked—"

"Lower your voice, young man. I am well aware of what you asked. You're being rude."

I had learned something about history in school, and now at home something about trying to discuss such things with Mom. So I retreated into that familiar and comfortable silence. It was safer.

With Dad, it was different. Not better, but different. He knew about the other side of issues very well. As the company's appointed negotiator with the unions, he had to know the other sides in order to deal with them. He also knew they were wrong.

And he loved to negotiate over the differences. I hated those things. Years later, shopping for my first home, I sought his tactical advice on one place.

"What do you like about it?" he asked.

"It's got a swimming pool," I said, full of enthusiasm.

"A pool? Oh, good. So tomorrow you ask them how much they think it would cost to fill in the pool. After all, you've got children and it's very dangerous."

"Fill it in? But I like the pool."

He looked at his stupid son. Dad was being very patient because I had demonstrated an eagerness to learn. "Well," he said extremely slowly so the lesson would sink in, "they don't know that."

Talk about uncovering new worlds. But there was one difficulty. "I already told them I liked the pool."

"You what?" He sighed. "All right. You liked the pool yesterday. But on second thought you're worried about your children and the pool. You are concerned for your children's safety, aren't you?"

"Well, yeah, sure. But—"

"Well, there you go."

Dad would take six months to buy a new car because he loved the haggling so much. Once, he determined to get more on an old trade-in than the $730 he had paid for it used. That one took eight months, but he showed me the eventual bill of sale; he got $731. He was delighted. The car dealer offered him a job. Dad was even more delighted.

You could tell when Dad was delighted. He rubbed his hands together and cleared his throat. That's how I knew before anyone when we had a room at that night's motel. He would come walking out of the office rubbing his hands and clearing his throat.

Sitting in the car with Mom, I wanted to be first with the news. "We've got a room," I'd tell her.

"How do you know?" she'd ask.

"Well," Dad would say, sliding back into the front seat, "we've got a room."

Mom would look at me in puzzlement. I would smile smugly. It worked every time.

Even sitting in the backseat, I could tell when Dad was smiling: his right ear moved a little. "What's so funny?" I'd say.

The ear would move again. And Mom would look at the side of Dad's head and then back at me. Sometimes that made her smile, too.

But rubbing hands and clearing throats did not happen much during union negotiations, which were like a fifth season of every year, a season worse than winter when clouds, tension, and fatigue ruled the family skies. "I hate those people," Mom would say, never having met any of them. One year was very tough; Dad admired the union negotiator, who made it very tough. By the next year, he had been promoted to foreman. "If you can't beat 'em," Dad said, "have 'em join you." Only one year was easy; the union negotiator was arrested for molesting children in a public bathroom. "That's too bad," said Dad.

So Dad did not become emotionally involved in the discussions I initiated. It was no threat to him if I examined the Nazis' platform; Hitler was dead and they lost. You want to think about the Democratic Party's philosophy? Fine, go ahead. Any intelligent person—and he was sure I was going to be intelligent, someday—would come to the inevitable conclusion: the Republicans were better. But people remember things better, he said, if they discover them themselves instead of being told. That had been the trick to being a consultant engineer, he said. Find out why a plant or department wasn't working right. Subtly suggest a solution. Then go away. When Dad returned in a few weeks, usually someone would say they had figured out the problem. They hadn't needed him at all. They would show off their solution. It was his, of course. He would marvel at their ingenuity and go on to the next assignment.

Between us, it wasn't a question of my challenging Dad; it was skillful use of an unwritten textbook on tactics, like a vigorous game of basketball between a slowing but wily pro and his inexperienced but eager son. We could argue back and forth and it was kind of fun—in those years, anyway—to push and shove each other verbally. "Oh, you men. Honestly," my mother would say, fearful that the heat of the exchange might grow too great, as it often does when males get competitive.

But, of course, we didn't. And it didn't. And if I somehow got the upper hand, as I did accidentally once when I started talking about muckraking American journalists of the early twentieth century, then he would grow silent. I would back off instantly, realizing this Canadian immigrant didn't know what I was talking about. He had never thrown my ignorances up at me, never taken my head and ground my face into something I had missed seeing or some freshly uttered stupidity. And I would not, could not, give him a lecture. Sometimes now he seemed to need protecting, which I quickly forgot. But maybe now and then I missed a couple of shots on purpose.

Dad and Mom liked what was happening to me, or at least they liked not hearing a steady flow of academic failures and occasional disciplinary imbroglios. Of course, Mom didn't say anything, but I was hearing more from her friends that she would talk about me and my accomplishments and my famous overnight career conversion. Dad would say, "Keep it up, knucklehead." And he'd award me a smile.

"If you're going to be a newspaper correspondent," Dad would say, "then your mother and I will give you the tools and it's up to you to make something of it." School was the most important tool. Then one Christmas came a good quality pen. And then a camera with appropriate lenses on following birthdays and a bag to carry it all. Then, one spring, the Parental Secretariat arrived on a weekend visit. "You really liked that European trip we took, didn't you?" Dad asked. Mom was quiet, knowing what was coming.

"Oh, yes," I said. "I never knew how different things can be."

"You're going to need to speak French in your career."

"Uh-huh." I was getting a little excited, but wary.

"Is that French?"

"What?"

"Is 'uh-huh' French for something?"

"Oh, no. Sorry."

"Your mother and I thought you might like to go to Paris to study French this summer. There's a special course for Americans at the Sorbonne."

"Wow! What's the Sorbonne?"

"The University of Paris. And we'd have to find you a family to live with."

Incredible. On my own in Europe! . . . Uh, wait. On my own? Way over there? That was a very long way from Ohio, even farther from Indiana. Those French have a different word for everything. And I'd need a trench coat. So I had mixed feelings when the three of us arrived in New York City on that June evening before the ship sailed for Southampton. We had just gone to bed when the phone rang. Dad answered. His voice had a strange tone in the dark—short, sharp sentences and questions that got increasingly clipped and businesslike. He hung up.

"My father's gone."

Mom gasped. I was slower. Grandpa Malcolm was on a sentimental visit to the old country. Oh, no.

"You mean—"

"Yes. At sea. He always got so seasick and that must have set off his diabetes."

I wanted to know all the details. When? How? Where? What was happening to the body? I'd seen ocean burials on "Victory at Sea." But eagerness to know was inappropriate at a time of death. And the d-word moved the land mines to tricky new places. I remained silent.

Mom and Dad would leave by train the next morning to meet the body in Montreal. "Maybe I should go with you," I suggested.

"No. Thank you," said Dad. "He's gone. He wouldn't want you to miss this opportunity because of him. It's more important for the living to go on. Thank you, though."

Early the next morning we took a taxi under the river to Hoboken, New Jersey. Dad had the driver go through Times Square past *The Times*. "That's where you're going to work someday," he said. The band played at the pier. The huge brown hawsers were thrown off. And slowly the ship backed into the Hudson River and sluggishly idled down past the Statue of Liberty, outbound. I watched my parents on the pier for a long while. And I waved long after they had become specks, just in case they could see better than I. According to my diary, I wondered when I would see them again.

---

*The doctor plopped down on the end cushion of the old couch in his book-lined office. A huge steam pipe, heavily insulated and painted to match the color of the room, cut across the ceiling high above. The doctor rubbed his eyes, though it was barely* 11 *a.m., and looked toward the slush-covered parking lot through the dusty glass panes and the years.*

*He was remembering, as if it were that morning, another elderly doctor, a half-century before, warning his class of medical students about the future. In their hearts those Depression-era students smiled at the old man. They couldn't wait for the future. It couldn't be worse than the present, had to be better. It held all the answers, surely, if only they could finish these damned courses and get out there and do something.*

But the old man's impatience was tempered by experience. He issued a warning to them about medical advances, which drew a few quiet chuckles. They thought these new sulfa drugs were wonderful, he said, and they were. They would cure many of the things that had long been a scourge of human health.

There would be even more wonderful drugs, he said. And maybe machines that could breathe for people. And some dreamers even envisioned a day when parts of humans could be put into other bodies and survive outside of a Boris Karloff movie. But nothing would cure everything, he said. The mere prolongation of human life, the professor said, would itself raise a whole new set of medical, moral, and even ethical dilemmas. The elderly, freed by antibiotics from the fatal threat of respiratory infections, would be saved to die later from far more painful maladies still eluding miraculous cure; pneumonia hadn't been called "the old man's friend" for no reason. There were more diseases and conditions out there, he said, just waiting for people to live long enough to get them. And doctors, who once had no choice but to accept a patient's passing, would acquire awesome powers over when that final moment arrived.

Remember the Greek tragedies, the old doctor advised the eager young men sitting before him. Remember that the enemy there more often came from within than without. Remember, he said, you are not gods. Don't get so caught up in what you can do that you lose sight of what you shouldn't do. Remember, he said, your oath says nothing about "saving" lives, just relieving suffering and doing no harm.

Sitting on that couch, the once-young doctor looked over at me and smiled sadly. He and his classmates had left that lecture hall long ago, he said, laughing behind the old man's back. Now, whenever this doctor's colleagues faced a hopeless situation with a patient who was not going to make it and a family that would not accept it, they would call him in.

*And he would listen to their fears and then he would tell a story about an old medical professor in a class long ago and the warnings he gave.*
*The doctor said he wished he could thank that old teacher.*

---

As the ship labored toward Europe, I fell into an offbeat schedule, sleeping late and spending much of the night prowling the quiet ship, marveling at the power of its laden movement through those immense, sullen waters that implied how very large was this world. I got a crewman to take me down to the engine room that was so full of sound. I knew no Spanish but caught the gist of the boilermate's explanation about the huge, shiny drive shafts whirling away the length of the room. I asked so many questions of so many crewmen that late one night an officer took me to the bridge, an eerie place that reeked of even more power because of its silence. The men stood there in the commanding darkness looking for something amid all the nothing outside the thick glass windows. The radar screen glowed green on one face. Other dials were dim. The officer let me steer for a minute. Such power was frightening. And he told me to push one button, which caused the loudest steam horn blast. I jumped about six inches. Everyone laughed. But apparently none of the slumbering passengers heard the horn, except the captain, who telephoned.

I asked how the steering worked, how fast we were going, where we were on the map, where other ships were around us, how to read the radar, why the men became sailors, how the radio worked, how deep the water was right there, and how far we went in a day, which enabled me to win fifty dollars in the next day's passenger pool on the ship's mileage. "You not only guessed the closest," said the amazed purser, awarding the money at dinner that night, "you guessed the exact mileage." This reporting business had its fun parts.

But my favorite time, as usual, was alone on the stern right above the propellers. When I held the salt-sticky handrail, I could feel the blades' power from below. The water swirled back in behind the ship, silently at first. Then about two seconds later the wake exploded to the surface in a swooshing, tumbling turmoil of black and green and white. I could watch that violence for hours as it fell back behind us and grew calmer and calmer until it was gone. And only I had seen it. Barely moments later, it seemed, no one could tell that all this humanity had ever passed by. And that was a little scary.

Sometimes I took my portable radio out there. If I touched the antenna to metal, it turned the whole ship into an antenna. And I'd listen to Radio Luxembourg, the BBC Overseas Service, the Voice of America, Canada, and even a commercial New York station or two. Every night, I wrote a dated note on ship's stationery with my address and mooched an empty liquor bottle and cork from my new friend, the bartender (What's the most popular drink? Who drinks more—men or women? Do Americans drink different things than Europeans?). And I launched the note and bottle off the stern.

On Mom's birthday I sent her a ship-to-shore cable; I just knew she'd be as excited to get it as I was to send it. She said she got it. I went to the movies a lot, too; they had several showings per day. In one storm the ship was rolling so badly the theater curtains kept cutting off first one corner of the screen and then the other. I had the place to myself that night. Afterwards, I went out on deck to watch that fury in the same waters where U-boats once lurked. And there was no one to say, "Be careful now." Waves the size of city blocks rolled out from the plunging ship and hit new ones coming in. Together, they rose up in a momentary struggle so large it obscured the horizon. And then, exhausted, the waves melted into green swells of wind-whipped foam. My God, that was exciting. Just before dawn, as I crawled into bed with my pocket flashlight to avoid waking my cabinmates, I devoted an hour to practice describing that scene in my writing notebook, which I knew would be useful somewhere someday.

. . .

From my reading, I had imagined southern England as frozen
in an eternal gray as it was on D-Day. But not that intensely
gray. How could anyone launch an invasion that was the hope
of the world in that gloom? How could anyone get up in the
morning? I never saw hard drizzle before, and a gray that seeped
everywhere. The morning of my arrival in Southampton, it
seemed that the gritty docks, yesterday's front yard, had become
today's neglected backyard, like the crumbling neighborhoods
around American railroad stations. A forlorn little band vainly
sought to generate some commercial cheeriness at the foot of the
ramp. And I wondered if this summer-on-my-own business was
doomed to depression in a foreign land where I didn't know the
TV channels. Those being the years when terrorism was still
domesticated and confined to the French in Algeria, the Algerians
in France, and a place called Indochina where President Kennedy
was sending a few American advisers to get things under control,
the customs and immigration inspections were perfunctory. Who
but a student living on the cheap would take nine days to waddle
across waters being traversed in six hours by jet? I checked my
bags at the Channel ferry terminal, dubious of their security,
and, unwilling to reveal my tourist's ignorance, I walked a good
ways to downtown.

The safest place I could find was an old bookstore where the
new volumes lined worn wooden shelves, their plainly printed
spines waiting for the careful shopper to find them instead of
standing straight out, as at home, so the colorful jackets could
scream to be purchased. I bought *The Count of Monte Cristo*,
which seemed longer than the movie. I ate a brunch of eggs and
toast, cut diagonally like my grandmother's, and spent much of
the afternoon in a movie watching *Giant*, studying again that
volatile silence of James Dean and reaffirming my secret love
affair with that Elizabeth Taylor. The candies sold there were
familiar from Canada, which was comforting.

For a while after teatime I sat on a park bench and was joined by an elderly woman in a black dress and those high-topped granny shoes my Grandma Bowles used to spend so much time lacing up. We got to talking. She came to that bench every day at this time, she said. Her husband, a fireman, had been killed in the blitz some twenty-odd years before. He had just rescued a child from a burning building and when he went back in, right over there in that vacant lot, the walls had fallen in.

"I had a cousin in the R.A.F.," I said eagerly.

"Ah," she said, smiling as if she knew each member of the home team, "those were the lads." But she had to be going; every evening, she went to a home to help entertain some "old" folks.

I trudged back to the docks then and boarded the little ferry to Le Havre to plunge, up and down and up and down, into the foreignness of France. I sat up all night to stay alert and save the two-dollar charge for a bunk.

There was a brief flutter in my stomach when the French dockside authorities descended on a young man in front of me and, seizing both his arms, forcefully escorted him back toward the pier. His crime seemed to be having an Egyptian passport. "*Où est le train au Paris, s'il vous plaît?*" I had practiced that for some time and was quite pleased when the customs man understood my Indiana French. Unfortunately, I had not practiced understanding the rapid-fire reply. But, being French, he waved impatiently as he talked, so I headed off in that direction and gradually zeroed in on the correct train, which delivered me into the central cacophony of Paris. I awarded myself a taxi ride. "*Onze, rue du Regard, s'il vous plaît.*"

"*Comment?*"

Why was this driver with *une cigarette* drooping from his mouth asking me how to drive there?

"*Onze, rue du Regard, s'il vous plaît.*" He stared at me. I smiled. Maybe my R's were wrong. Maybe this would be a friendly Frenchman. Maybe all wars would end tonight. "*Rue du Regard, s'il vous plaît.*" I showed him a piece of paper with the address.

"Wah, wah," he said. "*Quel arrondissement?*"

What what? What's a rondissement? A rondissement. A quick check of the pocket dictionary. Nothing under R. Try A. Oh, zone! Oh, uh, ah. "*Seizième.*" And he turned and started off silently.

"*Quel beau temps.*" But I guess he didn't hear me.

At my new home, I paid the fare on the meter plus 10 percent, which was obviously insufficient for his many kindnesses. He wanted more because the suitcase had taken up half the front seat.

The building was a somber six stories tall, in French. Gray stone, soiled by long age. Push the doorbell and the front door popped open. Some security. There was a short dark alley. The door of the concierge. An ancient woman—a cousin to Madame Defarge, no doubt—eyed me suspiciously and pointed up. Another big help. "*Quel étage, s'il vous plaît?*"

"*Seizième.*" No, I said to myself, it couldn't possibly be the sixteenth floor. I rested at three. And five. On the sixth floor, the seventh back home, there was the name on the door, which opened in a moment. "*Allo, Madame Brisset. Je m'appelle André Mal—*" But the little woman had turned and was walking away.

She did not slam the door, though, which I assumed meant "*Bienvenue.*" These Parisians were as warm and friendly as New Yorkers. I followed her into a dark foyer, then down a dark hallway to a dark room. It had a cupboard, a sink, a small desk, a creaky bed with a log pillow, and a large window with doors, locked tightly against any invasion by sunlight. They stiffly opened on to a cramped courtyard far below and an air shaft that funneled up all the sounds seeping from surrounding apartments—the kitchen clatters, the dining-room chatter, the disagreements, the laughter. I tuned my portable radio to a talk show to begin soaking up the language as I unpacked. Every once in a while I caught an "*eh bien.*"

An abrupt knock startled me from a nap. *"Servi!"*

The minute hand on my watch had just swept past noon. In the dining room a small crowd had gathered around the table, which was covered by one of those large lace doilies that have so many holes they don't really do anything except make the glasses sit crooked.

"Ah, M'sieur Malcolm," said a regal woman seated at the head.

*"Bonjour, madame."* Who the hell was she?

She introduced me to the four others, who shook my hand—one quick, fishy chop of our joined hands—and then they all sat down. I took the empty seat next to a dark-haired young woman, who passed me the potatoes. Potatoes? At noon? Hey, this might be all right after all.

"My name's Joanna," she said. The first words of English I'd heard all day, an islet in a strange sea.

"I'm Andy."

"I know."

*"Mes enfants,"* said the queen, *"il faut parler français seulement."*

*"Excusez-moi,* Madame Brisset," said Joanna.

Madame Brisset? She was the landlady who wanted her first month's rent two months in advance?

I smiled. It always worked back home. Nothing. I looked around the table and aimed a great big friendly all-American smile at everyone. Nothing. I looked to Joanna. She shrugged, and smiled back.

I got the platter last. Fish! For lunch? But it wasn't Friday. Still, I was pretty hungry. It didn't taste half bad, although the wine was very sour. They must have thought I was twenty-one.

After lunch Joanna showed me the stack of mail on the hall table. I had two birthday cards and a letter from home, which I hungrily consumed in my bedroom. They were two sentimental cards about what a good son I was, some extra money for a birthday meal on the town, and a newsy note from Dad about Wendy and the cats.

The summer passed quickly. Weekday mornings of classes in musty lecture halls whose hard wooden benches had been buffed shiny by so many generations of bored bottoms. Then a brisk walk home for the day's main meal. Possibly a nap or some sightseeing. In the early evenings I began hanging around the oily offices of *The New York Times* International Edition, watching every moment and movement and using some pauses to ask questions. I ran errands to earn their interest. Dinner was a ham sandwich on French bread. By the 2 a.m. closing time, the subways were closed, so I'd make the hour-long hike through the empty streets and the bustling vegetable market back to the apartment alone. I'd slide the morning paper under Joanna's door, add the day's events to my diary, and maybe, just before crawling into bed, watch the sky start to lighten over the rooftops. I liked the night better; it was a freer time.

I tried the museums. I really did. But I preferred the streets of today, the vibrancy of these people, any people, going about their everyday lives with their own revealing patterns and peculiarities. I'd pick a bus, any bus, and ride it to the end, eavesdropping on every conversation I could and surreptitiously looking up overheard words. My own assignment was to use them in conversation within twenty-four hours. I'd walk around the new neighborhood for hours, practicing observing and practicing remembering. Later, I would confide these observations to my notebook and see how much I had absorbed. Then I'd take the same bus back home and consider it an exciting afternoon. Soon I bought a motorized bicycle to putt around the city on long afternoon tours into the factory districts, the parks and fashionable areas, the working-class rows of houses. When the newspaper closed in the post-midnight darkness, I would hop on my moped and zip off to the Place de la Concorde, buzzing round and round that traffic-free circle alone and triumphant amid the gushing fountains and bright spotlights. Some nights I whooped out loud, so exhilarating was it to be emerging from the cocoon of youth.

Then I'd wheel over the empty bridge toward the government buildings and my room beyond. Frequently, two gendarmes would step out of the shadows and flag me down. The first time they waved me over, I thought they were very friendly and waved back. But when I heard their shouts even over my smokey little motor, I stopped. They wanted to check my papers in that age of plastic bombs. I would pretend to understand very little French, which was less true as time went on. I enjoyed listening in on their conversation, and when one grumbled about the stupid American, I smiled dumbly, knowing inside who was really stupid. That kind of secret power felt very good to have, well worth all the time and practice.

The intervals between my letters home had grown somewhat longer. There was so much to do and think about elsewhere. Once a week or so, I'd draw material from my diary to fill enough pages for a letter to Ohio. That was becoming harder, however. The feelings of awakening to things my parents had not taught me were hard to put down on paper, although my enthusiasm spilled out even through my hurried left-handed scrawl. I imagined these precious pages being fingered by so many strange hands en route to my parents' house, and then being opened and read over coffee where I would never know their real reaction— stunned silence at the maturity of my impressions, a slight smile at their cuteness, a mocking laugh at the ridiculousness of such thoughts. Often, I thought I could get away with just a postcard, which wasn't sealed so it needn't be confiding. I favored nighttime shots of the Arc de Triomphe or Mont-Saint-Michel, the medieval cathedral perched on a point of rock on the Atlantic coast and surrounded by water at high tide. I walked the five miles from the railroad station the weekend I saw the cathedral; I wanted to see it the first time as a medieval voyager might have, wending his way through some wispy woods, rounding a bend, and then suddenly spotting this dark mass of rock, shaped by man centuries ago, looming high and huge over the countryside. Now this was what I called history, still alive and touching spirits, not captured and confined to a musty room or book.

I wrote my teen-serious impressions in a short article and sent it back to my newspaper adviser, who printed it in the summer-camp paper, complete with a Paris dateline. When the paper arrived, I stared and stared at my first foreign dateline, my first dateline, period. I was addicted.

Then one day I went to buy a train ticket to Florence. I noticed as I walked away that the man had sold me one to Firenze instead. I returned to the window a determined fellow. *"Excusez-moi,"* *j'ai dit, "mais je voudrais à aller à Florence."*

*"Florence. Firenze,"* he said, *"C'est la même chose, m'sieur."*

The same thing? I could understand different pronunciations of the same name. But one place having different names in different languages? Damn! Why hadn't I known that? This was going on all around me for years and I knew nothing of it. I felt very stupid, and very determined that this sort of gap was going to become very rare in my life, though it was not necessary to tell anyone else about it. Most Sundays and Saturdays became devoted to consuming British magazines and French newspapers with the radio on. I had virtually no knowledge of the political parties they wrote about, the factions that maneuvered, many of the historical references, even the places. I was disgusted. For breaks, I went to a café. So they served their Coca-Colas warm; I would nurse that drink and eavesdrop on every conversation my ears could find. I began following Madame Brisset everywhere she went, talking, talking, talking. And the poor maid could not make a salad or more fish without recounting her life story and how she came to be in this kitchen. I went shopping with her. What's the word for this? For this? For this? And this? What is this? What did that man say to you? What was that you replied? Is that slang? When the family went on a picnic, I even tried lark's liver, although that was nearing my limit.

I bought a French-style jacket and burst the pocket seams with my thick bilingual dictionary. I browsed the bookstalls along the Seine. It seemed terribly intellectual; it still does. I went to churches, watched weddings and funerals. Once in a while, I went down to the American Express office to feel superior and Canadian, observing the Americans in their wash-and-wear travel clothes and sensible shoes getting on and off the buses, trying to decipher the foldout maps and funny money, and desperately dropping to each other the names of all the cities they had seen already. When a Paris traffic cop pulled me over one midnight for unsuccessfully trying to squeeze my moped through on a yellow light when he and I were the only living souls in sight, I argued with him, using my new phrases, the hand movements, the rolling eyes. He was stunned and delighted with the boredom-breaking exchange. He smiled and shooed me on my way. And I was delighted with my performance.

The following summer, I returned to Europe. Dad said he would pay my room and board if I could earn my airfare. I sold just enough stories to American newspapers in advance to raise the six hundred dollars. The pitch to the papers was to have their own young American reporter wandering the exotic spots of Europe; I may have forgotten to mention exactly how young the reporter was, but that was okay because one of them forgot to pay me. I wrote a French-language newspaper in Bruxelles and offered my services, very cheaply (free, to be exact), as an apprentice reporter. They were intrigued. I went out with the reporters and the photographers. Then I was on my own, interviewing suburban police about a murder, helping to review a new strip show ("Very compelling—Malcolm, *La Dernière Heure*"), and the next day showing up at the negotiations for Britain's entry into the Common Market, which I had read all about by then. "Excuse me, Minister Heath, any progress this morning?" So what if a nervous me had to find bathrooms frequently? I had the football in my hands. I was busting through the line. And God help any linebacker who got in my way on those days.

One day I took a city bus to the scene of the Battle of Waterloo. The anniversary was approaching. I had read the dramatic historical accounts—Napoleon's painful kidney stones delaying the attack just long enough for the German reinforcements to arrive and seal his doom; the bodies so thick the wheeled cannons could not be moved. The dusty diorama was very disappointing, the tourism aura depressing. I set out to walk the battle lines across the fields and ended up at the farmhouse on the British right flank where the British and Napoleon's brother had struggled. The ancient stone house had a television antenna perched on its roof now. The placid pastures were spotted with more overgrown memorial markers than livestock. And there stood the farmer, living his life today where so many had ended yesterday. I interviewed him about what that was like; he knew little of the battle's details, but he knew much about what camera-toting tourists did to his fields. As we talked, he mixed paint in an old German helmet hung on a string. The story I wrote appeared on page 1 of *The National Observer*. The day the laudatory letter from the editor and the clipping of the Waterloo story arrived at my Belgian boardinghouse, I memorized their contents. That night I got around to reading my parents' latest letter. At first, the excitement of that prominent newspaper display on hundreds of thousands of copies overwhelmed the seminal professional realization that behind every big story there are even better tales about unknown individuals, more compelling by their human detail and simplicity. And sometimes the unknown individual's simple personal story can point to the history. And I could uncover all this merely by being my genuine self and assembling endless questions in strategic order to make the subject both relaxed and forthcoming, which was always a challenge though not always easy.

The rest of my formal schooling seems, in my memory, to have gone quickly. I was at home briefly; in one thirty-six-month period, barely thirty nights there and they were spent in my old room, frozen in time with the passionately pursued icons of a thirteen-year-old, in my old bunk bed beneath the fading pennants of my childhood. I didn't mind when my vast comic-book collection, which today could have financed a child's education, was tidied into oblivion by my mother; those things seemed irrelevant then. I don't know what happened to my BB gun with the worn wooden stock; I assume it was tagged "Working" and went, unnoticed but not unpaid for, to some stranger during one of my mother's epic garage sales that turned clutter into many times more cash in a day than she had earned in a month of peddling handbags. Mom said she was tired of dusting my short-wave radio, so it was stashed in a closet; I still get it out now and then to wander the waves of static with nostalgia. Dad simply turned Grandpa's .38 into the police when the new registration laws came in.

However, I was stunned for a while when, on a walk by the lake at school, my mother casually mentioned that Wendy was gone. Approaching adulthood, I knew the code. "A car?" I asked. She nodded. "When?" A few weeks back. "Why didn't you tell me?" They wanted to tell me in person. And that was that, after all that love and play, the hours she waited for my school bus, and her blind devotion to those two scrawny puppies. Gone but barely remembered. "Gone." That definitely was a better word. Safer. It inserted that cushion of distance and implied choice that made memories pliable and sighs sufficient. But Edgar, the cat, was still doing fine.

The school newspaper adviser came to dominate my existence, discussing immediate personal events and practical problems my parents never knew of, teaching me the annoyance of editors and how to handle them, letting me learn through stumbles and falls, and not rushing to soothe the bruises. It was becoming more important in my mind to hide bruises and less acceptable to run to someone for soothing. My high-school teachers always nudged us to do better, to try this or that, never to be completely satisfied because there was so much for us all to learn together. With a few exceptions, my university professors knew it all; they had everything right there in their notes or stored in their skull. It was amazing to me how neatly packaged history or politics or even literature could become in a lecture hall. If I wanted to peek into that tidy world and gather dates and insights like walnuts for the approaching winter of my adulthood, that was fine, as long as it was Wednesday; they had regular office hours then. Sometimes I did. And the bubbling enthusiasms of youth warmed their weary veteran hearts, especially the journalism professors, who were more aware of the real world's messiness, merging yesterday's dreams with this morning's tragedies and tonight's deadlines.

I immersed myself in the arcanities of the university's daily newspaper and its lonely late-night workings at the printshop. I remember fondly my father's visit there one night. He was passing through Chicago on business. We ordered a pizza delivered and I showed him my job in considerable detail. I know he was very impressed; he only watched me as I jabbered away. And I know he was troubled, because when I asked how his work was going, he said too quickly, "Fine." And then he changed the subject.

On winter Friday afternoons, the Chicago Symphony had student-price matinee days, which I treasured, usually alone; I particularly enjoyed Wagner, Mahler, and Bruckner, and almost anything powerful with massed violins. I felt I had no time for frivolous social life, even a halting one without fast dancing. I was far too busy. And anyway Friday night was laundry night. Some Friday evenings I would simply fall asleep, fully clothed, and not awaken until Saturday. On others I managed to pore over the week's *New York Times*, watching the movement of the bylines and datelines and noting the styles of stories and approaches. I also received a few replies to the bottled notes I had launched in the Atlantic. One turned up in an Icelandic fishing net and another bobbed from near Newfoundland to an island beach near Bordeaux. The sender and the finders eagerly corresponded for a few years.

One summer I lined up a job with United Press International in Detroit, writing twelve hundred words of state news every hour from 6 a.m. until 3 p.m. for the radio-TV news wire. It taught me panic, watching how quickly the machine consumed my precious words and demanded more and more—now!—enough to fill twenty minutes of transmission time every hour at sixty words per minute. I also began the long, painful, still-incomplete process of learning not to expect much praise and to be suspicious of what you did get, because something else was likely behind it. When President Kennedy was shot that fall, I immediately interviewed several students and phoned the UPI bureau with notes on the campus mood and the school president's reaction; the editor thought they had a few more important things to do at that moment.

The next year I wanted to see the South. I became a junior reporter for the Memphis *Press-Scimitar* in the tumultuous civil-rights summer of 1964, when being in the South without a Southern accent was not the best place to be. It was an exciting time, though I wasn't fully aware of its import. Every week I mailed clippings of my stories, long and short, to my parents. And when I would phone home, Dad would comment on his favorites; Mom hadn't had a chance to read them yet, but she always found time to urge me to "be careful!" So I was. Whenever I went into Mississippi on assignment in my little red, very used Valiant (my twenty-first-birthday present), I would borrow a friend's Tennessee license plates to replace my inflammatory Ohio ones.

One day, long before searchers found the bodies of the three missing civil-rights workers, I thought for a few terrifying moments that my journalism career, even my life, might be considerably shorter than I had envisioned in my forty-year master plan. I had driven into Oxford, Mississippi, to cover a federal court hearing on that humid Wednesday morning. I circled the square to get the lay of the land. I parked the car, casually fed sufficient coins into the parking meter, and turned toward the courthouse. I noted four very large men watching from a nearby bench, so I walked slowly, real Southern-like.

"Hey, boy," one of them called. I couldn't hear him.

"Hey! Boy!" Walkman radios with their soft, insulating earphones had not yet been invented as an urban safety device. So I busied myself with checking my pockets. "Hey, Red!"

Then I heard footsteps. "Hey! Stop!" And then a hand on my shoulder. Oh, God. I whirled to face certain destruction.

"Hey, boy," said the huge man, smiling. "You don't gotta put coins in the meter. It's Wednesday."

I did not die that day. I covered the hearing. And I also learned a little something about my own prejudices. But when I told Mom and Dad that story, they didn't get it, a comprehension gap that seemed to be happening more in those days.

That was the summer I wrote Eric Sevareid again. He was back in New York by then; I kept track. I recalled our previous exchange of letters years before, and said I wanted to give him a progress report on my career and the French studies he had suggested, and to get some more advice. It was presumptuous but, as Dad always said, it only cost a stamp to ask. He wrote back of his pleasure at my progress. We made an appointment, which was very exciting because it seemed an unofficial recognition that I could have a journalism career. Mom said she always did like him. And I drove the eleven hundred miles to shake hands with an idol and have a fifteen-minute conversation about which I remember very little. Except he thought I should spend some time in New York now.

The next summer, perhaps to relieve the mailroom of the burden of sorting my frequent missives, _The New York Times_ hired me as a news clerk.

That was also the summer I got a naïve little letter from myself. As a matter of routine, just before his men graduated, my high-school English teacher had each of us write ourselves a letter about our thoughts and dreams. He tied them into a bundle and put them in his top left-hand drawer with three other bundles. Then, four Junes later, he pulled out the oldest bundle, looked up each person's current address, and mailed our letters to us. He said it would teach us how our minds had grown in just forty-eight months. My letter told me that I was going to work for *The New York Times* someday. I wrote my English teacher back a thank-you note, on *Times* stationery.

By that time, my parents had moved out of mother's dream house in the country and into a high-rise apartment in Chicago, where Dad had been transferred with his latest promotion. They, of course, took Edgar and most of Mom's other antique treasures. It was an entirely new decorating challenge for her and it meant forging a completely new network of friends, which she did through Dad's work and their church. But there was a wistfulness when, on an infrequent holiday visit of mine, she would reminisce and wonder, out loud, about going back to the country someday. Dad didn't have much to say then, unless it concerned his unpredictable, occasionally tyrannical boss or Dad's politics, which seemed to have grown more rigid and doctrinaire. He would make provocative statements he knew I disagreed with, and hope for an argument or an excuse to give a little lecture. I sought to avoid such talks. Even when I telephoned, he sometimes didn't get on the line. Mom said he was busy. But we had some good safe phone talks then, she and I.

And then one day I got a delightful surprise. Understandably, a multicolored collection of juvenile pennants did not figure into Mom's high-rise apartment-decorating scheme; neither did posters of Paula Prentiss or Kim Novak. But I was always welcome to use the guest room with its accumulating knickknacks, its antiques, frills, and green theme. I have always preferred unannounced visits. They gave me more control, and I couldn't be late for a surprise visit that I myself was directing. One night in my freshman year, before they left the country in Ohio, I set out to hitchhike the three hundred plus miles home unannounced. It took all night, four rides, an understanding state trooper, and a friendly ex-Marine, who went twenty-five miles out of his way. But by 4 a.m. I was sneaking unobserved into my old bed. Around nine, I heard Mom mumble, with a note of concern in her voice, that she hadn't closed the door to my room. Dad opened the door tentatively. "Morning!" I chirped. Their surprise was worth my fatigue.

Now here I was, three years later, enacting another surprise visit that would end up surprising me, walking down the side street near their apartment. It was unusually noisy and crowded. In fact, it was packed with perhaps a thousand excited girls, who were focusing their fervent attentions not on me but on an exclusive little hotel. Police were everywhere and remarkably jolly.

"What's all this about?" I asked.

The officer leaned toward me. "I said," I said louder, "what's all this about?"

He looked as if I'd just arrived from another planet.

"The Beatles."

Since I was so very sophisticated, the Beatles were, of course, beneath my interest. But a mob of screaming young females could provide some interesting passages for my writing notebook. So I started scanning the crowd. All were excited. Some were crying and clinging to each other for emotional support. Some were laughing. Some waved photos, as if they would compare the glossies with the real things should they ever emerge. And then, suddenly, they did. Or seemed to. Several men jumped into a limousine by the front door. The mob surged forward in a wave. The car got only a hundred feet before being surrounded and halted. The girls were pounding with desire on the car.

I noticed the police. They weren't doing anything but smiling, which was suspicious if you weren't busy screaming at the celebrities' proximity. I looked around. Out the side door came two men with wires running from their ears. They were quickly followed by four mop-headed young men who jumped into a small car and raced the wrong way down the one-way street.

Too late, the mob realized its mistake. Screaming, it washed down the street behind the fleeing car. Smiling, the Beatles waved out the back window. That was good fun. And I had just learned the old phony-limo side-door trick that could be useful covering something worthwhile someday.

Then I saw her. Mom? Mom! Mother? Here? My little mother standing in a mob of hysterical Beatles fans smiling and waving shyly at the disappearing car.

"Hi, Mom."

"Hi."

*I was silently pleased with my developing string of stories on the impact of medical technology on humans. It was brand-new territory for daily journalists. It required curiosity and sensitivity and some skills at convincing people to talk about what they were trying so hard to forget. It was very satisfying to pry the door open a crack, to chat, and then to have the door opened all the way.*

*I was starting to get hesitant phone calls from many people around the country who had a story to tell, an ax to grind, a side to explain, a fear to share, a guilt to shed. Stories like a hospital that would not remove a life-sustaining respirator from a man dying of five fatal diseases, because its officers thought it was their job to prolong life as much as possible —even for just another football season, as one put it. And with the accelerated fraying of the fabric of communal trust that had characterized a once-rural society, medical people feared serious legal trouble and the heavy cost of insurance protection. If parents could sue an entire city for a faulty playground swing, they sure as hell were going to take on an individual doctor over a fault they perceived in the medical warranty which he or she had never really offered. Medical malpractice suits were cropping up like dandelions as these angry and disappointed consumers challenged yet another area of authority once sacred; the image of omniscience, always based more on the white coats than facts, was coming home to roost. And one district attorney got murder indictments against two doctors who seemed a little too quick pulling the plug on a patient passing away.*

*What puzzled me was how both sides were willing to talk; usually, it's just the aggrieved party. The one playing defense has little or nothing to say. But here were the wife and children, the doctor and nurses, and everyone's lawyers, and they were all willing to sit down and explain their thinking. "We're not sure what's right," they all said.*

*"Mom, did you see my story last Friday?"*

*"No, I don't think so. What was it about?"*

*"It was on the front page. It was about the development of ethics committees at hospitals."*

*"Effects committees?"*

*"No, ethics. They're committees that meet to discuss the problems of modern medicine in a hospital, like whether a patient can ask not to have every treatment the hospital can provide because he'd rather die than go on. It was very interesting. I went—"*

*"Well, I must have missed it."*

*"Only sixty percent of all hospitals have one and—"*

*"My neighbor loves the crossword puzzles, so I give her the paper when it comes."*

*"My story wasn't on the crossword page. Do you read any of the paper?"*

*"It's an awful lot to read, Andy. And my arms get tired holding it."*

*"Well, maybe we'll let the subscription expire. It's a waste of money if you don't read it. And your neighbor can buy her own copy."*

"Oh, no. No. I put it on the coffee table for a day or so. Your father loved getting it."

"If only I knew his Zip Code now."

"What?"

"Nothing, Mom."

Whenever a story took me anywhere near her apartment, I allowed extra time to spend with her. I'd arrive brimming with enthusiasm from having spent a day or two inside the lives, or deaths, of a family or a hospital ward. She'd pick up on the enthusiasm part right quick and it would spark a memory. "Do you remember that night you called us from school when you decided to be a journalist?"

"That seems like a very long time ago."

"Really? It seems like only yesterday to me."

But the details of my current accounts eluded her, even when it didn't concern Hitler. There was little point, then, in trying to discuss the issues I was probing, the fascinating pros and cons of a society trying, haltingly and fearfully, to work out a new set of rules for an age when technology was developing around-the-clock, much faster than the values of the people who slept one-third of the time and, even when awake, paid little attention to plans for unpleasant events.

After a few minutes of my bubbling babble, trying to compete with the ubiquitous television, Mom's eyes would glaze and she'd remember it was time for a pill or she needed another pack of cigarettes. Or, worse yet, she might have missed a minute of "Jeopardy!"

"Gee, I'm sure glad I came all this way so I can watch you watch 'Jeopar—.' "

"Oh, this woman was on yesterday. What? Don't be ridiculous. It's great to see you. You can play, too."

"I don't want to—Mom, did you know this show was taped weeks ago? They do several shows in one day and they have to coach the players to say 'yesterday' even though it was really just an hour before?"

"Is that so?"

"Yeah, I had a friend who worked on one of these shows. He said—"

"Oh, darn! I knew that one."

*Even when she did remember a detail or two about my work, it somehow got twisted in her parental boasting and I would hear later from a family friend, a declining number of whom were still around, about how I was investigating a hospital. When I got back home that time, a message was waiting. I was to phone a doctor at a hospital I had never heard of.*

---

There was a keen competition to become editor of the university paper. And a keener disappointment when my competitor was selected. I was to be executive editor, second in command, and writer of a regular column on campus affairs. I felt betrayed and shattered. I congratulated him with a firm handshake. I went back to my apartment. I threw a book against the wall. I called Mom and dissolved into tears; the telephone was safer for her and me too. I poured out my disappointment and sadness in an emotional flood, which she accepted without admonition.

"Mmmhmm," she said. I pictured her pondering the squalid details of my pain, squeezing her lower lip between her thumb and forefinger.

"Oh, my. Yes, I see. . . .

"Uhh-huh. Oooh. That would hurt. . . .

"Yes, I understand. Yes. What did you say? . . .

"Well, that was good. What kind of fellow is this other person? . . .

"Mmmhmm. I don't like the sound of him either. . . .

"What does an executive editor do? . . .

"Well, you could, I suppose. But I don't think your father would approve of quitting, do you? . . .

"No, I understand. I wish I knew what to tell you. . . .

"You sound better now. . . .

"Yes, I know. It does. I don't know what to say. But let me try to get word to Dad. He's in Texas somewhere. How long will you be at your apartment? . . .

"No, now, don't talk like that. You'll survive this and worse in your life. . . .

"I know. Why don't you take a nap?"

An hour later, as my fury mounted, Dad called. Reign it in for the paternal presentation.

"Hi, knucklehead. What's up?"

I poured it out again, though more organized this time and the pressure of the anguish was reduced.

"That sounds a little sneaky."

"Uh-huh."

"It doesn't sound like there's any appeal to the vote. . . .

"All right. All right. Pull yourself together now. . . .

"Take a deep breath. . . .

"Now, when does it take effect? . . .

"Well, that gives you some time to think and see how it goes, doesn't it? . . .

"You're both paid, right? . . .

"Do you think you can work with this guy? . . .

"What will he be doing? . . .

"And what will you be doing exactly? . . .

"Your own column? . . .

"That'll give you some impressive clippings for your résumé. . . .

"Well, which would you rather do, spend a lot of time on budgets and writing editorials, or write a column and work with the reporters? . . .

"That's what I thought. . . .

"Why don't you give it some more thought? Go to a movie. Sleep on it. I think you may well have gotten the better deal, frankly. But it's your decision, obviously. I'll be home tomorrow night if you want to talk some more. Remember, you can do whatever you have to do."

---

*"Yes, Mr. Malcolm," said the doctor, "thanks for calling me back. I've been reading your articles. You've struck a raw nerve that many, including some of my colleagues, have successfully tried to ignore, though we deal with these things several times a day. How would you like to come to our hospital and spend some time with us, around-the-clock, kind of get a feel for what it's really like? No rules, except patient confidentiality."*

*He was as good as his word, even better. For five weeks I followed him, the nurses, the patients, their families, his colleagues. They were kidney specialists, often called in near the end when the body's ability to cleanse itself fell too far behind its ability to produce waste products. These toxins would build up in the blood supply, and without regulation by real kidneys or kidney machines, the poisons would trip the mortal alarms in other organs. I sat in on their meetings to decide who was a good candidate for transplants, for dialysis, the kidney machines, and who was too far gone. I overheard the late-night consultations as the team sought that delicate, shifting balance between maintaining enough blood pressure for healthy survival and not overloading the ailing systems with too much pressure or liquids. Captopril seemed a frequent prescription.*

*I made rounds with them: "Well, good morning, Mrs. Lewis, how are we doing today?" In the hall afterwards I took notes, like the medical students gathered round, as the doctor asked what they had seen and pointed out what they had overlooked about Mrs. Lewis. And I listened to their post-mortems as they munched deli sandwiches and discussed after a death what might have been done differently. I became such a regular presence that after a while they called me Dr.*

Malcolm and pretended to seek my opinion on certain patients. My standard response: "Take two Captopril and call
me in the morning."

But levity was a scarce commodity in those hallways. "Did
you know," the doctor said, suddenly turning toward me in
one meeting, "there are nearly a hundred thousand people
on dialysis in this country today? And every year fifteen
percent of them voluntarily quit that treatment. That's a
death sentence, you know. Suicide, actually. Now, suicide
is legal. But assisting a suicide is a felony in most states. Do
you think we're assisting a suicide if we let them quit dialysis?"

"You're asking me?"

"Yes, I am."

"Well, no, I don't think so."

"Why not?"

"Why not? Well, uh, that's a private decision between
doctor and patient."

"So you can guarantee that no district attorney in a tight
race for re-election will ever seize on a case like this and
prosecute you as a mercy killer?"

"Uh—"

"And can you guarantee that the patient's wife will see it
that way when he's gone?"

"Yes, I think so."

"You think so? But you've never met her. You didn't grow
up together in the same town. You've never even seen her
before yesterday, when you were called in to consult on her
husband. This is her first adult exposure to impending death.
It's your third of the morning. You better do more than think,
Mister. If you're wrong and she sues, your career as a doctor
could be over."

"Ah, well, uh, no, I'm not sure, I guess. So I'd involve
her in those final discussions to make sure. And I'd keep
detailed notes for documentation."

"What about tests?"

"Tests. Right. Well, I'd order up every conceivable medical test from here to Zambia so I could show later that I tried to think of everything."

"It's sad, isn't it? But you're learning, Dr. Malcolm, you're learning. And if she even hinted at any doubts about her husband's decision to withdraw treatment?"

"Then I'd continue treatment no matter what he said."

"Gentlemen, Dr. Malcolm is a very quick study. Now, if it was you who was so sick, can you guarantee that your wife would agree with our mutual decision to let you go?"

"I think so."

"You think so. Why do you think so? Have you ever discussed this with her?"

"No. I've never been that sick."

"And you're never going to have a stroke or suddenly be in an automobile accident, right?"

"Does anyone here have any Captopril?"

———

My last undergraduate year went quickly and smoothly. As executive editor of the paper, I did work with the younger reporters and practiced developing a presence in print through my own column. I soon came to believe that I had gotten the better deal in the editor's competition. My classes were all on a challenging level, especially in political science and journalism, where the advertising and radio-TV majors had been separated from "the writers," which seemed to earn us a special promising status among the professors; we knew this because they allowed themselves to reminisce in our presence after class. Unlike most of my classmates, I decided to go for a master's degree; Dad had one and he had warned that I would never go back later. Better to do it now in case I ever wanted to teach, because, no doubt, there would be a young woman and then a family and no time or finances for more school.

*A proud mother*

The young woman had already appeared, in a writing class. My tentative gestures of interest, most often expressed obliquely over the phone, were not rejected, which was heady stuff for the inexperienced. As time went on, she seemed genuinely interested in me, which was even headier.

Except for the last weeks, the graduate year went even quicker—thought-provoking seminars on urgent social issues, a thesis on foreign reporting, three months entombed in the political hothouse of Washington. I had been on my own, psychologically, for nine years already, so I was puzzled when I had to pull over and wipe my eyes as I drove away from my parents' apartment building after final graduation and marriage. I looked in the rearview mirror, as if I could see something there. It wasn't as if I wasn't ever going to see them again; that might be the case on some distant someday that I need not contemplate now. I had a career, a full-time job as a clerk at the *Times*, a closet-sized apartment in New York City, which the silverfish were prepared to share, and a heavy metal box in the car trunk. It was a brand-new tool kit, all kinds of tools, nails, screws, and wires, carefully assembled piece by piece from experience by my father as a wedding gift. He said in my own life as a father and husband I would need those kinds of tools, too.

---

*"Good morning, Mr. Anderson, Mrs. Anderson. How are we doing today?" The sixty-nine-year-old Mr. Anderson had entered the hospital two days before, thinking he had a back problem. Now he was about to be given a choice on how to die, possibly very soon. It was one thing to have a discussion over lunch about treatment options in hypothetical cases. It was quite another to confront that unexpected decision one day in a hospital bed with the consequences being almost immediate, and final.*

The doctor was getting very good at these secret negotiations, these delicate discussions that are so filled with pressure, euphemisms, pregnant pauses, sports analogies, even a little humor—anything to avoid using that word: death. The patient would have no time to practice. He would be involved in only one of these talks. And the lessons would die with him, unless someone wrote about them.

"Mr. Anderson, this is Andrew Malcolm. He's a newspaper reporter and a friend of mine. He's here studying how we work. I trust him. I'd like him to sit in with us this morning. If he ever writes about this, he won't use your real name. But if you'd feel better, I'll ask him to leave."

"No, it's fine."

Mr. Anderson had undergone surgery at a small rural hospital for a disc problem. That, they can fix, along with so many other diseases, conditions, maladies, and complications that once formed the horizon of doom. Now, thanks to the combined effects of technology and refined skills, that horizon is higher. Not gone, which many people choose to ignore. Just higher. But Mr. Anderson's hometown hospital was uneasy treating an abnormally high level of calcium in his blood, which alone could prove fatal if not controlled. The doctor had his immediate suspicions but told the patient nothing of them; he had ordered a full battery of tests. He knew he could be wrong. He hoped he was.

The doctor knew from three decades' experience that patients do not want to hear doctors admit how little they really know about so many things in the human body. The patients are frightened and want help from someone who knows exactly what he or she is doing, someone they can forget about if they get better, and blame if they don't. The doctor also knows how, when confronted by too much bad news at once, patients and family become confused and forget key points. So he eases into talk of terminal situations with generalities *and digestible pieces of information, never opening with the atom bomb. He avoids words like "cancer," preferring the gentler "tumors." He doses out the information like medicine, bitter but better for you.*

*The shifting, ambiguous line between doing everything medically possible to prolong meaningful life and doing everything necessary for comfort but nothing to prolong the dying process has not been universally taught in medical schools. There, a patient's death has been a defeat, another digit in the old loss column—not, perhaps, a relief for everyone concerned. It's harder to teach careful judgment and grays in a world that needs old films colorized and remote-controlled channel changers to save time. Students look for clear lines when there are just murky areas. How do you teach accepting defeat in a society where every team, even those down by twenty-four points with eighteen seconds left, is expected to use all remaining time-outs to stave off the inevitable?*

*Deciding how aggressively to treat and how passively to accept fate is usually left to the accumulated experience, sixth sense, and basic personality of individual doctors, who can steer the unquestioning patients and families toward reality or something else. People who will note the dirty fingernails of a waiter and vow never to dine at that restaurant again will blindly give up complete control of their life to a stranger in a white coat with an authoritative manner (and very clean hands). "Whatever you say, Doc."*

*Others, who would barely notice if their restaurant dinner was still moving, will treat this professional with the courtesy and trust reserved for door-to-door salesmen of Dr. Sam's Life-Enhancing Elixir & Furniture Oil. Displaying obvious signs of suspicion, because that's the way to show one is an alert consumer in today's trust-free, mall-pocked society, these frightened folk will demand to know every single detail of their medical care, which is their right; it's their body.*

Then they will make no effort to understand, but just accumulate the pieces for possible shuffling later into suspicious scenarios if the health-care warranty fails to materialize. They will expect a guarantee and then confuse a doctor's honesty about the limits of modern medicine with ignorance, which is no encouragement for honesty in a competitive world. To justify all this, they will recall a friend who said he had an inept physician once. And maybe he did. And the frightened fraternity of physicians did little to police its ranks.

This hospital doctor had seen all that so many times in what was developing into an "us" and "them" scenario. "All shapes and sizes," he'd say, "and the minds that go with them." But he tried, amid all that fear and ignorance and confusion, to remember why he had become a doctor.

"I took the Hippocratic oath to do no harm," he said before entering Mr. Anderson's private room. "And we must always be careful. But I think with all this medical technology at our disposal today, we can often do harm by using everything every time." The doctor also had braced himself with a cup of coffee.

"I'm not off to a very good start today," said a pale Mr. Anderson. "My bones hurt a lot."

"Uh-huh," said the doctor, nodding, knowing full well why the bones hurt. The tests had revealed that numerous cancerous tumors were dissolving them, hence the high calcium level. "Well, you've been poked and probed a good deal here."

"You'll have to speak up," said the patient. "My wife's hard of hearing—and so am I."

"That's right," said his wife. "Don't blame it all on me." And the four of us chuckled nervously.

The doctor did not relish having a sensitive and confidential discussion at a near-shouting level. He went to the door and nodded an invisible do-not-disturb sign at the floor nurse, who nodded back. He shut the door and returned to sit on the bed, which he hoped signaled more empathy than standing regally with his arms crossed. The elderly couple was silent, expectant.

"I'll be as straightforward and honest as possible with you," he said. "You said you wanted that. I have a feeling you already know what's going on in your body. But let me tell you what we know and you can begin to think about what we do next."

He spoke carefully chosen words, using pauses and firm gazes to emphasize his seriousness. He reviewed the patient's records and all the tests. And then got to the point. "There are many holes in your bones. Some of your ribs are broken. There are lumps on your kidneys and bladder and lungs. These are tumors. And they're spreading. You kind of thought that, didn't you?"

Mr. Anderson nodded. Mrs. Anderson clutched her purse for safety.

"Can we do anything?" the doctor continued. "Maybe. We don't know yet what kind of tumors these are. There are hundreds of kinds. A few respond to treatment. Some go away." He paused to let the real meaning sink into the frightened minds before him: more don't respond to treatment and most don't go away. Then he said it outright: "Other tumors we can't do much about." Another pause.

"We'll be very honest with you about the outlook. But I won't have all the information for a day or so. Any questions?"

"No."

"You knew it?" asked the doctor, hoping.

"Yup. Keep right on it, Doc."

"I will but—are you a football fan? Well, it's fourth down, Mr. Anderson."

"Thank you very much, Doctor."

"I don't know," the doctor said softly, "if 'thank you' is the right thing to say."

"What did you say, Doc?"

"Nothing," said the doctor. "I'll be back later."

Outside at the desk, the nurse handed over the three-ring notebook with all the patient's charts. She did that automatically and without speaking, like an acolyte who'd helped the same priest serve communion for years. The doctor wrote in the time and described the conversation with the patient. Then he added: "Family and patient still have some hope. Pls do not give final negative prognosis yet. Perhaps tonite or tmw."

That afternoon the doctor telephoned the cancer specialist, a woman he knows only by sight and reputation. The two professionals needed only eighty-five seconds to agree the cancer was too widespread for effective treatment and that Mr. Anderson had perhaps two months to live. The cancer doctor thought radiation might ease the pelvic bone pain. But they knew that within two or three days this would also increase the calcium level, producing a foggy consciousness and then a sudden heart stoppage. The two also agreed that given a choice between two months' cancer pain or a few days of grogginess, each would choose the latter. But, of course, it wasn't their choice.

That evening about eight, after yet another coffee, the doctor returned to Mr. Anderson's room to unload a little more reality. The patient was dozing. "Oh, good morning, Doctor," he said. "How are you today?"

"Nurse," called the doctor, "what have you got him on?" The answer was morphine; the pain had been too great. "So much for rational discussion this evening," the doctor said to me.

The next morning alertness had returned. "I've talked to the oncologist," said the doctor. "We can only treat some of this pain with radiation. That will raise the calcium. And

*then we can clean your blood every couple of days with an
artificial kidney machine. But you might find this a miserable
prolongation of things. I'm afraid things are not going to
improve. The outlook is, uh, well, the two-minute warning
is in."*

"I understand," said Mr. Anderson. "We've talked about
it. And I want to go home. I appreciate everything you all
have done. It's been the greatest care in the world."

"I wish I could do more."

"Me, too," said the patient, smiling. "It's a very poor deal.
But I'll try to put some more points on the board."

"I'm sure you will." And the doctor kissed the patient's
forehead.

"I'm sure I'll see you again," said Mr. Anderson. But the
doctor did not respond.

Outside the room he spoke to Mrs. Anderson, who was
about to enter the alone zone. "I don't want to give you any
false hopes," he said. "We're talking a few days to a week."

"I thought so," she said.

"I wish there was more I could do."

She nodded, drifting away now that the hopelessness could
no longer be dodged.

After arranging the immediate transfer back to the rural
hospital and consulting with Mr. Anderson's family physician there, a grim doctor walked down the hall past some
laughing visitors and a patient who would recover. "I don't
know what's right," he said. "I just do my best."

That was Thursday noon. Sunday morning at the rural
hospital, about three hours before dawn, Mr. Anderson's
heart stopped. The couple had signed a formal "Do Not
Resuscitate" order. It was written in Mr. Anderson's charts
in code: DNR.

When the monitor's alarm sounded, the nurses turned it
off.

Early in my journalism career when I thought I knew more, I saw my parents two or three times a year. Letters were rare. Phone calls were easier—and cheaper after 8 p.m.—and they saved time. My parents had moved again, this time to Milwaukee where Dad's new assignment was to rescue a plant which, like many others in the aging Rust Belt, was dying. Mom went along again, of course, and, when the painters left, was able to put her classy touch in every room of the new apartment overlooking Lake Michigan. Constructing yet another network of friends would be much more difficult. Dad talked of the challenge at work, but his voice did not carry much enthusiasm. He thought the company was trying to polish up a facility to bring more money in a quick sale. The workers were no longer eager, conscientious immigrants. They were at least second-generation, comfortable, speaking English only. For many of them, life began after quitting time and everyone wanted the same two weeks' vacation in the fall to go out in the wet woods and blow red holes in the sides of fleeing deer.

Then, one August Thursday, Mom called in midafternoon. "Andrew," she said, "it's your mother." Whoa, I could tell right off this was going to be an important call. "Could you come visit us this weekend? It may be the last time we're all together."

What? *What?*

I went. Dad acted pleased to see me. Mom was desperate. She had to talk to someone, anyone, even me. We went into the bedroom, her haven. "Okay, Mom. What is it? What's wrong?"

But she didn't want to talk. "No, I can't."

I wasn't all that eager myself. "Okay, then don't."

But she had to. "But I have to."

"Okay, what is it?"

Long, long pause.

"Okay, look you don't—"

"Your father is drinking."

There was a pause while I tried to figure out how not to figure out what was happening. "He always drinks, Mom. He has to have his martini at five-forty-five. And you have to have your Manhattan."

A deadly look. "I don't *have to have* a drink. You don't know what I've been through, young man."

"No, you're right. I don't."

Pause.

"Am I supposed to guess?"

"Sure. You're so smart. You guess."

"I don't want to, Mom. Just tell me what's wrong."

"Your father is drinking."

"You said that."

"Too much."

"What do you mean, 'Too much?' "

"He gets drunk!"

"Drunk? When is he drunk? I've never seen him drunk."

"Of course not. He's very careful. Only around me. Why do you think he won't get on the phone sometimes when you call?"

"This must be something new."

"No, it's been going on quite some time. I've tried to protect you."

"Me? Protect me? From what? I'm not here."

She gave me a you-are-very-stupid look. "I didn't want you to think less of your father."

"Oh, but now you do?"

She looked hurt. "No. I don't know what to do, Andy. He says the meanest things."

"Well, what you need to do is get some help, that's what."

"Oh, heavens, no. No!"

"No? What do you mean, 'No'? You obviously can't go on alone like this. You need help." I still didn't believe her.

"I didn't think you'd believe me."

"Oh, really?" Geez, get me out of here.

"So I took some pictures here."

"Oh? Pictures of what?"

"Your father drunk."

"Mom, no, wait, look, I believe—"

But she had already spread the colored squares out on the table. These were no family snapshots of fun around a picnic table or washing the car in the driveway. Nothing to do with happy Thanksgivings or new babies peeking out of blue blankets. There was Dad in sodden color leaning on the bookcase. Dad sitting on the rug like an Indian, eyes half closed. Dad on one knee staring at the floor. Dad staggering toward us, his shirt out, one hand reaching toward the camera, his eyes bright, red dots from the Instamatic flash.

"Oh, God."

"It's true, Andrew. I've checked the bottles every night."

"Oh, God."

"Don't take the Lord's name in vain, son. I know it's not pretty, but it's true."

"Why did you do this?"

"I knew you wouldn't believe me."

"I believe you. I believe you. Put them away." I felt sick.

"Mom, what have you done about getting help?"

"Nothing."

"Nothing? NOTHING! You haven't gone for help from somewhere?"

"Shhh. Don't raise your voice to me, Mr. New York Times. We can't tell anyone about this. Dad might lose his job. That's all he's got."

"CAN'T TELL ANYONE?"

"I'm not going to talk with you if you continue to raise your voice."

"YOU'RE THE ONE WHO WANTED TO TALK! All right, you're the one who wanted to talk. You take a roll of colored pictures of a drunk man for posterity. You take them to the drugstore for developing. You fly me out here to see them. You say you can't take it anymore. But we can't do anything about it? What—do you like what's going on?"

"Don't be ridiculous."

"Then we've got to get some help for him."

Silence.

"And for you, too."

"Me? I don't need any help. It's not my problem. He's the one with the problem."

"Well, Mom, it doesn't sound like things are getting better by themselves. Does it? I'm not saying you've got to put it on a billboard, but you two definitely need some help."

"No, I don't. And don't tell your father I told you this. He'll be even angrier the next time."

"Does he hurt you?"

"Oh, heavens, no. He would never harm me. He just talks crazy and angry about work and me. And the next morning he doesn't remember anything. But I do. I can never forget some of the things he says."

"Mom, he doesn't know what he's saying. I'll talk to him."

"Please don't tell him."

"Mom, you don't think he figures something's up already? You alone invite me out here for a weekend. I suddenly appear on a Friday night. And you and I go off into this room, alone, to talk. That's pretty strange, don't you think? He may get drunk, but he's not dumb. I'll talk to him."

"He's probably sneaking a drink right now."

When I left the bedroom, I heard the distinctive clink of glass on glass in the kitchen. But I decided Dad was emptying the dishwasher.

I succeeded in putting it off until Sunday. We all feigned normality rather well—reminiscences, civil discussions, dinner out. "Dad, I've gotta go to the airport in a few minutes. But I wanted to talk."

"Sure."

"How are things at the plant?"

"Fine."

"Good. Good."

"Yes, it is."

"Yes. Well, um, Dad, I had a long talk with Mom the other night."

Silence. The great stone face.

"And, um, she's very worried."

Absolute quiet.

"And so am I, actually."

He had adopted the classic passive possum defense, which is effective in avoiding anger and hiding exactly where a weakness lies. Just sit there and let the kid probe and probe. He doesn't want to be doing this anyway, so he'll quickly tire and go away and everything will be fine again around the burrow.

"She thinks you're drinking too much sometimes."

Nothing.

"Hey, Dad. Are you?"

"Am I what?"

"Are you drinking too much sometimes?"

"Maybe."

"Why?"

Nothing.

"Why are you drinking too much sometimes?"

"If I am, I don't know."

Not much to work on there. I thought I'd try the other flank. "Mom says you say some pretty mean things sometimes. What's the point?"

"I don't remember that."

"Oh. Well, look, I've got to go. But maybe you could be a little more careful, about what you're doing and saying. Huh?"

"Sure."

"Good. Good. That's great. I love you."

"I love you, too."

"I'll get my bag."

I gave Mom the okay sign. She decided to stay home. Dad

drove me to the airport. We talked about the upcoming football season, my work, everything but the real issue. And I escaped into the plane's aluminum cocoon and back into my own life where time still seemed as boundless as the sky we flew through.

---

*"Would you like to see the other side now?" the doctor asked me.*

*"Sure, but why do I think I don't really have a choice?"*

*The Friday-night date had begun full of promise for the couple, both in their twenties and both healthy. Then, for reasons no one will ever know, their car veered across the center line. It slammed into an oncoming pickup truck.*

*Around the country the lives of seven not-so-healthy individuals would be affected by the crash, another opportunity for medical technology to be useless and useful at the same time, unable to repair one person but able to try with seven others. When the ambulance crew reached the scene, they found the truck's passengers not severely injured. The young man was dead. The young woman was badly hurt; she had several fractures and a serious blow to the head.*

*Through the night, as beeping machines monitored the woman's condition, dripped nutrients and medicines into her veins, drained urine, and pumped oxygen into her lungs, her parents waited at the hospital and prayed for a miracle. By morning, it appeared their prayers would go unanswered.*

*Although the final outcome was clear to them from the start, the doctors dropped no big bomb on the family. Carefully, cautiously, always watching for anything contradictory, in frequent and worsening reports, they used terms such as "herniated brain stem" and "grim prognosis." The woman's lack of responsiveness continued. And the mother and father slowly began to realize that they were facing a situation with their child that they had always thought their children would face someday with their aged parents.*

*Because death seems so distant for young people, the woman had not executed a Living Will. Now recognized in more than three-quarters of the states, such a document contains advance instructions on the general degree of aggressiveness and the kind of medical care desired, and not desired, by the signer. Only about 15 percent of Americans sign such papers. In the absence of such a document, doctors must look elsewhere for direction, or to themselves.*

*"We always said we never wanted to live on a machine," the woman's father told me. "And we began to think that maybe the healthy part of her should progress into another life." The nurses, despite their common discomfort at raising such issues at a painful time, had reminded the family of the possibility of donating organs, a reminder required by a growing number of governments. In fact, about 80 percent of those asked do agree, finding solace in some goodness emerging from such sadness.*

*More tests confirmed that the young woman had suffered irreversible brain damage. At 2:50 p.m. the beeper went off in the purse of the hospital's transplant coordinator. Doctors thought the patient was a suitable donor; unlike her male friend, the woman's body had not been denied oxygen for any time. The coordinator began the tissue classification process, matching the woman with the hospital's waiting list for kidneys.*

*Then, just as casually as if she were phoning her mother to inquire about Sunday dinner, the coordinator dialed the unlisted number of a computer in Pittsburgh. "Hello," said the computer's voice, "I am going to give you a list of words. Please repeat the words after each tone." The computer then ran through a vocabulary of about twenty-five words and numbers. It recorded her voice for reference later in the conversation.*

*"Which list shall I search?" the computer asked, "Say 'One' for East Coast, 'Two' for West Coast, and 'Three' for all*

*regions." The machine also asked for the potential donor's age, sex, height, weight, and blood type. It searched its memory and, one by one, produced a list of nominees to receive various organs. Once, when the coordinator's response was a little slow in coming, the computer inquired, "Are you still there?"*

*"Yes," replied the woman. And within minutes she had alerted hospitals at the University of Alabama and University of Pittsburgh. They began to mobilize traveling surgical teams.*

For years early in my career, I buried myself in my work, flying here and there, asking hundreds of questions, and then writing about it, practicing a developing writing style that Dad could spot even when there was no byline. He subscribed to the paper and kept a growing mountain of his son's clippings, which he read and commented on in detail. And when he would discover some local paper lifting parts of his boy's writing to include in their own story, he would complain to them by phone, officially. Mom read some of my stories. She preferred to show them to guests. "Your parents are very proud of you," I heard later.

I reported to them on most of my trips and doings. They both came to visit at my current domestic or foreign assignment. In Japan, they marveled at my rudimentary Japanese, and that made me feel very good. Even in those exotic climes, Mom seemed to prefer staying inside over wandering the city or countryside for hours. We'd spend an hour or more getting somewhere and then she'd profess the need for a rest, a long coffee or two or three that would wipe out a good chunk of the day. When we returned from three years abroad, they had three young grandchildren, including a shy little girl adopted from Korea. Dad planned an all-day excursion to Disneyland from their retirement apartment on a West Coast waterfront. At the last early-morning minute Mom decided not to go, seeking someone to stay with her and donning sunglasses to hide presumably tear-swollen eyes as if we had left her out. She said she didn't understand why we had to go so far just to be together. "You all just go ahead without me," she said, "and have a good time." So we all did.

We had a great time, in fact. Dad plotted a park itinerary. The boys flew their airplane rides with abandon and climbed in the ersatz tree house. My daughter, who squished new Mickey Mouse ears down over her pigtails, didn't speak English yet but had fallen into a mutual love affair with her grandpa. Their hands rarely left each other's. And late that afternoon when fatigue set in, or seemed to, he hoisted her up in his arms and carried her all the way to the car. "I've got you," he said.

At the apartment on our return that evening, the adults had to temper their enthusiastic reports of the day's doings. We found Mom already in her dressing gown in a rocking chair, sunglasses still on in the gathering gloom.

The next day, as the youngsters sought excitedly to describe by word and action the previous day's wonders, Mom was obviously not interested. She was preoccupied that their enthusiasms would knock over some precious knickknack. "Well, that's very nice," she would say, "here now, watch that table." And the eager young outpourings slowed to a dribble.

---

*An hour later the transplant coordinator was by the crash victim's bedside. Her condition was hopeless, continued bleeding into the brain.*

*In a small meeting room the family had only two questions. Could their daughter's heart and breathing be maintained mechanically until her brother arrived the next morning?*

*"Yes."*

*And would organ donation involve any visible disfigurement?*

*"No. No one will know if you don't tell them."*

*The parents endorsed the donation forms. Even if the vic-*

tim had signed the back of her driver's license authorizing organ removal, the hospital wouldn't do it without a survivor's signature. "Dead would-be donors don't sue," one doctor told me. "Living relatives do."

In the darkened intensive care unit, nurses worked through the night, delicately balancing drugs, machines, and that individual's particular body chemistry to keep blood and oxygen flowing through the organs without overdosing them with chemicals. Four surgical teams were converging from around the country.

By Sunday noon, family and relatives had gathered for a tearful bedside farewell and religious service. The priest's prayers mingled with the slow rhythmic whooshing of air from the respirator while the relatives said "Amen" and eerily reminded themselves that it was that machine over there that was making the chest go up and down over here.

The patient was officially pronounced dead, although the respirator was not stopped. While two surgical teams watched football on a nearby lounge TV, the surgeons began. In situations like this, repeated all over the country every day and treated by participants now as routine, if rarely witnessed by the uninitiated, precise timing is necessary. The heart must be in a new recipient within four to six hours, the liver within twelve, the eyes within twenty-four, and the kidneys within forty. So at 6:20 the Alabama heart team stepped in for the first organ removal. A team member telephoned an operating room 1,120 miles away in Birmingham, where the recipient was being prepared. "Go," he said. And the two heart removals began simultaneously.

Within fifteen minutes the donor's heart was in a helicopter headed for the airport and a chartered race to Birmingham and the chest of a fifty-year-old woman. Soon the Pittsburgh doctors left with the liver for a sixteen-year-old girl with chronic hepatitis. By seven, local doctors had removed both kidneys and a lymph node to help tissue matching. The body *was closed. Eye-bank doctors removed the eyes. And the body was released.*

*Within twenty-nine hours, even before the funeral, all the organs were operating in other bodies. While I watched, the kidneys went into a thirty-three-year-old mother of two who was having adverse reactions to repeated dialysis treatment and into a retired postman, in simultaneous two-and-a-half-hour procedures in operating rooms across a basement hall from each other. Although the midnight implants were punctuated by some everyday chatter about restaurants, Chinese vegetables, and children at home likely staying up too late, most talk was clinical with considerable teaching going on, too.*

*With the kidneys connected, the artery clamps were removed and the recipients' blood flowed into the organs. "Nice and pink," said one doctor. "Good, good," replied his colleague as rock music played softly on a nearby tape player. "You know," he said to one nurse, his voice mask-muffled, "I sew better to Lionel Richie."*

*Two hours later, the doctors left for home and a brief sleep. One recipient told me later, "I feel like a fish released in the open ocean in spring. I go down on my knees to thank the donor's family."*

*"Our prayers for a miracle were answered," said the donor's father. "Our daughter does live on."*

*But neither family will ever meet the other.*

---

In their visit to my house in Canada, my parents went to dinner at the old restaurant where Dad had proposed so long ago. And Dad even danced again. He was very well behaved at those times. I never actually saw him drink too much, although when I phoned at an unexpected time, his talk was slurred sometimes and slightly incoherent or, at times, even belligerent. Mom would never comment in detail, except to confirm, in a whisper, that he was still drinking. One time when I pressed her about getting help, she got very angry. It seems that Dad had gone to a counselor for a while and for some incomprehensible reason the counselor had asked to see her too, which she had reluctantly agreed to, once.

"But that, that . . . woman," she said, "had the nerve to suggest that *I* was part of your father's drinking problem. Imagine."

I thought I could, frankly. But her voice seemed strangely frightened; I didn't push it. "So what did you say?" I asked.

"Nothing," she replied. "I walked out."

"Gee, that's too bad," I ventured.

"What's too bad," she shot back, "is that your father is an alcoholic. That's what's too bad."

"Yes, of course, Mom. But isn't the point to get over it any way you can with some professional help and not cling to bitterness?"

"Easy for you to say."

"Yes, I suppose so. But being easy to say doesn't make it the wrong thing to do."

"I beg your pardon?"

"Being easy to say doesn't mean it's wrong."

Stony silence.

"You still think you know everything."

"No. How's his counseling going?"

"It's not. He stopped right after that."

"Oh."

"He said I wasn't helping. I was his problem. And he felt uncomfortable with the kind of people in those groups."

I raised the subject with him now and then, mostly then. He said he was working on it. "Good," I said, like countless millions of alcoholics' children who don't want to see but do want to believe. "That's good, Dad. It's bad for you, you know. And Mom."

. . .

Mom, meanwhile, began developing a series of outside interests. Someone—I never actually heard who—had suggested she should be a model. So Mom began classes at a professional modeling school. I was not aware of a shortage in that profession, especially a shortage of aging women who claim to be five feet one inch tall (and don't you forget that sixty-first inch). Mom began taking an even closer interest in her wardrobe. As far as I could tell, Dad encouraged her to buy anything. I saw it as a materialistic penance. "Flair" became a popular word in Mom's vocabulary. Dad thought this school thing was a great idea; he said so in every phone conversation. "Did your mother tell you about her latest triumph?" he'd ask.

In the background I'd hear Mom. "Oh, Ralph, honestly. Don't bore the boy."

"Be quiet," Dad would say. And then to me, "The director of the school said your mother walks like a professional."

"Ahhh. Ohhh. Well, my goodness, that sounds wonderful. How does a professional walk differently from a regular mom?"

"Yes, I'll say." And then, away from the phone, "He says, 'That's wonderful.' "

I'd hear Mom: "And the makeup teacher said I have a real natural touch."

"And the makeup teacher says your mother has a real natural touch."

The reporter in me cried out, "What the hell does that mean? Since when does my mother need all that goop on her face? How much are you paying for these classes? Do the compliments cost extra?" But the wiser son in me won out. "Gee, that's great, Dad. Congratulate her for me."

"He says, 'That's great! Congratulations!' Here, Andy, you tell her yourself."

"No, Dad, that's okay. I've got—"

"Hello, Andy. Well, what do you think of your old mom?"

"Gee, Mom, it sounds great, just great. So you're having fun?"

"Oh, yes. But I'm a little nervous. I've got a test this week on runway walks."

"Runway walks? Oh, I wouldn't worry, Mom. Just watch out for the planes."

"What?"

"I said, 'Watch out for the planes.' Airplanes. Runways. It's a joke, Mom."

"This is special, Andrew."

These classes and reports went on for months. I was delighted, in part, for probably the same reason Dad was: because these lessons and practices seemed to obscure any evidence of other problems. And Mom, for the first time I could remember since the family famous house-tour week, was so enthusiastic and, well, outright happy. That was from a distance on the phone, the way most of us absorb the nightly television news, so safe, neatly packaged, and comprehensible through the insulation of the one-eyed, one-way lens. But up close, in person, the smells and passions of the actual events forge a different, less benign reality for the few who live it live.

"Wait right here on the couch," Dad said.

"Why? What for?"

"Mom's going to do a show for you."

"A show?"

"A modeling show."

"Oh, hey, Dad. She doesn't have to do that. I—"

"She wants to."

"But I—" But he was gone, behind the scenes. I recalled Mom sitting patiently through a backyard circus or two with my friends as performers, so I waited too now. It seemed like nearly an hour later this woman walked stylishly from the bedroom. Clad in a cape and fancy new dress, she swished across the room, stockinged legs flashing atop shiny high heels, hips swaying from side to side. Her fingernails were bright red. And, my God, what happened to my mother's face? It was all painted up like some bizarre hooker. Red everywhere and eye shadow and rouge to sink her cheeks and lipstick thick enough to hang a coffee cup on. My God, how long her eyelashes had grown since Christmas; they fluttered in the glare of the living-room lights where Dad had removed the lampshades. Mom also wore the cheesiest smile I had ever seen on any mother of mine. "Hello, there," she said, looking down as she swished off the cape, hung it on a forefinger, and flipped it over her shoulder while whirling across and around the room so her son could check out her lines.

For me, it was a nightmarish vision. This was not my mother parading around like a show-biz phony and this was not my father applauding fervently. And this was not me sitting there on the couch, first with my mouth hanging open and then with a frightened smile frozen on my face, slowly clapping, putting on a show, too.

I had seen my mother turn into a stranger once before, at a professional hockey game that pitted the Canadians of her beloved Toronto Maple Leafs against another band of Canadians playing for the honor and paycheck of an American city. I felt like getting on the arena loudspeaker then and announcing to the throng, "Attention, please. The wild woman yelling and screaming at the referee from Section B is not my mother and never has been."

After the hour-long fashion show in my parents' living room, I was still clapping slowly, smile frozen, when they turned to me, all eager, like twin youngsters seeking parental approval after the school play. "Well, what do you think of your mom?"

"Wow!" I said with genuine enthusiasm. "That was really something! Really something!" They both glowed at the success of the one-woman show for the two-man audience. Then, like the old days, we went out for a long Sunday drive, except now instead of little Andy practicing reading every single road sign out loud, my mother and father read every single road sign to each other out loud. Who were these people? And what was I doing amongst them?

· · ·

Not much seemed to come out of Mom's Modeling Era—not to the naked eye, anyway. She got one or two modeling jobs, one as a senior-citizen shopper, for which she had to spend the better part of a morning in an elevator with a camera crew, proclaiming to another passenger the attributes of a local bank. She relished the union crew taking frequent breaks while Mom, the tireless trouper, was ready to slog on, so excited and pumped was she. And when that ad finally appeared on television, my parents were so excited. It was as if the TV and all the professional attention had somehow finally confirmed her existence.

She sought and got a job selling in a fashionable dress shop at one of those suburban malls. And she did quite well. I went out, unannounced, to watch her at work a few times and was impressed. Instead of just standing around and letting the customer wander aimlessly and then, perhaps, settle on one thing, Mom was right in there with a flurry of questions. What's the occasion? Afternoon or evening? Any favorite colors? Then she hauled items from all over the store to mix and match, providing countless variations. And if you just added this extra scarf to set things off, it made another whole outfit. The scarves were on sale. Now, how does that look?

"That looks very smart" was the highest accolade. "Very smart indeed."

If a customer's taste didn't quite measure up to hers, she could be tactful, or silent. "Well, that might work." She really hustled and bustled out there on the floor, as if it were a fashion show. It didn't always go over too well with the slower-moving salesgirls, but it sure did with the owner, who started calling her in whenever someone fell ill or whenever he wanted to boost sales or just whenever. And this too boosted Mom's pride. Someone openly needing her. As soon as one customer was rung up and bagged, Mom's next smile was starting to form and her eyes were searching out any approaching quarry, the next chance to prove herself to herself. "Good morning, sir, may I help you?"

"Yes, ma'am. I was looking for a little something in green— say, a five-foot-one-inch mother who might like some lunch."

"Oh, funny boy. Come here a minute. Rosa, I'd like you to meet my son Andy. Beverly, my son Andy. Debbie, this is my son Andy. Oh, Mr. Parks. This is my son Andy."

"How do you do. You work for *The New York Times*."

"Yes, sir. But don't hold that against me."

"Not at all. Your mother has told all of us all about you."

"Yes, she has."

"Umm-hmm."

"And she's shown us the family photos, too."

"Oh, no, not the one of me naked in the bathtub. Mom, you promised not to."

"Andrew!" She went to slap my arm, but held up. "My son is quite the joker."

"What brings you to Milwaukee?"

"This famous store."

"Oh, Andy. Actually, he's doing a story on the governor's race for the *Times*, aren't you?"

"Actually, I'm doing a story on the governor's race for *The New York Times*, aren't I?"

"Who do you think is going to win?"

"I'll have to ask my mother over lunch." Chuckles all around. "Actually, I wouldn't mind hearing what you think about it, Mr. Parks. Have you got a minute? Let's go over here."

My parents didn't need Mom's earnings to survive. So she saved them. She eventually bought her own new car, a huge bronze boat where the long-lashed eyes could barely peer over the steering wheel. The ship would slowly swing around the corner like the *Queen Elizabeth* and consume every square inch of a vacant parking space before its door popped open like a huge wing. Then after checking her hair in the mirror, out would step this tiny little captain who marched away.

Mom pushed Dad to take long, leisurely vacations to Europe, which they had done together several times. He said he couldn't take that much time off right now. She should go by herself. So she did. For a few weeks during several summers, I received regular postcards of obscure Irish coves and crumbling British castles with cramped little notes on the back in Mom's distinctively illegible scrawl, telling of busy social doings and travel plans, how long yesterday's bus ride was, people she'd met, and what some had said about her courageous travels alone. I took to sharing these with Dad; I wasn't sure if he was getting any.

He would come visit my family for a long weekend at least once during Mom's vacations. He was very relaxed and pleasant. He would arrive with a gift for everyone. He would assign himself a home-improvement project, always involving shaping wood of some kind. And he would take the kids to any traveling carnival within sight. He loved accompanying them on the rides, standing by, his big hand gently holding their little backs on the merry-go-round as the horse went up and down or helping to drive in the dodge 'em arena. Once, he told his oldest grandchild that he would take him on the little diesel train for as many consecutive circuits as the boy wanted; I recall they stopped after No. 13.

At their apartment Mom and Dad had saved two dozen red plastic coffee-jar lids in a basket in the living room. Sometime on every visit, Dad would start to stack the lids on a wobbly TV table. As the plastic tower grew taller and taller, the little boy grew more excited. Dad feigned ignorance of the approaching attack. But at some point when the glee could no longer be contained, the young hand reached out and shook the table. The lids came clattering down. The little boy ran off. The Grandpa pursued. Then they started it all over again. Mom watched all this with silent interest and sometimes a faint smile. Once or twice she said she had no idea how to play like that with children. She said she didn't know the words or games. I suggested that it was the adult's attention they sought; the specific games were irrelevant. So was my suggestion.

One time, looking out the window, Dad spotted Kareem Abdul-Jabbar, the professional basketball player and an occupant of their apartment building. He grabbed a grandson and rushed downstairs for an encounter with fame. I watched the athlete unfold out of his Mercedes and double over to shake the hand of the youngster who barely reached his knee. Looking out that window, I was transported back a good number of years to the businessman's luncheon where the entire Cleveland Indians team appeared, along with a father who worked his way the length of the head table with a pen and a hurriedly purchased baseball, which he presented to a redheaded little boy at dinner that night. Though the ink of the signatures has long since faded, that ball resided in the safest corner of my sock drawer for many, many years. Now, back inside, Dad was rubbing his hands and clearing his throat. The younger youngster was vowing never to wash his right hand. Mom was complaining, as we were late for lunch.

At breakfast, the dining-room table contained an array of a dozen little boxes of cereal for the children to choose from. Grandpa kept track of who had the last first-choice. He also got stuck with the leftover raisin brans. Those little boxes continue to cause emotional flashbacks, even in crowded grocery-store aisles many miles and years later.

Except for her private vacations, Mom and Dad seemed to remain fairly close, or as close as ever, in those last few years before his retirement. I never ever witnessed any arguments, which seemed normal to me until my marriage began hitting rough spots. In one week's phone conversation, Mom said, simply and softly, "Edgar's gone."

"Oh, no." That cat, which I had trained to shake hands, had been around for twenty-four years of companionship, his own special Christmas dinners of chicken livers, and some habits whose peculiarities love made endearing; he always preferred, for instance, sitting on paper—just-discarded Christmas wrapping, an overlooked newspaper page, even a letter on a desk or a fallen napkin. Dad said that was because he came from a paper-box factory, which made sense as long as you like cats. Edgar even had his own cozy chair, known as Ed's Chair. I had not seen him in many months.

"He was very old, Andy."

"What happened?"

A long pause. Dad was not in on this conversation either. "We had to put him to sleep," she said, quickly adding, "We hung on as long as we could. But he was so old, Andy, too old to go on. He could hardly hold his head up and he couldn't control, you know, himself."

"Ah, bless his little furry soul." And thank God I wasn't involved.

"Yes. He had a wonderful life. But he was suffering a lot."

"Yes," I said for her sake, "I'm sure." But I wasn't. How could anyone be sure for someone else?

---

*The two veteran doctors, the four would-be doctors, and me, the outsider, had gathered in the glass-enclosed nurses' station looking out on six standard hospital beds, all occupied, arrayed around us in a half-circle. Three patients were sleeping, their slower heartbeats dutifully reported on screens along the desktop. Two heart rates were normal; those patients had visitors who appeared, through the thick glass, to speak soundlessly to each other with overly sincere gestures. They were opening a package with a large ribbon.*

*One heart rate was greatly elevated. He was the subject of the conversation.*

*"Which one is he?" I asked.*

*"Guess," said the doctor.*

*I glanced through the glass. "Oh," I said. The man in the corner bed. Half propped up. Two nurses hovering. Curtain partially open. Oxygen mask strapped over nose and mouth. Hair tousled. Face sweaty, contorted. With each breath, more of a gasp, his body convulsed in an involuntary half sit-up.*

*"Now, what's the story here, Bill."*

*"I told you before."*

*"Well, tell me again. For our friends here."*

*Bill sighed. He glanced around the group. This was his patient. But he had sought the older doctor's advice. It was proper protocol to guard against any oversights, though he knew full well what his senior thought was right. Bill also knew what he had to do. And they weren't the same thing. The patient is forty-seven, he said. An electrician. Advanced leukemia. Blood gasses not good. His kidneys were failing quickly; the creatinine level, one measure of the kidneys' effectiveness in cleansing the body's waste products from the blood, was up to five. At six they'd have to do something. Or they could give up, sedate him some more for comfort, and wait with the family for the end.*

*Bill wanted to operate on the man as soon as possible. He would cut into his arm and implant a shunt, a plastic valve. This would enable technicians to hook the man up to a kidney dialysis machine at any time at his bedside. At first the machine would cleanse the blood daily and then several times a week, although the patient likely had less than a week to live, no matter what. It was hopeless, of course. The machine could do nothing about the relentless real problem, leukemia. But it would keep the patient going a while longer.*

*"Bill, why are we doing this?" said the senior doctor.*

*"C'mon," Bill said, visibly squirming. "You know as well as I do."*

*"Indulge me." The students' heads turned back to Bill.*

*"We're doing it because the family wants a full-court press. That's why."*

*"Fair enough. Did you tell them the realities of our situation here?"*

*"Of course. They didn't hear a word of it. They think eight days is better than seven."*

*"Would you like eight days of this," the doctor said, nodding toward the corner, "instead of six or seven?"*

No one looked. No one spoke.

*"And what does the patient think of this?"*

*"He's out of it."*

*"I don't suppose he has a Living Will or said anything before?"*

Bill laughed lightly. The senior doctor was pretty good at these little stage plays when he had a young audience.

*"No,"* he said simply, feeding him the right lines.

*"Well, let's take a closer look at him, shall we?"*

The nurses parted as the doctors surrounded the bed. The senior doctor reintroduced himself to the patient, who may have nodded during one gasp. *"These are my colleagues,"* the doctor said. *"I know you've had a lot of people look at you. We just want to check a few things again."* He patted the man's hand. As he idly straightened the sheets, the doctor asked the nurses under his breath about the medicines and dosages dripping down tubes from nearby stands and about any changes they had noticed in his condition. They agreed his breathing seemed more labored.

The doctor wrapped the blood-pressure sleeve around the man's arm and inflated it tightly. *"We're just checking your blood pressure here. It'll feel a little tight for a moment."* He squeezed the end of his stethoscope to warm the metal in his hand before placing it on the man's skin. He listened closely as he let the air seep out of the sleeve. A nurse wiped the man's forehead with a cool cloth. The doctor read the numbers out loud, so everyone could follow along. He leaned over, placed the stethoscope on the man's chest, and listened again. He motioned for one student to follow suit.

*"Hear it?"* he asked.

The student nodded.

*The doctor straightened up.*

*He put his hand on the man's. "We'll do everything we can to make you comfortable," he said. The man's eyes were looking at the ceiling. The doctor stood there a long moment before leading the group back to the nurses' station.*

*"Now, gentlemen and lady," the doctor said, "why are we doing this?"*

*No one answered. No one had to.*

*"Here's what I would do," said the doctor, giving his friend Bill some room, because this family would be out of his life in a day or two but the two men would have to work together daily for the foreseeable future. On the other hand, these youngsters would be around somewhere too for years to come; the doctor had to get them off on the correct foot. "I'd meet with the family again. Are they around?"*

*"They're in the waiting room."*

*"Good. I'd take them into the private room, tell them again, and frankly, that we have a very serious situation here. I'd ask them if they understand how serious it is. Let them answer; make them answer. Let them get down here in the mud with us. It's too clean and comfortable and safe up there in the owners' boxes. Sure, we'd all like our fathers back. But at some point sooner or later it ain't gonna be, folks, no matter how hard we hang on. This isn't a body shop—recharge his batteries, put a fresh fender on, new valves, send him out of here nearly new. It's not that simple anymore, if it ever was. And we're not in the wish business. We can continue to keep him comfortable, relieve his pain, ease his passage, if you will. But we can't make the family's pain go away. I'm sorry. I'd love to switch the channel too, myself. I'd ask them, very slowly, if they really want to put their loved one through an operation at a time like this. I've told my kids I don't want this." He paused, letting the image of a haunting father, or father figure, hang in the air for these young minds.*

*"We let them know there is a choice here, even if they successfully avoided it until now, and it's all right in this case if they decide not to authorize this procedure. If they still insist, I'd say, 'Fine.' And I'd take my time setting up the shunt. Do you understand? Maybe late tonight or, better yet, tomorrow sometime if the O.R. is busy, as I'm sure it will be at this time of day. We've got some time left before we get to six. And, meanwhile, we'll keep him comfortable and see what happens." And then the ace reliever stuck his hands firmly into the pockets of his white coat.*

*His eyes scanned the group as the mind of each reviewed the presentation for gaps. The students made mental notes. Bill nodded slowly, acknowledging acceptance and respect. It was a compromise. Safe. Above all, safe. And also conveniently decent.*

---

My parents spent a year researching retirement spots and settled on the West Coast, which had no snow but couldn't have ended up much farther from their son's shifting assignments. They were in good general health; Dad had stopped smoking, though Mom did not. They were very enthusiastic about their new locale and thought that California would be an attraction for us to visit. It might have been, but every time the son and wife and three children piled into that apartment, it was more like visiting a china museum with a bunch of kindergartners; something or some rule seemed certain to be broken every instant.

For the visits, my parents always brought in all the favored foods, the potato chips, soft drinks, and radishes, even the little cereal boxes. Dad was into cheese after all these years; he had a half-dozen little aerosol cans of different kinds, which he would *psscht* onto crackers and consume in one gulp. "Try this one," he'd say. "It's hot."

But an awful lot of time was spent sitting around watching Grandma sip another cup of coffee. And an unfamiliar city's

*Wife of a retired man*

cable TV system, and scanning the horizon for whales that weren't due for two more months, can only hold youngsters' attention for so long. My parents' idea of getting out then was a long drive followed by a long meal in some pretty location and an only slightly shorter drive home, which is fine for adults. Mom acted hurt when I would take the children to do something separately, something that involved movement and energy.

Mom had found another small, fine women's clothing store to succeed in. She regularly won the salesperson-of-the-month-award, which was cause for another dinner out, when Dad would have three bowls of his beloved vichyssoise and skip the main course.

Dad seemed to be spending a lot of his time waiting around for Mom to get off work, where she was soon employed full time. He did the errands and shopping, which he always loved. He had a regular shopping list, a regular route around his regular store, and a regular checkout girl, whom he chatted up so much that she allowed him to redeem coupons on an item or two that did not, in fact, happen to move from his cart down her conveyor belt that day. One afternoon a week he worked on the financial books of a day-care center he had adopted. I imagined him also playing there with some of the enrolled toddlers, who don't get to spend their pre-school days at home.

Then one night he announced on the phone, "I've gone back to school." He said it in that casual, dismissive tone that really meant, "Ask me more about this."

"What school? Why?"

"I need it for the hospital."

"Hospital? What hospital?"

"Oh, didn't I tell you? Two days a week I'm volunteering at the Veterans Hospital. I operate the sundries cart."

"Hey, that's great. You'll meet a lot of people."

"Sure."

"But why the school?"

"For Spanish."

"For Spanish?"

"Is there an echo on this line?"

"What's the Spanish for?"

"A lot of the patients speak Spanish and no one comes to visit them. So I want to be able to chat."

Then, suddenly, two years in a row Dad—with Mom in tow—flew off to Colombia and the Dominican Republic to spend several weeks advising local paper-box makers in a kind of businessman's Peace Corps. He loved it. Travel. A little money. Foreign sites. Trying out his Spanish. His presence requested. His thoughts in demand. His driver waiting each morning. Helping eager people. His letters were gushy, his photos full of people. His mind full of ideas, and Mom kind of came stumbling along behind, quietly pleased at his joy but grumbling a lot about the heat. Mom fell ill with some bug in the middle of the Caribbean trip and confined herself to the hotel room. Dad loved to sweat. He was out there every day at dawn, excited, ready to do his factory motion studies and eliminate wasted time and materials, to make that world run more efficiently. The factory owners assigned an assistant to stand at Dad's elbow and take down every word and observation; sometimes by the next morning his suggestions were already in effect. I pictured him walking back into the hotel at night, clearing his throat and rubbing his hands together.

But Mom's illness, never definitely diagnosed, did not seem to improve despite a local doctor's visit. Visiting the British Isles is one thing; needing another language in the Dominican Republic, and not having it, made for another kind of trip in a place that was, well, rather dirty. She wanted to go home, sooner rather than later. Dad stalled two or three days and then reluctantly asked to leave early. Everyone was understanding. He phoned me before leaving. He was disappointed to be going, but delighted with his impact and was thinking maybe he could return the next year.

A few days later he phoned from home, a different man. He

was exhausted. He should never have tried that last assignment, he said.

"But you had such success," I said. "Wouldn't you always wonder if you hadn't tried it? And they've already invited you back."

"Yes," he said. "But was it worth it?"

"Worth what?" I asked. "A few days' rest and you guys'll be fine."

"Sure."

"Is Mom back at work?"

"Oh, yes."

---

*The doctor hustled down the hall toward the ward. Two women, one older and one younger, perhaps twenty, leaned against the pale-green wall, hugging each other and sobbing. The young one's mascara was all over her cheeks. Next to them, occasionally patting their shoulders, was a young man, maybe eighteen, extremely ill at ease, trying to find something to look at, something else to think about amid all the oblivious bustle of continuing life around him.*

*Although the evening shift had come on in the ensuing eight hours, Bill was back at the nurses' station, signing some documents. The two doctors stared at each other through the glass. Bill nodded toward the corner. It was dark over there. The lights were out and the blinds closed against the winter night. The bedside curtains were pulled to block the view for any other patient. The bed was no longer tilted up. The sheets were smoothed. The oxygen was off. The bags of medicine were disconnected. The monitor screen was dark. No more convulsions. No more gasps. No more life.*

*The shunt operation had been scheduled for midnight.*

---

There was no one day when it suddenly happened. I just realized over time that it had been a long while since Dad and I had had a long conversation on anything substantive. Once, he would have inquired how work was going. I would tell him the pleasures and some of the frustrations. He would offer some insight from his experience, usually involving far more patience than I could imagine mustering. In these phone conversations he always wanted detailed individual reports on each grandchild. Two days before each birthday, the cards and gifts would arrive, always at least one silly one and one serious. He was also aware, and sympathetic, as the storm clouds continued to build in my marriage.

But I realized slowly that our phone talks every few days were occupied less and less by subjects of conversational consequence and more and more by minute details of his daily doings, his friends' illnesses, his empty errands, and Mom's success at work, which he almost begged me to congratulate her about the next time I talked to her. Otherwise, he went here. He went there. He saw this doctor and that dentist. He watched some seals or a whale. He bought this and that. He had the car tuned. I found myself no longer asking his advice; the experiences he drew from seemed dated and no longer related to the decisions I had to make. When the subject did stray from the mundane, he seemed to pride himself on being outrageously curmudgeonly, going on and on about a topic he well knew I disagreed about. It was frightening in a way, as if he were drawing away a little, just out of reach for safety's sake. Or, worse, pushing away a little. We were still linked by talking but not through content.

Then one day Mom phoned, which was unusual. "Your father's in the hospital," she said. "He has been for several days. He told me not to call you, but I am anyway." Dad had grown frighteningly short of breath the previous Sunday. He had long since quit smoking. But not soon enough. His lungs were brittle. He was gulping for air at the slightest movement. He would be okay, for now. But an oxygen tank was going in by Dad's bed for occasional use in easing his breathing.

I called Dad's doctor and put on my reporter's hat. The doctor sounded nice, about my age. He was factual and forthcoming and realistic. "Emphysema does not go away," he warned.

"Emphysema?" I said. "Dad didn't call it that."

"I'm not surprised," he said.

It took several weeks for Dad to recover his strength, if he did. On the phone I was acutely aware of his every intake of air. "It was nothing," he said. "I'm fine."

My parents' life seemed to grind down into lower gears. Mom still worked many hours at the store, racking up commissions and bonus points and employee discounts. On some of Dad's "bad days" she would stay home with him. On regular days he would wait around for her quitting time. Often, instead of cooking dinner, Dad picked Mom up after work and they ate out. It seemed easier.

At a great distance, I was preoccupied with my own life in those days. My marriage had dissolved and I was numbly stumbling through the process of establishing a working-single-parent household with three children. My parents were very supportive, especially Mom, which was a pleasant surprise. She gave me cooking directions and recipes so we could have a familiar-tasting Thanksgiving and decent Sunday meals when the housekeeper was off. She provided a sympathetic ear on a few late nights. And one time asked a puzzling question: "I don't suppose you would have listened to any warnings before the wedding, would you?" One night she called to say she was mailing a substantial check. It was a gift, she said, something she had earned and wanted to enjoy giving me now when I could use it and she could know it. I was deeply touched.

Looking back, there was an obvious sense of inevitable decline over the next few years, although at the time I was not aware of the playing field tilting slightly to one end. Even if I had been aware, I would not have wanted to see it. I was, however, more strangely aware of covering myself and my future thoughts in case something untoward, something sudden, would happen to my parents. It was another one of those lessons that my high-school English teacher was always teaching. I had been out working in the world for some years. I was writing a story for the newspaper about how old-fashioned windmills were disappearing from the nation's countryside. As I sat in that motel room and then in the back of an airplane above the prairies, I vividly remembered that haunting discovery about the sledding passage from *Ethan Frome* in that teacher's classroom on that cold morning so long ago in Indiana. I copied the writing style. Form contributes to content.

When I wrote about the new electric pumps that were appearing on more and more farms, I used short, sharp sentences and lots of impersonal company names and cold model numbers. When I wrote about the old windmills, those graceful ladies of the prairies with their weathered, wooden blades whisking through the wind to provide power and water down below, I used long, lush phrases. And when the story was published, I quickly mailed a copy off to that teacher, who still kept generating four piles of letters in his drawer from seniors to themselves.

He sent back a thankful note. "To think that a student would remember one particular lesson of mine is gratifying," he said. "To think that student would then use that lesson in his own life is very exciting. To think that he would take the time to tell me is deeply touching."

I sent back a reply: "To think that it could be any other way when it concerns you and your class is outrageous." I liked the parallel construction of the notes. Then I added a P.S.: "I still carry my writing notebook in case you want to check it someday."

Two weeks later that English teacher died. Boom. Gone. Final. Though I had not seen him in years, I was stunned by the loss of this intellectual parent and by the crisp, cold finality of it all.

There had been no appeal for my grandparents either. But they had been obviously old. There were signs of decline in them that even a youngster could detect. My English teacher was too young to be gone. His death meant that cruel injustice still stalked the earth with a priority and a secret list of unexpected appointments. It could strike, silently, anywhere at any moment right out of the black. It also meant I was getting older. And then I realized what it really meant; it meant my biological parents, who were even older than the teacher, could go too, at any time. Thank God, I had not postponed writing that story and letter of appreciation and sending them on before it was too late, before I was stuck forever with a heartfelt message that suddenly had become undeliverable.

Over those next three years, I prepared myself—or, rather, covered myself—for my parents' departure. Like physical exercise, if I just practiced it enough, I was certain I could be prepared; even boys who were Boy Scouts for only a few weeks knew that. At first, I had only intellectual inklings that my parents might possibly die someday, the way getting a flat tire anytime is always possible but seemingly unlikely. But simply by keeping a spare tire back in the trunk hidden out of sight and mind beneath the dusty floor, we can almost always prevent needing it. That's part of the deal we make with the Fates. Touch wood. It's that one time you leave without the spare that you end up needing it.

I became fairly confident about my mechanical preparations. I never allowed any phone conversation with my parents to end on an unpleasant note. In every letter, I told my parents how much I loved them. "Thanks for everything," I kept saying. In my visits I tried to be more attentive, even when they read every road sign and uttered the minutiae that now seemed to consume their minds. I began asking questions about my childhood, trying to align the mental scraps with the real chronology, so they could be handed down like the family Bible with its pages of female handwriting of obscure but vital family dates—the weddings, births, and eventually the deaths of people, some of whom I had known. I had my parents rebuild the good times and the bad times, so I could trace them all accurately onto my own mind, the little boy concentrating, tiny tongue captured by his front teeth, still trying to stay within the lines. I would listen to them closely and then excuse myself to visit the bathroom, where I jotted down key dates and phrases. Emerging from that mirrored sanctuary one time, I overheard an annoyed Dad talking to Mom. "Why the hell is he asking all these questions?"

"What does it matter?" she replied. "The answers are true." She couldn't have been more helpful. She had answers and memories for everything. Dad was great for teaching baseball, but Mom was in her element on those days, keeper of memories, storehouse of relationships: Official Rememberer. She was in Heaven already; she was needed, sought after for her mind. I couldn't possibly keep up. I was constantly excusing myself to go down the hall. "Are you all right?" she asked.

"Sure," I'd say. "Now where were we?"

Whenever my parents drove me to the airport, I lingered with them by the gate until the last few moments.

"You better get on," Mom would say. "Can't miss your plane." I'd give her a hug and a kiss. And I'd do the same with Dad, adding a firm handshake as we parted. Down the ramp, just before the turn to the door where the kerosene fumes were seeping in, I'd look back. And there they'd be, framed by the concourse door, still standing together, watching, waiting. I'd wave a little too long by normal farewell standards and then walk away.

"It's not good, Mr. Malcolm. Not good at all." The voice belonged to Dad's doctor, but this late-night call was about Mom. "It's lung cancer," he said. "There's no doubt about it. And I'm afraid it's the most virulent kind."

"Gee, I had no idea. They didn't say it was this serious. Just some kind of lung infection."

"Yes, I suspected that. But I wanted you to know. We're starting radiation Monday. But, quite honestly, I don't think there's much of a chance."

"Of what?"

"Of her getting through this for long."

Suddenly, I found myself sobbing softly over the phone to a man I had never met. I did not hear him taking notes.

But when I got there, I found no signs of gloom. Like a reporter feeling out a new source, I asked my mother all kinds of questions about her condition, including ones I already knew the answer to. The doctor had told her almost everything. "It's too bad," she said, lighting up another cigarette, "but we'll just have to see what happens."

"Well, I know what's going to happen," said Dad. "We're going to beat this thing." Even in private, just between the two of us, right kind, he would permit no pessimism. "We're going to beat it, that's all," he said. "We can do anything we have to do."

Every morning they got up together. Dad made some breakfast: toast and coffee and marmalade, just the way Mom had eaten it every day I had known her. Then, by the door, he would take her arm as if they were headed for a midmorning ball and off they would go to the huge hospital on the hill.

I thought those dark, dingy rooms with the impersonal tile floors and the air-circulation system whooshing away were fairly depressing and certainly intimidating. The patient was to undress and lie still on a chilly table while technicians maneuvered the massive machine's arms overhead from a control booth behind lead walls. Click, grind grind grind, click click. The arm moved jerkily above, its nose pointing down at my mother, aiming its invisible rays at the unseen enemy deep within. The room lights dimmed. The machine lights came on, making a stark target + on the pale white skin of my mother's chest. I could see the technician through a window, consulting sheets of film for the correct coordinates.

"Okay, dear," came the voice from the ceiling. "Hold real still for me now, please. Good. Good."

The big brown envelopes were stacked in order of appointment. All day long, the machine clicked and ground. The + moved. The rays were launched. The cancer cells were killed. So were a fair number of others. "You may get dressed now, dear. Next." Life went on, for most. For the others, the big brown envelopes didn't come down anymore.

By the time the technicians in the white coats with the plastic name tags were aiming at Mom, Dad was done talking them up. "Well, you have work to do," he'd say, and step across the hall to the cafeteria to get Mom's post-radiation snack ready. "*¿Qué tal*, Juan?" he'd say.

"Oh, Señor Malcolm. *Buenos días.* You are early today, no?"

Two coffees. Two corn muffins. Three butters. Two napkins. Two knives. All precisely arranged at the usual table in the large room that was still ninety minutes away from the institution's lunch-hour rush. Then back across the hall to the radiation room, where Mom was probably back in her clothes by now and the next target was hanging clothes on the worn metal hook in the tiny cubicle behind the stiff plastic curtain.

"See you tomorrow," Dad would call out as he and Mom closed the door. But they were busy again. "Hold real still for me now please, dear. Good. Good."

At the cafeteria table Dad had to fill Mom in on all the news he had learned already—the technician's new baby, Juan's daughter, who was now in college, how he got the last two corn muffins. "You better save us *dos* muffins tomorrow, Juan."

"*Sí, sí,* Señor Malcolm."

After the second cup of coffee, Dad would announce the day's surprise itinerary. Mom was on leave from the department store. So every day Dad would plan a different scenic drive. During her time on that chilly table, Mom was supposed to think about other things, to wonder where she would be whisked this time. Some days there was a small corsage next to the corn muffin. Dad would pretend not to see it until she did. "Well, where do you suppose that came from?" he'd say, with a little smile. He would pull out a map and outline the route going, the luncheon destination—of course, reservations had been made—and the different return route. This would get Mom home for a nice nap while Dad prepared a small dinner that was preceded by a brief cocktail hour highlighted by a half-dozen cans of cheese spreads to spray on the usual crackers just in time for the evening news.

It went on like that every day for weeks. "We're going to beat this thing," Dad would say. By the end, Mom was pretty much in agreement. "Your dad says we're going to beat this thing," she'd say, "and I don't know as how I have much choice." She had lost some more weight.

Then, as if the thought had just occurred to him, Dad would stick his head out of the kitchen. "We can do whatever we have to do." And so they did. Months later, in another late-night call, Eastern time, the doctor confirmed to me what my father had predicted after the initial diagnosis. "I can't explain it," the doctor said, "and I can offer no long-term guarantees. But for the moment it looks like your mother has beaten the cancer. I'm impressed." And as the doctor spoke, I pictured a young father proudly showing his little boy a piece of paper confirming the sale of the family's used car to a dealer for $731.

———————

*He had spent his entire life—all 163 days of it—in a Plexiglas cocoon that kept him warm, quiet, and apart from worldly germs. To his parents, Stevie was a dream come true, a very little bundle of live warmth that they had worked so hard, so privately, for in recent years.*

*And he was a nightmare come to life.*

*To the nurses and doctors he was another in a long line of little loved ones who are wheeled in and out of their ward-*

sized work lives in the neonatal intensive care unit. They labor so hard so long to preserve every one of them; it is their job and their love and their pain. They put colored drawings next to the infants so they will have visual stimulation. They touch them, through the confining hand holes, to give them human warmth. They talk to them. They try not to care too much, of course, because there are no guarantees in life, except one. And there's a limit, or should be, to the pain of loss. But, of course, they do end up caring too much anyway. When they go home after work to their own families and problems, they leave the premature babies behind. But they carry with them the memory of those wee ones, lying there so wide-eyed and helpless, wiggling.

The nursing supervisor had called me. Stevie had also become an issue. "People think we have all the answers," she said, "but we don't. Believe me, we don't." She wanted me to write about the case, the kind that was fast, and silently, becoming more common in hospitals across the land. Doctors at a nearby hospital were even about to implant a baboon's heart in the chest of a troubled infant to see if they couldn't prolong a brief life a little more that way. Stevie's parents wanted me to write about their case. So did the doctors. No one had thought it would come to this. No one had the answers. No one had compiled the questions beforehand. How could they know?

Stevie had been born sixteen weeks early. If he had been born just four years before, when his parents married, his chances of survival at twenty ounces would have been nil. Now he had a 20- to 40-percent chance of making it—and, if he did, a 50-percent chance of not being handicapped somehow, blind or deaf maybe, or retarded.

When the labor started, the doctors had managed to stall the natural process. They pumped in medicines and chemicals to keep the birth on hold and push the infant's development as fast as possible for as long as they could thwart the contractions. The lungs were the main concern. They aren't needed in the womb, so they are among the last things to develop. But they are among the first things needed after birth. And without adequately functioning lungs, Stevie's chances would fall to zero.

It did not look good ten days later, when the mother's body overrode the medicines and expelled the baby anyway in the middle of the night in a Los Angeles suburb. The doctor said he was going to leave the couple alone for a while. They knew what that meant: decision time. Before leaving, he told the exhausted pair it was a boy, a little larger than expected, with a good heartbeat, but still very small.

They were confused, tearful. "There was so much racing through our heads," said the new father. The night seemed almost a replay of the previous year when another premature baby of theirs, a girl, had expired after forty minutes, unable to process enough air in undeveloped lungs. They recalled their own agony for long months afterwards, the sadness and hollowness and the sense of guilt that somehow they were responsible for the baby's death, although there was nothing else they or anyone could have done. In those days, they were still thinking in terms of doing everything.

They wanted nothing so much as their own child, a living symbol of their love and their hope for the future and their ability to leave something lasting behind, fully loved and finally on its own. Driven by such primal urges, helped by technology and new medical insights into the reproductive system, and aided by the uncontained ambitions of the specialists carefully climbing their own career ladder, they, like thousands of similar couples, had worked very hard at becoming parents. They had willingly discussed the most intimate details of their lives with those caring strangers, willingly taken the pills, and willingly—and, they hoped, nonchalantly—handed over the counter the sterile bottles of urine or semen in the crumpled paper bags, then turned to face the waiting room full of silent couples, with all the intent eyes and minds and organs, who had just done the same thing. And, like all the other desperate twosomes sitting there pretending to read the stale magazines, they had willingly turned their lovemaking into a process, timed not to the urge but to the carefully monitored ripening of an unseen egg, which they bracketed with precisely aimed ejaculations.

And now after all these wearing months, and the last few exhausting days, here they were together in the recovery room, alone with their hopes and fears. Who could have planned for this eventuality? Who would have planned for such difficult decisions before being forced to? They knew the statistics of premature infant survival were against them. "We were very concerned about our child's chances," said the father, "but also about the quality of his life. Is a severe handicap better than no life? He was twelve inches long. He looked normal, but there was no way to tell about internal organs. We were told the baby didn't have the capacity to breathe himself. He was on a machine. We pictured an artificial being, a potential vegetable, whose prolongation of life was basically an intrusion into his life. And we decided to let nature take its course."

When the doctor returned, it was still dark outside. They told him of their decision. "We want him in God's hands," they said. "There should be no heroics."

The doctor paused. Then he told them of his own, more important decision. He was going ahead with full treatment. He believed the child might be strong enough to survive. He had anticipated what they were going to say. And he had the telephoned court order to enforce his wishes.

The parents, who did not fight the decision, felt devastated. Not only did they face the likely loss of their long-sought new child. They now faced a long—and costly—ordeal beforehand. And they faced the doctor's defiance of their wishes. They had become spectators to their own lives, with no control. _Because the doctor could, he would. In their decision, the parents felt they were being careful, sympathetic, and realistic, according to their own beliefs and means. So did the doctor, who could go home, come dawn, to a normal life._

_And who was to say who was right in an inattentive society which had delivered the marvelous machinery without including the instructions?_

---

It began with a pain in the left arm, one of those deep bone-aches that survive despite any movement or stillness or aspirin. Then a couple of pimples emerged, like a warning. And a few more. And several others. They itched. Then they exploded in size and number all over her back and chest like some overblown atomic-age measles, the size of silver dollars. They oozed. They stung. They ached. They smelled.

"Shingles," Dad said on the phone.

"Gee," I said, "what's that?"

"You don't want to know."

That sounded very much like "Someday you'll understand, son." But I wasn't a little boy anymore. I was probably going to be elderly someday. I thought I wanted to know these secrets now. No more Firenzes.

"Of course I do. She's my mom. Tell me."

He was right, though. Once I knew, I didn't want to. He said he gagged, silently, at the sight of her back—the pockets of puss he gently bathed each day, then dabbed dry, then covered in ointment. The doctor had prescribed some medicines and more Valium.

More Valium? "I didn't know there was any to begin with."

Silence, as if some awful secret had just escaped and if Dad only waited long enough, the words' fumes would disappear on the wind and he could deny having uttered them.

"Well, she takes them now and then. For her nerves. The doctor prescribed them."

"Since when?"

Silence. He was getting in deeper. He knew it. If he'd known this was coming, he would have avoided the conversation altogether and not gotten on the phone. Reach out and don't touch someone. This son could be a definite pain in the ass sometimes, even in adulthood. Especially in adulthood, because simply issuing an edict didn't work anymore. There was only one way out now, the truth, right kind.

"Since Milwaukee."

Milwaukee! Then out loud, more calmly, "Since Milwaukee? You know Valium is a depressant. Mixing that stuff and booze can have some powerful effects."

"Oh? Do you drink now?"

"No."

"Have you ever taken Valium, doctor?"

"No."

"Have you ever had shingles?"

"No, Dad."

"Well, then let's not be quite so quick to rush to judgment here. Your mother's in a lot of pain most of the time."

"Hey, Dad, I know. I know. Constant pain is terribly draining. I'm not judging at all. But you don't have to be an, uh—you don't have to drink a lot to know that mixing booze and pills can make you feel mighty funny, even if it's just occasionally. She could fall down or something and really hurt herself. Or somebody. Is she still driving?"

A pause that reeked of patience. "No. I drive, of course."

"Does the doctor know about the pills and the daily drink? How often does she take those Valiums?"

The phone line from sunny California was freezing up. The ignorant son, the pushy, know-it-all reporter, was being frozen out again. "Okay, then. Well, is Mom there? I'd like to say hi."

"Sure. Just a minute."

But several come and go. An extension phone is picked up. And dropped.

"Hello? Hello? Andy? Is that you? Aren't you a dear to phone."

"How's my favorite mom?"

Mumble. Mumble.

"Hello? Mom? I can't hear you. Speak into the phone."

"Oh, sorry, Andy. It's hard to hold this heavy phone all the time."

"You should get one of those Speakerphones. You just push a button and talk at the box. Nothing to hold."

"A what?"

"A Speakerphone. You don't have to hold anything."

"It sounds complicated. We'll see. It's up to your father. This thing is very heavy."

"Well, I won't keep you—"

"No, no. It's great to hear you. How are the children?"

I quickly run down the latest unreported doings, oldest to youngest. "But how are you doing?"

"Oh, not too badly. This getting-old business is not much fun. Golden retirement years. Ha!"

"Well, it's nice that you don't have to work to survive. You guys are comfortable."

"I'm not very comfortable right now, I can tell you that. And I'm missing a lot of work."

"Well, you're such a super salesman. I'm sure they'll save your place until you get back. The important thing is to get well now."

"Yeah, your old mother didn't do too badly, did she?"

"No. You did great."

"You really think so?"

"Uh, yeah, sure, of course, Mom. You did great. I heard about your monthly sales awards and all. Very impressive."

"Oh, he told you, did he? He's sneaky. They really seemed pleased."

"Who did?"

"Pardon me?"

"Who seemed pleased?"

"Mr. and Mrs. Barker."

"Oh. You're pleased too, aren't you? I mean you did all the work."

"Yes, I suppose."

"You were so good I think you could even sell me a dress."

"You want a dress? What?"

"Uh, never mind, Mom. Pretty soon you'll be back there selling up a storm again."

"I hope so." Mumble. Mumble.

"Mom, speak into the phone. I can't hear you again."

"Sorry."

"No, that's okay. What did you say?"

"What?"

"What did you say? Just now?"

"What did I say? I think I said, 'I hope so.' "

"No, I meant after that. You said something else after 'I hope so.' "

"I did? I don't remember. Sorry. I must be getting old."

"That's okay. Getting old is better than the alternative. I didn't want to miss anything you said."

"Aren't you nice? You're such a good son."

"Well, I had a good mom, didn't I?"

"Andy, I can't keep holding the phone up. My arm hurts too much."

"Oh, I'm sorry. Well, I'll let you go."

"No, I didn't mean it that way."

"No, Mom. It's okay. I understand. I have to go to work anyway. I'm going to Nova Scotia in the morning on a story."

"Where?"

"Nova Scotia."

"Oh, isn't that nice? He's going to Nova Scotia for a story."

"It should be a good story."

"He's going to Nova Scotia for a story. Well, do be careful, son."

"Mom, Nova Scotia is not exactly a war zone."

"Funny boy. You know what I mean."

"Maybe I should wear my Malcolm plaid jacket."

"Oh, do you still have that? Yes, remember when we got them? We were in Scotland."

"I remember, Mom. We never did get a parade permit. I hope you're feeling better soon. You do what the doctor says, now."

"It's hard to keep track of everything I'm supposed to do. A lot of pills to take. He says I'm doing pretty well."

"That's real good, real good. Hey, one thing, Mom. Don't take a Valium when you have your cocktail. Okay?"

"What?"

"Don't take a Valium when you're having a cocktail. Pills and booze don't mix. Okay?"

"Yes, fine. You, too."

"What?" Sigh. "Well, you take care, Mom. I love you."

"Thanks for calling."

"Sure. Bye now."

"I love you, too."

"Me, too. Bye, Mom."

"Bye. Thanks for calling."

"You're welcome. Bye."

"I love your calls."

"Me, too. Bye."

"Bye."

"Goodbye, Mom."

---

*Twice a day, every day, Stevie's parents scrubbed their hands and donned the surgical garb to visit their son. After five and a half months, he weighed four pounds eleven ounces, not quite as much as his file of X-rays. From both sides of the glass-enclosed crib, they stuck their hands through holes to touch the baby. They adjusted the knit cap that kept his* head warm. They checked the plastic tubes that blew oxygen into his lungs lest he forget to breathe, like many preemies, and the plastic tube up his nose that constantly dripped the chemical nutrition into his stomach. They waved at him. And he stared back with the eyes that seemed frighteningly older than proper. Through their masks and the glass they talked to him, and sometimes his tiny fingers would seem to grip Mommy's forefinger. And her husband would wipe the tear off the glass.

Shift after shift, the doctors and nurses worked at keeping that delicate breathing balance between getting enough air in for survival and growth but leaving enough work to be done by the slowly developing lungs themselves, lest they get dangerously lazy. They even weighed the diapers before and after to monitor how many grams of moisture were going out so they could adjust the amount going in.

The parents hoped that in another six weeks, perhaps by Christmas, they could take Stevie home for the first time to the room they had specially decorated so long before. The nurses would be there full time. And there, for a year at least, their child would breathe from an oxygen tank and every minute electronic monitors would check his vital functions and watch for normal infections, which for him could prove lethal. And through the days and nights the parents would listen for the alarms or That Cough. "Steven," said the doctor, "is a tough little guy. His outlook at this stage is very good."

---

"Hello."

"Is this Andy?"

"Yes, who's this, please?"

"This is Betsy. One moment, please. Your mother is calling."

"Betsy who? What?"

"Hello, Andy. How are you?"

"Hi, Mom. Who was that? Have you guys hired a secretary now?"

"Funny boy. Betsy is our nurse. She comes in a few times a week to help out. She's very nice."

"Oh. Well. Betsy, eh? I'd like to meet her sometime. Where did she come from? What do you know about her?"

"The agency. She's a dear. But listen, Dad's in the hospital, Andy."

"The hospital? What's wrong?"

"He'd be furious if he knew I was calling you."

"Why? I don't count all of a sudden? Why would he be mad? Wait a minute, what's wrong with Dad?"

"I forget what it's called. Beverly, what is it, you know, that's wrong with Ralph?"

Mumble. Mumble.

"A what? Oh, yes, that's it. An aneurysm. It's when—"

"I know what it is, Mom, a weak spot in an artery. That can be very dangerous."

"No, it's when there's a balloon in the vein."

"Yeah, right. What happened? Did it burst or what?"

"No, I don't think so."

"Mom, can you please tell me what's going on here? Maybe Beverly could explain it."

"No, she was off Monday."

"Monday? This happened last Monday! And you didn't call me!"

"Your father didn't want me to. He said we shouldn't worry you."

"Worry me? Geez, Mom, I'm your son like it or not. Anyway, what happened?"

"Well, they found this aneurysm a couple of weeks ago and your father decided to have them fix it. So they did."

"So they did? That's it? It's fixed? Nothing else? That's a major operation. Right kind here?"

"Yup."

"You're sure?"

"I think so. But don't you ever tell him I called you. He didn't want me to. But you two were so close."

"Were? That's what I thought. Where was it?"

"The usual hospital."

"No, where was the aneurysm?"

"Gee, I don't know, Andy."

"How can you—Is it the same doctor as before?"

"Yes. He's so nice. Why?"

"Oh, just wanted to make sure."

---

*Little Steven did make it home, though shortly after Christmas. It was exhausting for the parents and exciting. Finally, they were becoming a family—an unusual one, to be sure, because there was always a third adult in a white uniform hovering in the background. But it was better than the alternative; they had allowed themselves to hope for a long while. Several times they had to rush Stevie back to the hospital when something got out of balance. But the couple was beginning to believe it was all going to work out.*

*Stevie's father had spent many hours talking with hospital personnel. He had taken his case before the institution's new ethics committee. It had become a mission for him that these kindly, well-meaning people understand the actual human impact of their instinctive decisions. The committee had been receptive. Its role was to debate and discuss and promote careful thinking outside that room. It would never formally condemn the doctor's decision, though it did revise the hospital's rules to make sure that future families were not similarly misled. And the committee set up numerous meetings between the father and a wide variety of hospital workers so the employees could know their work and decisions echoed outside the hospital. Hypothetical cases were much easier to discuss and decide until the real person showed up and faced them with the unexpected details and the hollow eyes.*

*Meetings might help the future. But not the now. The trips back to the hospital were becoming more frequent. The stays longer. Stevie's lungs were larger, but they had been scarred by the respirator's constant pressure. His heart was a little bigger than a peanut now. But it was working very hard all the time. And it was falling behind.*

*After fourteen months he got very sick. And very weak. And after a meeting, one of those unseen gatherings that have become such common landmarks in the lives of so many modern families now, the doctors reluctantly agreed that their ability to fight the good fight apparently had exceeded Steven's ability to take it. The parents, who had tried to avoid inflicting that struggle in the first place and then dared to hope, even starting an album of photos and memories and noting the first sneeze, tearfully agreed to what they had decided 426 days and $1.2 million in medical care before.*

*And they left him in God's hands, again.*

---

"Good morning. ICU."

"Is this the intensive care unit?"

"Yes, it is."

"I'd like to speak with Mr. Malcolm, please. This is his son."

"Oh, I don't think you can. I'll get his nurse."

"What do you mean I can't talk with him? Just put him on, please. Hello? Hello!"

"Hello, this is Nurse Williams. May I help you?"

"I sure hope so. My name is Andrew Malcolm. I understand my father is there, and I want to talk with him."

"I'm afraid that's not possible."

"What do you mean 'not possible'? Look, I'm a whole damned continent away. I just found out he's ill and I want to talk with him right now. Just put him on, please."

"I'm afraid he can't talk. He's still on the respirator."

"The respirator? But the operation was last Monday. Is there some other problem?"

"You'll have to talk to Doctor."

"I will. I will. Believe me, I will. But I'd like to talk with my father first."

"He's right here."

"Can you put the phone by his ear?"

"I'm afraid not. There's a lot of equipment and hoses here. But I could pass him a message, if you like.

"Hello. Mr. Malcolm? Are you there?"

"Yes. I'm here. Is my father awake?"

"Yes."

"Well, um, tell him it's his son Andy, and I love him very much."

"Mr. Malcolm, your son is on the phone. Yes, it's Andy. He said he loves you."

"Very much."

"He loves you very much. Well, now isn't that a big smile? That's the biggest smile we've had in this room all week. He's smiling."

"Good. Good. Tell him all his grandchildren send their love, too."

"Your grandchildren send their love, too. He nodded."

"Um, ask him how he feels? No, wait. Um, how is he?"

"We're doing a little better this morning, aren't we, Mr. Malcolm? I said, 'We're feeling a little better this morning, aren't we?' Yes, indeed. He nodded."

"If I was a newspaper reporter, I'd say that means that he hasn't been very well before now. Is that right?"

"Well, we've had some difficult moments. But there is always someone here by the bed. And I think we're beginning to improve. But you'll have to talk with Doctor."

"When is the respirator coming off?"

"I really wouldn't know, Mr. Malcolm."

"I really appreciate all your good care for my father. I really
do. Tell him I'll be out there by tonight or tomorrow."

"Your son says he's coming out to see you tonight or tomorrow.
Yes, he's coming. Won't that be—No, wait. Mr. Malcolm! No!
You can't!" The telephone hit the floor. "Mr. Malcolm. Calm
down. Mr. Malcolm, you must stay still. Lie down. Could I
have some help in here, please? Lie down! Mr. Malcolm, you
can't get up. Now, calm down, please, Mr. Malcolm. Here, no,
I've got this one. Get the other arm. You're going to pull out all
these needles, if you're not careful. Calm down, please, Mr.
Malcolm. Everything is going to be all right. Yes, it is. All right.
That's it. No, the one on the table there. We're going to give
you a little medicine now to make you feel better. Boy, it seems
we're always sticking pins and needles in you, doesn't it? Sorry.
There we go." A muffled pause.

"Hello, is this Mr. Malcolm's son?"

"Yes." I wasn't feeling so good myself.

"Your father got a little excited, but he's fine now."

"It doesn't seem like he wants me to visit."

"No, well, that's not really uncommon in these kinds of cases,
especially with fathers and sons. Sometimes fathers don't like
their sons to see them like this. Have you ever been in an
ICU?"

"No."

"Well, it's not pretty sometimes."

"I see."

"Your father's been through a lot, Mr. Malcolm. He's not
really himself, I'm sure."

"I'm sure."

"Are you all right, sir?"

"Sure. Sure. Tell my father—is he all right now?"

"Yes, we gave him a little sedative. He's taking a nice nap."

"Well, tell him I won't be visiting, if he doesn't want me to.
And tell him I love him. Very much."

"I'm going off duty in a half-hour, but I'll ask the relief nurse to give him the message."

"Thank you."

---

*For months I had been talking with the lawyers of families all over the country. I wanted to write about the process of negotiating a death. I knew how it worked in general. But I wanted real people as the subjects, no pipe-sucking overview from the musty confines of some social museum. I wanted to walk across the battlefield with the actual participants recalling where they were when and what they did over there. And then I would sit down and choose the words and the tempo and the details to paint the landscape. I was trying to find at least one couple who would talk to me in detail about how they made their decision to unplug a medically hopeless relative—presumably a parent.*

*I was once-removed from the issue, as professionals are supposed to be. But I assumed it was a difficult decision with many factors involved. I was intensely curious about how these hidden social moments came to be. But, unlike that day in Paris after the old man died in my arms, I was in charge of questions now; if my parents or one couple wouldn't answer my queries, there were surely many others elsewhere to ask, to bargain with, to flatter, to promise anonymity to, to cajole to get their story out for the benefit of everyone. Nothing personal in their repeated rejections, nothing personal in my determination to go over or around them to reach the goal line.*

*I believed that this process, these unexamined times, would carry lessons for others—not me, of course—but for readers unable to dodge such difficult situations. And I could be the bearer of the news, the one who rode into town and was surrounded by the crowd eager, or maybe just willing, to listen because I knew at least some of the turns that waited down the road for all of us. That was the wonderful thing about being a reporter. I always got front-row seats to the real-life dramas. When the curtain came down, I got up and went out to honestly tell everyone the story the best that I could and then I went home. Nothing to clean up afterward; it wasn't my mess. And it was safe, unless the front-row seat was to a war or a prizefight, in which case you were likely to get splattered a bit by flying blood and spit.*

*But none of these people in the ring would agree to talk with me, even without their names being published. My understanding of their wishes and fears did not prevent my jaw-clenching regret; if so many felt the need to hide whatever it was they were hiding, there must be something important there to write about—perhaps more than I could imagine. The more families declined, the more I wanted to know about it. I was professionally tenacious at all hours, putting out lines everywhere, through friends, doctors, friends of doctors, and every lawyer and hospital counselor I could find.*

*The counselors were useless in this process. The last thing these institutional guards wanted was to help some nosy reporter track down a case everyone had buried in the secret cement of forgetfulness and open it up to daylight. The hell with lessons for the future; someone in the here and now not interested in their institution's welfare or their own career might find some obviously innocuous details, but just by ending up on the printed page the details become acutely embarrassing, or worse. Death is surrounded by such swirling, unpredictable emotions. Unpredictability makes people uncertain. Uncertainty breeds fear. And safe silence. Especially in big institutions.*

*But lawyers deal in stories, too. They understand the questioning and digging. Telling stories by asking questions is what they often do for a living. And if they can protect their*

client and still help a good story to unfold, they might help
persuade someone to talk to me.

The lawyers told me, confidentially, of the guilt and dark
emotions they saw in these families, sometimes even years
after the unplugging. There had been divorces and other bitter
recriminations, they said, as part of the fallout from these
negotiated deaths. Typically, they said, the wife would be at
least willing if not eager to talk with me anonymously about
letting a parent go. But the husband would forbid it or ignite
such an argument that the emotional price would become
too high for his spouse to proceed, no matter how important
for society the faceless reporter said it might be.

And then one lonely husband sent word that he would
talk. About unplugging his wife. I flew there immediately. We
spent a day together. He was a gentle soul, very forthcoming.
He answered every question, sometimes painfully, sometimes
eloquently, but always fully. I was professionally alert but
personally impressed.

They had married somewhat later in life, as was becoming
more common. A two-career couple, physically active, cul-
turally involved. He had a grown son from a previous marriage, but she wanted her own child, their own. Two girls.
And then some minor muscle problem that inexorably over
the years became disaster. ALS, amyotrophic lateral sclerosis,
or Lou Gehrig's disease. A gradual but steady decay of all
muscle control except the bowels. And the mind. The mind
stays as sharp as ever. She became imprisoned in a slow,
suffocating paralysis that changed the way family, society,
and husband saw her.

There is no medicine to stall or halt ALS, although a
respirator can take over the breathing when the lungs go.
There is only one way out of ALS. Because neither husband nor wife wanted to face defeat, they never discussed
at what point existing was no longer living. So that when

*that Saturday morning arrived and he came upon his wife
in bed gasping, her eyes rolled back, the husband had seconds to decide. She seemed to nod. He summoned emergency
help.*

That launched the family on a two-year ordeal of insti-
tutionalization where family members who once shared a
bathroom simultaneously could only meet during certain
hours which the institution, for its own reasons, set aside as
permissible for visiting. There were countless visits, at first
twice daily, then daily, then every other day, then three times
a week, then twice, and then weekly. The motionless invalid,
hooked to a whooshing machine, would be wheeled out to
watch with eager eyes her two girls perform for a silent, one-
woman audience, to show her crayoned drawings of a family
without a mother, and to talk at her some rehearsed report
of a school event.

And then, the husband told me, came that unexpected
day when, using her head and a special keyboard and printer,
his wife tapped out the message: "I WANT TO DIE."

At first the husband refused to help her die. Then when
he finally agreed to seek help, the hospital refused. Over the
course of many weeks, a sympathetic social worker steered
him to an organization which led him to a lawyer who put
him in touch with a doctor who agreed after a bedside visit
to administer a sedative and disconnect the portable respirator during his wife's routine home visit. That doctor also
referred the husband to another doctor, who said he would
sign a normal death certificate so there would be no autopsy.
And the hospital's lawyer indicated his institution would look
the other way so long as it wasn't involved in any fashion.
The husband spoke to me in pained awe that such a benev-
olent conspiracy was necessary to accomplish something he
had always thought was so natural and inevitable. It had
become awfully difficult just to die.

*Would he please ask the doctors to speak with me?*
*"Yes, of course."*
*I talked with each about their role. They said it was more common than anyone knew. The death-certificate doctor said he was worried that many seriously ill patients in recent years seemed more afraid of what a doctor or runaway hospital would do to them than what the immediate disease might do. The doctor said he had many patients with* AIDS. *Right after the initial diagnosis, he told each of them that they could halt treatment at any time and, if desired, he could provide pills that would make their* AIDS *death quick instead of prolonged. He said not many patients chose that route, but each seemed relieved to feel they were once again in control of their lives and not on some medical disassembly line, rolling by treatment station after treatment station as each new station was invented and tested. The death-certificate doctor said maybe the public inevitability of death with* AIDS *would finally force society to face these decisions in advance.*

*I also asked the husband to have the lawyer talk with me, too. He did.*

*The lawyer described his personal methodology for developing evidence that could prove the patient had desired to die, how the relatives were merely accommodating those wishes, and how he kept everyone and everything separate and compartmentalized in case anyone tried some tracking later. He even went to an assistant prosecutor, a former law-school buddy, to discuss a "hypothetical case" that bore a remarkable resemblance to the real one at hand. This allowed the lawyer to establish an unofficial record of his intentions, and it let his classmate note, off the record, that such a hypothetical case held no interest for his office, as long as it stayed out of sight of the media.*

*And I asked the husband, as a conscientious correspondent*

*wary of everyone's claims, "Can I also see the death certifi-*
*cate, please?"*

*"My God," he said, "you reporters have to be very careful,*
*don't you?"*

*"Us, too," I replied.*

---

Dad's choice, as his doctor explained to me, was to replace the weak section of artery wall with a nylon fabric tube, fairly close to the heart, or to leave it alone. Without the repair, nothing might ever happen. Or tomorrow it could burst and that would be it. Dad, the industrial engineer whose career was built on fixing problems, had chosen the repair route. So they did it. A routine procedure these days in operating rooms where the time is booked to the minute and patients are wheeled in and out for myriad repairs beneath the bright lights and sterile sheets.

It went well for Dad, at first. But at some point in the recovery room, just as he was regaining consciousness, the incision burst into a different emergency. "It was," said the doctor, "like trying to sew together two pieces of wet bread." The muscle tone of Dad's abdomen was nonexistent. And then his already weakened lungs had started to fill with fluids, and that meant other organs began to stall without adequate oxygen. The pros behind the green masks had done a superb job of rebalancing everything. Now it was just a question of watching him closely and letting things settle down. He'd recommend waiting a while on my rushing out there. Yes, the nursing supervisor had mentioned something. Well, there really wasn't anything I could do by being there anyway, and the goal was to get him better and home. I could check in with the ICU nurse anytime and the doctor would call if there was any change.

Two weeks later Dad went home, paler and lighter, and began spending more time in his bed. Mentally, he was as sharp as ever, which may have been a handicap, given his physical condition. He understood too much about it. His abdominal wall was very weak. Inside, there was little left to hold his organs in their proper place—in effect, a huge hernia. So the body's insides gave in to gravity. The result was, standing up, my father looked about four months' pregnant. To sit down, he bent over, winced, and then slowly sank into the cushion as if he feared a miscarriage. To walk, he tilted his spine back for leverage on the heavy front load.

He grew increasingly self-conscious. He gave up cooking—too much standing and moving. And my parents subscribed to the blessed daily deliveries from Meals on Wheels, despite the fish dinner every other Tuesday. Their sacred jaunts through city and country grew less frequent and shorter. And when my second wedding day arrived, they could not make the long trip. So as we signed the official register at the ceremony in the same church where they had wed forty-three years before, we phoned from the rector's office. They could hear the bagpipes in the background. "Thank you," they said.

When we visited soon after, the two of them were eager to meet and impress their new daughter-in-law. One year later they had changed considerably.

---

*The ALS story was published, after the newspaper's lawyers read it to make sure the tracks to my sources were obscured. The story aroused considerable comment. I was pleased professionally to have gotten a difficult story and told it all the best I could.*

*I kept in touch with the husband, as I often do with story subjects out of interest. One day we were chatting and he said, "Sometime I'll have to show you the diary."*

*What diary? I asked.*

*His wife had kept a diary from just before her diagnosis right up until the end. It was too painful for him to read yet. But not for me. It was a revealing, detailed, human look inside the disease and the treatment of a terminal illness today, even after the victim herself wanted out. The diary led to even deeper involvement in that case; I wrote a book about it, half about family and society looking in at and eventually away from this once-vibrant woman, and half of it about this still-lively mind looking out at the world eventually treating her body for its own good, not hers.*

*The book became a television movie and the day after it was broadcast, I called my mother to see what she thought about the story and her son's book being on national television.*

*"Boy," she said, "they sure didn't show your name for very long."*

---

When my wife and I got off the plane for that holiday visit, there were no familiar faces in the crowd of searching faces by the security checkpoint and the baggage-claim area. That would not have been a good sign if I had wanted to notice. Two out of every three airport visitors are not traveling; they are greeting someone or seeing them off and my parents were no exception. It was a matter of family protocol for that generation, especially at the holidays, a sign of eagerness to see someone and reluctance to let them go. Hadn't it been such an occasion all those many days and years before when we had greeted Grandma in her fur coat at the train? One time when I was in university and my parents traveled through Chicago, I had organized some friends as fake reporters and photographers; when Mom and Dad came through the gate, we descended on them as a noisy, nosy, news-hungry throng, microphones waving, flashbulbs popping. A crowd of curious onlookers gathered; Mom and Dad loved it. But I had been through so many airports closely searched but ungreeted by then that I thought nothing of not being met that afternoon, not until we arrived at my parents' apartment.

We found the two of them in their pajamas. Mom was eager, almost desperate, to see us. Dad was friendly, loving, but somehow strangely apart. When I went to hug him, over his distended stomach, he winced. That was silently frightening to me. Now a hug, a sign of love, something we had done routinely and thought nothing of for all these years, now it caused pain. For the next few days I created occasions to repeat that hug, hoping to get it on my personal record that the greeting wince was an aberration. It wasn't.

They both visibly moved with uncertain balance and pain. At times, they even sat with it. Mom had suffered a broken hip that fall. She was just home, using a walker to keep her balance on the thick apartment rug, and undergoing physical therapy. The hip had cracked in a fall during a mysterious blackout in the hallway one evening around dinnertime. She had spent some weeks in the hospital and had come home, in a wheelchair, to find Dad becoming ever more tethered to his cold, metal oxygen tank in the corner and to his bed, which relieved his increasing back pain. "What," he had asked my mother late one afternoon, "did I ever do to deserve this?"

"You drank a lot," she replied.

By that visit, Mom's job was a memory. Soon afterward, so too was the fine Ma-and-Pa clothing store, it having succumbed to the modern drive for mass marketing, mail order, and chain stores. Mom and Dad were going out only by appointment—doctor's, dentist's, hairdresser's, or, rarely, a short evening at the home of one of their few surviving friends, where everyone would decide by 7:30 that it was getting late. So without much outside life, why go through the tedious and sometimes painful motions of getting dressed?

I had phoned two weeks before to announce our surprise holiday visit, thinking it would be a treat for everyone. For Mom, it was. From her hospital bed she had gushed with excitement. But Dad was different. After the sixteenth ring, when he had finally answered the phone, I told him of our plans—five days there, a nearby motel room, taking them out to dinner. There was dead silence. "I don't think you should come," he said.

"What?"

Silence.

"Why not? What's the matter? You don't love your son anymore?"

"I really don't think you should come."

"Why not? Dad. Mom'll be home. We can all be together." I felt like a little boy pleading to go to the baseball game. There was something fishy here. Maybe the nurse was still right, decaying dads didn't want sons to see them.

"Dad, I want to see you."

"No."

"Well, how would you know what I want to do? I love you."

"I love you, too. But I don't think you should come. Absolutely not."

I changed the subject to give me time to think. He wasn't wavering, so being coaxed was not his intent. "You know, your birthday is coming up soon. Maybe I'm going to arrange for another pretty girl to come sing to you like last January and this time I want to see her, eh?"

Nothing.

"Well, look," I finally said, "I would like to see you very much. Connie would like to see you. Mom said she wants to see us. If you don't want to see me, that's okay. It hurts, frankly, but I respect that. We'll just spend our time with Mom and I'll try and stay out of your way. I don't understand this, Dad. If that's what you want, okay. But I'm coming out there."

"Oh, no. Please. Don't."

"I love you. I have to go now. I hope you're feeling better soon."

The visit was necessary, but it was not a highlight of my existence. It was like baby-sitting with two children too close in age. There were numerous one-way spats, little annoyances that caused one partner to sigh and shake a head while the other acted oblivious. Someone always thought the coffee was too hot. There weren't enough cookies out. The television was too loud. The television was too low. It was time for a pill. No, it wasn't. Wasn't it time for dinner? Yes. But he or she wasn't hungry.

"I'm going to lie down a while."

"What?"

Nothing.

"He said he was going to lie down for a while.'

"You just got up."

"Mom, it's okay. Maybe he's tired."

"Funny time to be tired. You're not going to be here all that long."

"It's okay. Talk to me."

One evening the four of us were sitting in the living room. The newlyweds sat on the old, short couch close together, always touching each other, often giggling. The elderly couple smiled and chatted individually with the youngsters from their separate chairs. At one point Dad reached out with his spotted hand to hold Mom's. Without speaking, she yanked it away sharply. Dad looked bewildered, crushed. My turn to wince. My wife pretended not to see. It was awful.

Soon after, Dad complained of his back again. He went to bed.

———

*By that final fall of my detached research the first right-to-die case had made its way to the Supreme Court, a young Missouri woman in a hopeless persistent vegetative state for years after an automobile accident. Of course, she had left no instructions. The family had hoped for recovery, stood endless vigils watching her limbs atrophy, and now wanted her at peace. The highest Missouri court didn't rule on the peace argument. A majority said that allowing her to die in this day and age would be tantamount to killing her.*

*The issue was becoming more emotional, like abortion, though at least it was moving into the open. Now, instead of removing respirators and antibiotics, the issue was removing the nutrition pumped into her stomach through a surgically implanted tube. Without it, a patient would expire within days. The state court said every form of human life was precious, no matter how limited; the family said they knew their daughter and this was no life she'd want.*

*I telephoned the death-certificate doctor to see what he would call it. "Who is this?" said the receptionist.*

*I gave her my name. "He'll recognize it," I said.*

*There was a long pause. Too long.*

*"Hello?" I said.*

*"The doctor is dead," she said.*

*My turn to pause, puzzled.*

*"What? How? When?"*

*"Two weeks ago. Who did you say you were?"*

*"I'm a friend. Or an acquaintance, I guess. He helped me with a book I did on death and dying."*

*"Oh, yes," she said. "He had AIDS."*

*AIDS! AIDS? But that's a long, long illness. "I just saw him a few weeks ago," I blurted out, "and he looked fine."*

*Her silence answered the how.*

---

Sometimes Dad would lie in his bed and call down the hall, "I can't hear what you're saying."

"What?" said my mother.

"Well, why don't you come out here and join us?" I'd call back. "Four people can't fit in that bed." And I'd feign a laugh to soften the implied criticism.

Other times when I walked by their bedroom door, he would be moaning softly about some pain or the burden of it all. From his bed, he showed me the ancient bruises that did not heal, the many sores that came and went slowly, and the reddish scars that now lined his misshapen body. He would point to the display of medicine bottles arrayed on his dresser. With the twin, clear-plastic oxygen tubes aimed up his nose, he talked of the pain. He craved much sympathy. He got some. But the scene was not attractive.

I did not want to be his parent. When I was little and clumsy, I often fell harmlessly. "Well, get up," he would say. "You can do it if you want. Just get up." So I would. Now I stood by this old man's bed and thought, Get up. You can do it if you want. Just get up. Instead, I said, "Maybe if you took a little physical exercise once or twice a day, you could slowly build your strength back up. Walk down to the mailbox and back, things like that."

"I couldn't leave your mother alone."

"She's alone now, Dad, in the other room. You can't build every minute of your life around what might happen."

"Easy to say, boy."

"Yes, I suppose so."

He told me, as the doctor had, that his condition would only deteriorate. Then he looked up at me and offered a simple con-fidence. "Sometimes," he said, "I would just like to lie down and go to sleep and not wake up."

It was a frightening thought, so I dismissed it as silly. Obvious-ly, he was just depressed. It was understandable after all he'd been through. But I knew better than not to talk when it was necessary. Hadn't I slipped that letter to the English teacher in just under the wire? I had to say something to Dad, to have one of those father-son talks, except now I was talking like a father and he was acting like a son. I procrastinated. I kept hearing his voice in my head: "Do it now! Do it right the first time. Always do your best. Never lie. You can do whatever you have to do."

For days I circled like a hawk waiting for my prey to be in-attentive for just one moment, to create a window of vulnerability. I waited for him to be alone, for the women to be elsewhere, for the time to be right. It never was. I could always find some reason not to speak the words waiting to be born to the old man waiting to die. Until the night before we left, just before saying goodnight. I could not put it off any longer. His lessons were too firmly embedded in my mind.

"How you doing, Dad?" I sat down on Mom's bed.

"Okay. And you?" Cough. Cough.

"Fine. Just fine. This has been a terrific visit. It was really good to see you. I'm glad we did it. Thanks for letting us come."

"It was good to see you, too. You have a special lady there, son."

"Yes. Yes. I do. I do. . . . Uh, well we're off early in the morning. We won't come back to wake you. But I, uh, wanted to, um, talk with you about something, Dad."

"Sure. Go ahead."

I remembered for an instant that terrifying dark hole in the floor of that house under construction thirty-five years before. I told my father how much I loved him, how sorry I was about his physical condition. I described all the things people were doing to help him. But, I noted, he kept eating poorly. "Man cannot live by canned vichyssoise only," I said, attempting a smile. He listened intently. The soft hiss of fresh air seeping up his nose was barely audible.

He was always hiding in his room as if he were playing some kind of adult hard-to-get. And, I said, I suspected he was violating other doctor's orders; he knew the code phrase for drinking again. No amount of love could make someone else care about life, I said; it was a two-way street. Everyone was running around caring about him, but he wasn't caring about him. He was taking all the care and concern, but not giving anything back. He wasn't doing his best. The decision was his.

He had looked impassive throughout. I took a deep breath. "There," I said, "I've said it."

Dad said he knew how hard my words had been to say and how proud he was of me for saying them and how much he appreciated the thoughts behind them. "I had the best teacher," I said, smiling. "You can do whatever you have to do."

He smiled a little wanly. And we shook hands very firmly. It was the last time.

Three days later on the phone with Mom, I asked to talk to Dad. It was two days before his sixty-ninth birthday. Mom said he said he was too busy to come to the phone at the moment.

The next night, at about 4 a.m., Mom heard Dad shuffling about their dark room. "What is it?" she said.

"I have some things I have to do," he replied.

He paid a bundle of bills on his desk and stamped them for mailing. He packed up a broken electric shaver to mail in for repairs. He composed for my mother a long list of legal and financial what-to-do's "in case of emergency." And he wrote me a note.

Then he walked back to his bed and laid himself down. He went to sleep.

Five hours later, the phone rang in my distant house. It was Mom. But I could hear the voices of others in the background.

"Andy," she said, "your Dad's gone."


After that, I did all the right things for Mom. Maybe not as often as some would have and certainly not as often as she would have liked, but as often as I could bring myself to do all the right things. From my home I called her every few days, at least once a week, unless I was on vacation, when I abandoned all lists of chores. At those times I sent postcards full of safe daily news that sounded as if I was keeping her fully up to date but really contained nothing of me. If at times I let my guard slip and said something about my feelings, I got all the familiar warnings and advice and kicked myself for opening up, though it did give her a chance to talk. If I failed to call in a period of time that seemed proper in her lonely mind, then she would greet me on the phone with, "Well, hello, stranger."

And immediately I'd be on the defensive, which was the point. A few times I remarked pointedly, "You know, these days the telephones work in both directions. You could call us sometimes." Occasionally, she did during those nearly seven years, which gave her another chance to ask why I hadn't called. Since I had not registered my calls with any public agency, it was her word against mine for as long as we cared enough to bicker, which was less and less on my part. Always, Mom called moments after the cheap evening rates went into effect on the West Coast and inevitably it was during our dinner. Now I know who invented the microwave oven—someone with a mother in a different time zone. Then when Mom got the phone bill, she'd announce how expensive it had been and how she couldn't afford to do that too often, given her finances. Dad had, in fact, left her in quite comfortable shape.

After his funeral, when my wife tried to show her how to do the checkbook, something Dad had always done with his impeccable script and notations, it became immediately clear that carrying over balances was not her forte. Nor is it mine. "You and your mother are very much alike," Dad would say, and I hated hearing that. So I found another widow, a kindly woman with many clients in Mom's situation, who would come in once every week or two, pay the bills, do the books, and keep close track of income and outgo. Those occasions, along with the nurse's thrice-weekly visits, became the social highlights of Mom's life. Along with the hairdresser's and any doctor's or dentist's appointment. Mom got the nurse's home phone number from the agency, claiming an emergency one day. She took to phoning her there for a last-minute summons to an extra visit, especially on Sunday evenings, which seemed particularly long to her.

That was when Mom's arm seemed to bother her most, a deep abiding pain, sometimes handled by the powerful painkillers the doctor prescribed, sometimes not. The doctor said he could find no physical reason for the pain—nothing to simply fix, the way patients had come to expect. If you can fix the problem, he told friends, they turn you into a paid god; if you can't, then you're incompetent. I heard about each of these visits from Mom in the minutest detail—who said what to whom when and what she thought about it. I didn't really care, but I let her talk on and on and feigned interest. At the end of each conversation, which usually came about fifteen minutes after I thought it would, she would be so appreciative of my call. "I enjoyed it, too," I said.

I tried to get her interested in new things—a new book, a new magazine subscription, getting out more, asking a friend over for tea, even adopting a kitten for living and loving company. But at this age Mom was still Mom, only more so. Of course, she never said no outright. She simply never did anything of the sort. Her few social friends became telephone friends and then they became dead. One day when Mom would phone them, the number would no longer be in service because some son or daughter had had to fly in and close up the apartment and the bank accounts. They had buried their mother with their father as quickly as possible and, not knowing her surviving friends, had gone back to their own busy lives elsewhere, unable to notify anyone except maybe the church, which put the passing in the next newsletter.

I tried to convince Mom to visit us, to see her grandchildren in their own exciting lives. At first, she used her physical condition as an excuse. Then it really was. Year after year her X-rays showed no recurrence of the lung cancer, despite her continued smoking. But her back was becoming ever more bowed. And now she preferred to use a wheelchair when going out.

Once, I took her oldest grandson to visit. Three times I took my wife. But then I decided no one but me should be forced to endure those mind-numbing sessions, day and night in the same smokey living room with the beautiful water and clear sky so tantalizingly near and so ignored. And I didn't go there any more than necessary.

As always, I would arrive as a surprise, which turned me into a walking gift. It also seemed to make her more effusively appreciative. Being a very busy newspaper correspondent, I said, I only had a day or two to spare, which was generally true. On my arrival, she'd maybe get up, surely cover her mouth with surprise, and probably shed a tear or two. "Oh, Andy," she'd say. I'd hug her gently. I would bring my own soft drinks; somehow I never became interested in the harder stuff. And then I would sit on the once-long sofa and be talked at by her while the TV blared. She always had something to say, and while she talked often she'd nervously squeeze her lower lip with her right hand. "Mom," I'd say, "relax, okay."

Somewhere around 10:30 or eleven my eyes would slip closed again, and this time she would notice. "Oh, you're tired," she'd say.

"Yeah, a little," I said, "it's nearly 2 a.m. my time."

"Well, you go on to bed and I'll be along."

I would race through a shower, but no matter how quickly I was ready, she was back in her bed by the time I emerged. And she was ready to talk some more. Even feigning sleep in Dad's separate old bed did no good. She would ask me a question or verbally prod me until I awoke.

"Mom," I would say, "I'm really exhausted. Maybe we can talk some more in the morning. Okay?"

"If I'm feeling well. Mornings are not good for me."

"Well, maybe we'll go for a drive, get some fresh air, see some pretty scenery."

"I can't sit that long."

"How long?"

"What?"

"How long can't you sit for?"

"You're not making any sense, Andrew."

"I'm making sense. It's you who aren't making any sense."

"That's not a very nice way to talk to your mother."

"It's a real simple question, Mom. We'll go for a drive for as

long as you can sit. How long is that? How long can you sit for?
We'll be home by then. Do you understand?"

"Well, now I know how you really feel. Thank you very much."

"Aw, c'mon, Mom. Look! Mom, I'm very tired. You don't
seem to be making any sense to me. I'm going to sleep now. I'm
sure we'll both sound very intelligent in the morning."

"I'm glad your father can't hear you talk to me like that."

"Mom! Dammit! I'm very tir—"

"Gotcha!"

I sat up and looked over straight at her. "What?"

She said nothing. She smiled sweetly.

"What did you just say?"

"Gotcha."

At that moment I fully expected her head to turn completely
around.


Out in public, she was saintly and, wearing her wheelchair,
received the kind of obsequious deference that made that appa-
ratus a welcome accessory. I saw the wheelchair as a temporary
convenience, something to be used briefly while working on the
body to resume its normal duties or to save time so that it wouldn't
take thirty minutes to move from the parking lot to the restaurant
table. Mom saw the wheelchair as a badge of her suffering, and
waiters and customers solicitously moving chairs and other tables
out of the way to accommodate her had somehow become a sign
of respect, something to enjoy, and expect, and get annoyed about
if it wasn't properly displayed. I was properly attentive, especially
at the times she made the effort to forsake the paraphernalia and
walk in by herself. But I could offer nowhere near the fussing or
paid patience she craved.

Mom had religiously renewed her driver's license and she kept
her boat-length car although, thank God, she never drove alone
anymore, there being enough motorized murder and mayhem
by semi-alert drivers. But the driver's license was an official token

of her preserved mobility, even if she really preferred to be waited on instead. And her special state handicapped tags along with the spreading number of up-front ever-empty parking spots they entitled her to use everywhere were official respectful recognition of her endurance, like a war veteran's service. Those specially marked parking spots had become for her a right to be enjoyed, as if the establishments had kept these numerous spaces open in the hope that Mom would deign to stop by today. It annoyed her very much that on our little sojourns I refused to park in these slots.

"Here," she said. "Park here. No, right here. Oh, you missed my place."

"It's not yours, Mother. I'm not handicapped—yet. We'll leave that place for someone who really needs it, someone who is *really* handicapped."

"Well, your mother is," she'd say. "But apparently you don't care about that."

"Well, today I'm along and I can probably manage to push you all the way across this lane. Anyway, you're not handicapped for long though. Right, Mom? We're going to get a lot better soon. Right?" And I was so damned chipper and optimistic and smiling I'll bet it drove her crazy. I knew her buttons as well as she knew mine. She had to resist my hopefulness in silence.

The nurse would take her along on errands, until Mom took to staying home during those short trips to avoid having to get dressed. "Betsy parks in my spaces," she said, a little pouting. And, like a parent reluctant to criticize another adult in front of that little girl, I said, "What Betsy does with your car is between you and her."

On my visits I would drive us both out for a fancy dinner. Mom would talk about how little she normally ate; she said the portions delivered by Meals on Wheels were so enormous that she couldn't eat them all. Sure enough, her refrigerator shelves were packed with plastic-wrapped partial portions of meals, some of which had been stashed there so long that the nurse or I would throw them out before they decided to break out themselves. Then, after all the dainty demurring talk, this five-foot-tall and shrinking woman in the wheelchair would proceed to pack away two or three lamb chops, potatoes, vegetables, a salad, some rolls, coffee, and a piece of pie.

"I guess I *was* hungry," she'd say, lighting up a cigarette.

"Mom, why don't you quit those things before they kill you?"

"There's not much left in life I can enjoy."

"Do you enjoy killing yourself?"

Silence. And I thought, She's probably right; if she doesn't care, why should I?

"Mom, why don't you come visit us? You could see all the kids in their own lives."

"There's nothing I would rather do, believe me, nothing. But I'd have to sit so long in the plane. Eight hours is a long time."

"No, Mom. It's six."

"I think you're mistaken, Andy. It's at least eight."

"No, actually I'm not this time. It's six. I flew it just yesterday. Remember?"

"If you know so much. But six is a very long time anyway."

"Mom, you spend that long sitting in front of the TV on most days." I earned a glower for that one. "This way at least you'd be getting somewhere. You could see the kids. They could see you. And you could stay as long as you like. You won't get a better deal anywhere else. C'mon, whaddya say?"

"We'll see." That familiar and most useful of predictable parental rejoinders crosses the generations. "We'll see." Meaning, "When Hell freezes over, but I don't want to say so right now."

But she was not above trying to obliquely orchestrate a visit of my entire family. One year, by saying I don't know what, she convinced her bookkeeper and her doctor to write me, separately, of what a good idea it would be for Mom's health for all five of us to give up our holiday at home, to store all the animals and find a house sitter, then fly across the country to rent an expensive resort hotel room or two by a beautiful blue pool, so we could sit with the windows closed against the midday chill inside Mom's beautifully decorated apartment overlooking the water for several days of watching her watch "Jeopardy!" and listening to her recount the stories behind the acquisition of each of the countless knickknacks that were so precisely placed on every horizontal and vertical surface in sight.

I wrote back, a bit defensively, saying I had decided not to inflict any more such visits on my family, that I would be there whenever necessary, but that I wanted my family to remember her the way she was before, which, frankly, was not all that different from now.

The knickknacks were revered objects and some of them were quite valuable, she said. Once, she would have fussed over the precise placement of each, outraged that some defiant dust had dared to settle on her property. Every time Dad passed one of Mom's decorative hallway tableaux, he tipped one of the feeding geese so it appeared to be crowing into the sky like a rooster. The little goose was barely three inches long, but on her next regular patrol Mom immediately spotted the disturbed scenario, exclaimed her outrage, and reordered the scene. On his next foray down the hall Dad tilted the goose again. He called it teasing.

But less physical activity naturally led to less strength, physically and mentally, and more narrow interests. Instead of fussing herself, this Mrs. Tidy of family fame took to ordering anyone around to replace some disturbed item on the spot anointed by the gods. And she wanted to tell me, time and again, where each came from, because "Someday you'll want to know and I won't be here." I was interested in the family's old oil paintings, especially a moody little seascape Mom had done as a young woman. She gave it to me with great pleasure. But I never could keep straight which of her uncle's other brothers had done what portrait when—to her eternal frustration still, I'm sure.

"I know you don't want to do this and you don't care," she'd say during a lesson.

"If you're so sure I don't care about this," I'd reply, "then why are we doing it?" She'd ignore that and go on with the lecture. We each knew our lines.

Instead of cooking, on most nights, she'd offer a leftover from the refrigerator's stash of prepared foods, all to be consumed on a tray in front of the television that had become her main link to and filter from the real world that seemed so far away from inside that door. The television was always on "Max Vol," and only one person was dumb enough, once, to suggest she use her new hearing aid instead. "I SAID," I said, "WHY DON'T YOU USE YOUR NEW HEARING AID INSTEAD?"

Mom also was not eager to visit Dad's grave. It was a lovely site, she said, but she'd stay home this time. Every time. I felt I should go once each visit. But she was always too tired. "How long will you be?" she'd ask. To be honest, I rather enjoyed those visits. They got me outdoors, away from that smokey place. I'd take a few flowers and savor sitting on that inevitably sunny hillside with the stubby dry grass, making a mental report to him on my life since the last time, repeating how much we missed him, just looking at that broad view that I hoped reminded him of the prairies, even if it did have a hill. I was out in the open there, but it felt good.

Afterward, I'd buy a loaf of bread and feed it to the sea gulls and pigeons in the park before returning to duty in the apartment. Two days was about all I could stand.

Each winter, along about the anniversary of Dad's death, Mom slipped into a lengthy depression. Then each spring she seemed to slide out of it like a drab daffodil warming to the sun of longer days. But that last spring her interest in travel and dressing up was gone. Even her interest in going out on a dinner date with her son was gone. She began skipping meals, which she had never allowed me to do. My kidney-doctor friend had shrugged when I once asked about old people not eating. "Did you know," he said, "when salmon leave the sea for the last time to return to their home river to spawn and die, they never eat again?" That had seemed rather Delphic at the time, but I filed it away as a warning sign to watch for. Now here it was in my own family, and I instinctively sought to overcome it, urging her time after time to eat better.

Skipping meals obviously did nothing for her nutrition, but it also made some of her medicine more potent. Her speech and thoughts seemed slurred at times. She began skipping pills, too; not the pain pills, of course, because they created a warm mental fuzz. And not the Valiums, which calmed her but also contributed to the depression. She sometimes gave up the diuretics because they made her go to the bathroom more, and that required regular effort and made her uncomfortable. But fewer diuretics lead to a buildup of fluids. And, one morning, to a desperate shortness of breath and a dash to the hospital, where everyone goes now because busy doctors don't make house calls.

For a day, the doctor thought she was going to die, so weakened was her condition. And, he warned, a sizable spot of new lung cancer had appeared. We agreed not to operate; he was sure she would not stand such a procedure. When they stuck just a needle into her chest to suck out the fluids, her lung collapsed, so delicate was the balance now.

Mom wouldn't eat. So naturally they pumped that nutritional chemical slurry up her nose. She pulled the tubes out. So they tied her hands to the bedside.

I was puzzled. Several times I had gone out of my way, conversationally, to describe my medical and ethical stories and then probe gently for her feelings about life-prolonging medical treatment. I started the discussions by saying what I would want and then, seemingly as an afterthought, asking her. "Your father was lucky," she replied, "he went quickly." Or, "I don't like all those machines." One evening, she said, "I don't want to stay past my time." I gave out a mental sigh. At last some wonderfully clear directions until, later, I realized who was going to be left to figure out whose time it was or wasn't.

But then, on that frightening morning when she got so short of breath, so alone, she summoned not one, but two ambulances. "Just to be sure," she explained later.

How could I be sure if she wasn't?

---

*Ka-whoosh, ka-whoosh. The fresh hospital room was filled with the stereophonic sound of a tiny heartbeat, unseen for now but enlarged electronically. Ka-whoosh, ka-whoosh. "Everything's going to be fine," the nurses were saying as they bustled about preparing my very pregnant wife. The baby was not due for some weeks. But he (we had an ultrasound snapshot of him floating upside down with, as the technician called it, "the plumbing that always accompanies male babies") had decided not to wait.*

*In this scenario, the doctor had appeared a little too quickly for my tastes. Yes, of course, I wanted him there, but his dropping everything else transmitted a disturbing note of urgency that fed my fears. The anesthesiologist appeared quickly. Ever had any problems with any anesthesia? But I thought we were going to do the breathing bit. Or, failing that, a spinal tap—the mother unfeeling but conscious while the pale husband describes the joyous event to her. Ka-whoosh. Ka-whoosh. Ka-whoosh.*

*The doctor patted me on the arm and nodded. "I'd like to get started," he said to the nurses, "Now!"*

*The bed was quickly wheeled down the hall through the wide, shiny doors that can see beds coming. I had scrubbed*

up, *as instructed, and donned one of those goofy green gowns.
I went to follow.*

"Uh, the doctor would like you to wait here until they get
organized in the operating room. He'll send for you in a few
minutes."

"Oh, sure, fine."

"You can wait right here in the room, if you like."

*What if I don't like?*

*Something was wrong. This was the old "Tell-'em-the-
ten-percent-you-can't-avoid-telling-'em-but-nothing-else"
line. She shouldn't have said anything about a few minutes.
That gave me the peg to begin asking questions soon. Leave
it open, uncertain. Promise zero.* Nada. *Say nothing you
might have to take back. This is part of the institutional
power game. First, get the uninitiated undressed. They're
frightened anyway. But nakedness takes away all their protection, exposes their vulnerabilities, makes them pliable. Let
the family see their now helpless member wheeled off in a
gown designed not for modesty but for easy access by strange
hands. Then imply the existence of another proper code of
behavior, special rules whose clauses they will parcel out as
they want. There are special things going on that you
wouldn't understand. Out of consideration for you, we, the
pros, will protect you. That keeps the patient and frightened
family in check, out of the way, under control.*

*Five minutes.*

*Ten minutes.*

*Fifteen.*

*Twenty.*

*I check the hall again. No one, of course, is coming near
this room. Too busy with important matters.*

*Twenty-five minutes.*

*Thirty.*

"Mr. Malcolm?" *A disembodied voice from around the
corner.*

*"Coming."*

*"No. The doctor decided to do a cesarean after all. If you'll just wait here, he'll be out as soon as he can."*

*That brought us up to maybe 30 percent. "Okay. Thank you." Then a little fishing. "Is there some problem?"*

*"Oh, I don't know. I wouldn't think so. I was just passing by the O.R. and they asked me to tell you."*

*"Well, that was very kind. Thank you."*

*No problem, my ass. Cesarean was not the plan. Frankly, I had not been eager to be in on the birthing process. How could I help my wife breathe—puff, puff, puff, that's it, dear, very good—while I'm holding my breath? Or fainting on the sterilized floor? I had been in on those awfully named organ harvests and on the kidney transplants. I had no problem watching them turn the unconscious patient's belly orange with disinfectant and then draw a line where the knife would go while they talked about the football game. But that had not been my wife's belly. And it had not been my would-be kid, already named, waiting to make a grand entrance one way or another.*

*Forty minutes.*

*Forty-five.*

*I paced. I muttered. I checked the automatic doors down the hall. They were still automatic.*

*"Mr. Malcolm?"*

*"Yes, I am!"*

*"Would you like some coffee?"*

*"Uh, no. No, thank you. Say, do you know what's going on down there?"*

*"No, I'm sorry. I don't work in the O.R. But I'm sure everything is fine."*

*If you don't work there, how can you be sure? If everything is so swell, why are they operating when that wasn't the plan? If things are fine, why is she there and I'm here and no one is in between to explain? Too busy doing important things with pieces of paper. But, of course, they'd keep all the information compartmentalized. Better control. No mixed signals. They hope. Contradictions have a way of turning back and biting you in this litigious society.*

*Fifty minutes.*

*In her room. There's a newspaper. So what? That's what I want right now, another eleven-hundred-word analysis of South Africa to get my mind off the here and now.*

*Fifty-five minutes.*

"Mr. Malcolm?" *A man's voice. I run.*

*Jesus, there's a crowd in the hall, all still wearing masks.* "Hello, Mr. Malcolm."

"Yeah. Sure. Hi. What's going on?" *The crowd was still moving slowly down the hall. I followed along. Why were we walking like this? Was there some rush?*

"This is your son here."

*Here? Where? Oh, Christ, they've got him in a glass box on wheels.*

"We have some problems. And I don't have much time. He wasn't very active at first. He seems to be coming around now." *The other masks were pulling away down the hall with the glass box on wheels.* "I thought you'd want to see him. But we have a lot of work to do." *The doctor started to move off, too.*

"Right. Well, thanks for all your good work." *I didn't know who the hell this guy was or what the hell he had done or what he was about to do or could do, but I wanted to be on the good side of the good guys in white. Then I remembered the key question.*

"What was his Apgar?" *The doctor froze. Ha-ha. I had just guessed the guest's occupation on "What's My Line?" Didn't think a dumb civilian would know that key measurement of vital signs at birth, did ya? Eight is the best. Four or five acceptable.*

The reporter stared right into the target's eyes. I wasn't
giving him any room to fudge. He had gray hair, so he was
some kind of boss. He couldn't feign ignorance about the
Apgar. He returned the gaze.

"Zero."

Oh, shit! I wanted to know this. But did I need to know
this? But how can we make an intelligent decision without
such information? Intelligent decision? What intelligent decision? Who said anything about a decision? Not me. Not
the doctor; I'd kill him if he did. We're talking about saving
my boy's life here. Everything is not enough.

"Ah. Well, by God, you do everything you can."

"We are. We will."

So they did. We had sealed the deal with smiles. We were
all agreed on the goal and I had the best damned medical
team in the world out there for him, for me, for us. I had
never seen this guy before in all my years and I had just
turned my child's life over to him and his masked staff and
machines. And I felt awfully good about it. Frightened, but
good. There was no choice about it. These were real pros, I
could tell; they acted as if they knew more than they were
saying, which was comforting now. They were in control,
and that was super with me.

I watched where they went. I went off to report the good
part of the news to the other children; no sense in worrying
them, obviously. I visited my awakening wife, the new
mother. "How is he?" she demanded.

"He's fine," I said. "He's fine. But he only has ten fingers."
She paused, then slapped my arm in mock outrage at the
admission of our shared concern.

Then I wandered down the hall. The doctor looked at me
and nodded a boundary line at the doorway. I watched. The
nurses bustled about, cleaning up the newcomer, who was
awake but quiet under the heat lamp as the women's gloved
hands moved in and out of the warmth.

*There was visibly less tension now. I ventured a question.
"How much does he weigh?"*

*"About five pounds," said the doctor.*

*"Five pounds six," said the nurse.*

*"I gather this was not your first delivery," I said, smiling.*

*"They're all exciting and wonderful," he replied, his eyes
not leaving the child and the beeping and lighted monitors
arrayed all around.*

*"Boy, that zero on the Apgar scared me," I said, hoping
for a confidence-restoring reply.*

*"I wasn't too pleased myself," replied the pro. "But he
seemed to come around pretty quickly. He was up to four at
two minutes. And that's usually a sign that they weren't
without oxygen for very long. You want to be very careful in
these cases."*

*"Careful. Yes. Very careful. Good idea."*

*And so we all were for hours and then days and then weeks
in the infant intensive care unit, where all the observed
occupants wear tiny socks, undershirts, mittens, and slip-
on caps to preserve warmth. At first, the bowels wouldn't
work. Then the kidneys were slow to flow. Often, he choked,
silently. Twice he stopped breathing, a common forgetfulness in such cases, we were told, but one that required intensive testing to check that diagnosis. As soon as the little
lungs paused too long, the alarm went off. The nurse, one
for every two infants in the glass boxes, quickly stuck her
hands in the side holes and jostled the baby, alternately
watching the chest and the lights for confirmation of the
restored rhythms.*

---

I put Mom in a convalescent home—or, rather, the doctor
did, and I didn't object. I thought the company and stimulation
of others might do her good, get her mind off herself and her

painful arm at times. And when she got strong enough, she could come live in a similar place nearer us.

Once, Mom had several other interests. For the first few years after Dad's death she even tried to study her investment income as closely as she watched her outgo. She read the financial pages of the newspaper many days and might drop into our conversation some mention of a national business development. "See," she'd say, "your old mom knows a few things."

"I'm impressed," I'd say.

Dad had left her in good financial shape. Like most sons of the Depression, he had his savings in safer cash, certificates of deposit in reputable banks, which were federally insured. And that was coincidentally the best place for earnings then, too. Mom's bookkeeper and I had lobbied later for a little more diversification, and she had reluctantly agreed after, she pointedly pointed out to me, she had heard the same thing on an evening radio talk show.

The argument happened when I was least expecting it, which I suppose is why it happened, although I couldn't keep my defenses alert every second. She had called, she said, to seek my advice about an investment. I was flattered momentarily. She had inherited Dad's investment in his lifetime employer. For years he had bought a few shares here and there in the company, *his* company. It was an emotional investment, not the most aggressive but certainly safe, if sedentary. And also a significant size. Now, after years of unimpressive performance, the company was suddenly the target of a takeover. Mom was flustered. She'd gotten letters from all sides seeking to buy her nest egg. They had set deadlines. What should she do?

"Nothing," I said. "The action is just starting. The purchase deadlines are weeks away. Just wait and see. With this many people after your shares, the price is unlikely to go down."

"But it worries me," she said.

"What's to worry about?" I said. "You've hardly thought about them for years. Now other people want them. Maybe in a few weeks they'll want them even more. Just wait and see."

"Well, I don't know. The price is back up to what your father paid. I was thinking of selling them. They've set a deadline to decide, you know. I might lose everything."

"You're not going to lose anything, Mom. You own the shares. Nobody else. Do you understand? It's just bullying. They can't take them away from you. They can just buy them. They want them for as little as possible. And you want to sell them for as much as possible. You're in control here. This isn't the Depression. Stop worrying."

"I think I should sell them and get this over with."

"For God's sake, Mom, don't sell them. Not now, anyway. Those deadlines are phony. They'll change them next week, I bet. They're trying to scare you. And it sounds as if it's working. Dad worked so hard to get these shares."

"But they haven't increased in price in all these years."

"Well, they are now."

"I don't like this uncertainty."

"Mom, there's opportunity for profit in uncertainty. Forget about it for now. Just forget it. I'll watch developments and recommend something later. I'll take care of it, believe me."

"I think I'll sell."

"Mom, c'mon, don't sell Dad's shares. That'd be stupid."

Sudden silence. Oops. I'd just stepped in something. Quick, rewind the tape. What had I said? What was she waiting to pounce on? Damn! She hadn't called for advice. It was a trap. Gotcha! And I had walked right in, all earnest and hopeful. Or hopeless. How could I have missed it? After all these years.

"Well, thank you, young man. Thank you very, very much. After all these years, now I know what you really think of me."

That's what you think, bunky. "What are you talking about? I thought we were talking about stocks here."

"You think I'm stupid."

A little dense, perhaps. Crafty, for sure. Sometimes a Princess of Darkness. But not stupid. "I never said you were stupid."

"Yes, you did. You just did."

Okay, gal. You want a shoving match, I'll give you a shoving match. "No, I didn't. If, for once in your life, you had been listening to me, Mother, you would have heard my exact words." Turn on your hearing aid, lady, here comes the message. "So I'll say them again, real slow, Mom. It . . . would . . . be . . . stupid . . . to . . . sell . . . Dad's . . . shares. . . . Now, anyway. That doesn't make you stupid." Unless you do it. "It makes selling the shares stupid. Do you understand? There's a big difference. Whether you see it or not. Okay? I've done some stupid things in my life, too." One of them was getting suckered into this argument. "But that doesn't make me stupid." I wish. "But I did not say you were stupid. Do you see the difference here? Mom? Hello? Do you see it?"

"I think we had better end this conversation."

"You asked my advice. That's my advice. Don't sell now. If you didn't want to hear it, why did you ask?"

"Goodbye, Andrew."

"Why did you ask, Mom? Answer that!"

"I never thought you would talk to me this way."

"Talking to you can be very frustrating."

"I'm going now."

"Okay. Good to talk with you."

"Goodbye."

"Bye, Mom. I love you."

I was shaken. I felt pale. Thank God she couldn't see me. Once before, in my teens, I had spoken to her with similar bluntness. She had slapped me, knocking my glasses across the room. Females were frightening folk. Well, I had thought then, now I know what you think of me. But she couldn't reach across the entire country this time. And, this time, I was all she had left in the world.

. . .

Soon after that confrontation, for the first time I went over Mom's holdings with the bookkeeper. Then I mentally divided the home's $3,600 monthly cost into Mom's pension income and remaining savings; we were all right for now. But the apartment might have to go soon. A few weeks before that illness, perhaps in one of those eerie premonitions the elderly seem to have, Mom had said, "Someday I suppose I'll go into one of those homes. But I'd miss this apartment so much." I had silently agreed with both parts, especially the eventual need: once, the nurse had found Mom in bed, oblivious to a forgotten cigarette on the covers. The doctor, nurse, and I agreed she could no longer cope at home alone. Also, many days when the nurse would arrive, with her infectious cheerfulness, there seemed to be an extra pain pill or two missing from the bottles. But when I gently raised the issue, Mom acted so contrite, so little-girl innocent—even embarrassed—that I couldn't bring myself to press the issue. In the convalescent home, the pills would be out on the hall cart, not beyond her call but beyond her reach.

Mom seemed to recover fully from her breathing difficulties, although X-rays had revealed the quarter-sized spot of new cancer. The doctor told Mom he didn't want to do anything about it then; she translated that into, there's nothing that can be done about it. "It's going to get me," she told the nurse.

Mom was weaker, easily tired, and, by 5 p.m. daily, confused. Sundown syndrome, they call it among the minds that study aging minds but don't always understand them. At those times she could be easily annoyed at the people closest to her. Somehow, though, the reservoir of charm still managed to flow copiously on the odd occasion of a visit by an outsider, perhaps one of the kind volunteers who had delivered her Meals on Wheels.

Mom was angry at me for not phoning the first few days of

her breathing difficulties. "Wouldn't you think a son would call his mother in the hospital?" she said to the nurse.

"Why don't you call him?" the nurse suggested.

"No!" came the reply. "Let him call me first. I'm his mother."

"But he doesn't know you're in the hospital."

No excuse. Her son's ignorance of the need to call was a minor inconsistency, easily ignored.

"Hi, Mom. How ya doin'?"

"Hello, stranger."

"I've been calling the apartment, but you were never home. How are you doing?"

"Better, thank you. I was very sick."

"Yes, I heard. That's awful. I understand you were not taking all of your medicine. You can't do that, Mom."

"What makes you say that?"

"I was talking to the doctor."

"*You* were talking to the doctor?"

"Sure. How do you think I found out where you were? I know all your tricks." Or many of them.

"It was very exciting."

"What?"

"It was very exciting."

"What was very exciting, Mom?"

"The ride in the ambulance. They had their, their—oh, what do you call them? You know what I mean."

"Their lights?"

"No! No! They had their zoomers on."

"They had their zoomers on?" Oh, God, what time is it?

"It was very exciting."

"I'll bet."

"All the other cars pulled over and we went very fast."

Wait a minute. She's so sick she needs oxygen, but then she's alertly noting traffic patterns through the window? True to Mom's desperate summonses, two ambulances had rushed to the same apartment. My mother had tied up half her city's ambulance corps for a joyride with sirens. I owed someone an apology.

"Mom," I said, like an embarrassed parent trying to be patient, "what if there had been an emergency on the other side of town and no ambulance to help because you called in a spare?"

"They didn't seem to mind."

"What—are they going to give you a lecture about false alarms while you're gasping for breath?" Then, in a flash of insight, I knew how to prevent a recurrence.

"Did you know it cost three hundred dollars?"

"What do you mean?"

"Each one of those ambulances cost three hundred dollars."

"You have to pay for them?"

"Not me. You."

"Well, it turned out fine."


A few weeks later, I arrived to close up the apartment, selecting which few belongings went to dress her and furnish her room at the convalescent home and the remaining three tons of goods that went into boxes for storage at my house. I stayed nearly a week. It seemed like a month.

With much trepidation I entered her semi-private room, all phony cheery, the way middle-aged people get when they walk into those places, look around, and see into the future. So we focus on just this one bed with a real big heartfelt hello and a TV-sincere smile for all the unseen people watching out there at home. We feel good about putting the old folks in a special place for good care. We even arrange for her visiting nurse to visit still. But it's so exhausting to be jolly in those places. I remembered Mom's unpredictable fury over the years when she thought I'd overstepped my bounds. So it wasn't until the third day of my visit that I announced to her what I was doing at the apartment.

"What apartment?" she said.

With her in bed and me in an uncomfortable chair by the bed

rail, we spent long hours making conversation; she was clearest about the more distant past. She'd doze off. I'd read the newspaper, several times, even the news from Latin America. She'd wake up for an hour and share more memories. I tried to recite only the good ones.

"This is really a nice place," I said.

"Oh, yes," she said.

"They've even got a bunny out in the garden. You can feed him. Do you remember Herman?"

"Oh, my, yes. Dad and I were so worried about how dirty he might be."

"Maybe this one is another cousin."

Quiet.

"That's a pretty water fountain they've got."

"I've got a pitcher right here."

"What?"

"If you want a drink, there's water right here."

"No, I mean out in the garden there's a big water fountain, you know, shooting water into the air and splashing down. It sounds real pretty. And they have lots of flowers."

"Oh, really? I haven't seen that."

"Sure, you have. You were there with Betsy when I got here Monday."

"She's on vacation. She's always on vacation."

"Betsy? No, Mom, she has Wednesdays off."

"If you say so."

"It's not me who says—Never mind."

"You know the same cat always sits in that tree out there."

"What cat, Mom?"

"That big cat. Sitting in the crook of that what's-it tree."

"I—I don't see him, Mom."

"Well, just look. He's there."

"Maybe it's just the shape of the branch and the shade there."

"No, it's a big cat. He's always there."

"It's probably a pal of Edgar's, eh?"

"Oh, my, yes, wasn't he a special creature?"

"Let's go for a walk, Mom, in the garden. I'll get the wheel-chair."

"I don't want to get cold."

"It's nearly eighty degrees out there."

"Sometimes they make it so cold in here, I need an extra sheet. They're probably saving money on heating."

"You really think so? Let's see—well, it says it's seventy-two right now. Are you cold?"

"No."

"Maybe if you got up and moved around more, it would help your circulation and you wouldn't feel so cold."

"No, it's the heat."

"All right."

"I'm just waiting to die."

"Oh, come on, Mom. We're all waiting to die. Let's go out for one last meal, whaddya say?"

"No. They'll bring dinner in a few minutes."

"I thought I might eat, too."

"I'll give you some of mine."

"Sure, probably the beans."

It hurt one time when she said she didn't remember how many grandchildren she had, though their photo was by her pillow. Mothers knew buttons too, I thought. Then, an hour later when an acquaintance arrived, Mom rattled off all the names and ages. And I wasn't so sure.

It was a very clean, clinically caring place. Every meal came at the same time every day. On plastic trays. With pleated paper cups containing that eight hours' proper dosage. Mom didn't spend much time in the common rooms, watching the big TV screen. She always seemed to eat in her bed. It was easier. Once, I was a little late returning for the second of my three long daily visits. Dinner had been served. I walked briskly down the hall and into the East Wing's common area. About fifteen white-haired men and women were eating or being fed in front of the

TV. A few were talking to each other. Several were talking to themselves or others unseen. The tall man was complaining about the food that he hadn't eaten again. He was a famous opera singer, my mother had whispered that morning. The nurses were ignoring his insults, again.

Being the sole activity in the room during the commercial, I was watched closely by many old eyes. I found it a pretty pathetic scene and turned to hustle away from there into my mother's room. Two steps later I froze. I whirled. My mother was sitting in that pathetic crowd. She was eating very properly for a Toronto lady, fork in one hand, the other in her lap. And silently watching the people around as she chewed demurely. I felt sick.

Several minutes later, she noticed me. "Oh, Andy, come here," she said.

"That's okay," I said, knowing what was coming. "I'll wait in your room till you're done. No rush."

"No, Andy, come here. I want you to meet these people. This is my son Andy, everybody."

"Hello," I said, with a friendly smile.

Not one face turned or acknowledged the introduction.

"The potatoes are good," Mom said.

"Excuse me," said one woman, who obviously wasn't speaking to us. "Is that your husband?"

"I thought you weren't coming back."

"Hey, you," said the woman, louder. "Is that your husband?"

"No, it isn't," said my mother, turning to me and glancing at the ceiling. "It's my son."

"My husband doesn't visit anymore. He's dead."

I looked over at her and chose the United Nations approach: do nothing that might arouse anyone, even those in another world. I nodded.

"I thought you weren't coming back," said Mom.

"I can't stay away from my favorite girl. Besides, I covet your beans."

"Well, here have some."

"No thanks, Mom. I hate beans."

"That's what I thought."

"Eat them," I said to my own mother. "They're good for you."

The evenings were endless. By seven, people were preparing for bed. Naptime. Mom would lie there. I'd sit next to her and talk or daydream. She'd doze off. If I walked away to stretch my legs, she would wake up. On my return, she'd say, "I thought you had left."

"No," I said, "but I will if you want me to."

"No. No. Sit down."

So I would. I pretended not to hear Mom's roommate talking with her husband. They had been married nearly a half-century. Now she lived here. And her husband lived in another wing, a wheelchair ride away.

"How was your day?" he'd say.

"I said," he'd repeat, "how was your day?"

She must have whispered. "That's too bad," he said. He held her hand and they talked about their medicines and discussed their naps. Once, I saw him lean over in his chair and place his forehead on her sheets. With effort, she lifted one hand and stroked his head.

Before eight, the nurse arrived. "I'm sorry to break up you two lovebirds," she said, "but it's bedtime."

"Well, goodnight, sweetheart," he said. "See you in the morning." And he wheeled himself away.

I looked back at my mother. "Mom," I said, "I want to ask you something."

She didn't move a muscle.

"One time we were all sitting in the living room and Dad reached over to hold your hand." She nodded.

"Why did you yank your hand away?"

"Your father never knew his own strength," she said. "Sometimes he would hurt me."

"It seemed like such a cruel thing to do. I think he wanted to love you a lot." Me too, Mom.

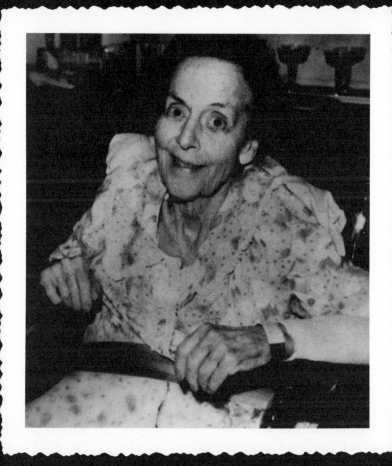

*A widow*

Silence. "I could have been more affectionate in those last years," she said. "I think your father needed more affection than I gave him."

I nodded.

She nodded.

"You know," she said suddenly, "I never wanted it to drag on like this."


The next day, before lunch, I had Mom sign a durable power of attorney. I told her the truth; that document named me specifically to make medical decisions if she wasn't alert anymore. She didn't seem to care much, one way or the other, though she definitely liked my fussing around about it. Down the hall, I found two witnesses, complete strangers, who came to her room and swore Mom was of sound mind and body when she signed. "A lot of people seem to be doing these," said one witness. "Oh, we did one for my Ben before his stroke," said the other, whose husband still sat in a chair back in his room, eyes open, mind too, both seemingly blank. "Thank you very much, both of you," gushed Mom, the hostess, as the two witnesses walked out of her room and life.

Later, a state ombudsman independently visited Mom and ratified her document. At that time Mom also added special instructions; she said she'd prefer not to donate any organs, but left the final decision to me. For an instant when that completed document arrived in the mail, I started to imagine what it really meant, me at the control panel, me parceling out pieces of my warm, defunct mother to be placed inside strangers I'd never recognize when we passed on a sidewalk somewhere someday. Then I successfully cleared my mind of those thoughts, because I knew no doctor outside of cadaver class wanted anything to do with organs from someone with cancer. Except maybe eye bank researchers. "Can you imagine," one doctor had said to me, politely not targeting newspapers, "what the eleven-o'clock news could do with that headline: 'DOC GIVES WOMAN CANCER ORGAN'?"

I thought all my preparations for Mom were terribly efficient. If I'd had a brother or sister, I could have let them make the arrangements or we could have both dodged them together until it was absolutely unavoidable and then, in our fertile fears, we could have fought over everything and resented it all and each other. But, as usual, I was alone. I could do it because it had to be done. And if Mom was aware of the implications—she didn't resist. She always did like being cared for. And the fussing was safe for me.

I thought the durable power of attorney was very good, more decisive, clear-cut. It was flexible; no way could anyone anticipate every potential medical and family situation, so it put the legal power to decide in one mind—mine, unfortunately. I knew that most states had not created such powers. I knew too that most states now recognize some form of Living Will, which merely states treatment preferences to anyone who will listen, but is often open to interpretation and being ignored, especially if feuding relatives are around. Americans plan their babies. They plan for college and taxes and their retirement. But they let somebody else worry about—and control—their own end.

I knew lawyers were drafting a model state law setting out an array of standard rights for the terminally ill and a priority list of relatives to consult (spouse first, then oldest child, and on down). This would negate the need for individual action on individual wills. But it would never come in time for Mom, or me. And anyway, they all still leave the doctors as guardians (or obstacles) at the last gate, silently studying the motives of imminent survivors, no doubt silently a little afraid for themselves each time.

I had felt out my own family's doctor on this matter. I wasn't still arising at 4 a.m. to do extra writing and then going to a regular job to have my family's future drip out of me someday into a plastic urine bag beneath a bed that could be cranked to sit me up when I couldn't do it myself. "I don't regard one in ten thousand as a realistic chance of emerging from a coma," I said. "What do you think?"

He said he had threatened his wife with his return should she keep him going under such circumstances. Good, I thought, we're agreed, although that is but one closing scenario. But, of course, I reserve the right to change my mind when I reach The Big Door, especially if Cleveland has yet to win the Super Bowl. Giving up is for the next illness.

Years before, Dad and Mom had made me the eventual trustee of their trust account. "You don't know how good it is to have a son like you to trust," Mom had said.

"Well," I replied, "you haven't seen me do my checking account."

I described Mom's remarks to her doctor on the phone each time he and I talked. He was very careful in this preliminary dance. So was I. We had never met. He said he had been unclear about her wishes during that spring's breathing difficulties. The two of us had already agreed and written into Mom's medical charts a "Do Not Resuscitate" order in the event of heart failure. Logistically, we were so prepared.

"Andrew," said the man on the phone. Oh, God. I knew that voice. My secret dancing partner. I pictured him standing at a nursing supervisor's borrowed desk, with the photo of her children cuddling in a man's lap and the free calendar from the drug company, each day carefully crossed out leading up to the next vacation. The curve of a stethoscope would be peeking from the pocket of the doctor's white coat, his eyes darting around the somberly busy hall, checking his mental bases. I was right; it was him.

"I'm afraid we have a serious problem with your mother."

You, too? I thought. It was unkind. But it postponed the issue a few more seconds. "Oh?" I said warily. I was entering the minefield. No more procrastination. No more dodging. No more mental games. This is it, Andrew. Isn't it? Think! Do it right the first time, the only time. You can do whatever you have to do. Can you observe everything that needs seeing? Can you remember everything you've learned? Ask all the right questions? Provide the correct answers? Do the right thing for her? For yourself? Show her the compassion you do not feel? Give her a gift of yourself, even if you're unsure how? And do it all so well that no shadow of a second guess will ever haunt you, or your observers. At least until that murky day of your own? Nothing lives forever, son. Someday you'll understand.

But how do you know when someday comes?


It was such a gentle whoosh. But so decisive. No room for any human pause in this rhythm. It was set for forty pounds of pressure. Whoosh. Click. Hiss. Pause. Click. It would deliver forty pounds of pressure. Whoosh. Click. Hiss. Pause. Click. Or the mechanic would know why. I was very frightened. And I knew why.

It was night. And I had waited an extra day before traveling. No sense in rushing. Mom wasn't going anywhere, not on her own anyway. Her condition was the same, they told me every few hours. It was more important for the living to go on, even one son's football game. She would want it that way. No, she wouldn't. Well, wait, maybe she would now. How the hell would I know what she wants? I never have before. It was me who wanted to be at that game, to celebrate the young and living and my former youth, and not to be standing watch somewhere else for someone who no longer knew what day it was. Then, after my son's interception, after the band played, when the scoreboard went off, then I'd go do my duty.

And if she was gone when I arrived—well then, phew, that was the way it was meant to be. Now the plane had been late. The rented car smelled of glass cleaner. I had walked from my motel room ("Clean Rooms, Cable TV, Free Movies") across the hospital's back parking lot, where the employees' Toyotas sat locked safe and cool and the grinding garbage truck consumed dumpster after dumpster of I didn't want to know what.

The ambulance idled by the emergency room entrance, its back doors wide open, its lights still silently blinking. A frightened family huddled on vinyl benches. A hurried paramedic had paused briefly. "ICU?" he said. "Uh, third floor, I think. Right, Linda? ICU's on three?"

The hallway was dim. Silence seeped from all the darkened rooms. A sweatered nurse sensed my unauthorized approach outside visiting hours. "May I help you?" she said, meaning, "What are you doing here now?"

"Is the ICU around here somewhere?"

That was the code word: ICU. Flexible visiting hours. If the patient is sick enough for ICU, she may not make it to the next set of formal visiting hours.

"Only immediate family," she warned.

I'm her only immediate family, I thought. I nodded.

She looked for a second at an open, unmarked door. Then she sent me way around to the unit's front door. It was locked. No window. A "No Unauthorized Entry" sign. Just a telephone that was silent when raised. This was the control game. I could hear the faint rings behind the door. No answer. No answer. No answer. No answer. But I knew ICUs; there's always someone there. Likely very busy. Probably checking me on a little TV camera, too. Yup, there it was up in the corner.

"Hello?"

"It's Andrew Malcolm. I'm here to see my mother."

Pause. Checking the charts. Had permission been properly entered?

"Have a seat. I'll be out shortly."

"I just got here from the airport." A useless bit of information, but it implied urgency, politely. Of course, I did not sit down. I had no desire to imply patience, since they were watching. I paced to create motion on that screen somewhere. Several minutes later the door opened. The nurse was already walking away from it. "She's in there. I'm over here, if you need me." What if *she* needs you?

And there she was. "Mom?" I said. "Mom, is that you?" Why was I tiptoeing?

"Hi, Mom. It's Andy."

Nothing.

"Mom, Andy's here. Hi, it's Andy." Anyone home?

The head turned toward me slightly. Eureka! "Mom, it's Andy. I'm here."

The mouth formed an "Oh."

"It's Andy, your son. The one with the red hair. You may remember me. I've come to play 'Moon River' on my drums."

Was that a faint smile?

"I just flew in from New York and, boy, are my arms tired."

Yes, it *was* a little smile. Well, this wasn't as bad as I expected. I could do a little Spike Jones imitation. She'd laugh once again. And everything would be fine.

"It's Andy." I checked around the room. No one else there. Good. "Do you remember me?"

A nod. Well, of course. Good.

"Are you in pain?"

A headshake. Good. Good.

"Can you open your eyes? And look at me. Come on. I'm not that ugly. Open your eyes."

The eyelids fluttered, but lay closed.

"Everybody said to send their love." Which was, as Huck Finn would say, a stretcher. But acceptable under the circumstances. In case she didn't remember everybody again, I ran through the family, giving brief activity reports on each, except me. That took six—no, seven minutes. No response, of course.

Now what?

I looked around the dark room. Wow. It was a full-court press. The first sign had been a sudden temperature that no one took seriously at first because Mom had not complained. Had she known? Pneumonia. Bad pneumonia. Septic shock, simultaneously the other organs were stunned by the bacteria's assault. Plunging blood pressure. Pump in the drugs and fluids to get it back up. Whoa, not too much. Now everything was backing up with fluids. More drugs to flush them out. Back and forth. Find the balance. Hope the hardworking heart holds on. The other organs shake it off. And watch the blood gases. That magic E.T.-type light on her forefinger monitoring whether the smokey old lungs were processing sufficient oxygen into the blood to keep everything fueled. Wait till the son gets here. And then watch.

Nothing happened in more than an hour. "Well, Mom, it's nearly 2 a.m. my time. I'm going to bed now. I have a room right next door. I'll see you in the morning. Okay? Mom?" Nothing.

I patted her bony hand. I thanked the ICU nurse.

"Can you let me out, please?"

"Oh," she said, "you can use the back door. It's always open."

So I walked out the open door past the sweatered nurse who'd kept that entrance a secret: See, I'm in now. And then I tried to sleep.


The doctor looked younger than I expected, even early on a Sunday morning. He was very sympathetic, looked me in the eye, and listened carefully. So did I. I knew nothing then of his late father's painful struggle with leukemia. The son had been summoned to the hospital by his suffering father. "I don't want this anymore," said the man. So his son had negotiated with another doctor. The respirator came off. And his father died. "We're getting better every day at keeping people alive," said the son, "but not making them better." So after every one of his patient's first encounters with a respirator, the doctor now asks, "If it's ever necessary, do you want to do that again?" Most say, "No." Some say, "Yes." And so they do. And some say, "We'll see." And then no one knows. So, of course, to be safe the professionals do everything and a few months later the doctor sees them in a nursing home, staring at the wall. "That's not what I'd want," says the doctor. "But that's what they chose by their inattention."

This doctor and I were now carefully reading each other in person. I let him see me recoil again at the sight of her. "Doctor, where did all these bruises come from on her arms?"

"Well, whenever the sedation starts to wear off, she pulls the tubes out and we have to put them back in. So we put these gauze strips here to hold her arms down. It's understandable, her pulling them out. They're uncomfortable."

Pause.

"There could be another reason."

Pause.

"That's right," he said, very businesslike.

We—or, rather, she and the medicines and machines—had pretty much defeated the pneumonia. It was the sepsis that still bothered the doctor and the weakened lungs. He was watching the heart closely. No serious faltering yet. And the kidneys; the creatinine level was not bad, though it could have been better.

"Do you suppose we could untie her hands?"

"Sure. But last time she went for the tubes."

"Tying her down really bothers me. I'd like her to feel free."

"I understand."

"What about the respirator?"

She needed it now. The next day, we would start trying to wean her slowly. Today we'd back off a little on the sedation. See if that, combined with my presence or at least my voice, could bring her around a little.

But that was not to be. I could get no recognition, no nod, no shake, not even a faint smile. At one point her right hand went slowly toward her face. The respirator technician went to stop it, worried about the tubes up her nose.

"No, wait," I said.

Her hand moved slowly to her mouth. The forefinger and thumb squeezed her lower lip. That was my mom all right.

"See," I said, "she does that all the time."

"Does what?" he said.


I fell into a numbing routine and felt I deserved it. Three or four very long visits a day broken by restless recesses in my room, staring at the TV. Once a day I would call my wife and report mechanically. I even felt guilty being able to walk in and out of the hospital. I would talk to Mom and at her. I reminisced in these one-sided conversations. Memories aren't so bad to have, Andy. Better than nothing. I had recently driven past her old dream house. "I saw our old house the other day," I said. "Remember the Christmas trees we planted by the garage? They're twice as tall as the house now." Never any visible reaction.

When I read the newspaper, I turned the TV on for her, though I couldn't remember which station was her favorite. That was probably the first time the ICU nurse had ever been asked what local channel carried "Jeopardy!"

Sometimes I'd just stare at Mom and think. A few weeks before, I had tried to go through the boxes with all her possessions from the apartment. So much of it should be thrown out. How can anyone force themselves to keep someone else's keepsakes? How can anyone throw them out? There were newspaper clippings with hairdo tips from 1947. Dresses. Underwear. Favored purses. All my letters from school, neatly bundled. Mushy Mother's Day cards. There were little notes in Dad's handwriting, pleading for another chance, repeating his love for her, vowing never to drink again. In one box I found a Tom Thumb dinner bowl I hadn't seen in forty-three years. That's when I gave up. There I was doing the chores of a survivor when the deceased hadn't officially left yet. Those boxes could stay packed forever, along with the memories.

I brought nacho lunches from the nearby 7-Eleven store to eat in her room. "Hey, Mom," I said. "Maybe I can get them to pour some coffee into these tubes. I'll bet you'd like that." What was I doing here saying all these forced things like some kind of TV host in a scripted interview? "Someone told me you really like coffee." I stayed in the room to talk while the nurses turned Mom and tapped on her chest to loosen congestion. But I very quickly found something else to do somewhere else whenever they came to vacuum her mouth.

One specialist suggested they could run a tube up inside an artery and check out one heart chamber. He meant well. It would tell him something. But I didn't care. I had no intention of authorizing any heart operation—any operation, period. I prevented invasive procedures, allowed others. I was on self-appointed guard duty here and nobody was getting by without my permission.

I held Mom's hand a good deal, not so firmly that it might hurt, but enough, I hoped, for her to feel. When no one was around, I stroked her face and arranged her hair. "Everything's going to be okay," I whispered. I felt extremely uncomfortable doing this, very emotionally awkward. One time I leaned over and hummed "Silent Night" by her ear, though it was afternoon. I couldn't remember the words. Then I walked to a nearby restaurant and ordered far too many courses of food. I ate them all. I went back to my room and threw up.


"Sir?" she said. "Excuse me, sir? Sir. You cannot use that door. It's for ICU staff only. You must come through the front door." It was the weekday nurse.

"I'm just visiting my mother over here."

"Fine, sir. But visitors must use the visitors' door."

"I did. But the weekend nurse said to just come in this way."

"Well, I don't care what she said. This is not a visitors' door."

"I'm really sorry. Do you want me to go all the way around there now?"

"No. You may stay this time. But next time you must use the visitors' door."

There was Mom. Same room. Same pajamas. Same whoosh. I walked right on stage. "Hi, Mom. How ya doin' today? Well, today we're going to try to get you off this breathing machine a little bit. The doctor's going to turn it down a little, not so many breaths every minute and a little less pressure when it blows. Okay? Now it's very important that you help, okay? I— we want you to breathe more and more on your own, okay? Because otherwise your lungs are gonna get all lazy on us with the machine doing all the work. I hope you understand. It's very important that you get with the rhythm. You take as deep a breath as you can and the machine'll help you a little maybe, and then you blow it all out, okay? In and out. Don't try to fight the machine. Go with it. It's very important, Mom. Okay? Oh, and don't fuss with the tubes, okay? They're taking medicine and food in for you to get stronger and you need them right now. So don't pull on them, all right? Then you'll get stronger and we can take all this stuff off you and get you some real scalloped potatoes."

"He's right, Mrs. Malcolm." It was the respiratory therapist. He had one tone of voice for the audience, the patient. That's part of the two-tiered conversations that are so common in those institutions—one level for the patient, who may or may not be hearing. With them we're bright, cheerful, confident, forced, like high-school actors concentrating on our lines, not their meaning. And another tone for colleagues or family, which is softer, like two nursery-school teachers dressing the youngsters for recess while discussing real life in adult code.

"How are we doing today?" he asked me softly.

"The nurse said she had a quiet night."

"No, I mean how are you doing?"

"Oh, fine. I'm hanging in there." Then louder. "Mom, you have a male caller. He wants to know how you're doing."

"It's a beautiful day out, Mrs. Malcolm," he said as his eyes scanned all the dials and connections. Oh, wait a minute, that's the trick of a hospital veteran. See, he talks to her but he never talks as if he expects an answer. I should remember that, care a little less. Then I won't feel so awkward. The technician's eyes lingered over the light on her forefinger and its numbers on the screen. "Her color looks good, though.

"I'm not being fresh, Mrs. Malcolm. I just need to listen to your chest a minute. We're always doing something to you."

"How does it sound?"

He said nothing for a full minute, moving the stethoscope from place to place before taking the plugs from his ears.

"Sorry?" he said.

"I said, 'How does everything sound?' "

"There's some fluid there." Then he prepared to change the machine. "We're going to attach a different machine in a minute, Mrs. Malcolm. Okay?" He acted as if she had a say in the matter. "It's a little more sophisticated. Okay? It's going to watch and see when you need a little help with a breath or two and then it'll leave you on your own. We've got to make your lungs do some work, too." He disconnected the tube. Almost immediately, she began to fuss. "No, it's okay. We'll have you back on in just a minute, dear." He punched in the instructions and pressure settings. Instead of ten breaths a minute, he set her for eight, later six. "There you go." She visibly relaxed.

So did I. And we went through another day.


But it was not a very good one. Something about the little green numbers bothered people. They returned to check more often that day. Mom moved her legs and arms more. "Mom, can you hear me? Can you open your eyes? Want to go for a run?" No response.

I stayed around until 10:30 or so that night before returning to the motel. I was just stepping out of the shower a half-hour later when the phone rang. I'm standing naked in an air-conditioned room, dripping all over the rug trying to sound calm and assured with the doctor. Mom's kidneys didn't seem to be working as well as yesterday. But these things fluctuate. And she was fighting the machine, breathing against its rhythm. So the hard-pressed lungs weren't getting as much air as before. The machine was more efficient than Nature.

"I think we should give it one more day," he said.

"Sure. Fine," I said, feeling neither. The edge was coming.

I didn't have much else to say at her the next day during my visits. I dragged up some more memories. I repeated the latest chapters in each grandchild's life, so much to be proud of. I was bored hearing me, so she must be, too. But I'm sure she didn't hear a word I said. Which wouldn't have been the first time.

I wasn't eating very well, which gives me headaches. I drank considerable amounts of caffeine. I was rather antsy, not sitting still very long. I struck up conversations with anybody who happened by, and kept them going at length. I never talk to people on airplanes, yet here I was on another type of journey dredging up childhood memories and funny experiences that I hadn't thought of for years. I was certain that I wanted to talk about them. And here were some empty ears for me to fill.

The weekday nurse was especially kind. After her lecture about the visitors' door, she said, she checked Mom's records and saw I was the only relative and decided what the hell difference did it make what door I came through and what hours I came through them. "At a time like this," the nurse said, "your mother needs you. And I think you need her."

Well, I know she was right about the first part anyway. But what had changed her mind?

Some nine months before, she said, she had been hospitalized, right down the hall. For the first time, she was the patient. And she realized that much of what a hospital does to people is for the hospital, not the people. "We tell you when to wake up, when to eat, when to sleep, when to visit, even when to pee," she said. "We don't mean to be so stiff. It's supposed to be more efficient, but we're so into control. Like when you came in that door. You were threatening my control. It's silly."

That was very interesting, I said. Were there a lot of staff aware of that?

"No, not unless they've been patients, too. It's very hard to train young men and women to do it all, and do it efficiently and omnipotently, and then tell them, 'Well, wait now, there are some times we don't want you to do it all.' "

The nurse said there is a similar lack of awareness among patients, especially the men, and among spouses and relatives, especially the women. "Everybody thinks that by not thinking about their end they can put it off. So when it comes, as it always does, they're suddenly faced with terrible decisions and unprepared. I've seen couples married fifty years, the husband has a stroke, and the wife doesn't have any idea what he wants. They never discussed it. Without advance thought, it's very hard for healthy people to let go of a dying relative. So we end up 'treating' these folks for days, weeks, even months not for the patient's sake—he or she is finished—but until the family can face up to reality."

The doctor came by again about six. He'd talked to the therapist. He read the numbers. Essentially, nothing had changed. I was a little impatient. Let's get the show on the road here, I thought. Although what the show was, where the road was, and where we were going was unknown to me.

"Well," he said, "let's get together in the morning and evaluate everything one more time. I'll call your room when I get here around seven."

At three I was still staring at the ceiling. I couldn't watch any movies; they all made me mad, even the comedies. What would she want? Did I miss any signs? Which signs to read? At five, I thought it was time to get up. At 5:45 I did. By six I was sitting on the edge of the bed, dressed, wishing there were some woods nearby instead of a few lonely palm trees. Were we trying to glue the autumn leaves back on here? Or was there still some meaningful life left in the old tree? At 7:10 the phone jangled.

"Andrew," said the voice, now so familiar we no longer needed to identify ourselves. "I'm here."

Three minutes later I was, too. Mom's room light was on. The friendly nurse and the respiratory technician were bustling about. The doctor motioned me into the hall. "How are you?" he asked, looking into my eyes.

"I've been better," I said. "You got any Captopril?" He didn't get the nervous joke. Wrong doctor.

"How is she, Doctor?"

"Uh," he says. And I know right away. "There's no improvement. Maybe a little deterioration. The creatinine is up to three, still no immediate danger, but it does seem to point in the wrong direction." There was some more fluid on the lungs. The heart showed signs of fatigue, but no failure yet. She was still resisting the respirator. He'd hoped that backing off the sedation would produce more alertness. But her organs and mind weren't getting sufficient oxygen to work well.

"What's the outlook?"

Several months of respiratory therapy, which just might get her lungs functioning enough to maybe get adequate oxygen to the brain to regain consciousness. If nothing else went wrong in the meantime. And then eighteen to twenty-four months down that uncertain road was the lung cancer's likely spread.

"Could she ever return to the quality of life she had in the nursing home?"

Pause.

"I doubt it."

"How much do you doubt it?"

"Very seriously."

Pause. He was watching me closely. So was Dad. You know, son, sometimes when creatures get old and sick, their minds get muddy and they do strange things that can lead to their death. In a way they're ready to die. We may not understand, because we're not ready yet, but we must learn to accept it.

"Geez, Doc. I'd love to have my mother back. But I wonder about the point to all this."

"I understand. I understand. My experience in cases like this has been families instinctively, wishfully, plunge into aggressive treatment, and then weeks down the road when problems are cascading down on us, they wish they hadn't."

"It's so hard to know what's right."

He nodded.

"She can't have any pain or choking."

"She'll be mildly sedated."

A deep breath. Oh, God, here we go. A swallowed sob. "I want to let her go."

Silence. No thunder. No lightning. No bells. No nothing. The doctor's hand went to my shoulder and squeezed. That's it? I thought. I say, take the brakes off, so we do. Isn't someone going to berate me? Read me my rights? He turned to the nurse.

"We'll be taking the tube out."

I couldn't think of anything else to do. I watched. The technician removed the respirator tube. "I'll bet that feels better," he told her. "I'm going to put this mask over your nose and mouth, dear. It'll give you more oxygen in each breath. Just relax and breathe normally. Okay, dear?" He wheeled the machine out without looking at me. I just stood there. The silence was stark. I realized I never called her "dear."

Alone, I held her hand. I watched the numbers. Her heartbeat jumped to 140 as the body tried to adjust to its sudden new workload. And then it settled back to ninety and ninety-four. I talked to her occasionally. I said I loved her. I hoped she was comfortable, at peace. I stroked her face now and then. "Everything's going to be okay," I said, though I knew I was lying. An hour later her pulse was eighty-six. Still pretty strong. Should I be glad? Or sad?

Her face was turned away from me slightly. How perfect. Except for a little jerk of her head with each breath, she never moved. Never blinked. Never said anything. But once I saw a tear.

Her hands were cold. I tucked her in more. "She hates to be cold," I told the nurse. She would come in now and then to check on Mom. And me, too, I think. We talked a lot. Her father had died unexpectedly, young. "You're lucky to have had her so long," the nurse said. I nodded. That wouldn't sink in for a while.

The hours dragged by. The doctor checked in by phone. I told the nurse Mom's color wasn't very good.

"No," she said, "the heart is having to work very hard but the lungs aren't."

Well, fine, I thought. Let's get on with whatever is supposed to happen here. I made the big decision to let her go. Now she doesn't seem to want to. But I'm ready. The pulse was still eighty-two or eighty. My stomach hurt. And my head, too. The nurse gave me two aspirin.

More hours crawled by. My mind wandered from the woman who gave me life to my infant son; why couldn't my own mother just admit the baby looks like me? What would it have cost her?

It seemed as if someone had put a sign on Mom's door. No one comes to make any more tests. People whisper when they go by. The nurse brings me a fruit cup from some lunch tray.

I was holding Mom's hand. It was rather cold. So was the room. Why do they cool that world down so much that people must wear sweaters when they go inside? How can they so easily accept a moron manning the thermostat, but not the inevitable erosion of a human body? I can't get comfortable anywhere. The bed is too high to sit by. The chair is too hard to sit on. And my feet are tired from standing like a goof, an acolyte with the social graces of an eighth-grader and nothing to do in front of all those people. The chill of the stainless-steel bed rail on my bare arm was searing.

At one point in a bedside conversation, I saw the nurse's eyes dart over my shoulder to the monitor. "It won't be long," she said. I whirled. The pulse was forty-four. "How do you know?" Have you been here before? I turned back for an explanation. But she was walking briskly to the phone.

I looked back at the machine. Forty-two. Then, down at Mom. Mouth still open. Same little gasps. Forty. Oh, Jesus, she's dying on me. Thirty-six. I had been afraid it wouldn't happen. Now I was afraid it would. Wait. Stop. Mom, don't go! I'll play the drums. Thanks for the potato chips. And the wardrobe arrangements. I'm sorry about the nap fights. Have a good trip. Is this what you wanted? Oh, God, give her peace. And me, too, maybe. Please. If you have a minute. Someday.

Minutes later, the doctor appeared, relieved. He checked Mom. The pulse was thirty-four.

"She's ready, Andrew."

Oh, my. What about me? Uh. No. Wait. Are we sure about this? Me neither.

They left the two of us alone then. Mom, I love you. And at some point, she left, too. The pulse went to thirty to twenty-four. To zero. There were irregular heartbeats for a while. After all those years some parts found it hard to quit.

Nine hours and five minutes after I authorized removal of the respirator, my mother expired in a windowless private hospital room with the television on. We were both alone together then. And I felt terrifyingly small.

The death certificate said Beatrice Bowles Malcolm, the white, widowed daughter of Harry and Jenny Bowles and the mother of Andrew H. Malcolm, died at the age of seventy-five that day at 1710 hours.

It gave the cause of death as respiratory failure.

# *Epilogue*

There are cycles to life in the woods with its enduring trees and their soothing rustles of leaves or needles and boughs—the trees' vibrant lives, their waning strength, their invisible decay, and then their frightening fall before the winds. And so it was with Mom's end even within the synthetic shelter of a hospital. It came, appropriately enough, in the fall. And that same day several new lives began just down the hall.

There were those who walked by Mom's room and nodded in shared sorrow, those who paused to speak softly, and those who bustled on past, afraid to look. I was in a conscious coma, truly stunned by the difference between even an unconscious Mom and a dead one. I kept looking at her as if something would change. She seemed so—well, so empty. Which meant she had been so much more full of life than I had realized before. I was overwhelmed by the enormity of the moment, although enormous is too small a word for the feeling.

I did not want to leave her room, although what I was clinging to was beyond my grasp. Everyone was very kind, especially the nurse. "There's no rush," she said, and even her words seemed oversized.

"Somehow," I said, "I don't want to leave her alone."

"Maybe," the nurse suggested, "it's you who shouldn't be alone." But, of course, I was.

The technician from the eye bank arrived then and hovered respectfully at a distance. After a while, I left.

Guilt and doubt began to sprout almost immediately. I had

Mom's address book in my motel room and phoned her few friends, so they wouldn't be left out as Mom had felt in similar circumstances. They were all appreciative save one, who was very angry not to have been called even sooner and announced, as a consequence, that she and her husband would not be attending any funeral. Since the only person who would have cared was dead, I uttered no retort, as I might have in my other life.

I had not met Mom's minister, but he was very sympathetic on the phone and from experience in his business of aging parishoners, he picked up on all the code words. "You were very brave," he said. I instinctively went to contradict him. But he added, "It was the right thing to do."

"Do you really think so?" I said less desperately than I felt. And we prayed together for a moment.

The minister assigned to the small funeral was a woman. I silently recoiled. If there was ever a church traditionalist, it was Mom, who had at times successfully requested the old unreformed service of communion at home. But, of course, the woman minister was just perfect for the job. I asked her to read Mom's favorite prayer, the one about the wind always being at your back. She interrupted the graveside service to recount one memory of Mom in the hospital some months before, instructing the nurses on how she wanted her bedside table arranged. And that caused each of us—I was the only male present—to laugh in our sorrows and then, one by one, to share our own private memories of Mom, some not even relevant. But that didn't matter. We were talking to each other and sharing the moment and each other's company through those spoken words, and for a few minutes I finally understood how that is with women.

There were some weeks of uncertainty for me, and the fertile shadows of doubt loomed large. Had I made that ultimate decision for her sake as a suitable surrogate? Or for myself to feel that burden of hope lifted forever? Had I been too hasty in pulling the plug? Would a few more days or weeks have made any difference to her? To me? What would Dad have thought? What did others think?

I wrote an anguished article about the decision for *The New York Times Magazine*. It was painful to write so alone and uncertain. But dozens of friends and acquaintances commented on the article and then, in whispers, began to confide their own such confrontation. I got hundreds of letters from readers. The letters fell into two categories—"Thank God you wrote this, because I thought I was the only one who ever did that," and "Thank God you wrote this, because we never knew this was happening and now we've made arrangements so our children needn't make such decisions." I answered them all. Months later I'm still getting handwritten notes. Some people enclose poems written during similar bedside vigils.

I walked through the end in detail again with Mom's doctor and the nurse. I asked several other medical professionals about a hypothetical case that bore a remarkable resemblance to Mom's. What else could have been done? How would they have decided? Six months later, my family doctor saw through the exercise. "Look, Andy," he said, "medically your mother was going nowhere. Believe me, you did the right thing." And suddenly I was ready to believe.

I suspect some shadow of doubt will always linger somewhere on the fringes of memory, which is okay. Memories are not so bad to have. And there should always be some mystery; only humans think they must understand everything and codify it for others.

As it turns out, I could do what I had to do. Thanks to my wife, my little pocket notebook, and innumerable dawns at a wooden desk within earshot of many birds, I've written it all down on paper now, which makes things official in my mind. It was difficult to do and overwhelmingly sad at times. My mother had to accept her parents' deaths; I must always wonder about mine.

But it was also very satisfying to chisel, sand, and buff the words to the proper polish and put them in order, in case they might help others. It feels good and liberating now to have done it.

Mom and Dad are together on that hillside where it doesn't snow. I've planted some trees in their memory in the woods. Scars heal there, too.

# A Note About the Author

Born in Cleveland, Ohio, Andrew H. Malcolm is the National Affairs Correspondent of *The New York Times*. Over the past quarter-century, he has been a *Times* correspondent and editor in Japan, Korea, Indochina, Canada, Chicago, San Francisco, and New York. A graduate of Culver Military Academy and Northwestern University, where he earned both his bachelor's and master's degrees, he has won several major awards for national reporting, including the George Polk Memorial Award and the Page One Award of the New York Newspaper Guild. He is the author of *Unknown America, The Canadians, Final Harvest: An American Tragedy,* and *This Far and No More.* Currently, Mr. Malcolm and his wife, Connie, live outside New York City amid many trees and the pleasant chaos of three sons, ages twenty-two to two, a teenage daughter, and numerous animals, wild and domesticated, including a mischievous Husky.

# A Note on the Type

The text of this book was set in Electra, designed by W. A. Dwiggins (1880–1956). This face cannot be classified as either modern or old style. It is not based on any historical model; nor does it echo any particular period or style. It avoids the extreme contrasts between thick and thin elements that mark most modern faces and attempts to give a feeling of fluidity, power, and speed.

Composed by Crane Typesetting Service, Inc.,
West Barnstable, Massachusetts
Printed and bound by Arcata Graphics/Fairfield,
Fairfield, Pennsylvania
Designed by Virginia Tan